ALSO BY JOHN J. NANCE

# FIRE FLIGHT

## JOHN J. NANCE

SIMON & SCHUSTER

NEW YORK LONDON TORONTO SYDNEY SINGAPORE

SIMON & SCHUSTER
Rockefeller Center
1230 Avenue of the Americas
New York, NY 10020

This book is a work of fiction. Names, characters, places, and incidents
either are products of the author's imagination or are used fictitiously.
Any resemblance to actual events or locales or persons, living or dead,
is entirely coincidental.

SIMON & SCHUSTER and colophon are registered trademarks
of Simon & Schuster, Inc.

For information regarding special discounts for bulk purchases,
please contact Simon & Schuster Special Sales at 1-800-456-6798
or business@simonandschuster.com

Manufactured in the United States of America

1   3   5   7   9   10   8   6   4   2

Library of Congress Cataloging-in-Publication Data
Nance, John J.
Fire flight : a novel / John Nance.
p.   cm.
1. Airtankers (Forest fire control)—Fiction.   2. Jackson Hole Region (Wyo.)—Fiction.
3. Yellowstone National Park—Fiction.   4. Forest fire fighters—Fiction.
5. Air Pilots—Fiction.   6. Wyoming—Fiction.   I. Title.
PS3564.A546F57   2003
813'.54—dc22               2003059095

ISBN 0-7432-5050-8

*To Olga Wieser*
*My literary agent and friend for two decades*

# Yellowstone-Teton fires of 2003

# FIRE
# FLIGHT

# Prologue

Misty Ryan slapped the cheap ceramic figurine back on the shelf and moved as quickly as she could between the racks of loud shirts and skimpy bathing suits toward the front of the overcrowded tourist trap. She pressed her nose to the glass, straining to catch another glimpse of the face she'd seen moments before passing by on the street.

It absolutely couldn't have been Jeff Maze, she told herself.

Or could it?

Jeff was supposed to be back in California finishing the fire season in the cockpit of his four-engine airtanker. No way would he be in the Caymans. *No way!*

But then, she couldn't mistake those craggy features, that loping gait. It had to be him, or the nonexistent angelic twin she was always kidding him about having.

Or she was losing it.

She felt her pulse accelerate to a rising rhythm of anger and excitement as she stood on tiptoes in her sandals and looked up and down the street.

*Wait a minute. Could he have flown here to surprise me?*

It was a wonderful thought, but she knew better. Such a plan would never occur to Jeff Maze, since it would inevitably involve a spontaneous thought about *her* pleasure.

Not that he didn't care about her happiness. Twelve tumultuous and exciting years together had welded the reality into her brain that Jeff truly loved her with as much of his heart as he could spare for such feelings. But surprising her was not in his Martian-like programming.

Jeff had always waited for females to please him—the very reason he'd been alone for so many years before Misty decided to tolerate his tom-cattish self-indulgence in return for the good things being with him could bring.

Whatever those were. She couldn't quite recall any benefits just now.

She ignored an offended snort from a heavyset woman she'd apparently shoved aside, maneuvered quickly around the kitschy displays, and ran out the front door onto the sidewalk in time to see a lanky male disappearing around the corner some forty feet distant.

*Dammit!* "JEFF! JEFF, WAIT UP!" she yelled.

Whoever it was turned back momentarily, apparently looking for the source of the voice, his mutton-chop sideburns catching an errant ray of late-afternoon sun and completing the positive ID before he disappeared around the north side of the building.

Lithe and fit, Misty reached the same corner within seconds and rounded it at a dead run, then slowed and looked around in confusion. To her right was a building with two doors facing the street. He'd had no time to hide, but he was nowhere to be seen.

Misty was aware of the puzzled expressions on the faces of several tourists strolling by. She ignored their stares as the previous flash of anger returned to flush her cheeks.

"That dirty—" she muttered, choking off the rest of the obscenity as two small girls walked past, obviously wondering why such a strikingly beautiful American woman with an impressive mane of shoulder-length red hair would be standing in the middle of the street looking so furious.

There was a camera store along the side street, the only open door she could see, and Misty rushed inside. The store was staffed by a young island girl leaning apathetically on the counter in a state of terminal boredom. She listened to Misty's almost breathless description of Jeff Maze and shrugged with unfathomable disinterest. "No one like that came in here."

"You're sure?"

The salesgirl lost no time returning to the magazine she'd been memorizing, ignoring the question.

Misty left the shop and returned to the main street along the waterfront, standing for a moment and trying to absorb the details of what she'd seen.

*If he is here, I'll find him,* she promised herself. *But why* would *he be here?* There simply was no professional reason for Jeff to be in Grand Cayman before the end of the fire season; therefore, he *had* to be there to surprise her, even if it was a first.

Why had he *run,* though? That made no sense. They'd argued and snapped at each other barely a week ago, but that was life with Jeff, and one she'd come to accept. Maybe even enjoy. After all, they lived together most of the time, generating enough heat with their tumultuous couplings to equal the forest fires he fought, and although she was less than a wife, she was much more than a mistress. Every year during fire season she followed his camp, working seasonally as a dispatcher for the Forest Service while he did combat with burning mountains and tried—successfully, so far—to keep the geriatric airplanes he flew out of the mud. He had a responsibility not to run from her, at least before providing an explanation, and she was the girl to hold him to it.

*So where the hell would he be?* she wondered, feeling a flash of embarrassment and letting the images in her mind get mixed up with her always confusing desire for him. She always wanted more, and he had almost promised more a month ago, and she had sensed an impending proposal. But then, as always, the trees had caught fire somewhere in the West, and he'd happily gone back to his real mistress—fighting fires with aging airplanes.

She'd noticed a large cruise ship lying at anchor a half mile offshore, a typical scene for Grand Cayman. She'd watched it earlier as its tenders steadily shuttled the passengers to and from their day in town, and Misty wondered now if somehow Jeff could be on the passenger list. Maybe that was his surprise, to suddenly appear and pull her aboard to a waiting cabin.

*Dream on, girl!*

A cool breeze kissed her face and ruffled her red hair in a flurry of motion. There were fluffy cumulus clouds blocking the malevolent heat of the Caribbean sun, and they added to the luxurious, languid feel of the island. She felt the loose, knee-length dress she was wearing shift provocatively against her body as she reached up to coax her hair back into place just as a hotel minivan glided past her, slowing in the line of traffic. Misty's eyes absently took in the interior, noting a strikingly pretty young woman with long blond hair next to the window.

And Jeff, sitting next to her. He was trying unsuccessfully to hide his face.

*Dammit!* Misty thought. *He IS here! DAMN HIM!*

She shook off the shock of finding he wasn't alone and memorized the phone number of the hotel that was painted on the side of the minivan. It was rounding the corner as she yanked out her phone and punched the number in, still amazed that a U.S.-based cell phone would work in the middle of the Caribbean Sea. At least she could find out where it was taking them.

He would have registered under an alias, she thought, since he was obviously trying to avoid her, but she asked for Jeff Maze's room anyway. There was the predictable delay before the hotel operator reported that there was no Jeff Maze registered.

"Give me the bell desk, or whoever controls your van," she said.

A bellman came on the line with suspicious cheerfulness, all too willing to tell her that their driver was headed to the airport and would return in a half-hour.

*Okay!* she thought. *What more evidence do you need, girl? It's time to write the dog out of your life.*

But he was headed to the airport. Jeff was here and headed to the airport. If she hurried, she might be able to catch him.

She had a rental car and a map, but she also had her pride.

*I am absolutely not going to chase that grinning bastard down and make a fool of myself again, especially not in front of some little girl-toy on his arm. Nope. That's it. Kaput. Over.*

Misty pulled open her purse and rummaged for the picture of the two of them she always carried, moved a few steps to a trash can, and tore the photo into little pieces with open vehemence.

She closed her purse then, and suddenly found herself breaking into a run, dodging through traffic, and racing to reach her rental car—while what was left of her self-esteem helplessly screamed *No!*

The two-lane road to the airport was crowded and slow, but Misty caught up with the empty minivan as the driver was trying to pull away from the curb. She blocked his exit and jumped out, earning a startled honk as she fumbled in her purse for her wallet and another photo of Jeff, which she shoved in front of the driver through the open window.

"The man and the blond you just dropped off . . . is this a picture of him?" she asked.

"Uh, yes," the driver replied, clearly on guard.

"Are they together? The girl and this guy?"

"Ah . . ."

She palmed a twenty-dollar bill into his hand, and he glanced at it before looking up at her in alarm. "Are you . . . his wife?"

Misty laughed a little too sharply and shook her head. "Relax. He doesn't believe in wives. I'm a coworker."

"Okay," he said, smiling thinly. "Yes, they checked out at the same time. I do not know where they're going."

"You don't know which airline they're using?"

"No."

Misty thanked him and returned to her car. She reparked it along the perimeter fence just beyond the terminal building and closed the door behind her. There was a familiar shape on the private aircraft ramp a quarter mile distant, and she had to squint against the afternoon sun to make it out, but once she focused on it, the image was unmistakable.

*My God, a DC-6B!* she thought. It was the same model Jeff flew as an air-tanker captain. The DC-6B he flew back in Wyoming had a red vertical tail-fin with the ship number painted in white.

But the tail on this one was bare metal.

*Those old workhorses are everywhere, I guess,* she thought. *Probably owned by some freight-dog outfit in Miami.*

She turned and looked again. There was something about the tail that bothered her, and she squinted harder, almost convinced she could make out the shadowy remnant of red on the tail in the distance. Something *had* been painted there at one time, she concluded. Some sort of logo that had been stripped off. Maybe even large, white numbers.

But then, shadows of past logos typically haunted the metallic surfaces of old airliners, from the rakish red lightning stripe of former American Airline Flagships to the almost-discernible name "United" on a once proud Mainliner. Even the youngest DC-6B was forty-five years old, and many of the old Douglas ships still flying had served a mind-numbing procession of masters over the decades before ending up with some honest third-tier operator just trying to make a buck—or a peso—as the nationality dictated.

There was no way the DC-6B she was staring at could be one of the airtankers in Jerry Stein's fleet from West Yellowstone. The idea was just too bizarre. It would take all winter to patch them up after the beating they'd taken the previous season in the Yellowstone area alone, and then there was the new federal law prohibiting foreign use of the fleet.

*No. Not possible!* Misty concluded.

But, she reminded herself, here she was standing with her nose halfway through a chain-link fence because one of the living legends of airtankering had just strolled through beautiful downtown Grand Cayman with another woman, and a hottie at that, damn him. Jeff was supposed to be too busy flying important missions in California and had even canceled their long-planned two-week debauch in Hawaii because of the late-season fire!

Furious, she'd given herself the Caymans trip both as a consolation prize and as an in-your-face swipe at Jeff—who professed to hate the Caymans and the "snotty attitude" of the customs agents.

A fresh burst of anger flushed her face as she thought of the blond in the minivan. She should go into the terminal and find the rat and his new playmate so she could create an embarrassing scene loud enough to attract the local cops. Confrontations with errant lovers were usually no fun, but this one had the potential to be very satisfying.

Misty began to turn away when a distant motion on the ramp caught her eye. Someone was walking toward the old DC-6B.

No, it was two someones.

One was a familiar, well-built male carrying a flight bag.

The other was apparently the copilot—a woman with long blond hair lugging a map case.

# Chapter 1

Clark Maxwell mentally forced himself back into the cockpit of his ancient airtanker, leaving the momentary daydream behind. He had to remember where he was: in flight, in charge, and getting tight on fuel, with approximately four thousand pounds of fire retardant left in the belly. He reached down and grasped the small MP3 player and the earphone buds he normally used in cruise flight and stowed them safely in his brain bag, the square briefcase wedged along the left side of his command seat. The rest of the grand classical piece he'd been listening to would have to wait.

The smell of smoke was in his nostrils again, filling the airplane's cockpit with the incongruously delicious aromas of smoldering pine and spruce, the olfactory elixir that had incited the daydream to begin with: images of a smoky mountain cabin adorned by the exquisite feminine presence of Karen Jones wearing nothing more complicated than a smile.

At least he could dream. Of course, Karen Jones herself would never suspect she'd become his fantasy pinup girl in the four years since they'd met. In fact, he reminded himself, she might not even remember who he was.

An insistent male voice was calling over the air-to-air radio, using the slightly unfamiliar call sign of the tanker he was flying.

"Tanker Eighty-four, Lead Four-Two. You copy?"

There was a large "84" painted in white on the red tail, and a small placard repeating the same number on the edge of the glareshield to help the pilots remember their call sign.

*I guess I should get back to work and answer him,* Clark thought, watching his young replacement copilot squirming in the right seat over whether or not to say something about the captain's lengthy silence. Josh White was barely twenty-eight. Rusty Davis, his regular copilot, was in his forties, experienced and fearless when it came to telling his captain whatever might need to be said. Rusty would have already verbally slapped him for drifting, Clark realized, but Josh was just sitting there waiting for Captain Maxwell to return from the ozone. Not good. I'll have to discuss it with him on the ground. Copilots needed to be assertive, and this one wasn't.

Maxwell mashed the transmit button, his lips brushing against the boom microphone's gray foam covering in the process. His headset was beginning to hurt his ears again. It was one of the best—a noise-canceling model with liquid-filled ear pads—but when it began to hurt, it was a sure sign he'd been in the air too long at one stretch.

"I hear you, Four-Two," Clark replied. "That was a good dry run. Are you clearing me finally to follow you in for the real drop?"

"Roger," the lead-plane pilot said. "The zone is almost too smoky, and I need your remaining gates about two hundred yards downslope on the north side. We're going to try to keep the flank from jumping the ridge, and try to cool the line so the dozers that are working up the ridge can make some headway. It's going to be tricky, because there's a roaring updraft coming off the river that really bucked me. You saw the escape route when I flew it, right?"

"Roger, Sammy. I was right behind you at the time, if you recall. Down the valley and then left over the small draw."

"That's your engine failure escape route, too, Eighty-four."

"Okay, let's get this done," Clark said, trying to control a flash of impatience.

"Eighty-four, if you're lined up well, go ahead. Otherwise, we'll hold for the helo at two o'clock low."

Clark could see the helicopter approaching with a full water bucket, and he was in no mood to wait for him.

"Come on, Sam. Let's do it so we can get the hell outta here," Clark replied, his voice clearly testy despite his failed attempt to keep emotion out of it. Lead Four-Two was the call sign of Sam Littlefox, a friend and a former Air Force pilot who also happened to be a full-blooded Ogalala Sioux from Rapid City. There were times he could be irritatingly careful.

"You've gotta understand," Clark had explained to Sam over drinks the previous week, "sometimes we civilian-trained veterans don't completely appreciate such strict regimentation of what's always been a somewhat relaxed occupation."

"In other words, you guys don't like rules."

"No. Not true. We . . . just like to comply with them in our own way, at our own pace."

Not that Sam wasn't right about the need for checklists and better coordination and smooth teamwork. But it was a bummer to be told by an ex-military jock how to apply an art form invented by civilian pilots to begin with.

Even more irritating, he reminded himself, was the fact that Congress was threatening to give the whole show to the Air Force Reserves and wipe out an entire industry—seasonals and all—an event that would end his job as well.

Jerry Stein, the owner of the old Doug DC-6 he was flying, was completely panicked. Most of Stein's money came from the annual Forest Service fire contracts awarded to the lowest bidder. Stein had been frantically lobbying the entire Montana congressional delegation for months now, begging them to oppose the move.

*Not that I care,* Maxwell thought.

Well, he *did* care about Jerry, he corrected himself. Too many years of friendship not to. But he had reached the personal conclusion that it *was* time to bring in the military or some steady professional team with enough money for newer airplanes and decent training. The airtanker industry was falling apart, which was one of the reasons he'd given up dropping retardant four years ago and pledged to stay in retirement.

The other reason for his escape he remembered all too well: the constant feeling of being stalked by fate. Having survived seventeen seasons, the statistical realities were creeping up on him like a tiger in the dark. Clark remembered the night some four years ago when he'd fed the number of crashes and deaths into a pocket calculator and realized that after twenty years of aerial fire fighting his chances of survival would be no better than 50 percent. A chill had shuddered through him, and he made the decision to quit on the spot. Not even smokejumping was as dangerous.

*So what the hell are you doing here, Maxwell?* he thought to himself as he tweaked the throttles, the question finding no ready answer other than the memory of Jerry Stein's impassioned call for help two months ago. He was short three captains, Jerry had whined, and would face death-by-contract-cancellation if his "best captain" didn't relent. Clark's resulting snap decision to come out of retirement and roll the dice once more seemed very strange in hindsight. Jerry had never been that persuasive, but he'd somehow discerned during Clark's weakest moment that his early retiree was missing the fraternity and the danger and the smoke. With the realization, Jerry had played him like a well-hooked trout.

"Okay, Jere," Clark had said after the sixth phone call, "you wore me down. But only for this one season!" He'd replaced the receiver feeling both startled and pleased that he was going to get away from four years of chasing temporary flying jobs around the globe, an itinerant existence that had begun to wear on him.

There was still the dream of running the flight-training department of some college or university someday, but that would first require a return to the real world. Maybe another season of firefighting was a good beginning. Maybe, he'd mused, when the season was over, he might even muster enough courage to leave professional flying altogether and apply to an enormous state university somewhere to teach forestry *and* aerial fire fighting. Perhaps he could even teach a course about the history of aerial fire fighting, a little-understood profession barely fifty years old. Years back he'd spent almost one entire winter researching the origins of the idea, if for no other reason than to dispel some of the myths. It turned out to be a fascinating anthology. The idea of dropping incendiary things from airplanes in order to start fires and destroy things dated from World War I. But the idea of using the same air machines to put out fires was a relatively contemporary twist that began in 1953 with the combined efforts of the Forest Service and the state of California.

The practice of dropping parachutists known as smokejumpers to fight small forest fires was a technique first begun in the thirties and early forties, but there had been no way to deliver large quantities of water directly to burning trees in remote areas until a collection of old Air Force bombers was outfitted with tanks to carry water and, later, slurry.

There were no manuals back then to teach pilots how to fly heavily loaded airplanes down burning canyons at near treetop level, or how to survive the hellish columns of superheated air and amazing hazards such as exploding trees. Most of the techniques were figured out by dangerous trial and error, and the closest body of pilot expertise resided in the crop-dusting industry, a fiercely independent fraternity of agricultural pilots used to keeping themselves alive by their own wits, men who—as a friend of Clark's once put it as charitably as possible—held a healthy degree of skepticism for other people's rules.

Clark chuckled at the memory of his first encounters with the original airtanker pilots. Profane, brave, rough, and scathingly unimpressed with "college pukes" and "fancy, schmancy Air Farce dandies," they were a frontier bunch in a Wild West show. His checkout as captain of a modified DC-4—an earlier, shorter version of the DC-6 and DC-7—had been a single flight in the left seat with a tobacco-spitting owner-instructor, and his first flight to a fire had been with an assigned first officer who held only a mechanic's license and was slowly dying of emphysema. The man sat in the copilot's seat sucking on a medical oxygen bottle. The Federal Aviation Administration (FAA) would have had a collective coronary, but the FAA seldom got involved in airtanker business in the early days. The whole shaky affair was between the Forest Service and the pilots, and the FAA was more than happy to look the other way.

Slowly through the late fifties and early sixties, a dozen mom-and-pop aviation companies using ancient aircraft barely saved from the scrap yard began to form a small but very profitable industry. Buying old airplanes from the military for almost nothing and then retrofitting them with tanks and "gates" to release slurry, the airtanker companies began leasing their aircraft, along with pilots, each summer to the various governmental units fighting fires. Bit by bit, the training and the pilots became better and more sophisticated. Year by year the companies gained more political clout and snuggled in bed more closely with the governmental agencies using their services, quietly exuding the attitude that only they could be trusted to deal with an industry they had created.

And season by season, better techniques were developed for sizing up a fire and using lead-plane pilots to decide the best and safest method of laying down a line of retardant dropped from 150 feet in the air.

Clark had been there through much of the later learning process, as it slowly evolved into a rule- and procedure-driven business with safety considerations gaining more ground. It was discovered that lead planes flying test runs over a fire gave the pilot time to find hazards as well as to search for the best track and position and the best escape route a big lumbering tanker could use to get out safely. The lead pilot would fly a "dry" run with the tanker in formation behind him, and only after that would the real bombing run occur. The heavily loaded tanker would then roar over a ridge or down a valley just behind the lead plane, as if on an invisible leash.

"It gives the ground crews time to head off the fire front, or otherwise turn a massive fire toward a less catastrophic destination," Clark was used to explaining. "We don't put out the fires, we work with the firefighters on the ground to slow down and contain the fires, and we're most effective when we get there in the early stages."

Helicopters were added in the sixties to take it a step further, some carrying water in large buckets, and some ferrying helitack crews in to attack smaller fires by hand. One of the largest helicopters in the world, the giant Skycrane, was also recruited, an aircraft big enough to carry a tank the size of a small railroad freight car along with the pumps to rapidly suck from a nearby lake a full load of water that could then be dropped on a fire.

Year by year the abilities of the airtanker pilots as a group became more effective, and year by year—as Clark bitterly recalled—the maintenance and the state of repair of the aging tankers seemed to become progressively less reliable.

"Why on earth does anyone do this job?" a local reporter once asked him with his little tape recorder stopped.

"The thrill and the accomplishment and, to some extent, the money," Clark replied, speaking the truth, yet instantly worried that the reporter might print that off-the-record comment and unleash a typical firestorm of protest from the other pilots.

It was, after all, still a very hazardous business, as insurance companies continually reaffirmed by refusing life insurance to airtanker pilots. Having the wings literally rip off airtankers in flight was, while not routine, unfortunately not unknown. They could all recall the loss of two C-119 Flying Boxcars to wing failure in the early eighties, and every time Clark had to pull up hard from a dangerous run through a flaming valley, that same nagging worry about the metallic sanctity of his craft sat like a patient buzzard on his shoulders, as if waiting for the inevitable moment a hidden crack would suddenly enlarge and engulf the entire structure and remove *his* wings.

It was something they seldom discussed openly, since such occurrences were not survivable.

Clark shook his head to expunge the thoughts and bring himself back to the moment. The lead plane—a specially modified, light twin-engine aircraft crammed full of radios—was banking now a thousand feet below him and soaring over the emerald green carpet of coniferous forest. Clark pulled the four throttles of the DC-6B back and slowed, preparing to follow. He'd use the usual forty-five degree descending left bank to reverse course from east to west and line up on the leading edge of the fire, then eyeball the release point, while tracking the lead plane visually. When the moment felt exactly right and he had the wind conditions and drift figured, he'd toggle the remaining heavy red retardant out of the belly of the old converted Douglas airliner and pull up. Hopefully, the slurry would hit the threatened trees just beyond the swath of retardant he'd already laid down. So far, the line was holding, despite the size and intensity of a fire this big, and the dozers were getting closer.

They could still lose it, though, Clark thought. Leave it to the Forest Service to snatch defeat from the jaws of victory again by waiting too long to call for the limited number of available airtankers. This one had been another classic case of a young incident commander experienced only with small fires being reluctant to call for the airtanker fleet lest he be criticized. He'd needed a bigger fire before he could be sure.

Now he had one.

Of course, there were other factors increasing the annual forest fire stakes, and they all knew it. Wildlands all over the West were feeling the encroachment of new homes and cabins with the owners all demanding complete fire protection. Too often however, those beautiful surrounding forests were filled with dry tinder and brush and deadfall, which too many residents refused to clear away. That made fire season a formula for annual disaster, and a continuous, growing frustration.

How many times, Clark wondered, had he sat in the standby shack waiting for someone officially to call for airtanker help while a fire they all knew was going to be bad grew from a flicker to a blaze? Too often the call didn't come until the fire was threatening communities, cabins, and parks. He'd seen the same mistake, year after year, throughout his seventeen seasons, and he'd sat on the sidelines in retirement during the last four years watching the same nonsense until he was bone weary of it.

"We bomb no fires before their time," one of the pilots had put it with an appropriate eye roll and a toast. "No junior fires for us. Only full grown, manly, monster fires where dropping ten thousand gallons of retardant is about as effective as pissin' in the wind."

Like the fire he was fighting now, growing larger by the minute east of Jackson Hole.

*I'm going to need to nail it this time,* Clark thought. If the blaze jumped the ridge, not even a squadron of airtankers would be enough to save the area.

And, hit or miss, as soon as the drop was made he'd have to boogie back to West Yellowstone before the fuel got too low. The chances of running so low he'd have to suffer the embarrassment of declaring a fuel emergency and landing at Jackson Hole was extremely unlikely, but it was a reputational nightmare that kept his calculations sharp.

The other pilots would love something like that, of course. He'd be needled unmercifully by what he had laughingly dubbed the "FLOPPs"—the Fraternal and Learned Order of Perfect Pilots, of which he was a charter member—an acronym his fellow airtanker pilots had declared insulting.

*Fuel's tight but okay,* Clark decided, the low-fuel nightmare gaining ground. Sudden fuel leaks were not unheard of on these old birds. *Hopefully we'd notice the levels dropping before the engines got real quiet and she became a glider.* He glanced at the fuel gauges again just to be sure, wondering if they'd been calibrated or replaced since the last time he'd flown ship 84. He'd forgotten to check, and suddenly that seemed like a serious oversight. Few of the small items the pilots wrote up were fixed quickly. It was too easy to defer them until the end of the season, when the list of inoperative and questionable things needing repair became staggering.

*Should be fine,* Clark reassured himself, banishing the nightmarish thought of dead sticking a fuel-starved four-engine airliner into a geyser-infested Yellowstone valley. The prospect of living through such a forced landing only to boil to death in a superheated geyser pool was a bogus worry, though the FLOPPs loved to terrify new copilots and engineers with the possibility. Truth was, no crew member was likely to survive such a crash landing to begin with.

Maxwell's experienced eyes swept the engine instruments again in un-conscious routine. All the gauges on Tanker 84 that still worked were giving steady readings, and that was a surprise.

He knew intimately all of the DC-6s Stein owned by number and person-ality. He hated flying old T-84, since she was the least dependable of the fleet—a real hangar queen he'd been assigned only because his favorite, Tanker 88, had "gone out of service" at the last minute.

"Eighty-eight's in the hangar, Clark. You'll be taking Tanker Eighty-six, instead," the operations manager had told him at seven A.M. But at the last second, Jeff Maze and Jeff's longtime copilot, Mike Head, were switched to Tanker 86, and Clark drew the lemon of the fleet.

"When do I get Eighty-eight back?"

"Maybe tomorrow. If you're reasonably polite to me."

Out of all the DC-6s in Jerry Stein's geriatric fleet, T-88 was Clark Maxwell's favorite. He'd flown her enough to learn her myriad idiosyncra-cies. She was a creaky old metallic grandma with a quarter of her flight in-struments, and sometimes even the fuel gauges, inoperative. But she was also a flying battlewagon originally designed to carry an infinite number of airline passengers for an infinite number of years.

He trusted her. And that meant something, especially now.

When the wing box had suddenly collapsed on an old Lockheed C-130A over a California fire the previous summer, detaching the wings and killing three of his friends, Clark had watched the amateur videotape of the disas-ter on TV from the safety of his apartment in North Dakota, assuring him-self it couldn't happen to him. His old Doug was far tougher than any of the old 130s. In fact, he wouldn't hesitate to fly Tanker 88 again—assuming he was dumb enough ever to go back to aerial fire fighting. Everyone knew that the DC-6s were far better built than the old 130s.

All things were relative, Clark counseled himself. *So what* if the DC-6B's fuel gauges were unreliable, or even if half the forward flight panel was in-operative, as long as the wings stayed on.

He kept track of the fuel in his head anyway—a simple matter of how much fuel he'd departed with versus how long he'd been sucking at the tanks in flight and at what rate. As long as there were no serious fuel leaks in the wings, the calculations were always golden, whether or not the gauges worked.

*Besides,* he reminded himself with a grin he knew the copilot wouldn't understand, *when I can read the gauges, I don't trust them anyway.*

It was time to turn.

Clark Maxwell began banking the DC-6 back toward the west, completing the turn and steadying the ship on course in trail to the lead plane. He let the Douglas drop the last four hundred feet to the target altitude that would put him one hundred feet above the ridge a mile and a half ahead. He could see the lead plane disappearing intermittently through smoke plumes as it blazed the aerial trail, and he followed, urging his ancient airliner toward the same hole in the sky.

The lead plane was a Beech Baron. The Forest Service owned nineteen of them, but all had been grounded six months before for exceeding the maximum lifetime flight hours. Six of the Barons, however, had been specially inspected and returned to service to fly one final season on a waiver, and Sam Littlefox—Lead Four-Two—was flying one of them.

Maxwell glanced at Josh White again, wondering if Rusty was enjoying his day off. He fully intended to make Rusty pay for leaving him with a greenhorn like White.

Clark sighed, reminding himself of his instructor responsibilities. If White was supposed to do a better job of participating, maybe Clark should be a good captain and brief him every now and then, not to mention help teach him.

He hit the interphone button.

"Josh, I'm going to bring us across the ridge from left to right, then bank right, use left rudder and sideslip a bit down the slope, then bank back toward the slope, then do a tight *right* bank and pull hard just as I release the load. Then we'll roll out to the left and fly the escape route."

White was nodding, his eyes wide.

"Okay?" Clark queried.

The ridge was coming up fast, and White's eyes were riveted on the eighty-foot trees near the summit.

"Okay!" White replied at last, still fumbling with the interphone switch.

Insistent southerly winds had been assaulting Jackson Hole and the Tetons for the past few days, whipping up sparks laid down by a deluge of lightning strikes. It had all started with a dry, tightly wound thunderstorm packing far more energy in disturbed electrons than in water. The electrical storm had ignited a series of small blazes in an exceptionally dry forest filled with seventy years' growth of unburned debris, the legacy of the newly controversial American policy of trying to prevent all forest fires. Smokey Bear, according to some, had been setting us up.

The problem was far more complex, of course, than just a debate over the issue of whether naturally caused wildland fires should burn or be doused. But a century of preventing natural forest fires had helped to create vast regions of forests with heavy buildups of dead vegetation, dense stands of trees that hadn't evolved an adaptation to fire, and sometimes an increase in fire-prone plants. Forests unburned for three hundred years were primed to explode and just waiting for the next hot, dry summer. It was precisely the same situation that had sparked the multiple firestorms of 1988 in Yellowstone National Park, a monstrous series of fires that burned almost a third of America's first national preserve.

And in the summer of 2003, the stage had been set once again, with a tinderbox of dry, vulnerable forests, a record drought born of global warming, and sustained high winds from the south. Everything was ready and waiting for nature to strike a match.

Nature obliged.

The storm had crackled and boomed through the Jackson Hole valley on Sunday, but the first wisps of smoke hadn't signaled the inflammatory result for another twenty-four hours, and then the Forest Service had blinked once more, hesitating too long to launch the remaining airtankers.

"Until the media arrives, we sit," Jeff Maze, who served as the president of the Airtanker Fliers' Association, was fond of saying to anyone who'd listen.

The DC-6B was bucking now, its fuselage kicking violently upward as the wings struggled to follow and Maxwell fought to descend. The mountains and ridges—and the massive presence of the Grand Tetons looming ahead to the west—generated confusing wind currents that in turn spawned mechanical turbulence and bone-jarring updrafts and downdrafts. The DC-6B had to run the gauntlet of roiled atmosphere even before approaching the massive columns of rising, scorching air that could flip a plane on its side in an instant. Clark was familiar with the washboard of disturbed air, but one never got comfortable, and he could see Josh was sitting white knuckled in the copilot's seat and breathing hard.

Clark Maxwell began slowing the old Doug—as the pilots called any member of the Douglas family. He glanced at the airspeed, satisfied with 145 knots. Slow enough to make the drop effective, slow enough to minimize the beating the aircraft would take with the turbulence, yet enough kinetic energy to pull up and escape if he lost an engine or some other problem occurred.

He felt the massive old control yoke shake in his left hand as she bumped through the first of the ridgeline updrafts and then hammered through the combination of heat and wind, yawing to the left and right and slamming through the angry columns of air like a Laramie broncobuster.

"Here's where you just have to watch him pass over the release point, and then count yourself down to the same point," Clark said, his voice wavering in the turbulence.

Josh was nodding and trying hard not to appear rattled.

They hung on, Clark moving his thumb lightly on the smooth surface of the red release button and waiting for the precise moment when instinct and experience would triumph over training and tell him when to loose the retardant into its arcing, cascading trajectory.

In the lead plane, Sam Littlefox was already pulling up and turning right, having just passed over the initial release point and leaving the target to the airtanker behind him. Clark could see the target downslope and just ahead. He could also see the flames roaring up the ridge, but still only halfway to the top.

Maxwell banked right and nudged the rudder left, feeling his stomach protest as the heavy airplane dropped below the steep ridgeline and sideslipped with an alarming sink rate, the trees and boulders becoming intimate visions in motion below. He rolled back left suddenly and aimed his cockpit at the unburned trees above the fire, then rolled sharply right again and pulled hard, hitting the release switch when it felt just right.

"Now," he said to Josh, his thumb already to the hilt on the drop switch. He could feel the DC-6B shake loose the remaining slurry and perk up aerodynamically—like a good quarter horse suddenly promised the barn after a long day of riding.

They punched into a rising plume of smoke and the cockpit windows suddenly went opaque. There were more shuddering impacts with the superheated air rising angrily from below, and the wings of the converted passenger liner flexed alarmingly, torturing and twisting the 1946-vintage fuselage in the process. He could hear the airframe itself protesting and squealing loudly as he moved the throttles forward and held his bank through twenty-five degrees of turn, following neither vision nor instruments for a few seconds as he let memory guide them through his mental picture of the escape route down the narrow valley.

And suddenly they were in the open again, precisely where he intended to be. The cockpit filled with a fresh blast of smoke, but blue sky engulfed them in a comforting embrace as the adjacent ridges dropped safely away and the DC-6 leapt for thinner air, its commander mentally plotting a course for the retardant base at West Yellowstone.

"Wow!" was the only comment from the right seat.

"What?" Maxwell asked with a grin. "You thought we were in trouble?"

"No . . . I mean," Josh began. "Well . . . I couldn't see anything for a few seconds there."

"Tanker Eighty-four, Lead Four-Two," Sam was saying. "I don't care that I'm not supposed to report the results all the time. The crew boss is telling me on the air-to-ground that you guys nailed it. Nice job."

"Roger, and we're returning to base. Understand Tankers Eighteen and Twenty should be with you in five minutes?"

"Roger that."

Clark Maxwell strained ahead to see the approaching aircraft, which would be little more than dots on the horizon, if he could spot them at all. He'd already heard both pilots checking in on the frequency, but not knowing where they were in the smoky skies ahead was always a worry.

Only the lead-plane pilot had a traffic collision avoidance system on his panel, a newly installed TCAS that graphically displayed on a small screen where all the other air traffic was around him. The Forest Service didn't require TCAS units on the airtankers they used under contract, which meant there was no way the pilots were ever going to get them. Jerry Stein was too cheap to buy such expensive luxuries for his ancient DC-6 fleet voluntarily. As a result, Clark lived with a low rumble of worry that one day he was going to pull up through a plume of smoke and find another tanker in his windscreen. The mere thought of trading paint at a combined speed of four hundred knots could still bring him awake at night in a cold sweat.

Usually on such nights he could go back to sleep, like most pilots. She, on the other hand—if he was lucky enough to have feminine company— seldom could, and at least one relationship had been worn away on the lathe of that repeated nightmare.

Once again Clark snapped himself back to the present, this time aided by a strange shuddering that had momentarily rippled through the airplane.

"What was that?" the copilot was asking.

Clark shook his head slowly. "I don't know. It felt like number three or four." He checked the engine gauges, finding everything steady, and put his hand on the throttles, finding nothing amiss. "A transient, I guess," he explained.

"Sorry?" Josh managed.

"A transient problem. Flashes into being, then cures itself without a trace."

"Okay."

"We have a lot of those in this machine. Like warning lights. Keeps you guessing what warning light you almost saw go on and off."

Clark felt wholly dissatisfied with his glib dismissal. Obviously it *had* been something, and in older airplanes, anything out of the ordinary was a cause for concern.

"It was kind of a . . . a racheting feeling," Josh added.

"A feeling or a sound?" Clark asked.

"Feeling."

"Yeah. I agree."

"But I don't feel it now," Josh said.

"Keep a close watch on the gauges," Clark ordered, turning back to the task of looking for West Yellowstone Airport on the horizon and working to suppress the creepy feeling that he was missing something.

# Chapter 2

Karen Jones's already-limited patience suddenly expired.

She threw the dog-eared copy of *People* back on the small coffee table with a sigh and crossed with a catlike pounce to the small receptionist's window.

"Excuse me," Karen said softly, pulling the sliding glass open as she looked the startled, white-frocked young woman in the eye. She couldn't be older than twenty, Karen decided, yet she was trying to play the stern senior nurse. The effect was almost comical.

"Sorry to be pushy, but I've got to see the great medicine man right now," Karen told her. "No more delays, please. I just don't have time."

"Now, Ms. Jones, the doctor is with another—"

"No!" Karen's right hand snapped up in a stop gesture as she shook her head. The young nurse fell silent, eyeing Karen's hand as if it were a coiled snake. "No, I need him now. For just a minute."

Down the short hallway from one of the exam rooms, Karen could hear laughter. She could also hear the clock ticking loudly on the wall as she waited for a reply that she realized probably wasn't going to come from the startled girl.

"Look," Karen tried again, "I really don't want to be rude, but let me try to explain. We've got a mess of fires trying to bake Jackson Hole. I'm one of the people who needs to parachute in and put them out. But before I can do that, I need the doctor to sign my release form. No signature, no jump, no trees, no town. So I really do need you to go ask the doc"—Karen paused and chuckled at more muffled laughter from down the hall, recalling how good-looking young Dr. Rafferty was—"if he'll step away for a moment and sign this slip so we can get me back to gainful employment. That make sense to you?"

"Well . . ."

"He's having entirely too much fun anyway."

More silence.

"See . . . I'm not *asking* here, I'm more or less telling you that's what I need you to do right now. *Please!*"

"I have strict instructions not to disturb him."

"I can just imagine," Karen said, glancing down the hall again. "But in the interest of municipal security, you've got to."

"Sorry?"

"My poor smokejumping squad is leaderless as long as I'm on a medical, and that could be dangerous."

"Sorry?"

"I'm their squad leader. Our base is jumped out, and I'm on the top of the list again, and even as we speak, they could be arriving out there in town, prowling around aimlessly with chain saws, looking for fires to douse and terrorizing the local women. Poor guys."

The nurse-receptionist stared at her blankly.

"NOW, please!" Karen added.

The woman jumped slightly, her face betraying the progress of a brief internal struggle between policy and prudence, concluding with the decision that the patient before her might be dangerous—especially if she really was a smokejumper. She fairly leapt up from her desk and disappeared into the diminutive clinical warrens of the converted house, returning with the amused doctor in tow.

*He's almost datable*, Karen thought as he approached, instantly taken aback at the premature nature of the concept. Her marriage was dying, but she was not yet single.

Dr. Rafferty smiled. "Ms. Jones, are you terrorizing my nurse?"

"Someone has to, Doc. She should have been chasing after you with a whip and chair to keep you on schedule. I'm dying of boredom out—"

"What's the emergency?" he interrupted gently.

"Burning trees, requiring my presence."

"I'm not following you."

"A forest fire. I'm a smokejumper, remember? With a turned ankle? The initial diagnosis was in Boise, but I'm all repaired now and just need your sign off."

"Oh, yeah. I remember the paperwork."

She thrust the form at him with a pen, but he motioned her back to one of the exam rooms instead, where he began manipulating her right ankle.

"It's just fine, see?" she urged. "It's reasonably pink and I'm walking on it without pain. So please just sign me off and I'll get out of here."

"You sprained it?" he asked in an even voice.

"No, I just turned it."

He was probing around the back of her heel, and she worked hard to keep her foot still and suppress a cry of pain. Instead, she gave him a broad smile, which, along with her short blond hair and tanned, *Baywatch* look, usually worked to alter male attitudes. She'd winked her way out of more traffic tickets than most cops could carry using the "cute chick trick," as she called it. Maybe she could make it work on an overly cautious contract doctor.

"Doc, you sure all that touchy-feely stuff you're doing down there is medically necessary?" she teased.

He looked up and met her eyes without a flicker of reaction. "When I do this—" He moved her foot sharply to the right and once more she had to concentrate hard to keep her smile and not wince in pain. "—does it hurt?"

"Course not," Karen replied, her voice a bit too strained to be believable. She cleared her throat and tried again. "No pain, no problem."

The physician stood up and leaned toward her, studying her eyes so long and from such a close proximity she was half afraid he was thinking of kissing her. But he reached out instead and gently wiped an escaped tear from her cheek.

"Medical exams always make you cry, do they?" he asked.

"Huh?"

He smiled. "Or just painful ankles?"

"I don't understand."

"The tear got you busted. That ankle is still tender."

Karen sighed. "Well, big deal, Doc."

"Just because you're a brave girl and too tough to yelp when it hurts doesn't mean you're ready to jump yet."

"Now, look, Doc—"

"Maybe you are and maybe you're not. Ms. Jones, I'm not going to release you without a thorough exam, and I can't do that until tomorrow. I've got other patients waiting."

"Doctor, please! This really is an emergency. I'm needed in the morning."

"When?"

"Ah, by noon."

"Okay. Soak it tonight and come back at eight A.M. sharp and I'll take a good look at it before I take care of anyone else. I'll let you go if I feel it's ready."

———

Karen emerged from the building working hard to hide the slight limp from all the doctor's probing. She had aspirin and water in her car and was going to need them.

A familiar noise caused her to look up. One of Jerry Stein's DC-7s was rumbling off the West Yellowstone runway a half mile away from the physician's office. She watched the ancient pelican clawing for altitude as it climbed slowly southbound in the thin air of nearly seven thousand feet above sea level. The four engines driving the huge four-bladed propellers were at maximum power, producing a familiar and comfortable roar of massive airborne horsepower wildly distinct from the cacophony of fanjets. Everything about the old prop airliners was different, she thought, especially the sedate way they climbed. It was a startling contrast to the mental image she had of Boeings. Turbojets always seemed to leap into the air and climb more like missiles than airplanes.

*A far cry from our jump plane, too.* The thought triggered a rush of memories of the many times she'd stepped out the door of a jump plane in flight to the sobering yank of the opening chute and the breathtaking, green vista of the forest spreading in all directions beneath her.

Working as a fire crewmember for the Forest Service in the summer of her collegiate senior year had been literally a baptism by fire, and she'd loved the challenging experience and the exhausting work. But the most crystalline memory had been watching from the ground as the first smoke-jumpers she'd ever seen unfurled themselves from a passing airplane, their parachutes looking like white mushrooms against the deep blue of the sky as they floated down toward a distant ridge to do hand-to-hand combat with burning trees. The scene had become as indelible in her mind as the questions she'd asked her crew boss: "Who are they? What do they do?" And, "What kind of person would skydive onto a forest fire carrying little more than hand tools?"

"The best kind," he'd replied.

By late September she was asking where to apply.

Karen O'Farrell's acceptance the following spring as one of the fabled Missoula smokejumpers was in some ways more exciting than getting her bachelor's degree in forestry and being accepted to graduate school.

"But why on earth," a soon-to-be former boyfriend had asked the very evening of her impromptu celebration, "would any sane person *do* that? Especially a pretty *girl?*"

Karen's answer had surprised even her. "To help make history," she'd replied.

She'd been astounded to find that the very first smokejumper to skydive on a fire had done so no earlier than 1941. Before that, small forest fires routinely became large forest fires while fire crews tried to hike through inaccessible backcountry to reach them.

Smokejumping changed all that. Suddenly tiny fires spotted from the air could be attacked almost immediately, and she was thrilled to become a part of the tradition.

She returned to the present, smiling at the vibrant memories and pulling her new key chain remote from a pocket of her jeans before pressing a button to start the engine of her Suburban. The little remote was more fun than practical, but she took childish delight in starting the engine from across a parking lot when someone was standing unsuspectingly by her car. The look on the victim's face when confronted with an empty vehicle coming to life was always a hoot.

The little remote had been the only item on her Christmas wish list eight months ago, and her husband, Trent, had forgotten it completely. Instead, he bought her a bottle of perfume and two hundred dollars' worth of skimpy things from Victoria's Secret. Maybe she was being selfish, but the incident had truly hurt her feelings.

Karen slid behind the wheel and strapped herself in, trying to separate important thoughts from painful ones. It was over with Trent, and they both knew it, but she'd probably wait until the fires were out and the season was over to formalize it and get on with her life. She'd said nothing about her intentions when she'd seen him at the hangar an hour ago—his tepid hug was their first physical contact in the nearly five months he'd been living in West Yellowstone without her. Besides, she figured, if she brought up divorce now, he'd probably just start hitting her again out of anger—a startling propensity she never knew he had before January.

She'd warned him years before when they were married that if he ever hit her, the first blow would be the last. But after the brief battering in January, she'd elected to stay in their Seattle area house for at least the next few months, ignoring his apologies and growing increasingly uncomfortable with his anger, and his presence. When it was finally time for her to go to Missoula once more to take up her seasonal smokejumping duties, the departure was a great relief. Trent was heading off as well to work for Jerry Stein in West Yellowstone, and in truth, Missoula and West Yellowstone were only four road hours apart. Yet in the intervening time, neither of them had made the effort to bridge the distance.

She put the Suburban in gear and glanced at her watch. Then she put the shifter in park again, suddenly unsure of where she should go.

The original plan had been to head straight for the airport and fax a copy of the medical release back to the jump base in Missoula. But now she was in one of those momentary quandaries she hated, between an urgent mission and scheduled relaxation, with license for neither. There was really no reason to rush back to the airfield since she hadn't yet succeeded in getting the medical clearance. But suddenly kicking back and doing nothing productive seemed too much like loafing and letting everyone down.

Not that getting hurt in the first place hadn't let the squad down.

The injury had been her own fault, of course, and that was both embarrassing and aggravating. The jump two weeks ago into a remote section of forest eighty miles north of Boise had been routine—her eleventh jump of the season, and her second as squad leader. She was first out the door and stuck the landing in the middle of the small meadow they'd selected, a bravura performance she knew the others had seen but would say nothing about.

The fire had eaten away at only a few acres so far, and within eight hours they had managed to cut line rather easily around the south side and halt it with no need of helitack or tankers. The task accomplished, she decided they would camp in the black—one of the burned areas incapable of igniting again—and walk out in the morning. But she'd neglected to lace her boots tightly before hiking a few yards downslope in the dark to relieve herself, and what would have been a routine stumble over a small, unseen branch became a twisted ankle—though not bad enough to preclude the next day's ten-mile hike to the road.

She'd cinched her boot up as tightly as possible and decided to say nothing to her squad. But when she stepped off the bus after the long ride, the limp gave her away.

She had already developed a reputation when serving as squad leader of harping about proper medical clearance and the willingness to ground yourself if you weren't ready to jump, as well as warning against the dangers of too much "can-do" machismo. Once she'd been found out, turning herself in to the doctor in Boise was unavoidable—as had been the act of checking in with the designated physician in West Yellowstone.

The sound of her cell phone corking off triggered a flash of irritation. She knew who it was without looking at the screen, and almost regretted giving the jump duty officer her number so soon, especially since she had a few minutes to herself. Karen punched the call over to her mailbox. Her squad couldn't be used until tomorrow anyway, and if Trent was trying to find her through the jump shack because he'd lost her cell number once again, so much the better. She would just be out of pocket for a while.

*Okay, I'll relax. I'll relax for, let's see, two hours, then drop by Ops.*

The sudden urge to drive east into Yellowstone Park tugged at her as a possibility, but she rejected it. She knew she should go back to the hotel, ice the ankle, and pop pills for the rest of the day. But she wasn't into "should."

Was there a Starbucks in town?

No, she reminded herself. She'd searched on the Internet from Boise. West Yellowstone was still too small for its own Starbucks, although there was one espresso kiosk as a poor substitute.

Karen put the Suburban in gear once more and maneuvered out of the parking lot onto the street, turning away from the Stagecoach Inn just to the south where she was staying and driving past the other motel where Trent had been living for the past five months. She tried to push Trent's scowling face out of her mind. He had worked for Jerry Stein off and on for fifteen years. Karen didn't care much for the man, nor did she like his ragtag fleet of tankers and helicopters, though the men he employed to fly them were a fun bunch—a wild cross section of humanity ranging from quiet, professional family men to unforgettable characters with no fear and less restraint.

She passed the espresso stand set up in a parking lot and continued on for a block before deciding her caffeine deficit was too serious to ignore. Relaxation was fueled by coffee.

Her cell phone began ringing again, and this time she reached over and punched the "send to voice mail" button without looking as she rolled down the window to place her order.

"Grande nonfat, no-whip, double mocha," she said, amused at the puzzled reaction. "What? You don't speak Seattleese?"

"Sorry?" the attendant replied with a blank stare.

She rolled her eyes at him and chuckled.

"Okay, I'll go real slow. You do make mochas, right?"

"Right."

"Make one for me, please, but use skim milk, a double shot of espresso, no whip cream, and put it in the twelve-ounce cup. Got it?"

He look relieved and nodded, taking her money as the cell phone beeped to signal a waiting message.

She sat waiting for the mocha as she drummed the top of the steering wheel with the fingers of her left hand, her eyes falling on her ring finger again. The lighter band of skin was almost completely gone now, the summer sun having erased the evidence of her unhappy marital entanglement. Parachutists had no business wearing rings that could easily get caught on the structure of the aircraft they were departing, or on a tree branch or numerous other objects—mistakes that could literally yank off fingers. As soon as she'd heard the stories in jump school, she'd made a habit of carefully placing her wedding rings in a safe-deposit box every May before the season started.

She'd married Trent in an impassioned November fever, which began with a simple slow dance at an upscale Sacramento watering hole. God knows what she'd been thinking. Right out of graduate school and suddenly swept up by Trent's overpowering attentions, it had seemed a dream. He'd barely wrenched his B.A. from a tiny college in Missouri, but he was exciting and he kept calling and calling until he wore her down and she began to believe they were really in love. But by May—the first season his veteran smokejumping bride removed her rings—the newly married veteran fire-fighting aircraft mechanic was accusing her of having an affair.

"With whom?" she'd asked in anger.

"Hell, woman, I don't know. Probably one of the college studs on your jump squad. Maybe you didn't want 'em to know you're married."

"Oh, yeah, Trent," she'd snorted. "You broke the code. Now the whole world will know that we're not there to fight fires, we're just dropping in for an orgy, and I didn't want the rings to intimidate the studs."

"Well . . ."

"We only need a few hours to douse the fire, then we can spend the next three nights on the mountain boinking our brains out."

"Hey, darlin', I didn't mean—"

"Yes, you did. You meant the accusation: you just didn't think it through. Grow up," she'd sneered at him. "I take off my rings because I'm kinda fond of my fingers remaining attached, and my whole squad knows I'm happily married."

*Correction,* she thought now. *Was happily married.*

That was five years ago.

She felt a twinge of regret at how his face had fallen into a sort of lost-puppy look. He'd made a bumbling, if sincere, apology, and things had been good for several years. But the truth was, their fire had already begun to cool, the mutual loss of interest propelled into free fall by whatever had been eating him for the past two fire seasons. Karen knew she wasn't the problem, nor was there another lover. But something serious had driven him to a far-away mental place where she could no longer reach him—even if she still cared to try.

The night he'd hit her, however, had been the final evidence that it was way over.

She took her mocha and motored slowly away from the kiosk, ignoring her phone as it rang again. She lowered the ringer volume and sipped the drink, making the decision to think of herself for a change. At least for the next two hours.

Karen steered her way onto South Canyon Street heading north, then west on U.S. 20, turning off eight miles later onto a dirt road that wound its way through fields of late-blooming wildflowers as it meandered up a small mountain ridge toward the Continental Divide. She reached a clearing in the trees near the top of the road and turned the Suburban's nose toward the valley as she parked and killed the engine, leaving the window cracked open to the fresh breeze that ruffled her hair. She clicked on the accessory part of the ignition switch and fussed with her collection of CDs, trying to find the right track for her mood, as the radio came on and Karen Carpenter's voice suddenly filled her ears.

It was the wrong song to hear just then. "We've Only Just Begun" had been her hope chest song, the golden oldie she'd found as a starry-eyed teenage girl that presaged the kind of marriage she would have some day. The words were perhaps sappy and incredibly idealistic, but, then, so were teenage girls, she thought. "Working together," "side by side," "sharing horizons," and the feeling of two people with a world of time ahead.

*Yeah, right.*

And here she was pushing thirty, already in a failed marriage with no kids—not that she was ready for kids yet.

Karen realized she was leaking more tears, this time from a different class of pain.

"Dammit," she said to herself, rubbing angrily at the liquid emotion, but unable to force herself to hit the button and silence the radio.

That song had always made her cry. It wasn't just Trent and his failure to be what she wanted. Even if she'd married the perfect man, that song would have made her cry.

*But wouldn't it be nice,* she thought, *to have someone you'd want to be that close to forever? I wonder if it's possible?*

There was a faraway chirping noise coming from her phone, and this time she answered with a curt "Hello."

"Karen? This is Chris Levine in Ops," the male voice on the other end intoned. "Ah, could you come on out to the field as quickly as possible? We're going to need some extra help here."

"Chris, I'm not cleared to jump until tomorrow at the earliest, and my team won't be—"

"Karen . . . Karen . . ." he interrupted.

She stopped. "What?"

"We've had a terrible accident."

A series of images crackled through her brain, chronicling the better moments in the short anthology of her dying marriage, followed in a nanosecond by a glimpse of the guilt she was going to feel if Trent had somehow been hurt or killed.

"What's happened?"

"One of the DC-6s went down northwest of Jackson a few minutes ago."

"Oh, no!"

"I'm afraid so, and we're gonna need help in here with the phones and, you know, administrative stuff. Trent volunteered you."

*Then he's not hurt,* she thought, shaking her head to expunge the personal thoughts.

"Karen, it sounds exactly like last summer's disasters. An eyewitness said it came apart in the air. One of the wings."

"Oh, God! Trent said everything had been checked a hundred times over and it could never happen again!"

"I know. We don't have details yet. Can you come help? I know your squad isn't available until morning."

"I understand. I'll be there in about ten minutes."

"Good."

"Wait . . ." she added, not sure she wanted to ask the next question. "Who was aboard?"

A small shudder ran through her middle. There were no names she *wanted* to hear, but there were a couple of names in particular she prayed she wasn't going to hear.

"It was Tanker Eighty-six, Karen. Jeff Maze. Mike Head was the copilot."

"Oh, God!" Karen gasped, rubbing her eyes. *Jeff Maze.* She remembered the last time she'd spent a great evening in the company of the almost legendary pilot. Jeff and Trent had always been great friends. It had been just a year ago.

She sighed heavily. "All right. I'll be right there."

But the line was already dead.

# Chapter 3

News that Jeff Maze had gone down in Tanker 86 hadn't reached Clark
Maxwell in the air.

He left his DC-6 with the ground crew, expecting them to rush the loading of some twenty-five-hundred gallons of fire retardant at the same time
as they filled the cavernous fuel tanks with the prescribed fuel load. But he'd
hurried away before they could tell him the entire West Yellowstone airtanker force had just been grounded.

Clark checked his watch as he bypassed the so-called pilot standby shack
and pushed through the door to the building that held the Operations
Room. He was due to be airborne again in twenty minutes, and he glanced
up expecting to see the usual kicked-over anthill of activity.

Instead, the room was quiet and somber and populated by a collection of
ashen-faced people who looked up as if a ghost had just joined them.

*What's this?* Clark thought, looking around until he caught the eye of
Rich Lassiter, an old friend and the Air Operations boss. Clark had known
Lassiter for fifteen years and seen the same haunted look on the retired
Navy captain's face too many times before when disaster had struck and
they'd lost another pilot or crew. Clark moved quickly toward Rich, reading the scope of the disaster in the older man's eyes. There was no mistak-
ing the hunched shoulders and the grim expression. They'd lost one of
their own.

"What happened?" Clark asked quietly. Uncharacteristically, Rich Lassiter placed a hand on his shoulder, and Clark listened in stunned disbelief to
the headline version, his mind reeling as much over the fact that he'd been
scheduled to fly that particular DC-6 a few hours before as over the possibility that Jeff and his copilot might really be dead.

"You're sure. . . . I mean . . ."

"That they didn't make it?"

"Yeah."

"No, but the reports don't hold out much hope. The wreckage is burning," he said.

Clark shook his head, the imagined crash site vivid in his mind, intellect smothered by the raw emotion of unreasonable hope. There had been an eyewitness, Rich said, who'd sworn she'd seen a wing come off, and when such things happened with big airplanes, the fate of the occupants was inevitably sealed.

Nevertheless, hope always sued for an alternate ending.

"My God, Rich. How many more are we going to have?" Clark asked. Rich Lassiter started to answer, his voice catching, then shook his head and turned to attend to a ringing phone.

Clark recognized one of the Forest Service public affairs officers near the back of the crowded room, a validation of the seriousness of the moment. The man's counterpart from the Park Service would be arriving as well, he thought, as would the well-meaning Critical Stress Debriefing Teams sent in to help counsel those who wanted to talk about it.

*That would be all of us,* Clark thought, equally convinced that every pilot in the shack would try to tough it out rather than risk appearing vulnerable by openly seeking counsel.

Rusty Davis suddenly materialized at Clark's side, his face equally gray and grim. Rusty held up his hand to forestall Clark's question. "One of the guys called me," he explained. "What do we know?"

Clark repeated the basic details, his voice inadvertently accusatory, as if Rusty had somehow been complicit in the disaster. He'd felt the flash of anger slip past his reserve and regretted the tone instantly. But he was too distracted to apologize.

Three off-duty airtanker pilots were in the building, all of them equally grim, all of them friends of the downed crew.

Clark knew the routine in depressing detail. Even if they had a video of Maze's wing coming off, there was a procedure to follow. They still had to ground all aviation operations from the aircraft's home base and quickly test all the fuel supplies for contamination. That meant draining the fuel out of each aircraft, then reloading once they were given the green light. The frantic operation was already in progress on the ramp outside, deeply impacting the ability to support the firefighters east of Jackson Hole.

But far beyond the rote procedures, there was a collective chill affecting each of the pilots in the shack, a cold feeling of mechanical betrayal. Each of their old warhorse airplanes had supposedly been so thoroughly inspected following the disasters of 2002 that there could be no recurrence of wing loss—especially among the DC-6B fleet. And now . . .

Clark looked around to see Bill Deason approaching. The senior airtanker captain was now one of the grand old men of the profession, as well
as a good friend, and it was painful to see the anguish in his eyes.

"Clark, I just . . . I just don't believe this!" he was saying.

Clark nodded in sympathy. "I know it, Bill."

Deason's beloved, fifty-three-year-old PB4Y-2 was sitting in the dirt several hundred feet away next to the ramp, never to fly again after a Forest Service order in January permanently grounded all such aircraft for the very
type of wing failure that had apparently killed Jeff Maze. Deprived of the
airplane he'd named *The Aging Mistress,* Deason now flew an ex-Navy P-3
Orion with "10" on the tail, a turboprop machine far more powerful, modern, and safe—but anything but his favorite. The telltale indicator, according to his wife, Judy, was the fact that he'd yet to name the P-3. For years he
had taken immense pride in nursing his old piston-powered bomber along,
coaxing amazing feats of precision and endurance out of a ship few others
could handle. Modern turboprops like the P-3 were easy to fly, Bill maintained. But ancient air vessels like the PB4Y-2 were like sailing ships or steam
locomotives in their cantankerous complexity. Such ships were mastered
only by men willing to learn their unique language.

Bill leaned wearily against the Ops counter, shaking his head.

"Has anyone told Misty? Someone's got to take care of Misty."

Chris Levine, who had been on the phone summoning reinforcements
such as Karen Jones, shook his head sadly. "She's on her way back from a funeral in Florida and due into Jackson Hole late this afternoon."

"A funeral?" Deason asked.

"Her mother died last week. I'm trying to get someone to the Jackson airport to meet her when she arrives. This is going to devastate her."

Deason held up a finger. "Chris, call my wife, Judy. She can make that run
to Jackson Hole and get her. She's at the hotel. No, wait, I'll call her." Deason grabbed one of the phones and punched in the number as he glanced at
Clark. "I always expected that someday Misty was going to blow Jeff's head
off with a shotgun," he said softly. "It was shabby the way he treated her, but
. . . she's completely in love with him." Bill grimaced. "*Was* in love with
him."

Bill's wife answered, and he turned away to speak in low tones about the
unspeakable. Clark tried to turn his attention elsewhere, but Bill's voice carried, and he knew that husband and wife were also dealing with the reality
that it could just as easily be Misty Ryan arriving at Judy Deason's door with
news that she, too, had joined a long line of tanker widows who would get
few benefits, little support, and no public recognition for their husbands'
sacrifices.

Clark had known Bill and Judy for fifteen years. The couple had been happily married for thirty-six, and Judy had followed Bill through his hardscrabble crop-dusting days, which were endless years of tears and toil and paltry profits from spraying fields with poison from airplanes while trying to stay out of the power lines. She'd raised three good kids while he was doing battle with gravity, and she'd quietly taken the hardships in stride while Bill flew as an airtanker pilot and became one of the lucky few to survive more than twenty seasons. They were both good, caring people, highly respected by all the pilots.

*The whole community was filled with good, hardworking people,* Clark thought. That was one of the attractions that had drawn him back into it, even after he'd sworn never to succumb again to the temptation to bomb burning trees with pink liquids. Part of the attraction was the unspoken camaraderie that bridged personal and professional disagreements among tanker pilots. But even though the FLOPPs didn't think it manly to discuss, camaraderie was a distant second to the real narcotic of airtanker flying—the adrenaline high of dangerous aviating coupled with the instant satisfaction of seeing the fruits of your labor reflected in the trees below. That shared experience wove unspoken bonds among men who could be otherwise incredibly combative with one another, because together they shared a lofty secret: the knowledge that few mortals could do what they did and that, given the societal threat that massive forest fires posed, the risk was worth it.

For those who had never been in the military, some of that risk was shouldered as much for God and country as for the paychecks that could keep a pilot and his family fed all winter. Every year there was a war to fight, and, mercenaries or not, they were the heroes to fight it.

*The brotherhood had been tested too many times with crashes and losses like this,* Clark thought. Not that anyone would ever formally refer to airtankering in such warm, fuzzy, and collegial terms. But it *was* a brotherhood, with fewer than six hundred in the United States admitted to the inner circle of fire fighting as tanker, lead plane, jumpship, air attack, and helicopter pilots.

The standby shack, which was normally full of wisecracking competitors needling one another unmercifully about nearly everything, usually resembled some seedy civilian version of the SAC "molehole" flight-line alert facilities, which had been manned 24/7 for over forty years by the Air Force's former Strategic Air Command. It was heartbreaking to see that kind of testosterone-soaked, lighthearted atmosphere turn funereal and grim.

Clark moved to one of the windows, letting the image of the DC-6 he was flying—Tanker 84—coalesce in his consciousness. As a DC-6, she was

supposed to be far more sound than the lesser airplanes that had disintegrated in flight the previous summer. But the wings of aging airtankers
took a terrible beating each time they hauled a fuselage full of slurry into
that rough low-level environment. He trusted the DC-6, but now the shards
of metal still smoldering in a forest forty miles distant were from a sister
ship essentially identical to the one he was flying.

Or, he corrected himself, was about to go fly once again.

Worse, Jeff Maze's airplane was the same one Clark would have been flying, and it had apparently come apart in flight, leaving the fuselage a ballistic projectile destined for catastrophic impact with the ground.

Clark watched the ground crew in the distance waiting for the signal to
began refueling the tanks they'd just emptied. Once again they would unmercifully stress the wings and the engines and the airframe, bouncing
through shudderingly severe drafts and pulling g's.

So how strong were *his* wings?

He thought of Tanker 88 in the hangar, and shuddered uncharacteristically. Should he ground Tanker 84 and wait for Tanker 88 to be back in com-
mission? But if he did, what guarantees did he have that Tanker 88 wasn't
going to be the *next* one to come apart? Undoubtedly the Forest Service—
which moved far faster than the FAA—was probably moving that very
minute to ground all the DC-6Bs, at least the ones in Jerry Stein's fleet, regardless of the devastating effect that would have on Jerry's finances.

But, Clark reminded himself, there was the not-so-insignificant problem
of the growing forest fires east and northeast of Jackson Hole and the des-
perate need for every airtanker that could be coaxed into the air. He knew
Jerry would already be on the phone hammering out an agreement with the
Forest Service to let his crews go ahead and fly the DC-6Bs if the individual
captains felt safe. Jerry Stein could make such a deal secure in the knowledge that none of his pilots would want to admit to being concerned and
lose their paychecks in the process.

*Might as well suck it up and pray for survival and hope whatever I fly has at least
another week of structural integrity.*

Clark recognized the self-delusion. It was a decisional acceptance one
could never explain to a nonflying spouse or lover, and a direct kinship with
the faith and fatalism that had permitted so many young men to climb into
air machines in England during World War II, knowing their chances of returning as whole men were statistically slim.

With an almost trancelike surrealism, Clark Maxwell gathered the paperwork from the dispatch desk as his substitute copilot, Josh White, came in
from the ramp and moved to his side.

"They're waiting for the word to reload," Josh explained.

"Yeah, I was watching."

"And . . . I'm being replaced by your regular copilot."

Clark nodded, forcing a smile. "Yeah, Rusty told me. I'll miss you, Josh. You didn't steal my flight lunch like Rusty always does."

Josh White smiled self-consciously, the smile fading just as quickly as he glanced around the crowded room at the somber gathering. "One more thing, Clark. The mechanic I was talking to couldn't find anything wrong with either engine three or four. He said we could be describing anything from an impending failure to our stomachs growling."

"You think he's right?"

He could see Josh weighing his reply as Rusty came up silently behind him.

"You told him it was a racheting sound, right?" Clark added.

"Yes, I did, and . . . the guy I was telling is an engine mechanic, and I think he's right. He just doesn't have enough information to troubleshoot."

"Okay."

"And . . . thanks for letting me fly with you," Josh added, offering his hand, which Clark took.

"Good job, Josh. Just . . . work on not hesitating when you have something to say, or something that's worrying you."

"Okay. Thanks."

When Josh had walked away, Rusty inclined his head toward the ramp and Clark followed, closing the standby shack door behind him.

"What've you got?" Clark asked.

"I thought you might want to know what Boise's thinking," Rusty said, referring to the National Interagency Coordination Center. "I just sat in on a teleconference."

"What did Jim have to say?" Jim De Maio was a friend of Clark's, and was recently appointed Forest Service assistant director of Fire and Aviation Operations.

Rusty shoved his hands deep in his pockets and looked off to the southeast, toward the unseen fires chewing at the carpeted mountains adjacent to Jackson Hole.

"Lynda was doing the briefing."

"Gardner?" Clark asked, an eyebrow raised.

"Yes."

Lynda Gardner was a former smokejumper and now the intelligence coordinator and briefer at the Boise center. He was surprised she'd be doing the debrief over De Maio, but it was more than that. She and Clark had a history, Rusty knew, although the most information he'd squeezed out of Clark over too many beers one evening held that the Clark and Lynda story was little more than a brief and torrid rebound affair. It had arisen, he maintained, from mutual failed relationships and the convenience of summer proximity. They hadn't seen each other in years.

"Yeah, it was Lynda," he teased, "and she was looking hot."

"You could tell that on a telephone conference?"

"Okay, she *sounded* hot," Rusty said, attempting to lift himself out of the depression of the moment with the kidding, and equally aware it wasn't working. He sighed and continued. "She was basically telling De Maio and the others that the fire thirty miles due east of Jackson Hole airport—the Deer Creek fire—has the potential to jump the ridge and join a number of smaller fires, since the winds aren't forecasted to let up for the next forty-eight hours at least. You know where Highway Twenty-six is?"

"Yeah, the main highway from the east into Jackson Hole and the park."

"Right. She briefed that it could easily jump the highway west of Brecca Peak, and, if so, it had the potential to ignite Yellowstone. Only this time, if the fire starts, we could lose at least two towns and the east side of Teton Park."

"That's worst case?"

"Yeah, but a very real possibility, Clark. This is a really serious deal."

"What do they have committed to fight it?"

"You ready for this? Total of eleven airtankers, three Skycranes, a mess of light helicopters, and two more P-3 Orions on the way from California."

"Good grief! That's a huge effort."

"You can say that again! All of the tankers are coming here."

"What? West Yellowstone can't handle more than eight, tops. Not to mention the facilities—look at this room! We're falling all over one another right now with six birds outside."

"They're bringing in additional loading tanks and crews, Clark. I guess they're going to use Jerry's ramp, too."

"Lord."

"And they're really worried they didn't get moving on this fast enough. Again."

"What's Jim say?"

"De Maio? He says that Lynda's overstating the case about the slow reaction. But Clark, no shit, I could hear it in their voices. They're really sweating a repeat of the monster that ate a third of Yellowstone in '88."

Clark glanced through the windows of the operations room to the ramp beyond, taking in the doublewide trailer that served as the pilot ready room and fire retardant operations shack. Their aircraft sat on the retardant loading pad just to the west of the trailer, and Clark realized one of the loading crew was waving in the general direction of flight operations in hopes of snagging Clark's attention.

"They're ready, Rusty. Let's go."

Rusty nodded and picked up his flight bag, covering the hundred yards to the DC-6B as the mechanic held out a clipboard.

"If you feel comfortable enough to fly, you gotta sign this release first."

"Would you fly with me?" Clark asked.

"Hell, yes." The mechanic grinned, muttering the rest of the answer under his breath, "Someday, in a Piper Cub."

Rusty had already disappeared into the aircraft, and Clark hesitated for a few seconds after handing back the signed form. He scanned the horizon and the intermittent deep blue appearing between the altocumulus clouds in the summer sky overhead. The temperature was in the lower seventies, the West Yellowstone wind—not being a product of the wind tunnel created by the Tetons and the Canadian low sitting north of Missoula—was a mere breeze of six knots. But it was strong enough to bring a bouquet of fresh aromas from the wildflowers carpeting the nearby meadows and the pines on the slopes, a scent not so much smelled as perceived on the thin mountain air.

He could detect as well the aromas of an aging aircraft, from the sharp atomizing smell of aviation gasoline splashed on the leading edge of the wing and the concrete to the musty odor of oil staining the side of the engines. All of it was overburdened by the strong, occasional whiff of their perennial cargo: the thousands of gallons of red slurry made from water and fertilizers and carrying a unique bouquet of chemicals, including essence of dirty ammonia, a smell no tanker pilot could ever completely wash out of his clothes during the season.

Clark sighed and forced his mind clear of the horror in the woods forty miles away. He would consider Jeff Maze's death only when they returned. He put a foot on the entry ladder and paused involuntarily, his eyes raking the underside of the airplane where the wing and the fuselage joined. It was only sheet metal, of course. The serious fittings of metal to metal that held everything together was deep within, but he couldn't help but look, as if reassurance would flow from an unbroken surface.

*Stop it!* Clark commanded himself. He turned and climbed the ladder.

As Tanker 84's right outboard engine coughed to life and its propeller began rotating amid a cloud of bluish-black smoke, a few hundred yards away across the north end of the runway Karen Jones parked her Suburban and hurried toward the offices of Stein Aviation in search of her husband.

Jerry Stein's complex occupied the northwest side of the West Yellow-stone Airport, adjacent to the north end of the single north-south runway. The northeast side was occupied by the Forest Service, with a moderate concrete ramp, the fire retardant mixing and loading areas (and adjacent doublewide trailer), and on the east side of the ramp behind a low fence, a single-story government building housing a small Operations office, meeting room, and large parachute support facility for the smokejumpers.

Through the windows of the Operations office, the large ramp Jerry Stein had built across the runway could be seen fronting two large, new hangars. And in the maw of one of them, six of Stein's mechanics could be seen conferring urgently about something.

Karen looked closer, startled for no rational reason to see that one of the men was Trent. She moved quickly in his direction, giving a perfunctory wave when he suddenly looked up and saw her.

Tanned, tough, compact, and beautiful, Karen's approach instantly riveted the attention of the other mechanics, and Trent smiled involuntarily in a flush of possessive male pride. The desirable female coming toward them with such self-confidence bore his last name.

*For a while longer, at least,* Trent thought, well aware that breakup day was near.

"Here comes my little honey," he said for the others' benefit, not realizing that most of them knew better. Trent tried to give her an inordinately affectionate hug as she reached the group, but she patted his shoulder and spun expertly away from his grasp, standing beside him, but surreptitiously holding him at bay.

"So you guys must be this year's version of the fabled hole-in-the-head wrench gang," she said, her smile thin but sufficiently winning. Two of the faces were familiar, but she hadn't seen West Yellowstone since the previous September, and the names had faded in her memory.

The five other men nodded and introduced themselves, all but one raising a grease-covered hand to substitute for a handshake.

"Could you give us a minute?" Karen asked, inclining her head toward Trent. She waited for them to scatter before pulling Trent by the arm into a corner of the hangar.

"What?" he said, irritation replacing the show smile. "I'm busy."

She ignored the swipe. "Obviously, you've heard about the crash."

"Of course I have. We're all stunned."

"Stunned? That's decent of you. Jeff was a good friend, and they're saying a wing fell off," she said, her eyes boring into his.

Trent was visibly pale. "Eyewitnesses can be very wrong," he replied slowly. "It could have been anything. Even a midair."

"Convincing the wings to stay on is part of your responsibility, isn't it? I mean, your crew inspected that bird?"

Trent hardened visibly, his eyes narrowing.

"What are you getting at?" he asked, his tone approaching a defensive snarl as he looked down and kicked a small bolt toward the hangar wall.

She was looking for the pain in his eyes and seeing only discomfort.

"I'm asking you, Trent, if you're going to be in the crosshairs of the inevitable federal investigation," Karen said, squatting down to pick up the bolt he'd just kicked. She handed it to him with a neutral expression. "Here. Wouldn't want that to get sucked into a jet engine, would we?"

He took the bolt and slipped it in his pants pocket without comment, looking off balance. He cleared his throat, his eyes straying away from hers in a manner that sent a small chill up her back. It was the same physical response he'd shown for the last two years any time she probed for details about why his work seemed to be making him so secretive and distant.

"My crew did not do the major inspection work, Karen. Jerry had that done at another shop somewhere else. When I got here in April, everything was golden, the feds were happy, and my guys have done every required inspection on time since then." He snorted again, raising his defenses. "What are you now, anyway, an FAA maintenance inspector?"

"No. I'm just worried. I'm worried that *you* seem worried."

"Well cut it out, okay? It's all under control."

Karen tilted her head involuntarily, suddenly puzzled by the response. "What does that mean, exactly?"

"It means I know what I'm doing, Karen. Get off it."

"Look, I have a right—"

"LEAVE IT ALONE!" he barked, the raised volume of his baritone voice actually echoing off the metal walls of the hangar. "Just . . . just drop it."

He shifted the subject to the routine, with questions of when her jump squad would be in and when he could expect her back at the motel. She answered vaguely, wondering why she'd even bothered. Maybe she'd been looking to comfort him when she first walked over, but his attitude had irritated her, and her reaction had sparked him off again, and . . .

She sighed and shook her head.

*We can't even talk to each other anymore.*

Karen left Trent quietly and returned to her Suburban to motor around the north end of the runway to the grim atmosphere of the Air Operations office. She reached the door just as Tanker 84 broke ground three-quarters of the way down the runway and rumbled off to the north.

# Chapter 4

There were no more racheting sounds from the engines on the right wing as Clark Maxwell roared through twenty minutes of Wyoming sky, carrying his desperately needed cargo of fire retardant to the front line of the battle. The relative silence should have been comforting, but there was a pregnancy to the normal readings on the engine gauges, and it fed a growing concern that something as yet undetected was seriously amiss in his air machine.

He tried to write it off as mere paranoia, but the attempt wasn't working.

There was scant conversation between Clark and Rusty other than the normal, businesslike exchanges in preparation for descent and initial contact with Sam Littlefox in Lead Four-Two. The fire, they had been briefed, had already blown up and over the line all the airtankers had worked so hard to fortify along the ridge while Jeff Maze and Mike Head were doing load and returns.

The fire was now churning down the other side of the ridge into a dangerously contained cirque that could easily become a wind tunnel causing what firefighters called a "blowup," an out-of-control forest fire that crowns and quickly generates into a firestorm, pulling oxygen in from all sides and making its own wind.

The teams of weary, dirty firefighters rushed in from the Jackson Hole staging areas were somewhat stunned at having been chased off the ridge. Everyone had expected the line just below the ridge to hold, but it hadn't, and now the contingency position was to lay down a line of retardant—known as "tying line"—between a number of small lakes, and then set a backfire as the line of retardant was completed. If the fire got past the lakes and climbed the next ridge to the east—or worse, if it roared out of the narrow canyon to the north—stopping it would be improbable.

The massive, practiced coordination among the array of firefighters on the ground was combined with helicopters ferrying water from nearby lakes to spot fires, bulldozers and other heavy equipment coming in by road, and the airtankers in a concerted attack against the common enemy. Watched over from Boise, led by an incident commander, and supported by the Park Service and the Forest Service as the lead agencies involved, it was akin to a major military operation with much at stake.

Two small communities built on old mining claims in the national forest only four miles to the northeast would be in the crosshairs of the fire if it jumped the ridge. The flame front had already crested the top of the west ridge, the stiff south winds literally pumping in the oxygen it needed to crown and leap from treetop to treetop, causing the flames to jump hundreds of feet in the air.

The battle-hardened firefighters regarded such blow-up fires as malevolent, living things, and in their eyes the beast had indeed shown itself for a brief moment, standing two hundred feet tall at the summit in defiance and declaration of its omnipotence, as if shaking its plasmic fist at the army trying to defeat it.

Every member of the firefighting team knew that the larger stakes included Yellowstone National Park, and there was a common determination never to allow a repeat of the out-of-control firestorms of 1988.

The summer of '88 had begun innocuously enough with the Park Service following their new policy of permitting naturally occurring forest fires in the park to burn themselves out as a normal cycle of nature. But in mid-July, while only a tiny number of acres of the park and adjacent wildlands to the south were on fire, there were voices of caution warning that things were going too far. The extreme drought that had parched the entire area justified a policy change, they warned. A quick effort was needed to put out all the fires, whether naturally caused or not. But the voices went unheeded, and within two weeks Clark was on his way in from Idaho, along with a small air force of airtankers, because ten times the initial acreage had erupted in flame. Propelled by almost unprecedented dry, hot winds sometimes as high as seventy miles per hour, seven major fires blew up around the park, consuming three hundred years of dry, unburned forest fuels and becoming a roaring mass of firestorms that ultimately consumed 1.2 million acres of forest, including 36 percent of Yellowstone's 2.2 million acres.

The memories were still very fresh in Clark's mind. Never before or since had he seen such walls of flame, with fireballs leaping hundreds of feet higher in hellish bursts no one had adequately described in words or pictures. In the end, despite the largest recorded fire-fighting effort in American history—a joint civilian-military operation involving twenty-five thousand firefighters at a cost of $120 million—nothing could stop the fires except nature herself. On September 11, 1988, the first snows of fall began accomplishing what the exhausted force of firefighters could not, and the fires faded away and died.

Now the stage was being set again, and the remaining unburned two-

thirds of Yellowstone stood exposed, tempting fate and the laws of thermo-
dynamics.

While the fires gaining ground east of Jackson Hole were an increasing
worry, within Yellowstone Park itself, some thirty-eight miles to the northwest of the main blaze, there was a new threat—the spot fire started by Jeff
Maze's disintegrated aircraft. Ground equipment was expected to reach
that site just inside the southern boundary of the park within the hour, but
there were no roads. The flames had already passed the birthing stage and
were maturing into a running and torching front encouraged by the wind.

Clark couldn't keep himself from flying over the crash site, even if it delayed his arrival at the main fire by a few minutes. The wreckage was not far
from their route.

He slowed the big Douglas and began making the required radio calls. A
restricted area had already been placed around the crash site and helitack
crews—firefighters brought in by helicopter and able to rappel down to the
site—were already on the ground and working. Clark relayed his latitude
and longitude, speed and direction of flight before switching to a dispatch
frequency to report on the size and direction of the blaze started by the
crash. He stayed above a thousand feet over the blackened swath of wreckage in the forest, some eight miles west of the southern entrance to the
nation's oldest national park. The wreckage was still smoldering, even
though the fire it had started was busily burning northward.

Clark circled the crash site in a single left orbit, noting that the sole eyewitness had been right: The fuselage had gone in almost vertically, and the
right wing lay in identifiable pieces almost a mile to the northwest. The confirmation made him squirm internally, but he wrestled the incipient fear
back under control as he climbed back to a safe altitude, locking it away in a
mental recess marked "for ground use only."

Still, his ears had become more sensitive, his instrument scans more fre-
quent, and his airman's senses for anything amiss had become somehow
more acute. His very body was monitoring the pulse of his aircraft—the
subtle movements and subvibrations that a nonaviator would never per-
ceive above the throaty roar and rhythmic shaking of the engines and props.

Deep down he knew he was waiting, spring-loaded, for any return of the
odd vibrations they'd felt before.

Or worse.

———

Sam Littlefox was nearing the end of his shift, and Clark could tell the hardworking lead pilot was getting weary. He'd already fumbled two transmissions in a row before finally getting Tanker Eighty-Four's call right.

"Okay, sorry about that, Clark. Ahem. Tanker *Eighty-four* . . . you're cleared in to follow me," he said.

"Tanker Eighty-four, roger. Long day, huh Sammy?" Clark added.

"Roger that," he replied. "Okay, we'll turn inside Doubletop Peak and cross a ten-thousand-five-hundred-foot ridgeline. The start of the line we're cutting is at about ninety-four hundred feet above sea level about two miles from the ridge."

Picking the high ground as the best place to slow down a fire's progress was a tried-and-true method all airtanker pilots understood. The higher the altitude, the more rarified the air, which meant less oxygen and a cooler fire that couldn't move as fast from tree to tree.

Sam continued, "Then there's a very tight passage slightly to the right, in five miles at eighty-five hundred feet, and the terrain just keeps on getting lower from there. It's both the normal egress route and a perfect escape route, until the smoke fills it up in another hour or so."

"Gotcha."

Clark rolled off the downwind leg and reversed course in a broad turn, throttling back and descending two miles behind the Baron, his mind still back at the wreckage of Tanker 86. The distraction worried him, even though this drop would be easy once they had passed the ridge and descended to the right altitude.

The cirque was more in the shape of a sloppy Y, with the ridge they were about to cross at the southern end of the Y and the forks to the north, all of it surrounded by ten-thousand-foot peaks. Had the one forested canyon leading out of the cirque at the top right of the Y shape not been there, descending into it would have been too risky. Rusty had already pointed out the trap, a rising volume of smoke moving north that could cut off visual access to that escape canyon, leaving a heavy tanker too low to clear the ridges and with nowhere to go except into the side of a mountain.

As was customary, the lead-plane pilot was monitoring the firefighter's ground and command frequencies as well as those of the tanker and helicopter pilots and headquarters, all simultaneously. The airtanker pilots were normally monitoring only the air-to-air frequency, but Clark was well aware that Sam was dealing with as many as four frequencies and a confusing and constant volume of chatter that increased with the intensity of the battle.

"Hold . . . standby," Sam was saying, returning just as quickly. "Okay, we're going to need two runs, Tanker Eighty-four."

"You got it," Clark replied, checking his airspeed. They were approaching the ridge now, less than a mile away, and he'd forgotten to brief the copilot again.

"Rusty, I'll bring us in no more than two hundred feet AGL . . . above ground level, over the ridge—"

"You know, it's frigging amazing, but I actually do know what AGL means, skipper." Rusty smiled. "You really can talk in Av speak to me if you'd like."

Clark nodded. "Yeah. For some reason I keep confusing you with the greenhorn who took your place this morning. Nice fellow, but really . . ."

"Just off the turnip truck?"

"Naw. Just a newbie. Okay, two hundred AGL. We'll ride the tailwind over the ridge as a safety buffer. I wouldn't do it the same way if the wind was coming at us."

"Got it."

"Gear down," he commanded.

The copilot glanced over with a puzzled expression, and Clark grimaced. "I forgot to brief that."

"Roger, gear down." Rusty lowered the gear lever and the DC-6 shuddered and slowed appreciably as the large main wheel assemblies moved into the slipstream, producing a serious increase in aerodynamic drag. It was almost like hanging an open parachute out of the back, giving the ability to descend more steeply down the slope without picking up as much airspeed.

The cirque ahead was a little more than eight miles long, but if they followed Lead Four-Two at the end as it branched off to the right, and as long as they didn't lose visibility and blunder left, the descending terrain was enough to permit an easy escape without a frantic climb attempt.

They were close enough now to the steep sides of the glacial cirque to see the seventy- to eighty-foot-tall lodgepole pines to their left relaying the incredible heat of the advancing fire like a rock concert audience surfs one of its stars along the top of the crowd on outstretched hands. Adjacent treetops unaffected one moment were candling the next as the intense heat rolled downslope. Clark could see the process with startling clarity to the left in his peripheral vision as he kept his eyes on the target line in the valley ahead. Lodgepole pines as a species actually thrived on fire, relying on the monstrous heat of a forest fire to burn through the coating of their cones and release new seeds, and these were getting their prescribed dose of hell.

The fire was advancing as much as twenty feet a minute, and accelerating, while the stand of trees he was about to lubricate with the slurry was on the east side of the scratch line the hotshots had cut.

He leveled the ship out at less than fifty feet above the treetops and made the final mental calculations, ignoring the usual violent lurches of the heavy mechanical turbulence created by the interaction of wind and mountain—

"turbies" in the verbal shorthand of some of the lead pilots. But this time they weren't going to be directly over the fire, so the ship would be spared the worst effects of slamming through the rising heat columns that would strain every part of the metal structure and test the very limits of how much Mr. Douglas's marvelous design could take before coming apart.

"Gear up," Clark said. They were at the right altitude now, and the extra drag was unnecessary.

"Roger, gear up," Rusty answered, raising the handle.

Clark poised his thumb over the dump switch as the gear finished its retraction sequence. He counted to himself and pushed at the calculated moment, feeling the gravity-fed slurry jetting from the bottom of the plane at the same moment the ratcheting sounds from the right wing returned in force.

"What's that?" Rusty asked, the alarm in his voice clearly evident over the intercom. "Number four?"

Clark's eyes snapped to the instrument panel for clues before resuming the task of keeping them out of the trees ahead. He pulsed back on the yoke slightly to raise the nose and start climbing at the same instant he goosed the throttles, wholly unprepared for the sudden incredible vibrations that began coursing through the cockpit.

It was as if the entire DC-6 had fallen into the clutches of a massive paint mixer. It was worse than any turbulence Clark had ever experienced, the cockpit shaking so profoundly it was impossible to read the instruments or even make out the terrain ahead, and for a few seconds, with extraordinary internal calm, he knew the old airliner was going to disassemble itself in the air and kill him.

Somewhere in the back of his mind the knowledge flashed that only a broken propeller blade could cause such planetary-class shaking, along with the fact that whatever was causing it, the aircraft structure wouldn't take it for more than a few seconds.

And just as suddenly as it had begun, the horrid vibrating ended, and a bone-jarring *whump* and the sound of ripping metal took its place as the right outboard engine tore loose from its mountings and buried the remaining two blades of its propeller in the leading edge of the right wing. There was an impressive cascade of sparks, followed instantly by the unmistakable feel of an airplane in serious trouble.

Rusty plastered his face to his side window, aware of the trees passing entirely too close. The right outboard engine—number four—had literally twisted off its mounts and canted severely sideways and down to the right, instantly redesigning their aerodynamics. While the remaining three engines could have easily powered them over the mountains even before making the first drop, they were now flying with a modified barn door of extra drag pulling backward on the right wing. And they were well below the ridges of the mountain cirque and in a bowl that had only one escape route.

Clark rolled the control yoke almost completely left to counter the wild tendency of the DC-6 to roll right. His mind was alternating at high speed between what was needed to keep them climbing and what was needed to keep them right side up. Time was dilating, stretching seconds into what seemed like minutes.

"METO power on . . . on the rest!" Clark ordered, only marginally aware that his copilot had already done exactly that, pushing the old Pratt and Whitney recips to what was known as the "maximum except takeoff" setting.

The climb rate was anemic, and he watched the airspeed barely holding at 145. There wasn't enough distance left between where they were in the valley and the steep walls of the cirque to have any hope of climbing straight ahead. They would have to follow Lead Four-Two to the right and down the small canyon as planned.

"You want the memory items and the engine-failure checklist?" Rusty asked, his voice tight and thin.

Clark nodded. The words weren't coming easily, and his mouth felt like dry cotton. There was a rising level of apprehension he usually kept bottled up, but he could feel it now, boiling like a roiled stomach and threatening to distract him, and that in itself was a distraction. Nothing ever scared him in flight. Why this? They practiced engine loss. They just never practiced panic.

He checked his control positions. He was using half of the left rudder throw against the tremendous asymmetric thrust from the two large propellers on the left as they churned the air with double the normal power, pulling the single-engine right wing forward. The unbalanced power on the left wing was trying to roll them to the right even more, and he worked to crank in all the left rudder trim he had.

"Check METO!"

"We've got METO. It's checked."

He could see Rusty's hand jump back to the throttle levers as he watched the engine gauges and worked to spur on every last horse they had.

"No. My entire life and a few very steamy experiences flashed before my eyes a few times, but no lakes."

"Okay, I hate to screw up someone's fishing hole, but I should have pickled the load already. Punching it off now."

Clark reached over and set the dump rate to open all the remaining gates before hitting the main dump switch. He pushed up the throttles as more than fifteen thousand pounds of slurry sprayed from the belly, emptying all the tanks and causing the old bird almost to leap into a far healthier climb than before.

The cascade of red retardant fell in a vertical column from the belly of the old Douglas, the weight of the slurry keeping it together for part of the drop as the leading edge took on the shape of an angry wave and the back end spread out to resemble a gigantic plume of pink cotton candy, the man-made cloud moving downward until it landed on the trees below like a science fiction writer's vision of pinkish rain on some alien planet.

"I think we're okay, aren't we?" the copilot said, the mix of statement and question following Clark's own thinking.

"Yeah. We're flying and we're climbing, Rusty," he said, not sure which of them he was trying to reassure. "We'll be fine. Just run the engine-loss checklist and check the tanks for indication of fuel leaks on the right. Is there a lot of damage on the right wing?"

"It's . . . pretty torn up by the prop blades, but I don't see any fuel . . . I mean, I don't think it got the tank."

Another unbidden sparkle of fear shuddered through him, triggering an equally disturbing flash of anger at losing his internal cool. This time it had been the mention of the fuel tank, which held gasoline, which was amazingly explosive if given enough air and a spark.

Rusty began reading the checklist items as Clark watched the Baron disappear in a right turn around the corner ahead and into the canyon. They were at least fifteen hundred feet above the ground now, and still climbing.

*Speed 152 and coming up. Good!* Clark thought. *More than enough energy margin for a turn.*

The turn was about a mile ahead. Beyond the narrow escape pass there would be a broad valley falling off from eighty-five hundred feet to seventy-five hundred, with a small river in the middle. They could bank left and follow the river safely back to the town of Kelly, and all the way to Jackson Hole Airport, if need be.

But it wasn't looking that serious, other than the obvious damage to the right wing and number-four engine, which was literally drooping off the mangled engine mount.

"You want me to declare an emergency?" Rusty asked as he worked on answering the question of a fuel leak. "Lead Four-Two doesn't even know we've got a problem." His voice was as taut as his eyes were huge.

There was a microsecond of hesitation, Clark wrestled his fears to the mat with a combination of relief and bravado. No, thank you. He could

do without telling the world he was scared to death. At least for a few moments. It would be Rusty's voice, of course, not his. *Right now I'd be an octave
higher than normal,* he thought.

"Let's get safe first. Tight right turn coming up."

"Can we . . . make it?" Rusty asked, immediately regretting the verbal
fear he'd just banner-lined.

"Piece of cake," Clark shot back, working to show the traditional pilot
dismissal of danger as he gripped the yoke hard and muscled the heavy old
airliner into a thirty-degree right bank with the aid of a little less left rudder.
The view out front of the cockpit was filled with trees and rocks at first, but
slowly the scene melted into the image of the pass with the broad river valley beyond.

Clark felt his heart rate slowing at last. He was thoroughly in control.
There had never been any doubt, yet something had spooked him.

The canyon walls on each side were soaring at least fifteen hundred feet
above them, even with a steady climb. They were almost out and over the
broad valley ahead when there was another lurch and number four shifted
farther downward on what was left of its mounts. Clark could almost feel it
swinging on the remaining attach point. He gripped the controls a little
more firmly.

"It may well fall off, Rusty. We're going to be headed for a whole community. I'm going to get us up higher and try not to fly over any buildings."

"Roger."

Clark toggled the transmitter. "Lead Four-Two, Tanker Eighty-four.
Sam, we've got a problem. We puked the number-four engine, and we've
dumped the load."

"Roger, Eighty-four, you're cleared out of here."

"Just a second," Clark said, both hands on the yoke as he began a left bank
and continued the climb. "Help me with the yoke, would you?"

Rusty grabbed the copilot's yoke and added pressure into the left bank.
"Jeez, this thing is heavy."

"Sure is."

"May I ask you a question, O Captain, my Captain?"

"Okay. Provided you don't get sarcastic."

"Moi? Not possible. But shouldn't we declare an emergency and go into
Jackson? Like right about *now*?"

"The reason I don't want to go into Jackson Hole, Rusty?"

"Yeah?"

"It'll cost Jerry Stein three times as much to get this old tub flyable again
if he has to work on it there, and it's just possible, with too much scrutiny
around and not enough heavy maintenance, that she might never fly out.

This old warhorse could end her days rolling out of Jackson Hole in torched-up pieces on the back of a flatbed, and we desperately need her flyable. If we can safely get her back to Jones at West Yellowstone, he can probably patch her back together."

There was a contemplative silence from the right seat, and Clark glanced over, glad to see that the copilot clearly understood that their airplane was on the ragged edge of being scrapped, and what that meant. No airplane, no job.

"I'm talking safety, though, too. So what do you think?" Clark asked.

Rusty nodded. "I concur."

"But go ahead with the emergency declaration. I should already have let you do that."

Rusty keyed the transmitter and made the call, broadcasting their position and the fact that one engine was shut down.

"One thing," Clark added. "The turbulence heading back may knock the engine completely off, but it can't be any worse than it is now. We'll just be prepared for it."

"How do we prepare? Pray a lot?"

"Couldn't hurt." Clark looked over at Rusty and managed a strained grin, which was gratefully acknowledged with a nod.

"See any lakes ahead?" Clark asked.

Clark turned the old Doug toward the north, the ridgelines falling away on both sides as they climbed safely through twelve thousand feet with the valley spreading out below.

"Okay, Rusty, *now* you can take a breath and call Ops, in that order. Tell them what we've got. We're returning to base with an ETA of twenty-five minutes, but we're going to dogleg north to avoid any populated areas."

"Nice job, skipper," Rusty said.

"And good teamwork, as usual," he said, his mind racing ahead, trying to make sure the return to base was going to be no more complicated than setting course for the home base and keeping her in the air until they got there.

A mental image flared in his head, like a full-color, three-dimensional map, with the central feature the black hole where Tanker 86 had gone down. He knew precisely how many miles ahead it was, and he could see the glow of the new fire the crash had sparked as it undulated on the horizon. And it seemed, suddenly, that aside from any consideration of saving their own hides, the most important reason for working so hard to get home safely was the cold fact that his community couldn't handle a second loss in one day.

# Chapter 5

Jerry Stein replaced the receiver of his sky phone and sat back hard in the tiny cabin of his Lear 23. He already felt like a sailor trying to bail a sinking freighter with a tin cup, and now his ragged, battered corporate ship was taking on even more water.

He leaned forward just as suddenly as he'd sat back and cupped his chin in his right hand, his elbow on his knee, oblivious to everything but the need to plan for the onslaught.

"What now?" Diana Stein asked softly. After twelve years of marriage she could read her older husband very well, and it was obvious his stress level was approaching red line.

Jerry looked over as if surprised to find her in the seat to his right.

"What . . . what?"

"Something new has obviously gone wrong. What is it?"

He sighed and straightened up, running his left hand through his thinning sandy hair as his right probed for the stockinged texture of her shapely left leg, stroking it slowly. It was an annoying habit she'd learned to accept in public or private. She always wore skirts for him, knowing how much he hated pants on a pretty woman. And she was fond of eliciting scandalized reactions from her more sophisticated East Coast girlfriends with an explanation rooted in the reverse snobbery of marrying a Montanan: "Having a wife would make no sense to Jerry if she wasn't always receptive to no-notice intimacy. Skirts, for him, are an accessibility issue."

"Babe, Tanker Eighty-four is in trouble and limping back to West Yellowstone with number-four engine barely hanging on the wing. Clark Maxwell's the captain. You remember Clark?"

"Of course."

He shook his head. "We've lost two good men *and* a DC-6, and now we've trashed another very expensive engine I just overhauled, *and* the prop, *and* done major sheet metal damage to the wing."

She was sitting forward in alarm and searching his slightly craggy face. "He is going to make it, isn't he?"

Jerry nodded. "Oh, he'll make it, all right. I'm just . . . calculating the damage, in terms of money and contract compliance. And . . . the human costs, of course."

She watched him silently. "How much, you think?" she asked. He never seemed reluctant to answer her questions regarding the business, but the answers were seldom complete, especially when it came to his financial gymnastics. She knew he'd danced around the abyss of bankruptcy more than a few times in his career, so when things were tight, she was never certain whether the wolf was at their door, or already dining in their parlor.

He shook his head. "I don't know. More than we can afford, probably, but I'll think of something. I still can't believe we lost Jeff."

"And the copilot," she prompted.

"Of course. I've . . . just forgotten his name. Oh, yeah. Mike Head."

Jerry looked forward at his empty captain's seat in the cockpit of the small corporate jet. He usually flew the Lear on takeoff and departure, then came back and worked in the cabin, letting the copilot do the flying at altitude and returning before descent. The Lear had only enough fuel to stay aloft a little over two hours, but they could make Denver from Modesto in one hop.

Jerry's left hand flailed the air in a gesture of frustration. "They're gonna be crawling all over us now, the Forest Service and the FAA and the NTSB and Congress and God knows who. There's no way we're going to keep the DC-6s in the air past next week without another round of ruinous inspections."

"Even if the Jackson Hole fire continues?" she asked.

He nodded, and they both fell silent for a few seconds. Diana reached over and began massaging his neck with her left hand, noting that the muscles were as taut as steel bands. She saw the copilot cast a questioning glance back into the cabin, wondering if the phone call was going to affect his instructions. But she caught his eye and shook her head ever so slightly. He was a fairly new employee and very young, but savvy enough to get the message that now wasn't the time to interrupt.

Diana could always recognize Jerry's deep-thought mood. Most of his business career had been a marathon of trying to think a couple of moves ahead in a game that changed its rules from week to week.

Massaging his neck was soothing to her, too, and she let her eyes wander around the once-plush cabin of the tiny 1970 model Learjet as she worked. Like most of the aircraft Jerry Stein owned, the Lear had been purchased toward the end of its useful life for a bargain-basement price and was in great need of constant maintenance. The interior wasn't shabby, but it was obviously overdue for refurbishment, with cracking leather on the seats, stained headliners, and a tiny galley that didn't work. But when it came to getting them anywhere in the United States fast, the Lear did the job, and that was all he cared about.

There were, of course, bragging rights available to those who owned a flyable private jet, regardless of its age, and that meant a lot to a former debutante like Diana who could have married more steady money with her Swarthmore degree and her eastern connections—not to mention the twenty-one-year age difference.

But Jerry had been a lot more fun than the men she'd sampled in her postcollegiate years, even if social status, to his way of thinking, was based on how you survived rather than what you owned. According to Jerry, if they had social status anywhere, it was entirely because of what he'd accomplished in the aviation business, not because of how much he'd bought with the proceeds.

While his Wild West show of business management had been amazingly successful, his sartorial style was iconoclastic, and sometimes embarrassing. His penchant for jeans and western shirts versus business suits for almost all occasions was a trial to her, and a trademark to him.

She'd learned not to panic about his roller-coaster wealth, or the apparently endless company names that adorned first one, then another of the dizzying array of corporations and partnerships he owned. The name changes used to bother her, since she knew well some of them were to escape from bad dealings and rocky reputations. But now she took it in stride. Jerry was not a dishonest man, merely an artful dodger, and they had a prenuptial agreement she'd insisted on that made her family trust fund untouchable. At thirty-six and still beautiful, she was wealthy enough to survive any calamity Jerry might get them into—regardless of his ultimate net worth.

Of course, she was always guessing about his net worth, and often wondered if he was stashing money away in some off-shore account.

"Better?" she ventured, noting that his right hand had stopped massaging her leg and was merely sitting there.

"Um-hum." He was still lost in thought.

Predictably, her family had been scandalized by their marriage plans. But she had evaluated all the pluses and minuses and decided that he was the best of the field of those actively pursuing her. Love hadn't been a factor— until the morning some six months after eloping when she suddenly raised up on one elbow in their bed in Helena, looked at him sleeping peacefully beside her, and realized she had actually fallen in love. How, or why that could happen, she could never decide, but the feeling was still alive and well—as was their insatiable physical passion for each other.

Jerry patted her leg and leaned forward enough to be heard over the white noise of the slipstream at forty-one thousand feet.

"Jim, how soon to descent?"

The copilot turned. "About ten minutes."

He nodded and unsnapped his seat belt, leaning over to kiss her lightly. "The media could be waiting."

"I know the drill," she replied. "And don't get sidetracked by the business aspect. We have two funerals to help plan."

In Flight, Tanker 84

Clark Maxwell's left arm was aching from the constant twenty pounds of left bank pressure he was maintaining on the control yoke, and he desperately needed something to drink. Coffee, water, anything would do, but there was no time for either of them to run back to the ice chest. The last of Jackson Lake had already disappeared under the nose and another ten minutes lay between them and the field at West Yellowstone.

"Why don't you let me take it for a few minutes?" Rusty asked.

Clark nodded, relinquishing the yoke as the copilot substituted his own muscles.

It was easy to trust Rusty, and not just because they'd flown five seasons together before Clark's temporarily revoked retirement. Rusty's penchant for hauling old airliners around as a copilot and turning wrenches on airplanes as a mechanic belied the fact that he was a lawyer who hated lawyering and loved aviation. He'd tried to practice for nearly ten years in what he described as junior-partner hell in Denver. But the pressures had led to a major lifestyle meltdown and a couple of years of drifting, plus a lost marriage, and the scruffy beard he was wearing the day he enrolled in a junior college mechanic's course.

The junior college had been intimidated enough to try to keep him out when they found he had a B.A., a J.D., and an M.B.A. degree. As Rusty told it, he'd renewed his legal license by ten A.M. one morning, threatened a major federal lawsuit by eleven, and been in his first class by noon in coveralls carrying a Gucci briefcase with nothing but a sandwich inside.

Taking flight lessons and working his way to a commercial and instrument rating before qualifying for airtanker copilot had been another protracted struggle, but he'd loved every minute of it.

"Clark, close your eyes if you want," Rusty was saying. "Rest up a few minutes for the approach. It really is allowed."

"Thanks." He could see Rusty still looking at him as if waiting for an opening.

"What?" Clark asked.

"I'm wondering," Rusty began, choosing his words carefully, "how preventable this was, you know?"

"You mean, with all the special inspections this year, how the hell could a propeller blade fail like that? Or were those inspections just a placebo to make the FAA and Forest Service brass feel good?"

Rusty nodded. "Something like that. Look, Clark, I've figured out it was you who wrote that bombshell exposé article last year on tanker safety, and it scares me to think how right you were. This whole system's shot."

Clark gave him a worried glance and the copilot smiled and nodded more vigorously. "Hey, most of us really appreciated it. Not that anyone knew it was you."

"Why would you think that article was mine?"

"Deduction, my dear captain Watson. Only a guy with a butt full of saddle sores from too many years in the DC-6B, and a guy who's a true professional in this business, could have known the right stuff about what's wrong. Obviously none of the guys still flying on the front lines every year are going to risk their jobs to speak up in public, and that means the only cappie with both the necessary qualifications *and* the ability to do so without cutting his throat would be someone newly retired, and that left a particular birdman named Maxwell."

"So, that's your conclusion, huh?"

"Yes . . . that, and your speech patterns gave you away. You write like you talk."

Clark chuckled as he rechecked the gauges. "If I write like I talk, then I'm really in deep trouble."

"Actually, you do both very well, skipper. I was impressed."

The compliment registered with a small sparkle of pride. Rusty was a good writer with several national articles to his credit.

"Thanks," Clark replied guardedly. "But . . . how many others know who wrote it?"

"I'm the only one, as far as I know."

"Ah, you're . . . you're not planning on—"

"Broadcasting the fact that the old friend I requested to fly with threw an anonymous harpoon into the side of the tanker industry last year and scared both the general public and the administration? Hell, no. You were dead-on right. I just wanted you to know that I agree with you, and that I appreciate it."

"Well . . . I just don't see the owners ever having enough money to do it right, y'know? Maintenance, training, inspections, ancient planes . . . we'll just keep on using Band-Aids and killing people," Clark said. "And I still have a lot of suspicions about how the C-130s were being used in the off-season, things we've never really looked into. The only real remedy I can see is a government takeover of some sort. Heck, I know the Forest Service and BLM will continue to harden their oversight, but it's still brittle. They can't make exhausted old aerial wrecks safe by passing regulations requiring them not to crash."

"I admire your courage, Clark. I've seen this trait in you for years."

"Really?"

"Yeah. Like the time you tried to hustle that little redhead in Boise?"

"What?"

"Pure courage. You didn't have a prayer."

"Yeah, right."

"But the type of courage I'm talking about is the intestinal fortitude to tell it like it is regardless of the consequences. Did the queen bee ever figure it out and call you?"

"Sherry Lacey, you mean?" Clark asked, recalling the last time he'd spoken to the Forest Service's director in charge of wildland firefighting. Sherry was a lovely, intelligent woman and one of the Air Force's first female pilots. But ultimately she was in a highly political position, and there was little chance she would have liked his conclusions.

"No. As far as I know she never knew that came from me."

"Well, I salute your courage," Rusty added.

*Courage indeed!* Clark thought. He'd penned the article from within the safe haven of retirement and hadn't been brave enough even to sign his name. Of course, maybe it would have been better if Jerry Stein *had* known it was him who'd stirred up so much fury. If so, he hadn't a doubt that Jerry would never have begged him to come back. "The bastard who wrote that," Jerry had fumed to him on the phone, "is a traitor and a liar." Clark had murmured all the right sounds of passive assent and said nothing more.

Rusty was nodding grimly. "Clark, you know, honestly? How long have I been flying these tubs as costar . . . maybe eight years? I sure would like to stick around and upgrade to captain, but I'd rather find a new job or even stop flying instead of rolling the dice every summer and running the risks we run. I love it, but these birds are aging faster than Trent can repair them."

"We need to talk. There's more going on here than meets the eye, Rusty, and I could use a silent ally. Congress doesn't understand yet, even after the Blue Ribbon report last year, which was scathing and excellent."

"I'm ready, man. Because the way I see it . . ."

The shrill jangling of an alarm bell covered the last few words as both pilots jerked their heads to the right. There was a red glow on the forward panel, and Clark realized it was the number-four-engine fire light. Rusty pressed his nose to his side window.

"What now?" Clark asked.

"Jeez, number four's on fire!" Rusty said.

"Number four?"

"Yes!"

"Didn't we shut off the fuel and finish the checklist?"

"Yes, dammit . . . I know I did. . . ." Rusty was fumbling to reach for the checklist with his free left hand, across his lap, his right staying on the yoke.

"I've got her," Clark said, taking up the pressure on the yoke with his left hand as he reached for the engine-fire switch on the overhead panel with his right.

"Rusty . . . check engine-fire switch number four. Confirm number four."

The copilot looked up and nodded. "Ah, roger, number four confirmed."

Clark pushed the switch that isolated number four-engine from fuel and electrical power and discharged the fire extinguisher.

"Anything? Any change?" he asked.

"No! The fire bottle isn't going to help. . . . The engine's almost fallen off."

Clark ignored the unintended rebuke. "Can you see what's burning? Where the flames are coming from?"

"Want me to go back and look?" Rusty was already unfastening his seat belt.

"Yeah. Go."

Rusty tumbled and pushed out of the right seat into the narrow aisleway, bruising his leg as he struggled free of the center console and raced out of the cockpit door into the mostly empty cabin to look out of the windows on the right side.

He was back in less than a minute.

"I don't know, Clark, it's . . . the flames are coming from the front of the engine nacelle and over the top of the wings as well as under it."

"You think it's fuel?"

"Could be . . . God, if it is . . ."

The rest of the sentence went unspoken. The fuel tanks were half empty, but what remained was highly explosive aviation gasoline, and if the flames could somehow find a way in to ignite the fumes, it would be all over in a literal flash.

"How about oil, Rusty?" Clark said evenly, feeling a cold knot forming in the pit of his stomach and the same creeping fear oozing around inside. "Could it be just burning oil?"

Rusty nodded, brightening just a bit. "Maybe! The flames aren't that much . . . it could be burning the remaining oil leaking out of the engine."

"I'll call base and tell them we're on fire and to get the fire trucks ready to follow us down the runway."

"Can we make it back?" Rusty asked as he refastened his seat belt, his voice more pleading than asking, the knowledge that there were no parachutes on board an unspoken truth.

"What are the options? We're much closer to home than to Jackson Hole. Even the lake is a long way back."

Clark shoved the remaining three throttles forward to METO power.

"I'm going to goose the airspeed as high as I can."

"Try to blow out the flames?"

He nodded, adjusting the rudder trim and rolling in more left aileron as the ship responded, the throaty roar of the remaining power plants masking the extreme danger they were trying to overcome.

"Anything else I can do?" Rusty asked, the strain in his voice apparent.

Clark nodded and tried unsuccessfully to grin.

"Yeah. Get out the beads and start clicking."

"Beads? I'm not Catholic."

"Then . . . I don't know . . . maybe make a promise to God that you'll give up women if he gets us out of this."

Rusty looked at him with raised eyebrows. "*Excuse* me? *I'll* give up women?"

Clark snorted, finally forcing his mouth into a genuine smile. "Well, *I'm* sure as hell not going to, and I'm the captain."

WEST YELLOWSTONE AIRTANKER OPERATIONS

Clark Maxwell's familiar voice had somehow cut through the din of conversations and office noises and silenced everyone in West Yellowstone Operations and the nearby pilot standby shack. The short bursts of static on the frequency seemed to underscore the distance between the crippled DC-6B and the relative safety of the runway outside.

There were other voices over the radio crackling through the room, the routine background chatter of the mechanics and ground crews and the Operations personnel, but those in the room were practiced at tuning out anything but the radio exchange they wanted to hear.

Clark described his situation to the dispatcher, who was located at a small desk in a corner of the room.

"Ah . . . the flames are probably about . . . they're trailing behind the wing maybe ten feet . . . not a huge fireball, but we're really kinda worried about it getting to the fuel vents. I'm . . . gonna need the trucks ready to hose it down the second we slow up. Tell them to just follow me down the runway."

The dispatcher's reply was almost inaudible to the cadre of aerial fire-fighters collectively holding their breath.

"Roger, Tanker Eighty-four. We'll be ready. How far out are you?"

The microphone button aboard the DC-6 was pushed and once again the intermittent static coursed through their ears before Clark's voice returned.

"My . . . ah . . . handheld GPS says we're about ten miles out now, clos-ing fast. Speed's two hundred sixty."

"We're clearing all other traffic. The field's yours."

There was a tug on Rich Lassiter's sleeve as he stood next to the dis-patcher. He turned to find one of the younger Forest Service employees standing wide-eyed with a receiver to her ear.

"What?"

"One of the rangers at the south entrance to the park says one of our tankers just flew by on fire."

"We know."

She nodded. "Yes, but he says the whole right wing was on fire and he was going down."

Somewhere in the back of his mind Lassiter recalled an article about the extreme fallibility of eyewitnesses in aviation disasters, but it wasn't si-lencing the shrill voice of panic in his mind that they were about to lose a second one.

IN FLIGHT, TANKER 84

"I've got the field at eleven o'clock," Rusty said, pointing in that direction. He looked back out his window. "And it looks like it's diminishing out there . . . just sputtering, y'know?"

"Almost out?"

"Close. Not much flame left."

Clark nodded as he nudged the struggling airliner five degrees more to the right, aiming for a point three miles north of the field. The wind was out of the south, and he'd make the tightest left turn possible to final approach to minimize the time.

"Rusty, the only checklist I want to hear is the before-landing checklist. Take care of everything else silently."

"Okay. I'm still showing two hundred ten knots, Clark."

Clark nodded again without replying as he ran the visual calculations of just when and where he should yank the throttles back and slow before turning. There was an optimum point that would bring them down to the right approach and landing speed at just the right moment. Too soon and he'd lengthen the time they were exposed to the fire. Too late and he'd whistle in over the runway threshold too fast to land safely, and making a go-around with the fire still going could cost them their lives.

"We're five out," Rusty called.

"Roger that."

The throttles were suddenly in motion backward as Clark pulled engines one, two, and three to idle, and worked fast to take out the considerable amount of rudder trim he'd been carrying.

"Gear down."

"Roger, gear down," Rusty responded as his hand moved the gear lever. The sound of an immediate rush of wind filled the cockpit as the landing gear moved into the slipstream way above normal extension speeds. The DC-6B shuddered and began to slow.

"Four miles."

They were still almost perpendicular to the final approach path to the runway and moving over the ground at a hundred and ninety knots.

"Flaps ten."

"Roger. Flaps coming to ten."

Clark used every ounce of muscle he had in his left arm to crank the yoke over as he pressed hard on the left rudder, skidding and rolling the big aircraft into a left forty-five-degree bank. The nose came left as they slid through the final approach course, slowing and descending, the speed still above 170.

"Flaps twenty."

"Flaps twenty."

"Flaps forty."

"Roger, forty."

They could feel the ship rise on the added lift of the large flaps as they came farther out, and Clark pushed forward to keep them descending, the fuselage of the big Douglas now twenty degrees misaligned with the runway.

Rusty pressed the transmit button on his yoke. "West Yellowstone traffic, Tanker Eighty-four, emergency bird, two-mile final, full stop, Yellowstone," he said, releasing the transmit button and glancing at Clark. "Speed one thirty and slowing."

Clark banked back to the right slightly, aiming at the very end of the runway and coming over the threshold just as they aligned with it. He flared and let the mains settle onto the concrete almost simultaneously with the nose gear before pressing on the top of the rudder pedals to activate the brakes, metering the pressure but slowing rapidly as the waiting fire trucks flashed past. The firemen began racing to catch up as the DC-6 slowed below thirty. There was a taxiway just ahead on the right, and Clark steered the ship into a tight right turn to pull safely off the runway before letting it roll to a stop.

"They're already on it!" the copilot announced, just as an impressive stream of water and foam hit the right wing from behind.

———

An anxious team of mechanics led by Trent Jones himself materialized with an engine stand and tool kits. When the firemen were through cooling the engine and cleaning up, they pulled the stand up to the hanging remains of the eighteen-cylinder engine. The two pilots had run the shutdown checklist with calm, steady voices, but when Rusty climbed to the ramp minutes later and tried to walk, his legs had turned to jelly.

Clark seemed steadier, but he, too, was fighting the effects of the last half hour.

Trent Jones motioned for his lead mechanic to take care of questioning the pilots while he stood on the grimy surface of the asphalt chewing an unlit cigar and moving around number-four engine with an older mechanic in trail.

The scorched and damaged Pratt and Whitney R-2800 power plant was barely hanging on the twisted remains of the engine mount, which had broken at all but two weld points. The engine itself was almost touching the concrete and still swaying gently.

Trent moved several feet away and looked closely at the right wing. The two ruined propeller blades had chopped several huge gashes in the leading edge of the wing, but the main event—the wing spar—appeared untouched.

"If that had reached a fuel tank, they'd be gone," he growled to himself.

Andy Simmons, the other mechanic, scratched at his mountain man beard and stuffed a greasy rag in a rear pocket of his coveralls as he watched.

Trent Jones was technically his boss, but he was also a much less experienced mechanic. Andy hated management duties. He had worked for Jerry Stein for a decade before Jones came aboard, and he was perfectly content to let a volatile man like Jones spar and battle with Jerry while Andy came in quietly every day and happily did what he loved to do: convince complicated machines to run well. The amazing R-2800 was his specialty, a brilliantly designed engine first produced in 1939, full of complex reciprocating parts and eighteen cylinders that, when running smoothly, pulled itself through the air with the power of two thousand horses.

"Jets," Andy was fond of sneering, "are kid stuff. Real men maintain R-2800s."

He'd already seen enough of this particular version to know what it was going to take to repair it.

"So whatd'ya think, Mr. Maintenance Director?" Simmons asked, well aware that while Trent was a reasonably competent mechanic, he was a novice with the R-2800s, and completely underwater as a maintenance director.

Trent Jones made a rude noise and pulled the unlit cigar out of his mouth.

"What's to think? The prop's toast, the wing alone is a good two days' work to patch, and we'll have to either scavenge an R-2800 engine mount, or build one when the fuzz isn't looking. And we've got a wingful of soot and black to get off."

"You do know, don'tcha, that Jerry's on descent right now in that little Lear of his?"

"What?"

"Yeah. He'll be on the ramp in another twenty minutes, Trent, and heading for the hangar to help you out."

Trent whirled on him. "Thank you *so* very much for reminding me!" He shook his head in disgust. "As if I don't have enough pressure."

"You're welcome," Simmons said evenly. "I just wasn't sure you understood that Jerry always demands instant reports and instant good news fixes when the fit hits the shan."

Trent ignored him as pointedly as he could.

Andy shrugged and smiled. "I've been with him a long time, Trent. He's probably fired me and rehired me more times than you latched on to your mom's nipples as a kid."

"I wasn't breast-fed, not that it's any of your business."

"Aha! So *that's* why you're such a mean sonofabitch."

"Shut up, Simmons."

"Yassir, Mr. Boss Man."

Trent began walking around the back of the engine again, his eyes scanning every exposed surface of the machinery.

"You think we've got a twisted or broken shaft in there?" Trent asked.

"I can't answer you. I'm supposed to shut up, remember?" Andy replied, eliciting exactly the explosion he was looking for as Jones threw a rag on the ground and shook a finger at him.

"Dammit, Simmons! This is NOT the day for your comedy club audition, okay? I want your damned professional opinion."

"No."

"Don't you friggin tell me no!"

"I meant, 'No, I don't think the shaft is compromised,' " Andy said with exaggerated innocence.

"Oh."

"But we have to tear 'er down to be sure, Trent."

"Can't we clean it up and bench test it?"

"Nope. It's a tear down. That's the bottom line. I don't know how long she ran with only two blades beating her up, but even a few seconds can do a lot of damage, and even though that fire was obviously oil-fed, the heat may have finished her off."

Trent sighed. "Stein will never accept that expense."

"Maybe not, but if she's toast, as you called it, she's toast. I can't work magic. But somehow I suspect you already know that."

There was no answer since the sight of Jerry Stein's Lear 23 on final approach had commandeered Trent's full attention.

# Chapter 6

Precisely when his thinking was hijacked by the burning need to visit the crash site personally, Clark wasn't sure.

He'd left the battered form of Tanker 84 to the panicked mechanics and walked across the grass and the single runway toward the Forest Service ramp. A soft wind was whipping at him as he approached three of Jerry Stein's small helicopters parked on the south end of the Stein Aviation property.

The fact that he might have just cheated death limping back to base in a crippled, burning old airliner seemed more of an embarrassment than a cause for celebration.

Not that he wasn't happy to be alive.

It was the fact that Jeff Maze and his copilot hadn't been as lucky.

The freeze-framed image of the crash site he'd mentally recorded from a thousand feet up hours before seemed pitifully insufficient as an acknowledgment of their demise. Especially since, in some ways, they had died in his place. Not for a minute had he been able to forget the fact that Tanker 86 was supposed to have been his.

*There but for the grace of God, go I*, he thought to himself, rolling the phrase over in his mind to see the full horror reflected in the polished surface of its meaning.

*I need to be there,* he decided suddenly, his eyes focusing on the Jet Rangers ahead. His many years as a rated helicopter pilot made the decision simple.

Clark walked into the Operations building with Rusty in tow, instantly chagrined by the hearty round of applause and the backslaps. These were his colleagues. Pilots. Fellow airmen. Friends—some more so than others—but all of them needing to trivialize any near-death aerial experience, toasting the successful recovery as if the experience were nothing more lethal than a football game snatched from defeat in the last seconds of the fourth quarter.

And after the loss of Jeff Maze and Mike Head just a few hours before, the home team desperately needed a win—as the hastily wiped tears from several otherwise leathery faces clearly attested.

When the uncomfortable congratulatory air had subsided and the normal beehive of activity resumed, Clark quietly moved away to find one of Rich Lassiter's assistants on the crew desk, leaving Rusty with his hands flailing the air as he related the emergency once more in dramatic detail.

"I need one of the Jet Rangers," Clark said in a quiet voice, pointing to the grease board listings of Jerry's helicopter fleet.

The young woman looked up at him with a puzzled expression. "Were you . . . assigned that, Clark?"

"Effectively, yes, and I'm fully rated in the Bell 206. I'm on a special mission for Jerry. He needs me to go to the crash site to answer a specific question."

She cocked her head, studying his expression and looking for an indication that he was kidding, but Clark kept his face unreadable.

"What . . . question?" she asked. "You just limped in here. When did he talk to you?"

"Hey," Clark smiled, looking around, then continuing conspiratorially. "He has a phone in his Lear, and you've been here long enough to know that Jerry doesn't like all his reasons broadcast, right?"

She hesitated, unsure of herself, but unwilling to push too hard. After all, Clark Maxwell was the hero of the hour and one of the old dogs. She nodded then and quietly handed over the keys and the clipboard for one of the freshly fueled Rangers just outside.

"Thanks," he replied. "I'll be back in two hours."

Clark turned away from the desk, his eyes taking in the expected panorama of pilots and Operations personnel standing and talking while others worked the phones at small desks. His eyes locked on the exit door twenty feet distant, then jumped back to the right, to one of the desks where a blond woman with her back partially to him had a phone to each ear.

For a second he thought she looked like Karen Jones, but it had been a long time since he'd seen Karen. He peered closer as he moved a little to one side to get a better view.

It was Karen, he realized, her short, blond hair swinging luxuriously whenever she moved her head. The recognition triggered a small, pleasant shock, like a splash of cold water in the face after a long, hot day.

Clark watched her as she lowered one of the receivers and scribbled a note before disconnecting. She was just as beautiful, he thought, as the last time he'd seen her, some four years ago. Her body carried not an extra ounce, her skin was smooth and glowing, and he could imagine her infectious smile irradiating the room. Time had apparently been treating her very well.

He was still out of range of Karen's peripheral vision, but he watched her head come up, and she stared out the window as if somehow sensing that she was being watched.

Karen Jones pivoted suddenly in the swivel chair, spotting Clark, a smile of recognition spreading slowly over her face. She waved at him, her voice drowning in the tidal waves of sound washing through the room, but the import of her greeting eminently readable on her lips.

"Hi!" she mouthed.

"Karen!" he said in a loud voice as he moved toward the desk separating them and looked around before leaning as far in her direction as possible. *She is obviously on a mission and doing something administrative,* he thought. "How are you?"

"Well, very shaken," she replied, sweeping her hair back from her forehead. "Jeff was . . . a friend of mine . . . and, of course, a longtime friend of Trent's, as well. I didn't know Mike Head, the copilot, but everyone says he was a great guy. We hadn't even had time to accept their loss when you go and scare us half to death with an engine fire."

"Sorry," he grinned. "I just wanted to be noticed."

"Next time let me know, and I'll post your picture in the post office. It's a lot less wearing on the nerves."

Clark raised an index finger in a wait gesture and maneuvered around the desk to get closer as Karen got to her feet. There was a sudden uncharacteristic flutter of uncertainty in his middle as he tried to decide whether or not to hug her, but she solved the dilemma by extending her hand. It was a correct little handshake, until she reached out with her other hand and enfolded his.

"It's really good to see you, Clark!" she said, her smile warm and broadening. He was trying to keep an appropriately serious expression, but a small flare of excitement had ignited in him, and he was sure the sudden warmth was visible on his face.

Another heavy four-engine tanker was lumbering into the air and moving past the window behind her. The rumble of its pistons and props momentarily washed out all conversation in the building, but Clark didn't notice.

"How are—"

"What hap—"

They began simultaneously, both of them laughing at the result.

"You first," he said.

"I was just going to ask you about your engine. The whole place was hanging on to every word until you landed. Thank God you're back safely, but in the future, could you maybe not come in trailing a hundred feet of flame?"

"It was only fifty feet."

"How tough was she to fly?"

He shrugged. "I used a few muscles I'd forgotten I had trying to hang on to her, but otherwise it wasn't too bad. The Douglas DC-6 is a tough, reliable old . . ." his voice trailed off at the vivid memory of the DC-6 wreckage in the forest and the fire he'd just survived on his right wing. She nodded as he glanced away, understanding his slip.

"Normally it is," she said. "I know. From what I've been hearing, no one around here has any earthly idea what could have gone wrong with Jeff's bird."

He looked at her, suddenly aware he was chewing on his lip, which undoubtedly looked stupid. He forced himself to stop. "I'm . . . just getting ready to fly to the crash site in one of the Jet Rangers, if you'd like to come along . . ."

She shook her head vigorously. "No, thanks. I . . . I've got to help out in here."

"Understood. Dumb idea."

Karen moved her left hand away from his, and he realized they were still in the middle of a suspended handshake that was beginning to feel awkward. He gently squeezed and let her hand slide from his, feeling the loss.

She crossed her arms below her breasts, and he tried not to notice the alluring effect.

"I've . . . seen enough terrible things, Clark. Not plane crashes, really, but . . . other horrors."

"Really?" he said, immediately regretting the question and the haunted look that appeared on her face.

She inclined her head toward the southeast, rocking on one foot, then the other, looking for a way around the explanation. "When I last saw you, it was a bit too fresh to talk about."

"That was four years ago, then," Clark offered.

"Yeah, well. My first summer smokejumping was 1994, and my third jump ever was on Storm King Mountain in Colorado."

Clark's eyebrows went up at the mention of the peak near Glenwood Springs that had become almost as infamous to firefighters as the 1949 Mann Gulch tragedy in Montana. An uncontrollable firestorm had roared up the natural chimney of Storm King's valley, sending forty-nine firefighters fleeing for their lives. Three smokejumpers and nine hotshots were

caught before they could reach the ridge, along with two helitacks who had
been above the ridge but retreated the wrong way. Superheated gasses destroyed their lungs with a single breath long before fire could consume their
bodies, and several had fallen mere yards from the top of the ridge that separated the living from the dead.

"You knew some of the victims?" he asked, not expecting the response.

She nodded. "Two of my best friends died. I was one of the thirty-five
who made it. I had to identify one of my guys." She grimaced and looked
away, then sighed. "So, how are we doing on this fire?"

"Not well. Have they briefed you?"

She shook her head and told him about the summons to help with the
phones, and her inbound squad.

"So, you'll be jumping tomorrow?"

She smiled. "Maybe."

"Where are you . . . uh, you and Trent staying?"

A cloud of sadness crossed her face for just a second as she glanced away
and exhaled a little too sharply, then looked back as if there were no messages there to be read. "Oh, we're at the Best Western. He's already been
here for months and his room is a pigsty, so . . ." She hesitated, realizing the
implications of mentioning her separate room. "So we're there."

"Well, I'd better—" He began backing away from the counter, remembering suddenly to pick up the clipboard and key to the helicopter as she
smiled at his awkward retreat. "—you know, get going."

"Sure. It's wonderful to see you."

"Maybe sometime this week I could buy you a beer or something," Clark
said.

The smile intensified ever so slightly. "Maybe you can," she replied. "I'd
like that."

Karen gave him a parting wave as Clark headed for the door, feeling self-
conscious and suddenly aware of just how he was swinging his arms and
walking. It was the same effect, he mused, she'd had on him four years ago.
He hadn't wanted to admit it to himself, but Jerry Stein's plea to come back
for just this summer had become instantly more palatable when he'd called
Missoula and discovered Karen Jones might be there sometime during the
season to supplement the West Yellowstone Smokejumper base.

Clark picked up his flight bag and walked quickly toward the Jet Ranger,
calculating how much time he'd have to get to the crash site and avoiding
the subject of why staying away was impossible. He could see Jerry Stein's
Lear 23 coming to a stop in the distance on the Stein Aviation ramp, and the
ground crew closing in around it.

Diana Stein emerged first from the cramped interior of the Lear 23, an folded her perfectly trim supermodel body, and shook her mane of auburn hair—well aware that every male eye in the vicinity was carefully taking note of the boss's wife and trying to hide the fact.

She glanced back to see Jerry hanging up the sky phone. He motioned for her to stand back as he jumped out of the door like a large cat pouncing onto the tarmac, his eyes rapidly taking in who was there before pointing to his small Operations building and setting off at a pace that forced everyone else to jog.

Diana leaned languidly against the leading edge of the left wing, watching one of Jerry's employees clamber into the cabin to fetch their bags. She was expected to follow her husband into Operations on such arrivals. She was the walking validation of his status as the alpha male, the only one allowed to flaunt his elegant and sexy woman before the other men. It was a role Diana understood as clearly as she understood his immutable need for it.

She smiled to herself and shook her head almost imperceptibly before pushing away from the wing and following.

Jerry was already inside his Operations shack, shaking the outstretched hands of his employees and nodding at the offered updates as he moved toward the windows forming the wall of a small briefing room on the other side. He was oblivious to the Jet Ranger lifting off outside.

Pivoting, he pointed in turn at four of the contingent who were following him.

"James, Hawkins, Brown, and Jones. In here."

The four men moved nervously past him into the cramped room and began unfolding metal chairs as he closed the door behind them and plunked down in the first one offered, waiting for the others to get settled.

"You want the maintenance realities first?" Trent Jones asked.

Jerry Stein shook his head, his voice low and tense. "All right, listen closely. As we were landing, I got a call from a guy in D.C. who watches over us, so to speak. I pay him good money to keep his ear to the ground. He's got good sources in Congress, deep-throat sources in the FAA, Interior Department, and the Forest Service. He's plugged in, and he knows about the crash *and* the engine loss on Eighty-four *and* that damned Blue Ribbon report *and* the problems the retardant manufacturers have been generating. He also knows that the only thing we've got going in our favor right now is the fact that the forests near Jackson are burning and we have only so many airplanes."

"He's worried about us?" Bill James asked.

"Worried?" Jerry snorted. "Guys, are you in any way dependent on the money Stein Aviation pays you?"

They all glanced at one another before focusing back on Jerry and nodding nervously yes.

"Okay. You want to hear worst case? The secretary of the interior and the secretary of agriculture held a meeting this morning over breakfast. Know what they discussed? How to terminate immediately the contracts of all air-tanker companies and call in the Air National Guard and the Air Force with C-130Hs or some other more modern version."

"Can . . . can they do that?"

"Oh, it gets worse. They called in the Department of Justice and were asking for opinions on whether they could refuse to pay us for what we've already accomplished, and whether they could back charge us under the contract for hundreds of thousands in fees and penalties, as well as the possibility of attaching the airplanes to make sure they'll never fly again. Even the guaranteed availability money in the contracts could be tied up for years. That means instant shutdown, instant Chapter Seven liquidation bankruptcy, zero paychecks, and we're all on the street."

"Okay, but . . . is that likely?" Trent asked, his voice hesitant.

Jerry took a deep breath, feeling another burst of the occasional throbbing pain in his temple that had been worrying him increasingly over the past few days. He glanced beyond the men into the room, his eyes instantly finding Diana, who was standing in her usual alluring way by the counter, smiling in his direction. He tried to smile back to hide what was probably written all over his face: The possibility that he was truly on the verge of losing everything. Including her.

He turned back to his employees.

"The word I get? One more incident, one more accident, one more embarrassment, and it's all over." He let that sink in before looking at Trent.

"So, after all that good news, is there anything you can say to cheer us up, Trent?"

# Chapter 7

The column of smoke stabbing the azure sky from the crash-induced forest fire was visible as soon as Clark leveled the Jet Ranger at four thousand feet above ground level, the angular rays of the descending sun casting an elongated shadow to the east over the highest ridges of the Yellowstone Caldera. The flame front from the new fire was being whipped and shepherded steadily northward in the arms of the southern wind, growing ominously as it progressed, eating its way through the lodgepole pines and Douglas fir and the stately ponderosa, but the dark, cylindrical monolith of smoke was rising strangely, ascending vertically for many thousands of feet. It loomed, Clark thought, like a giant exclamation point above the dot of scorched forest that held the remains of Ship 86, at once impossible to ignore and easy to follow.

There was another flurry of radio transmissions in his headset, calls and answers coordinating the urgent progression of the fire-fighting fleet in and out of West Yellowstone. The fires east of Jackson Hole were growing steadily, and tomorrow would be even more intense.

Weary of the distraction, Clark reached up to the control panel and lowered the VHF radio volume, hoping to leave the muffled *whump-whump-whump* of the rotor blades and the high-pitched whine of the turbines as the only noises in his mind.

He knew there could be other helicopters already in the area, and missing a call from one of them could be dangerous, but he had his breaking point, and the noise had surpassed it. Nevertheless, he dutifully keyed the transmitter and called out his location and altitude in the blind.

Clark closed his eyes momentarily, letting the vibrations course through him, drowning out the almost overwhelming feelings of profound loss and confusion that had risen from nowhere to snap at his resolve in the past hours. This mission was as obscure as he felt. Unfocused. Upset. Unsure.

He made a small correction in the course, feeling the ship respond instantly, and was thankful for his ability to fly choppers. The Jet Ranger was like an extension of him, a natural connection that let him fly like most people breathed, the seemingly chaotic rhythms of the small galaxy of moving parts a well-understood concerto responding to his very touch in ways that fixed-wing pilots seldom understood. The flight controls of most fixed-wing airplanes had to be physically moved to affect the flight path. But a rotorcraft, Clark was fond of explaining, was as different from a fixed-wing aircraft as females were from males. Like most women he'd known, helicopters responded best to those who touched them gently, and they were equally intolerant of inattention.

To meld with a helicopter and produce the crude mechanical equivalent of a hummingbird's maneuverability, a pilot gently held the cyclic—the control stick rising from the floor—and merely *thought* his ship left or right, up or down, forward or backward, his feet similarly caressing the pedals controlling the left and right movement of the tail rotor. It was a delicate ballet in three dimensions, an intricate dance of feet, fingers, and thought accompanied by what, to the pilot, were the sweet mechanical murmurings of a living metallic bird speaking her language clearly and steadily, a constant monologue in her pilot's ear on the never-ending battle to best the wind and gravity with fuel and fury.

A sudden patch of turbulence caught the Jet Ranger and tested his skills for a moment, the ship settling down again just as quickly, as the weird Yellowstone landscape unfolded below in amazing detail through the Plexiglas. The steam of a hundred geysers rising in the distance off to his left and the carpet of green beneath were a natural expression of the contradictory geothermal hell roiling just below the park's crustal surface—the Yellowstone Hot Spot—the natural volcanic blowtorch that had progressively cut a path from the Pacific Coast to present-day northwestern Wyoming over millions of years of crustal movement. The North American tectonic plate had been the one in motion, moving slowly west at about the speed of a human fingernail growing. The hot spot had merely continued to pump molten magma from the earth's mantle, changing and scarring the surface that was slowly passing above.

And in Yellowstone's case, a vast, little-understood matrix of natural plumbing ferried superheated groundwater from the furnace below to the surface in the form of geysers, fumaroles, mud holes, hot springs, and other sulphurous discharges. It was nature and it was natural, unlike the forest fire Clark was looking at ahead of the Jet Ranger.

*About eighteen miles to go,* he thought, checking the GPS and remembering what navigating an airplane had been like before the network of GPS satellites had been launched. Dead reckoning was the basic phrase, and his fa ther, an Air Force colonel, had been a taskmaster at the basics of how wind corrections, combined with speed and time and careful record keeping, would tell you almost precisely where you were.

A side gust bounced the Jet Ranger, triggering a momentary slapping sound as the rotor blades sliced through the strong crosswind and settled down.

*I miss you, Dad,* Clark thought, the genesis of at least some of his upset suddenly becoming clear: the looming sight of the scorched and blackened crash site just ahead. Seeing it earlier from the cockpit of Tanker 84 had tugged at a locked door in his mind, a closet stuffed with awful memories of another crash site, a catastrophic melding of mountain and metal on Washington State's Olympic Peninsula in 1975 that had killed his father, Colonel William "Sax" Maxwell, and eleven others. The exhausted pilots of an Air Force C-141, returning home to McChord AFB from a wholly unnecessary trip to Southeast Asia, had accepted a descent from a controller. But the controller had made a lethal mistake they were too tired to catch: five thousand feet was too low to clear the ridge of a peak called Mount Constance. At the last second, the investigators figured, the crew had seen the onrushing granite and yanked the nose up, but the big Lockheed thundered into the rocks less than three hundred feet below the summit, killing all aboard fewer than fifty miles from home.

And Colonel Sax Maxwell had been the senior navigator.

Clark shook back the memory and nudged the Jet Ranger to the left, watching the wisps of smoke from the center of the wreckage as he set up an approach into the wind, slowing and descending at the same time, his left hand working the collective downward bit by bit. There was a momentary worry about whether a restricted area had been declared by the FAA around the crash site, but he dismissed it as unimportant and brought the ship to a hover three feet above a charred clearing a hundred yards or so from the main impact point, letting the Jet Ranger settle onto her skids.

There were two other helicopters at the site, both off to the east where numerous vehicles and fire trucks had made it in across country from the nearest access road. Clark waved at a small group of men as he secured the helicopter and took the key, trudging through the acrid aroma of freshly charred grasses and burning wood to reach them.

A park ranger whose duties had never included dealing with air attack firefighters stepped forward, his hand up.

"Sir, I need to know who you are and what you're doing landing here," the ranger said, not unkindly.

Clark held out his aircrew I.D. card from Stein Aviation and offered his hand, which the ranger shook.

"Okay, Captain Maxwell. That takes care of the who."

"I'm here for the owner, Jerry Stein. I don't need to touch anything, but I'm kind of the director of safety, and I'll be working with the NTSB. Are they here yet?"

The park ranger shook his head no, launching into an excessively detailed report on when an NTSB team was expected to show up. "We're just keeping the wreckage safe for now, as per their instructions by phone, but—"

"I'm just going to walk around it."

"Well—"

Clark raised his hand, palm up. "I'm involved in the investigation, remember? I'm not touching anything or even kicking tin. Just getting a feel for it. So, if it's okay with you . . ."

The ranger pointed back to the northwest. "We found the wing over there about a mile."

"I know. I saw it earlier from the air."

"Yeah. It's pretty gruesome. The bodies are burned beyond recognition, y'know?"

"I can imagine."

They stood in uncomfortable silence for a few moments before he spoke again.

"I heard this was an old airliner before they made it into an airtanker," the ranger added.

"Yeah. They can carry a lot." Clark was feeling increasingly antsy to be free of the man. The young ranger had obviously seen too much and was having his own problems dealing with it.

"You ever flown in one?" the ranger asked.

Clark sighed and looked at him, realizing he was only in his late twenties, his eyes somewhat sunken and distant.

"This was a DC-6B. I was supposed to be at the controls of this aircraft, but they switched airplanes at the last second."

The ranger looked him in the eyes for the longest time, Clark's words finally taking root as he backed away a step and inclined his head toward the main wreckage. "I'm so sorry. I understand."

Clark nodded without comment and stepped away, walking slowly toward the initial point of impact, noting the various shapes and identifiable shards, including the crushed pilot seats with what remained of his two colleagues blackened and shapeless.

He didn't linger.

The special stench of charred airplane and burned flesh triggered its own revulsion, and he walked to the far side to sit on a blackened log, looking back at the crushed and shattered cockpit and trying to imagine his body there in place of Maze's.

If he'd been at the controls when the wing fell off, he would have been no more able to save them than Jeff had been.

Somehow he'd planned to find the right wing attach points and examine them, but the impossibility became painfully apparent as he let his eyes wander over the twisted metal. Finding the right piece in that mess—let alone interpreting the damage correctly—was far beyond his knowledge, even with his airplane and power-plant mechanic license, also known in the vernacular as an "A&P." He could see the general area of what had been the right wing root, or shoulder of the aircraft. But beyond that, the experts at the NTSB would have to answer the question of why a plane supposedly inspected with unprecedented thoroughness could fall apart just a few hundred hours of flight time later.

*And just how many flight hours* had *it been since that inspection?* Clark wondered. He recalled the Hobbs meter on Tanker 84 indicating that about 180 flight hours had elapsed since the inspections. Tanker 86 might have had a few more or a few less hours on it, but there was no way a wing in danger of failing wouldn't have been discovered if the inspections had been done right.

*They must have botched the inspections. Or maybe Jerry found a confederate willing to cook the books and sign off on a damaged structure.*

No, he reminded himself. The inspections had been performed by Sandia Labs with the Forest Service's maintenance inspectors breathing down their necks. And Jerry was slippery, but not crazy.

*So, if the inspections were adequate, and there were only 180 hours of flight time on the bird since the inspections, and since that isn't enough to produce new cracks dangerous enough to take off a wing, then what else? What got you, Jeff, if not Jerry's bargain-basement approach to maintenance?*

Clark looked around, wondering if Jeff's spirit could be sitting nearby, looking with the same detached wonder at the same scene.

*What's the matter with me?* Clark thought. He wondered why he'd come in the first place—and was startled at the answer that suddenly seemed so obvious. He was, he realized, still looking for closure in his father's death so many years before.

The Air Force had refused to let Colonel Maxwell's ten-year-old son go to the crash site until the cockpit had been removed. But then access to Mount Constance in the Olympic Mountains of Washington State was denied even after the bodies were gone, and since the crash site was within a national park, the Air Force could make the order stick.

Mere hours after the crash, in the early light of morning, fog and cold had surrounded the grisly scene. The first rescuers to helicopter in quickly found the front portion of the C-141 broken away and deformed, but recognizable. The windscreens seemed mostly intact, and for a brief moment the first team member to shine a powerful flashlight inside had held a brief and futile hope that among the flight-suited human forms strewn around the interior, someone might still be alive.

But the impact had been unsurvivable, even for the two crew members ejected from the disintegrating cabin and found on the snowy slope.

It would be six years before Clark, as a young teen, could climb there on his own, camping for three days in a pup tent pitched at the exact point of initial impact. But that pilgrimage did not achieve the closure and communing he'd longed for ever since the dark hours after the crash. It was as if his father were still out there, still roaming in confusion, still needing his son to rescue him. It was as if little Clark were somehow responsible.

Clark shifted a bit on the log, aware part of it was still smoking from the fire. Overhead he heard the rumble of another airtanker returning to base to the northeast and glanced at his watch. He should get up, get back in the Jet Ranger, and leave. But he couldn't make himself move.

There was a connection here. It was the closing of a circle, he thought, or somehow the conclusion of a mystery. But the details were confusing. Was there a link beyond the obvious between his father's death so many years ago and this recent crash? This accident site he was visiting while the wreckage still smoked. The other had been forever barred to him by time and circumstance.

This crash should have been *his* last resting place, his remains crushed and burned. He should be dead. And somehow there was a symmetry between the two crashes that he couldn't completely grasp, even though he knew instinctively that when he did understand it, the knowledge would be comforting.

And in that second the clouds cleared from his mind.

Something, indeed, was changing profoundly within him, as if another door had closed in his life, one he had struggled to shut for nearly three decades. Clark stood, his eyes on the blue of the smoky sky. Jeff Maze's spirit was not here. Neither had his dad's spirit been waiting for him on Mount Constance.

And suddenly it was all right to leave.

There was a small shard of aircraft aluminum near his foot, thrown from the main wreckage by the force of the impact. He glanced up to make sure no one was watching and picked it up, noting the small serial numbers on the twisted surface, before slipping it into the pocket of his flight jacket. He was well aware of the rules and the dangers to an investigation of removing or even moving anything, but this scrap was hardly part of the cause, he decided, and he needed a tangible piece of Tanker 86 as a touchstone of mortality.

"This is a piece of the airplane I died in," he could imagine himself saying to startled friends in the future, waiting for their jaws to drop far enough before telling the rest of the story of fickle fate and unplanned redemption.

There was a small fluttering of something white flipping along in the wind, something torn from the body of the wreckage. Clark leaned forward and captured it, surprised to find a scorched business card in his hand. He peered carefully at the raised letters on the front, some of which had partially melted and run. But the name of what was apparently a bar or tavern was clear: LA ZORRA SECRETA.

He turned the card slightly to find a better angle in the sunlight. The name of the city was too blurred to read, but the country was still there: Colombia.

He shook his head. It must have been stuck deep inside a brain bag and forgotten. He wondered which of the pilots had been there over the years. Perhaps it had been an expansive vacation, and if it was a place Jeff had visited, Misty might have been there, too, and could tell him about it someday.

But then again, knowing Jeff, God only knew which female might have been partying with him at a bar whose name Clark roughly translated as "The Secret Vixen."

He chuckled at the memory of the wild-man legend Jeff had loved to nurture, his smile fading just as quickly. He pocketed the scorched business card and walked back to the helicopter.

————

The return flight to West Yellowstone seemed to last only a fraction of the time it had taken to reach the crash site. For the entire twenty-five minutes his ears were filled with the soothing strains of Vivaldi's *Four Seasons* through the MP3 stereo connection in his headset, while his mind played with the suddenly invigorating idea that somehow Karen Jones could be talked into meeting him for a beer. Her optimistic way of looking at everything was a balm he sorely needed right now.

He made a smooth, fast approach to the ramp against the wind and brought the Jet Ranger to a perfect hover just inches above the same spot where he'd found it. He sat there in the air motionless for almost a minute, blowing dirt and scraps of paper around on the ramp as he hovered with what appeared to be effortless ease. There were eyes peering from the windows of the Forest Service Operations building, and several people watching from beneath the P-3 across the ramp, and he enjoyed that. Clark knew he was showing off shamelessly, but he didn't care. There were some things he could do that they couldn't.

Tiring of the exhibition at last, he lowered the Jet Ranger to the tarmac.

Through the windows of the Stein Operations building across the runway he could make out what might be Jerry Stein engaged in some sort of meeting and paying no attention to his helicopter landing. *Jerry is the last person I really wanted to see tonight anyway,* he thought.

He locked the ship and took his flight bag, spotting two Forest Service men he didn't recognize heading toward Airtanker Operations.

"Excuse me. Would you guys drop off this clipboard to Lynda at the desk?"

"Sure," the taller of the two said, accepting the board with the attached keys.

He circumnavigated the building to find his truck in the parking lot, his mind already working over the problem of how to contact Karen without upsetting Trent.

Clark slipped his flight bag in the right seat of the pickup and drove around the runway to the Stein Operations shack. As he approached on foot, he could see that Karen was inside. So, too, he noted, was her husband, the chief of maintenance, who was wearing a more worried expression than he'd ever seen on the man. It was logical, Clark told himself, as he reversed course without entering and climbed back into the cab of his truck.

Trent Jones would be under immense pressure to immediately repair Tanker 84, the crippled DC-6 Clark had managed to fly safely back to base. At the same time Jones would be defending virtually everything the company had done to maintain the DC-6 that had killed Jeff Maze. He wondered whether Jones was given to resisting Jerry's penurious approach to maintenance, or facilitating it. The man was very hard to read in his brief contacts with pilots on the ramp.

Yet, the haunted look he'd seen through the window on Jones's face was worrisome, and once more Clark felt his mind tunneling back into the why and how of Maze's crash with the same inchoate worry that he was somehow still missing something important.

In fact, perhaps they all were.

# Chapter 8

Karen Jones slid the room key into the lock and pushed into the room, surprised by a blast of refrigerated air from the air-conditioning unit she'd left on.

*Damn! It was hot when I checked in this morning.*

She closed the door and turned off the air conditioner, then turned the small clock radio to an easy listening station and plunked herself on the edge of the bed, feeling decidedly off balance. She took a deep breath and pulled out her cell phone from the depths of her purse, scrolling to the very welcome message she'd received earlier and listening to it again.

> *"Karen. Clark, here. I know you and Trent are staying at the Best Western, but I wonder if maybe you'd have time for a beer over at the Coachman Lounge. That's where we flyboys tend to hang out, as you may already know, in the . . . ah . . . Coach, no, Stagecoach Hotel. I'm not staying there, by the way, because I've rented a house on the edge of town, so . . . I'm driving over, but . . . if you have time, I'm thinking I could meet you there about seven P.M. I figure we've got a lot of catching up to do. Oh, and, of course, Trent's welcome to join us, if he's around. I figured he'd be working late. . . ."*

He laughed, that deep, pleasant rumble of a laugh she remembered well, then continued, obviously flustered.

> *"I'm sorry. That made it sound like I'm trying to arrange some sort of illicit liaison, and I don't mean it that way at all. So, please, the two of you come on over. Or just you. Either way. I'd just like to get together and catch up."*

Her message in return had been purposefully cryptic and teasing, and she already felt bad about that. Clark Maxwell was far too nice a guy to mislead, and she was still Mrs. Trent Jones, and this was *not* a date they were arranging.

Karen forced her mind to other matters as she opened her bag in the bathroom and worked over her makeup and hair and perfume before laying out a dress, then hanging it up, then pulling it out again in aggravated confusion. She'd been in jeans all day.

What was wrong with jeans?

Pulling the dress off the hanger again, she slid out of her jeans and blouse and wiggled into it, worrying that just about anything she wore would send a wrong message one way or another.

*Hi! I like you, Clark, and want you to know I'm a girl, so I took off my jumpsuit and wore a dress and heels, even though the last woman to be seen in that bar looking like this was Jerry Stein's flashy wife.*

*I do look good in the dress though,* she thought. She'd splurged at Nordstrom's several months back and had hauled around the carefully packed little black cocktail dress for months with no place to wear it. It was required. The requisite LBD—little black dress. All young women should have one at the ready, carefully packed and checked, the way she carried her parachutes, instantly available for use.

She was pleased at the way it emphasized the curves that none of her squad would ever see under the bulk of her jumpsuit.

Of course, Trent had taken one look the day she'd bought it and snorted, making crude comments he thought were hilarious about the missing accessory—a coin-changer belt—and asking whether she'd reserved her street corner yet.

She'd tried to swat him, but he'd moved too fast, and what once would have elicited laughter and a rapid adjournment to the bedroom had ended in pique and rejection on both sides.

Karen did another turn in front of the mirror, simultaneously pleased and fully alarmed at the overt statement the dress was making.

*This is too much. He already knows I'm a girl.*

"Dammit!" she said out loud, even less sure what to do than before. She checked her watch again. A quarter till seven.

*Okay, okay. A fresh blouse and jeans. That's safe.*

She carefully repacked her dress and slipped into a fresh pair of jeans, smiling at the memory of how she must have looked four years ago when she and Clark Maxwell had met for the first time.

Her squad had jumped on a remote fire in southern Oregon that September and had spent two tough days cutting line to contain it when one of the more experienced jumpers tried to break the fall of a newly cut tree with his head. The concussion was serious, but whether it was life-threatening was unclear. The incident commander had radioed for a helicopter, and a Bell 212, the civilian version of the famed Huey, had shown up in the late afternoon with enough room for all but one of them to catch a free ride out and avoid an eight-mile hike. It had been no sacrifice for Karen to volunteer to stay behind to finish the cold-trailing of a small remaining area—a process of feeling for hot spots with her bare hand and using a small bladder bag of water called a Fedco to douse them. She was, after all, an accomplished outdoorsman, and the pilot had promised to return in the morning to pick her up.

She had already pitched her tent and happily settled down to wait for sunset, anticipating a luxurious evening of solitude by the campfire cloaked in the delicious privacy of the forest, when the distinctive sound of an approaching 212 had overwhelmed the mountain ridge once again.

The big helicopter settled in for the second time with the same pilot at the controls, and she watched while he secured his cockpit and climbed out, introducing himself as Clark Maxwell and explaining that his intent had been to fly her out before sundown.

"I'm afraid it's too late, though," he'd said. "I guess I misjudged the time."

He was a trim, good-looking man, just over six feet in height and in his late thirties, with established laugh lines on his face and deep green eyes that seemed to be taking particular note of her. She'd been more than a little suspicious of his motives and very aware of the remote surroundings. It was always possible, she figured, that he was a "player" zeroing in on an eligible female with the practiced self-confidence of a cougar stalking a rabbit. But Clark Maxwell proved to be a perfect gentleman and a welcome companion who'd even thought to bring dinner.

"Wait a minute," she'd said. "Dinner? I thought you came back to fly me out before sundown."

"Ah, well . . . the food was kind of a contingency," he'd explained with a shrug. "In case it got too dark."

"Uh-huh."

"Well, I was a Boy Scout. You know, 'Be Prepared'?"

"Right."

He'd picked up the food, he told her, by landing the 212 in a mall parking lot in Medford. "I confused a local cop. He was going to write me a ticket, but he couldn't figure out which law I'd broken."

The two of them feasted on an amazing dinner of beef bourguignon. He'd even brought wine. Nothing distinguished, to hear him tell it, just a naive little white Zinfandel in a Styrofoam "ice bucket." He'd brought paper cups to use as glasses, and a thermos of Starbucks house blend.

"It was next to the restaurant" was the explanation. "Starbucks."

They'd polished off the food and the wine and lain back on the mountainside nursing the coffee and talking until three in the morning. The night air was balmy in a gentle breeze as they lay under a canopy of stars with the Milky Way so incredibly bright and crystalline and startling that it had literally made her cry. Meteors and satellites marched across the starscape as the lime-green aurora borealis danced on the north horizon and purple flashes marked the passage of distant thunderstorms. The accompanying songs of the night owls and the distant cry of a persistent wolf had rounded out the symphony of ponderosa pine needles in the wind, singing their praises of the successful battle that had saved them from the flames.

Jupiter and Saturn sparkled overhead, Orion and Cassiopeia and the Big Dipper undulated with the sparkle of a million distant suns, and the planet turned beneath them as if set on its course specifically for the two of them—right then, right there.

She could still remember the subjects they'd discussed, the perfume of cedar wood smoke in their hair. From childhood toys to quantum physics, puberty to philosophy, and, most of all, the aching joy of being alive in such a place. They had found a kinship of wonder that was unlike anything she'd ever experienced with anyone, male or female, friend or lover.

He hadn't as much as touched her hand that night, and she smiled at the thought of kidding him someday that the reason had been the nightmarish image she must have cut in the starlight with her smudged face and dirty jumpsuit and hard hat–pressed hair. But it had been one of the most moving moments of her young life, and when they'd lifted off with all the chain saws, Pulaskis, and parachutes the next morning, there was a powerful, unspoken bond between them—as if they were the only two humans on the planet who knew what they knew about the cosmos and life.

She had never told Trent about that magical experience with Clark Maxwell, since he would have responded only with anger fueled by jealousy. Trent had already grown maliciously fond of maligning the other members of her smokejumping squad, and what that lone pilot-philosopher and she had shared that evening was far too beautiful to be sullied by the likes of Trent's discontent with life.

*Whoa! Gotta get going!* It was five past seven, and she'd been lost in her memories.

She opened the door, then closed it quickly to recheck her appearance in the mirror; then she rushed into the hallway and pulled the door closed behind her. Surely Clark wasn't going to turn and leave if she was stylishly late by ten minutes, she told herself. But nonetheless, being *too* late was also a statement, and one she did not want to make.

IN FLIGHT, EAST OF JACKSON HOLE

Sam Littlefox, the pilot known as Lead Four-Two, pulled his Beech Baron back up to a safe altitude some fifteen hundred feet above the ridgeline and leveled off heading south. His eyes searched through the purple haze and heavy smoke-filled valley to the east for the P-3 Orion retardant tanker just finishing its last drop.

"Tanker Seventeen is clear and climbing," the pilot of the four-engine Orion reported, still unseen.

"Roger, Seventeen," Sam replied. "I just got your marks from the judges. Eight-one, eight-three, eight-five, and a six-two from the East German judge."

The Orion pilot keyed his transmitter, chuckling. "Must've been the dismount," he said. "I think you've been up here too long today, Sammy."

"You got that right."

There were two clicks of the other microphone, a universal signal of acknowledgment, eliminating the necessity for words as the tanker pilots climbed and headed back to West Yellowstone for the night.

But Lead Four-Two had one more mission to accomplish before he, too, could head for West Yellowstone. The dispatch center in Bozeman, Montana, needed more than satellite data—they needed a short detection flight.

"Sorry, Sam, but our only call-when-needed detection ship is timed out," Dispatch had told him by radio. "You're all we've got for eyes."

"No problem," Sam replied, the ever-ready load-me-up response that had become his trademark—and a fatigue-inducing bad habit.

There was no so-called air attack platform—usually a larger aircraft orbiting at ten thousand feet and coordinating the battle on the growing fire. Supposedly, one would be in place by midday tomorrow, but the entire confusing, whirling mass of tankers and helicopters and the strategy to deploy them had been the responsibility of the lead-plane pilots all day long, and he was exhausted.

The thirty-six-year-old Native American banked the Model 58P Forest Service–owned Beech Baron back to a northeasterly heading, his eyes tracking the flames that an hour ago had jumped the lines along the middle of the Y-shaped cirque and crossed to the northeastern side, crowning at times and throwing firebrands downrange to light new spot fires. The ground crews had fallen back three times in one day, and were now moving like a routed army toward the same pass the tankers had used as an escape route all afternoon. Much hard work had been too easily overrun by the fire, and it was a major defeat, plain and simple.

*The valley's toast,* Sam thought to himself as he passed over the middle of the expanse and lurched through the superheated updrafts rising from the blaze on the eastern flank. The plan had been to contain the main fire in the cirque while attacking the spot fires that had broken out to the north and northeast, but the south wind had been relentless, and the broad expanse of partially forested valley beyond was already aflame. The fast-moving fire threatened to combine by the next day with a growing blaze in the high terrain six miles north. From there, mature forests that had gone untouched by fire for over three hundred years stood ready to explode, and if the wind shifted even slightly to the west, all of Grand Teton National Park was going to be in the crosshairs—not to mention the unburned portions of Yellowstone. Even the burned areas now full of dry, light fuels—the so-called "pioneer species" that had started growing rapidly to replace the heavy timber destroyed in 1988—were primed and ready to ignite.

He put the Baron in a gentle right bank, his eyes falling on the folder he'd left on the empty right seat and the piece of paper that had worked its way out. It was a pen-and-ink rendering of a mythical dragon, fire and fury snorting from its nostrils as its claws raked the air, the personification of forest fire he'd drawn for his five-year-old daughter, Kelly. Somewhere between the technically correct and scientifically sound details and the shorthand version normally fed to kids, his tribe's heritage of storytelling had shamed him into creativity. He'd given the beast name and form in a continuous story that Kelly seemed to love. The scientific details were there, too, and it had amazed him how fast she'd absorbed it all. There were insights there, he knew, about communicating with the open mind of a child, or with anyone, using pictures. But as a father, he was simply enjoying the profound connection. His lead plane was the dragon slayer, he the knight, and the beast was a respected part of the land. But sometimes, he'd told her, the beast had to be disciplined about taking more than its share.

Sam chuckled at his long-standing worry that a true elder of his tribe might sue for telling such wild variations from traditional versions. One day he'd have to research how the Oglala Sioux really explained forest fires. He had always been too distant from his heritage.

There was a muscle group in his shoulder that seemed to kink up and start hurting late in any flight, and he felt it now as it threatened to expand into a headache. Sam reached into one of the many pockets of the fishing vest he always wore in flight and closed his fingers around a small bottle of aspirin, working the cap open to pop two in his mouth. He fished a small bottle of water out of another pocket and drained nearly half of it, chuckling at the explanation he usually gave the uninitiated for why he wore the many-pocketed garment.

"That's why they call it a fishing vest. When you're always fishing for small items, it's the best solution."

He descended the Baron for a closer look at the new flame front marching across the second valley northeast of the cirque, riding through the violent turbulence to fly behind a small ridge. Vast areas of charred and smoking timber already marked its path, and he wondered if the fire would, in the language of forest fire fighting, "lay down" overnight, as most of them did, or whether it would keep on roaring.

The ultimate arbiter would be the wind. If the fire didn't lay down, they would be helpless to intervene until morning. The technology was far too expensive to outfit airtankers for safely picking their way through smoke-shrouded mountains in darkness.

He glanced back to the west, struck by the magnificent multihued, ruddy colors of the horizon as the sun dipped behind the Tetons, its rays diffused by the smoke.

The firefighters would attack again in the morning with a squadron of airtankers and helicopters carrying water buckets, as well as with several huge Skycrane helicopters capable of carrying up to two thousand gallons of water with each refill at a nearby lake. The air attack would be assisting the growing force on the ground. There would be smokejumpers and heli-rapellers as well, or so he hoped. They were sorely needed to reach the fourteen smaller fires now growing to the north where the mountains became all but inaccessible by road.

The engine of every one of the blazes was still the stationary low pressure gradient in upper Montana, which was sucking the wind and the flames northward and infusing the tinder box of brittle forests with the oxygen the fires needed to crown, join, and explode.

And if that happened . . .

He banked left, mentally calculating the route back to West Yellowstone as he punched an interphone button and pulled a small cell phone from its cradle. He mated a small connector to his headset cord before punching in the correct phone number for the Dispatch Center in Bozeman and pressing "send," his mind already turning over what phraseology would appropriately convey how bad it was. They needed bombers and jumpers and choppers and time, and they had far too little of any.

Keeping the fires from joining, he thought, was going to be the rough equivalent of a miracle.

# Chapter 9

Trent Jones could feel his pulse pounding in his ears.

It was happening a lot lately, and he was afraid of what it might mean to his FAA medical qualification and his continued ability to pilot the machines he patched together as a mechanic.

The hangar was quiet, other than an occasional metallic clank from all the activity around the damaged DC-6B, but the whooshing in his ears seemed loud enough for everyone else to hear. He thought about his upcoming flight physical, and whether he should risk mentioning the phenomenon to his doctor.

"It's stress, Trent," Karen had told him the year before in her absolutely-sure-of-herself mode. "You haven't figured that out yet?"

"Well, duh!" he'd fired back, irritated that she had to find an explanation or a solution for everything—and aware how screwy that complaint would sound if he voiced it. Men were always getting accused of trying to solve problems when a female just wanted sympathy, but the truth was, women like Karen could be just as irritating.

Of course, it wasn't sympathy he'd been looking for, just a receptive ear, and his solution had been to stop talking with her about work or anything related to Jerry Stein's business—especially during the fire season.

Trent glanced around in irritation, feeling exasperated that he couldn't get a complete sentence out between Jerry's incoming phone calls.

Stein was still pacing around in a far corner of the hangar, holding his tiny cell phone like a weapon and using a headset to chew royally on the caller with a liberal dose of profanity, his free hand gesturing for emphasis.

The cup of coffee Trent had retrieved like a glorified gopher for Jerry sat untouched on a workstand next to one of the mechanic's battered FM radios, which had just been turned on. It was adding to his irritation by blaring hip-hop garbage into the night.

Trent cautioned himself to keep his temper in check.

Like all the other calls over the past half hour, Jerry had answered this one instantly, cutting his maintenance director off in midsentence with an upheld index finger, as if he were merely hitting a "pause" button.

Trent glanced over at his team of mechanics working on the twisted and torn engine mount for the right outboard engine nacelle. They were looking grim. He tried to recall exactly where he'd been in his explanation to Jerry. There was an intricate nature to the battles they faced in repairing and reflying Tanker 84, and he needed at least a little of the owner's attention to explain it.

Jerry had apparently finished his call and was walking briskly back toward the DC-6B. "Sorry, Trent. Go ahead."

"I was saying, I think, that getting an engine mount located and shipped here is going to be impossible inside a week, and that's if we're lucky."

"Bullshit. This airplane's going to be flying tomorrow."

"How, Jerry?"

"Hell if I know. You're the maintenance director. Direct some maintenance. Make one if you need one. The frickin' feds aren't around at midnight."

Trent sighed again and rubbed his eyes before looking up. "Jerry, for God's sake, we've been having a version of this conversation for years now. You tell me, 'Fifteen minutes or die,' and I tell you it will take at least a day, and you . . . you *order* me to work a miracle, and I try my heart out, and it ends up taking a full day just like I said it would. In other words, all your pressure can't change the realities I have to work with, except to kill me with ulcers or a coronary."

"You have an ulcer, Trent?" Jerry chuckled.

"Not yet."

"Well, until you have your ulcer issued, I expect you to find a way to get this bird flying by tomorrow without cannibalizing another DC-6. We get paid, if you recall, by the hours we fly, not by the hours we sit on the ramp with broken airplanes. No flight hours, no contract, no job. Got that?"

Trent raised his hands in frustration. "I know you'll go ballistic at this, but Jerry, the truth is, I only live in *this* dimension of reality, and the answer in this reality is that I can't do it by tomorrow."

Jerry Stein simply nodded and looked down for a few moments as if checking his shoes for something disgusting. With equal unpredictability, he snapped his eyes back to Trent as he pointed to Tanker 84, his voice surprisingly controlled.

"Follow me," he said, moving toward the ladder leading to the cabin of the DC-6B. Trent trailed after him, noting how battered and ancient the old Douglas looked in the harsh glare of the hangar lights. On an anthropomorphic level he felt a growing kinship. He was feeling equally old and battered.

Jerry fairly bounded up the rickety metal stairs with Trent in trail and turned into the empty cabin. Now, more than a half century after its manufacture in Long Beach, California, the cabin reeked of the ammonia-based chemical essence of retardant instead of rich fabrics and fresh coffee. In the early fifties, eighty to ninety well-dressed passengers routinely had been seated in here, Trent thought, most of them puffing on their complimentary cigarettes as stewardesses in military-drab uniforms bustled around with pillows and drinks and chewing gum to relieve ear pressure.

There were probably ghosts in here, Trent decided—a thought that had softly tapped him on the shoulder more than a few late evenings when he'd entered one of the old Douglas airplanes and felt anything but alone. Thousands of fascinating human stories had to have shared briefly the space he was standing in.

Jerry had reached the rear of the cabin and was turning, his arms crossed beneath a pugnacious expression. For just a moment, Trent wondered if he was about to end up in a fistfight with his boss, but Jerry motioned him to sit on a plastic crate, his face deadly serious.

"I don't want anyone overhearing this. You heard what I said in Operations a while ago, right?"

"Of course."

"Paraphrase it."

"What?"

"Tell me what I said, because I'm not sure you got it, cowboy." Sharpness, almost anger, was creeping into his voice.

"Well, Jerry, you essentially said that there's a growing movement in Washington, D.C., to give our mission to the military, or have the government buy a new set of tankers that we'd fly and maintain on contract."

"Right. And what have I been racing around trying to get our senators to do?"

"I'm not following you?"

"Christ, Trent! Think. Why'd I send you to Arizona last year?"

"You mean, the trip to Davis-Monthan's boneyard?"

"Of course."

"Oh. Well, sure, we want to buy a bunch of the older airplanes they've got retired, like C-130s and maybe C-141s, and—"

"And for surplus prices! Especially since we'd have to refurbish them."

"Yeah. Okay."

Jerry threw his hands up in a gesture of extreme frustration, and Trent reacted with a hurt expression.

"What?"

"Trent, I swear, sometimes you're denser than a fence post."

"Thanks a hell of a lot."

"Look, man. You need to understand what we're dealing with here. The DC-6s and DC-7s are probably going to be grounded for the rest of the season now, and the helicopter fleet, most of which we don't own, accounts for over ninety percent of the fire-fighting capability nationwide, and while the Forest Service and the Bureau of Land Management like us a lot, they can put out their fires without us, and we don't want them figuring that out. If Uncle decides to use *their* Air Force C-130s with the portable tanks, they wouldn't need us at all. You getting this?"

Trent nodded, his face crimson.

Jerry Stein turned and paced a few steps toward the front before turning back.

"My political friends think they're doing me and the other owners a big favor pushing the bill that would have the government buy a fleet of tankers that *we'd* fly, like you said, but you know what? We can't make any money flying government airplanes. Even if it's the other idea which I had to say publicly sounded fine . . . where they give us low-interest loans to buy new planes and convert them . . . we still lose all the serious money. The margins would be paper thin, and it just won't be worth it. I, for one, would close down and sell everything."

Trent was struggling to control his temper and barely succeeding. Jerry's condescension was pushing him to the limits.

"Jerry, we wouldn't have all these maintenance headaches if we had newer airplanes—"

"Trent, dammit . . ." Stein's voice was rising, his gestures becoming more manic as he warmed to the rant. "I don't give a rat's ass about the maintenance expense for these old pelicans."

"What? Jerry, you ride me constantly about every damn penny!"

"Yeah, but those expenses are a drop in the bucket compared to what we can make each season with airplanes that were paid for decades ago. We get to sign these amazingly lucrative contracts that lease our airplanes to Uncle Sugar as if our airplanes themselves were worth millions, and costing us maybe fifty grand a month per bird. Instead, they're paid for and cost us nothing but maintenance. But, Trent, if we're forced to *really* buy new stuff and pay fifty thousand per month per airplane in principal and interest, we'd make peanuts and the game would be over. What about flying a federally owned fleet? Then we'd get even fewer peanuts, because we'd be just renting out pilots. And, of course, if the military takes over completely? We get shit. You got it now? They change the game, the game is over."

"Yeah."

"The only way I continue to make serious money to pay your inflated salary and bonuses and keep cute little Karen happy is if we keep doing things the way we do things now. Even then, we've got maybe a year, tops, before Congress screws us."

"A year, you think?"

Stein nodded fiercely. "In the meantime, if you hadn't noticed, there's a forest burning, a contract to fulfill, and a huge tub of money to be made. But if I can't deliver the goods to the Forest Service . . . if I can't provide the contracted-for airplanes because my maintenance chief wants to let a DC-6 sit in the hangar for a week rather than fixing and flying the damned airplane . . . the contract doesn't work and our golden goose gets barbecued."

"Look, Jerry—"

"You know what our margins are?" Jerry Stein leaned down, shaking his masticated, unlit cigar at Trent's nose.

"No."

"Absolute minimum, worst season? Eight percent. Best year? Forty percent profit. *Forty percent,* Trent, of millions. But I have to fly to get it. No dash, no cash."

Trent tried not to let his jaw drop in shock. Jerry was always bitching about being on the ragged edge of bankruptcy when he'd been making millions per season? *And you fly around in a ratty Lear 23,* Trent thought to himself, recalling equally disturbing yell-fests over the maintenance expenses Jerry Stein had just dismissed as trivial.

"You know *why* I make that much?" Jerry continued. "Because, as I said, these airplanes are already bought and paid for! As long as I can use these planes, we're a money machine. Of course, now I'm down by one whole DC-6, which the insurance company will almost pay for, and we've got two dead pilots whose families will try to sue and raise our insurance premiums some more, and we're going to have the damned NTSB and FAA crawling all over our frames for weeks trying to figure out why the wing came off."

"I know."

"So why did it?"

Trent looked up, startled at the sudden ambush. "Ah . . . sorry?"

"The wing. The long thing on the right side of Tanker 86 that should still be bolted on? Why isn't it?"

"I . . ." Trent snorted, both hands out, palms up. "Jerry, I haven't got a clue. That bird was given a very thorough, very expensive, and very monitored inspection last fall by Sandia Labs at the direction of the Forest Service, as you well know. They did eddy current, they pulled the wing bolts and X-rayed them. Everything."

"So why did it crash and kill Jeff and . . . and . . . oh yeah, Mike Head? You best be ready to answer that, because they're sure as hell going to be asking."

"I know."

"I need planes in the air, including this one, by tomorrow. Otherwise, man, we're on a slippery slope to oblivion."

Trent took a deep breath and stood up, his hands on his hips. "Jerry, I'll do my best."

"Good."

"But . . . given some of the things I've made happen for you over the past few years, maybe two other changes would be helpful now that I know you're not starving."

"Yeah?" Jerry replied, cocking his head in suspicious anticipation and already regretting his financial revelations.

"Yeah. For one thing, maybe you should be a bit less abusive when you talk to me. Okay? I'm not your lackey. And, second, maybe I should get a few more tiny percentage points of that eight-to-forty-percent gold mine I didn't know you'd been raking in. After all, if I'm not your most loyal, hardworking employee, I'm the most important."

"Or what?" Jerry asked with a carefully controlled sneer. "What would you do if I said no? Run to the FAA?"

Trent shook his head. "There is no 'or,' Jerry. I'm not threatening you, although . . . it probably isn't the wisest of moves to completely piss off someone who knows where at least some of the bodies are buried."

They stood and stared at each other for a few very long seconds before Jerry broke into a laugh and slapped him on the shoulder.

"Good bargaining, Trent. But . . . I really will see what I can do. You hang in there, meanwhile, and keep us flying."

"Yeah."

Jerry's smile was broadening. "Hey, cheer up. I only yell at you 'cause I love ya, right?"

"Sure," Trent said, keeping his anger in check and forcing a strained smile. "But I bet you say that to all the mechanics."

Jerry smiled at the I'm-not-mad-at-you humor and waved as he bounded down the stairs and out of the hangar.

When he had gone, Trent climbed down from the airplane feeling distracted and suddenly disquieted by something Jerry had said.

What was it, and why was it disturbing him?

He stood at the base of the steps trying to remember, the memory returning after a few seconds.

*Oh, yeah,* Trent recalled. Jerry had referred to his wife as "cute little Karen," and somehow that seemed like a red flag.

Or perhaps his reaction was nothing more than the pain of knowing what he was about to lose.

# Chapter 10

Less than a mile away from the West Yellowstone Airport, Judy Deason returned from the ladies room at the Grizzly Lounge to find Misty Ryan gone.

She quizzed the bartender and one of the waitresses in the adjacent restaurant, but no one had seen Jeff Maze's longtime girlfriend leave, and a quick check of the street outside turned up only a passing truck and a bizarre-looking teenage couple with more punctured body parts and tattoos than brains, judging from the nonsensical argument they were having.

Judy went back inside and pulled out her cell phone. Bill Deason was relaxing in their motor home, which was parked in a cluster of RVs belonging to eight other pilots, a parking area located near the end of the runway adjacent to the Forest Service ramp. Bill answered his cell phone on the first ring.

"How was she, before she pulled her disappearing act?" Bill asked when Judy explained she was gone.

"Well, she cried a river all the way in from Jackson Hole, but she'd settled down to just being numb. Maybe quietly distraught. She was definitely drunk. She's been knocking back straight Scotch as an anesthetic. You know our Misty. Just like she was at our tailgate party last summer. One minute she's saying Jeff was the greatest male who ever lived; the next she's calling him names that would embarrass a drunken sailor."

She heard her gentle husband laugh. "Now, wait a minute, Mrs. Deason, ma'am. Exactly how would a demure and proper lady like *you* be aware of what it would take to embarrass a drunken sailor?"

"We have cable."

"Oh, yeah. I tend to forget."

"Seriously, Bill. I'm sure she never for a moment gave up thinking that wild man was going to marry her someday. Her world has just been zapped into oblivion."

"You want me to come look for her?"

"Yes! That's what husbands are for."

"Okay, but first go down the street and check the Coachman Lounge. They used to hang out there together and terrorize the bartender."

The Coachman Lounge was just a few blocks away, and Judy pushed through the door just in time to see Misty onstage, trying to turn on the microphone, her body wobbling gently from the effects of the liquor and the pain. Her cascading mane of red hair seemed to be electrified and almost standing on end, her eyes glazed as she found the switch suddenly and overboosted the speakers, causing the customers to jump.

"HOW DO . . . I GET THIS DAMN THING . . . oh, *shit* . . . izz on. Sorr-r-r-ry."

Judy made a beeline for Misty, motioning her to be quiet and sit down.

"NO!" she boomed into the mike, pointing a weaving finger at Judy as she tried to hang on to her highball glass, which was sloshing house rum in all directions as she teetered. She looked around at the other people in the bar, most of whom were well aware of who she was and what she'd lost.

"THISSS . . ." she overboosted again, then repeated the drawn-out word more quietly as she pointed the glass at Judy.

"Thisss . . . wunnerful woman right here is Chewdy . . . *Judy* . . . decent. Izza different word, see, *Deason*, which izzer name . . . BUT . . . she's the most de*CENT* girl I know. AND . . . didja know that she has a husband? Yeah! How 'bout that? An' he's still alive."

"Misty, *please*, come with me."

Misty ignored Judy.

"I never had a hussand . . . hus*band*." She shook her head and looked around. "No-o-o-o sirree, Robert! Didn't. Jeff was *supposed* to be my husband, and he . . . he sure felt like my husband in bed . . . but didja know that 'cause his airplane went south for the winter and did stuff . . . he couldn't keep it glued together today and so . . . he's all gone! Still dead. Bur-r-r-ned up beyond recognition. You might say heezza *crispy critter*, see? Can't sleep with a crispy critter." She tried to laugh through a cascade of tears. "Well, a girl can *try* t'sleep with a crispy . . . critter . . . but charcoal'll get all over the sheets, see—"

"Misty, please!" Judy tried again to dislodge her from the microphone.

"NO, JUDY!" she boomed, wagging her finger, trying to look fierce. "NO! Stan' back and no one will get hurt . . . except . . . except for Misty, course. *I'M* gonna hurt. I AM hurt." She grimaced, the tears flowing steadily. "I'm frapping DESTROYED, an . . . all our friends here need to know . . . that . . . that fucking Jerry Stein killed my husband before he could be my husband, y'know? He's , . . an AC . . . uh, a CA . . . no. Stein plays . . . with the frapping CIA . . . agency, thing. I'm not supposed to tell, y'see, 'cause Jerry said I couldn't. No . . . *Jeff* said I couldn't." Her voice climbed an octave, becoming a squeak as her face screwed up into a mask of pain. "An' now he's dead. . . . *Y'know?*"

Clark Maxwell appeared at Judy's elbow and together they half carried, half guided Misty away from the microphone and out to the lobby, where they gently lowered her onto a couch. She didn't resist. The dam had broken again, and her soft sobs precluded any protests.

"Bill's on his way over," Judy whispered to Clark. "We'll put her to bed in our motor home tonight."

"You need any more help, call me," he said, satisfying himself that Judy had it under control. He hesitated, feeling momentarily guilty that he hadn't offered the extra room in the log house he was renting. It was far larger than the Deasons' motor home, but somehow the thought of being alone with a drunken, distraught Misty Ryan was frightening, and more than he could handle. Besides, she needed a woman with her.

Clark stood for a minute, processing what she'd said. CIA? The mere mention was chilling, especially after several government executives had been tried and convicted several years before for misusing former Air Force aircraft obtained only to fight forest fires. The entire community was convinced the CIA had been involved but had weaseled out of any public responsibility, letting someone else take the blame and go to prison. The stories—and attendant suspicions—had taken on a life of their own.

But there was Jeff's demise to consider, and the question of precisely how an otherwise carefully inspected aircraft could suddenly come apart. If the aircraft had been used clandestinely and extensively by some CIA front over the years whenever they were supposed to have been in New Mexico just sitting, the extra flight hours and possible abuse without corresponding maintenance could explain the sudden breakup. Misty's drunken reference to the CIA was worrisome, though it wasn't difficult to imagine Jeff Maze telling Misty anything he thought would get him out of an otherwise hard-to-explain situation. Considering his tomcat reputation, a bogus explanation of "I had to disappear for three months because I'm with the CIA on assignment for Jerry" could easily have come from his bag of tricks to cover nothing more than a side affair.

Clark moved back into the lounge where Karen was waiting at a table in the far corner.

"Sorry," he said.

"No, no!" Karen replied, reaching out to touch his wrist in a reassuring gesture that sent a small jolt of adrenaline through his body. "I thought that was very good of you. Frankly, the rest of us were too embarrassed for her to intervene."

"Poor girl."

"She waited a long time for old Jeff."

"Makes you kind of reconsider your own time line, y'know?" he said, looking back in the direction of the lobby. "Makes you want to reassess what's important, since it can all end so quickly."

She nodded, a faraway look in her eyes.

"Been there, done that, Clark. Got the souvenir teaspoon." She chuckled, her eyes reengaging his. "You never finished what you were telling me."

They'd been on their second beer when Misty had lurched in the door, and the interruption had been fortuitous. After they'd relaxed and both filled in the missing four years, he'd begun to get careless and had come close to telling her too much about his growing concerns, which inevitably centered on the maintenance department of Stein Aviation. Perhaps it was the instant level of trust he felt around her, or maybe the intense emotions of the day triggering an incautious need to talk. But drop-dead beautiful or not, Karen was still Trent Jones's wife, and if there was anyone pressing the limits around Jerry's operation, it had to be Jones.

"Well," Clark sighed, "what it comes down to is, no one alive knows how much our airplanes have taken in the way of overspeeds, and extra g-forces, and we don't have reliable ways to check every critical piece for metal fatigue and cracking. I mean, I know maintenance does the best they can, but all we're sure of is how many hours the airplanes have logged. We have no flight data recorders, no stress meters on the wings, nothing. And yet every low-level mission means the wing box is taking more severe flexing."

"No flight recorders? I thought they were required."

"On commercial jets, yes, but not on our ragtag fleet. We've tried. The Forest Service paid to install a few temporarily a couple of years back, and they worked too well. The readings we got scared everyone to death."

"You mean, some of you were putting too much stress on the planes and the recorders showed it?"

Clark chuckled. "Karen, the hot dogs—the really outrageous guys who'd fly into hell and flip off the devil—they refused to allow the recorders aboard their birds."

"Like Jeff?"

He nodded.

"Yeah, like Jeff. But those of us who try to stay somewhat reasonably conservative in our flying thought we'd see reasonable readings when those recorders were installed. Instead, we were coming back from every drop with digital confirmation of constant over-g's and massive overspeeds, and no way of knowing when the metal we were torturing so badly was going to break."

"Is that why you retired?"

He nodded, his eyes on a faded picture of the Tetons on the far wall. "Yeah, well . . . that was one of the—"

"Hey, Maxwell!"

Clark turned to see Joel Butler and Ralph Battaglia, two of the other DC-6 pilots, standing by the table holding their drinks and nodding to Karen, serious expressions covering their faces.

"What's going on, Joel?" Clark asked.

"Did you hear they're considering night ops out of Jackson tonight with the choppers? The Chinooks and Skycranes?"

"You're kidding!" Night operations were prohibited, except in extraordinary cases with firefighters trapped or communities threatened.

"I mean, they're only talking about it, but things are getting really grim," Joel was saying. "Some of the ground troops were being cut off on the other side of that ridge we were hitting this afternoon. And, by the way, Ops has given us all a seven A.M. show time tomorrow. Didja get the word?"

Clark shook his head in mock pain. He reached for his cell phone to check for messages, but found none waiting. "Seven A.M.? Really? I'd understood eight."

"Crack of dawn, dude. And they've got you posted for Tanker Eighty-eight."

"Joel," Clark said, looking askance. "Please don't call me dude, okay? You know I hate that."

"Which is why I do it." Joel smiled, leaning over the table toward Karen with his hand outstretched. "Since your ill-mannered boyfriend here won't introduce me, ma'am, for fear, I guess, that I'll try to hustle you away, I'd just like to make up for his manners. I'm Joel Butler, a genuine airtanker pilot who, unlike this rotorhead, doesn't go slumming around in helicopters. And this is Ralph Battaglia, also a real man and an airtanker pilot, and with that last name, I strongly suspect a mafiosa as well." He grinned back at his partner, who was rolling his eyes. Butler let her hand go and Battaglia leaned in to shake it while Clark sat back and watched in amusement.

Joel stood tall and cleared his throat with exaggerated formality. "Now that we're all introduced and know each other, and you have a choice in men, can we buy you a real drink and explain all about this business of fighting forest fires?" Butler asked.

"I'm a Missoula smokejumper," she said, watching the startled reaction.

"No! For real?" Butler asked, shaking his head and glancing at Clark, who was nodding. "Wow. I mean, you're the . . . ah . . . the best-looking smokejumper I guess I've ever met."

"Me, too," Battaglia agreed, matching his friend's somewhat evil leer.

"See," Joel continued, "most of your fellow smokejumpers aren't terribly interesting because they're kinda . . . seriously male, and—"

"Thank you, gentlemen, for the compliment and for being so polite, and for the interesting invitations. I know my husband, Trent Jones, Jerry Stein's director of maintenance, will be really flattered that you like his wife so much." She sat smiling as they looked at each other in confusion and finally made the name association.

"Oh, jeez! I'm sorry, Mrs. Jones. We just figured, you know, since you were sitting with Clark—"

"I'm kidding," she said.

They both stood in confusion for a few moments, cocking eyebrows in suspicion. "Really? Then, you're *not* Jones's wife?"

"No, I'm *not* kidding about being Trent's wife. I am. Please, guys. Sit down," Karen said, surprised when Clark popped to his feet to put a hand on Joel's shoulder.

"Ah . . . they'd love to stay, Karen, really they would, but they just can't." Clark began pushing the two backward in a modified bum's rush. "In fact, they were both just leaving. Weren't you, guys? Tell the lady how you were leaving, before her husband arrives with his shotgun."

The two pilots exchanged a look and started nodding as they backed up.

"Yeah, you know, *damn!* Look at the time. We gotta go."

"Yeah," Ralph echoed. "I forget we're due in . . . *where?*" He glanced at Joel.

"Tulsa."

"Oh, yeah. We're due in Tulsa in . . . jeez, twenty minutes."

"We'll have to hurry," Joel added, aping concern.

"Okay!" Ralph said. "Well, you two kids have a good evening."

"Absolutely," Joel agreed.

"We'll just go over here and do some . . . leaving stuff. And we saw absolutely nothing," Ralph continued. "We have no idea where you are tonight, or what you may or may not be doing to, or with, each other."

"No idea," echoed Joel. "We know nothing."

Karen was trying to stifle a laugh as the two bumbled away toward the other end of the bar while Clark sat down, puzzled by her broad smile.

"What?" he asked.

"You."

"Me? Me what?"

She was giggling audibly now. "You just gave those two characters every possible reason to think we were back here having a liaison."

"A liaison?"

"Yep."

"Are we?"

"I don't know. You tell me."

He paused. "I don't know, Karen. I don't think I've ever had one of those before. How do they work?"

"Well," she stopped giggling and leaned toward him, her eyes sparkling. "First, you . . ." her voice trailed off and he could see her eyes narrowing as she looked over his shoulder, spotting someone she didn't want to see.

"So, exactly what's going on here?" a somewhat familiar male voice asked. Clark turned to find Trent standing behind him. He stood in mild embarrassment and offered his hand, which Trent took reluctantly for a perfunctory shake.

"Trent. Good to see you. I'm glad you were able to make it."

"No one told me I was invited," Trent snapped, his eyes glaring at Karen.

"You don't check your messages, do you?" she shot back.

"I got back to the room expecting to see your things there," he said, ignoring Clark. "So where's your stuff?"

"Trent," she began evenly, her voice steady but taut. "Would you please wait over by the bar and let me finish my conversation here, and then we'll—"

"Screw that! Answer the damned question, Karen. I'm your husband. You're staying somewhere tonight, and it doesn't seem to be in my hotel room. So where's your stuff?"

"I have my own room here, Trent. I'm staying here by myself."

Once more he glanced at Clark, his eyes narrowing. "And where are you staying? Here, or . . ." he looked over at Karen.

"I'm not staying here, Trent," Clark replied carefully. "I rent a house on the south end of town, which is where I will be headed when I leave this bar."

Trent was glaring at him, and Clark paused, then continued. "Look, Trent, this has been a tough day for all of us, and I haven't seen Karen for the four years I've been away from airtankering. So there's nothing going on here but two professional friends getting reacquainted and talking shop and commiserating about losing Jeff today. Okay? So cool down. What you see in here is more or less a wake."

For the space of a few heartbeats Trent looked at Karen in silence, then turned back to Clark and without warning shoved him backward violently with both hands. Clark stumbled, almost losing his balance, and steadied himself with his hand on the wall as Trent's voice boomed through the bar.

"I know what you're up to. You get away from my damn wife, flyboy! Got that?"

Clark straightened himself to his full six-foot-one height and put an index finger in the air, his head cocked, his jaw set.

"Touch me again, Trent, and I'll deck you."

"Oh, really?"

"*Trent!*" Karen snapped, sailing around the table and getting between them. "*Cut it out. Now!*" She slapped her left hand firmly on Trent's chest, her right balled into a fist, staring him down. "You're acting like an ass!" she added.

"Get out of my way," he said, weakening, but trying to keep up the show.

"Trent! Sit down and shut up," she said, her eyes flaring. "I mean it!"

At least a half dozen of the men around the bar had slid off their barstools and quietly converged on the standoff as Mr. and Mrs. Jones stared each other down. Well aware he was awash in witnesses and potential defenders of his wife, Trent gave a sudden snort of defeat and grabbed a chair, flinging it back behind him against the wall where it clattered harmlessly on its side.

"Screw you, bitch!" he snarled.

"Not anymore, Trent," she shot back, turning away as he pushed past and stormed toward the front of the tavern.

Clark watched over his shoulder until Trent was gone. He turned, then moved carefully to where Karen was still standing and facing the wall, and placed a hand gently on her shoulder.

She turned sharply, her features softening when she saw it was Clark.

"I am so terribly sorry, Karen, to have put you in a . . . a . . ."

"Compromising position?" she laughed, as tears appeared. "You didn't. I did that to myself when I married Trent Jones."

She took a shaky step toward the table they'd occupied, searching for her purse.

"I'd better go now."

"Of course. May I walk you out?"

She nodded. "To the stairway."

With the other pilots and patrons returning to their drinks, Clark followed Karen to the hotel lobby, carefully avoiding the temptation to put his arm around her. She turned at the foot of the grand central staircase, a discreet distance between them.

"I sincerely apologize for my husband's stupid, boorish display, Clark. You didn't deserve that."

"Neither did you."

She looked at the ceiling and laughed sharply before looking back at him.

"There's a lot I haven't deserved. He's . . . he's not a bad guy. And he wasn't always like this, mad and surly and combative, I mean. Something's changed in a place he won't let me near, and it's destroyed us."

She looked outside again for a while and sighed heavily, returning her eyes to his. "The job with Stein is killing him, and I'm really suspicious why. It can't just be the normal pressures. There's something more going on."

"Maybe it's the chance that Congress will end it all."

"Could be. But that guy in there who shoved you? I don't know him. I didn't marry him."

"I'm sorry, Karen. I didn't know."

"Of course not. I guess, earlier, I felt it . . . improper to suggest to you that my marriage was over, since I didn't want you to think I was issuing some sort of invitation, you know?"

"Of course."

"But why hide it? We're history."

"Are you going to be safe tonight? I mean, he obviously doesn't know which room you're in, but—"

"Oh, I'm okay. He's not dangerous, just obnoxious. I'll be fine. I jump out of airplanes and attack forest fires, remember?"

He chuckled. "Yeah, I meant to ask you about that. Why *do* you smoke-jumpers do that? Is it kind of a lemming thing?"

She ignored the question, her eyes on his for an uncomfortable interval.

"We never really got to talk tonight, you know?"

He nodded. "I know."

"I've been wanting to tell you for a long time . . . four years ago when we met in Oregon, Clark, that night . . . that was so incredible."

"For me, too," he said.

"It was important to me. And I want us to try this again, okay?"

"Sorry?"

"Talking. Sitting down together and just talking."

"I'd love that." Clark pushed his hands in his pants pockets and examined the floor at their feet for a few seconds before looking at her. "Karen, I've got to fly a full eight hours tomorrow, but when I get back . . ."

"Call me, would you?" she asked.

"Okay."

"I mean, I may be in the woods for a few days with my squad."

"I'll find you. Just . . . try to convince Trent that—"

"Don't worry about him! Seriously. It is so over."

"Qkay."

"Tonight was the proverbial last straw."

She extended her hand, and he held it gently for a few moments before backing away with a wave and pushing through the door, forcing himself not to stare as she moved up the stairs and disappeared into the corridor.

# Chapter 11

At half past two A.M., Clark gave up trying to sleep.

There was an old-fashioned windup clock by the bed, and the ticking alone had become loud enough to rattle the windows of the sparsely furnished room. He rolled upright and sighed, feeling the bite of the cold air as the covers slithered off his unclad body. His mind was flatly refusing to relax, and it was too late to take a pill or even consider alcohol.

*This isn't supposed to happen to me,* he thought. Pilots were notorious for being able to sleep anywhere, dropping into a REM state on demand. But all he'd been able to drop into was restlessness.

There had been a fog, he decided, obscuring his thoughts all evening. A warm, feminine, enjoyable fog to be sure, but while Clark had indulged in Karen's presence, a deep part of his brain was working away in frenetic silence, and the focal point was the right wing of what had been Tanker 86. Now he found himself standing barefoot on a cold pine floor searching for his pants.

*I'm gonna be walking wounded all day,* he told himself, knowing all too well what that tenuous state of consciousness felt like. He'd flown with crushing, cumulative fatigue too many times over the years. Sometimes the memory of how exhaustion felt was enough to trump a bout of insomnia.

But not tonight.

It took almost an hour to shower, shave, dress, and stumble into the little kitchen for coffee and the proper breakfast he refused to shortchange. His favorite of three fried eggs, over easy, and half a package of crisp, smoked bacon had been derided as a "heart attack on a shingle," but his cholesterol was well within limits, and there were certain things in life he refused to give up.

Like women, he thought, though over the last four years he could have been mistaken for a practicing monk for all the feminine companionship he'd had.

The dishes rinsed and the kitchen shipshape, he was in his truck by four-thirty A.M. and parking at the field five minutes later. His black, six-year-old Chevy pickup would be all but invisible in the predawn darkness, he figured, and that was good. Best not to be too conspicuous.

Clark turned on a tiny pencil light and fished around in his flight bag for a larger flashlight and a tool kit. He left the bag on the front floorboard and pulled his parka on against the chilly mountain air, taking care to lock the doors manually and avoid triggering the loud chirp the antitheft device made when activated with the remote.

The northwestern end of West Yellowstone Airport's north-south runway was the location of Stein Aviation's facilities. Jerry's home base featured a more or less continuous asphalt ramp running from the small Operations shack past the two hangars to the south, paralleling the runway.

Jerry Stein had built a loft office for himself inside and along the back of his largest hangar, rather than put it in the Operations shack building, where he'd be too easily accessible to the pilots. Several of the Stein Fleet were on the other side of the runway on the Forest Service ramp, but two of the DC-6Bs were parked in front of the Stein hangars on the west side, and there was a long gray row of other flyable and nonflyable aerial hardware parked wingtip to wingtip on the grassy area just to the south of Hangar Two. The lines of old aircraft loomed like metallic ghosts in the gloom and the shadows, most of their bulk shaded by the hangars from the few sodium vapor lights on the north side.

Hangar One was ablaze with lights and maintenance activity, and Clark could see Tanker 84 still inside. Tanker 88, his favorite, was sitting in front of Hangar Two now, which was a good sign. Perhaps the bird was ready to return to service. Two other Douglas airplanes in various states of repair and reliability were also lined up in front of used-up ex-Navy P2V Neptunes.

Clark walked quietly toward the aircraft, crunching through the grass while considering the dark ironies.

The slurry-bombing Neptunes had been grounded six months before because their wing spars were cracking horribly and were essentially beyond repair. But the old DC-6 fleet had shown no such problems. Jerry, he'd been told, had sent every one of his DC-6Bs somewhere down south for the extensive inspection of the wing boxes, the attach points, and the wing spars—inspections required by the Forest Service. Reportedly, the entire fleet had been given a clean bill of health. Of course, there was no "thumbs up" from the FAA, since they more or less let the Forest Service make the airworthiness decisions on airtankers under contract to the government. All the pilots were disturbingly aware that the FAA's original approval was no more than a paperwork exercise. Undoubtedly, the guts of the old DC-6s had not been seen in decades by a real live FAA inspector.

Clark had tried hard not to question the quality of the inspections. After all, they'd been done under a Forest Service arrangement with Sandia Labs and there were stringent federal laws about honest record keeping for airplanes. There was also an unspoken acceptance of the opinion that Jerry Stein wouldn't be stupid enough to lie about a critical safety matter so easily verifiable as a major, federally required inspection series—especially when his business was on the line and so financially tenuous.

Clark stopped beneath the belly of the closest DC-6B and snapped on the flashlight, playing it along the aging and dented metal fairing that covered the point where wing and fuselage came together.

The tool kit he had wasn't sufficient. There were a host of partially rusted screws securing the metal cover beneath the wing, and removing them would take a substantial screwdriver and more time.

And suddenly that fact chilled him.

Clark looked more closely at the screws, trying to convince himself that they had definitely been removed during the previous year.

He couldn't. Some looked as if they hadn't been *touched* for years, let alone removed. He moved quickly to the other wing, coming to the same disturbing conclusion.

Clark leaned against one of the large main tires for a moment, almost in shock. *If these panels haven't been removed, no inspection's been done! And there's no way they would have pencil-whipped the inspection, so . . . I'm missing something.*

He moved quickly to the next DC-6B. This time the flange panel did appear to have been freshly removed and resecured on one side. Yet the other side appeared untouched.

Clark realized he hadn't come out here to find something wrong. He'd come out to fill in the blanks and find comforting confirmation that his worries were unfounded, maybe even silly. Why wasn't that happening?

*I've got to look inside those panels,* he concluded. There would be a risk of discovery by one of Trent's people and the prospect of mildly embarrassing questions, but that was a small worry at best. After all, he was one of the pilots and a licensed aircraft mechanic himself. It wasn't completely outlandish to think he'd want to be prowling around just before dawn with a tool kit and a flashlight. He was lucky they weren't locked in a hangar, since security had been considerably tightened in the wake of 9/11.

The thought of trying to explain what he was doing made him smile.

*Yeah, Jerry, when I can't sleep, I come out and inspect your airplanes. There's this recurring nightmare that I'm really an undercover FAA inspector!*

Clark looked around again, taking a deep breath of air redolent with the fumes of aviation gasoline, fire retardant, and engine oil. Even the tires of the old Douglas fleet were detectable by their aroma, and it was a comforting mix even in the frosty night air.

He took his largest screwdriver to the smallest of the flange panels, working up a sweat as he glanced over his shoulder to see if his flashlight had attracted anyone's attention.

*Really impressive security on this field!* he thought, equally aware that somewhere near the Forest Service complex there was a guard prowling around watching for anyone trying to fool with the airtanker fleet. *As far as Jerry's ramp goes, I could be out here planting bombs or loosening bolts and no one would have a clue.*

The thought crossed his mind that he should have brought gloves. He was leaving clear fingerprints every time he touched the old Doug's belly.

The last screw finally surrendered its grip with a squeal of protest, dropping past his hand as a last act of defiance to fall in the dirt. Clark wrestled the panel from its encrusted attach points and laid it on the ground. He climbed a small, rickety step ladder he'd found on one side of the DC-6B, balanced himself, and thrust his head and torso inside the cavity, working his arm and hand inside as well. He played the flashlight around the most critical structure of the airplane, where the wing and body met. The wing was fastened to the massive, beefy wing box with very large metal pins, but Clark knew that, like every other piece of advanced metal alloys in the structure of a modern aircraft, the pins as well as the flanges could deteriorate, corrode, crack, or otherwise give up their strength while no one was looking.

The interior bay looked dusty and undisturbed, as if thousands of hours of flight time had followed the last major inspection. Supposedly, eddy current boxes and X-ray devices had been shoved inside this space just a few months before. There was really no other way to carry out the inspections without opening the bay. So where was the evidence of the big inspection of the pins and the wing box?

Clark carefully lowered himself out of the bay and snapped off the flashlight. He stood there for a few minutes, sampling the darkness and the quiet, his mind accelerating the creepy feeling that he'd stumbled onto something truly sinister. Ten minutes earlier, Clark thought, the possibility of being discovered poking around in the dark was merely the stuff of mild embarrassment. Now he was sufficiently spooked to wonder if he could be in danger.

*No! Not possible!* he told himself. It made no sense that major inspections

the Forest Service had mandated could have been bypassed and the paperwork falsified. People were sent to prison for such things.

Of course, he had yet to actually see the paperwork listing the inspections. Maybe it wasn't falsified at all. Maybe it never existed.

Clark felt a cold rush spreading through his bloodstream as he considered
the possibility that the wings on the DC-6B he was supposed to have
flown—the one that killed Jeff—might not have been inspected after all.

But what about Tanker 88, he wondered, the one he loved to fly?

*I'm going to be out there pulling g's in a few hours,* he reminded himself. *This
is doing nothing to make me feel better! Have we all been lied to? How could Sandia
have been fooled?*

His mouth was very dry all of a sudden. He carefully replaced and resecured the flange panel, and returned the step ladder to its previous resting
place before moving quietly toward the hangars. Maybe the answer was in
the maintenance logs. At least the logs would show officially what inspections had been done. *At least they'll show what Jerry claims was done,* Clark
mused.

The thought was not reassuring.

There was a wooden stairway leading to Trent Jones's office on the second floor of the wooden structure built inside the maw of Hangar One. To
reach it, he would have to walk across an expanse of brightly lit hangar
floor.

There was, however, a door on the back side of the hangar, out of sight
and behind the office. Clark quietly circled the back of the structure and
tried it, relieved to find it unlocked. He slipped inside and stood in the shadows for a minute, tracking the mechanics as they labored frantically to get
Ship 84 ready to fly again. Somehow, he noticed, they'd managed to secure
a new engine mount for number four and were in the process of mating a
fresh engine to the wing.

When he was sure no one was paying attention, he moved into the light
and climbed the stairs, trying to look casual. The office door was unlocked,
and he entered quickly, keeping the lights off and watching through the
blinds for several minutes to make sure no one had noticed his entry. When
he was sure, he locked the door and moved to the file cabinets, using a small
penlight to look for what he needed.

Each aircraft had a large file section devoted to the records of its entire maintenance history. For a fifty-year-old aircraft, it translated to a
large quantity of paper, although he could see that separate, thin bound
maintenance logbooks had been established for the last few years for
each one.

The DC-6B he had just inspected on the darkened ramp was Tanker 74, and he pulled the book from the file cabinet and set it on the floor, careful not to let the light of the tiny flashlight hit the windows as he turned the pages.

The aircraft had been taken to a maintenance facility in Fort Lauderdale, he saw, a place called Southlight Aviation, a shop he'd never heard of. They had performed and logged all the required inspections, made some repairs, and signed them off. One wing pin had been replaced, another machined to get rid of corrosion, and there were even negatives of the X rays of the attach points and bolts appended to the file. The paperwork, in other words, was in order.

Clark looked closely at the flight hours at the time of inspection and checked it against the currently logged flight time.

*One hundred fifty-five flight hours since the inspection.*

The cold feeling in the pit of his stomach returned. There was no way the dirt and dust he had seen in that alcove of Tanker 74 could have accumulated in only one hundred fifty-five hours.

Clark looked around for the copy machine, but the sound of voices outside the office caused him to stuff the book back in the file cabinet and dash to the window blinds.

Two of the mechanics were arguing about something at the base of the stairs, one of them pointing up. Clark strained to listen, catching only a few words clearly. One of the men suddenly threw up his hands and turned to climb the stairs.

Clark quietly unlocked the office door and moved to the back of the loft where a small closet stood partially opened. He paused to close the file drawer and squeezed inside the closet amid brooms and boxes, securing the closet door just as the mechanic bustled through the main office door.

"Goddamned little prick!" the man muttered as he yanked open a file drawer and loudly rummaged inside for a folder he quickly located. He stood reading for a few moments.

"YES! Just what I thought!" he said, closing the folder and stuffing the file back and slamming the drawer. His exit was just as hasty, and Clark could hear a triumphant announcement to his partner downstairs that he was right and his partner was wrong.

Clark waited until their voices receded to the far side of the hangar before cautiously emerging from the broom closet to fire up the copier. He ran copies of the key pages he'd found listing the wing inspections for Tanker 74 as well as Tankers 88 and 84.

The records for Jeff's destroyed DC-6, Tanker 86, were missing.

*That's logical,* he told himself. *Jerry or someone would have already pulled them for the NTSB.*

He waited until all the mechanics in the hangar had their heads in various pits and panels before slipping out and descending the stairs, the photocopies folded and stuck inside his parka.

Back in his truck, he used the same penlight flashlight held in his teeth to illuminate the pages as he flipped through them, reading in far greater detail the same lines he'd barely spotted before.

The inspections had all been done in the fall of 2002. Clark made note of the name and license number of the mechanic who had signed off on Tanker 74, and found it was the same signature that appeared in the other logs.

*Jorge Dominguez, and a five-digit license number, meaning he's been around a long time.*

Clark glanced at the dashboard clock. It showed five-fifteen A.M., still an hour and forty-five minutes before show time. It was seven-fifteen in the morning in Fort Lauderdale. Probably too early, he thought, but worth a try. He pulled out his cell phone and punched in the number for directory assistance, waiting for an operator to find the number of the repair shop and connect him. When the process was complete, he sat listening to the number ring in Florida, fully expecting an answering machine.

"Southlight," a cautious voice answered, a Spanish-speaking accent distinctive in his pronunciation of the name.

"Good morning. Jerry . . . Stein here, with Stein Aviation up in Montana. I need to speak to Jorge, please, if he's in."

"Jorge?"

"Yes . . . one of the mechanics. He does still work there, doesn't he?"

"We have no Jorge here, I think."

"Look, are you sure?"

"I know many people named Jorge, señor . . . sir . . . but none work here."

"May I ask, are *you* an aircraft mechanic?"

"Oh, yes."

"And you have no knowledge of a Jorge Dominguez?"

"*Dominguez?* Oh! You mean *Jack* Dominguez. We call him Jack, so I have forget his real first name is Jorge. Sorry."

"Is he there?" Clark asked, feeling instant relief.

"No. Maybe by eight, I think. I can tell him you called, Mr. Stein."

"That's not necessary. I'll call back. Oh. One more thing. Mr. Dominguez did work on our DC-6B fleet inspection last fall, right?"

"Yes. We all did. That was a big job. There was another federal agency in-volved, too."

"I know . . . do you happen to recall when we picked the airplanes up from you and flew them home?"

"We were done in early October, I think, and the pilots flew all of them out the same week."

He thanked the man and punched the phone off, sitting in silence for a few moments to assess what he'd heard. So Dominguez did exist, did work for Southlight, and the mechanic he'd talked to remembered the fleet and the inspections. So far so good. But what did that prove? Maybe Southlight was a mill for falsified inspections. But that wasn't possible with Sandia Labs present. Maybe, he thought, they'd just been sloppy and missed one of the bays.

Or maybe he was misinterpreting the whole thing.

Clark sighed, knowing very well the weary sound he'd just made was the fatigue he'd be dealing with all day. His body longed to go find the nearest bed and drop out of service for a few hours.

The parking lot was still in shadow, the main illumination in his truck coming from the overhead map light as he scribbled a note to himself about the call. He finished and repocketed his pen, his eyes on the barely dis-cernible fleet of old metallic pelicans in the distance. Maybe he'd been pan-icking for nothing, and maybe not. Maybe Jeff's aircraft had sustained hidden damage unique to that airframe with a very hard landing someone didn't report, or a four-g pull up that somehow didn't break the wings off then and there, but could have started a fatal crack.

But what if the logs were falsified, and the inspections were a sham? If so, how could Jerry be behind it? Jerry Stein might be slippery, but he wasn't a criminal. Maybe Southlight had ripped him off. There were enough possi-bilities to make him dizzy.

A sharp knock on the driver's-side window caused Clark to jump practi-cally into the steering wheel. With his heart racing, he turned to see one of the veteran mechanics standing there. He fumbled with the ignition key and lowered the window as he shook his head at Andy Simmons.

"You scared the bejesus out of me, Andy."

"Sorry, Clark. I just saw you sittin' out here, and I was wondering if they'd kicked you out of the hotel or something."

He shook the man's hand and opened the door, raising the window and grabbing his flight bag in the process.

"No, remember the glorified log cabin where I threw a party about six years ago?"

"I sure do."

"I'm renting it again, so they can't kick me out. Why would you think that, anyway? I'm the last guy to get out of control around here. Well, after Bill Deason, maybe."

"Not what I hear."

They started walking toward the hangar complex together.

"So what *do* you hear, Andy? Am I getting an undeserved reputation?"

"Well, when you beat up Trent to protect his pretty wife, yeah, that would give you a reputation. A good one with us!"

Clark stopped and shook his head, his hand out in a stop gesture. "No, no, no, Andy. That's not what happened." He filled Simmons in on the minor extent of the scuffle and saw his expression droop.

"Aw, well, that's nothin' then."

"That's what I'm telling you."

"And here we were hoping he'd be in traction this morning in some far-away hospital."

"He pushing you guys that hard?"

Even in the subdued light Clark could see the look on Andy's face harden.

"There's a lot of stuff going on around here I don't like, Clark."

"Really? Anything I should know?"

"Considering you wrote that letter last year and know a lot about this system, I'd say yes."

Clark felt his head spin slightly at the surreal impact of finding yet another person who knew.

"God, is there anyone who *doesn't* know I wrote that letter?"

Andy brightened again and chuckled. "Yeah. Most of us. I just guessed, and you just confirmed it."

"Oh, shit."

"Don't worry, I won't be telling Trent or Jerry. But I want to talk to you."

"Sure. When?"

"This evening, I think. I know we're busy as hell but I need to unload on someone. I'll leave a note on your truck or something."

Clark waved and headed toward Operations but turned back suddenly.

"Andy, just a question."

He moved back toward Clark to keep his voice down. "Shoot."

"Over the winter, our sixes weren't flying any, I don't know, missions or anything, were they? I mean, I assume the only flight time they have since the inspections last year in Florida is what we've flown this summer. Right?"

Andy Simmons stared at him for several uncomfortable seconds before answering.

"Are you asking if we flew them out of *here?*"

"No . . . I know the airport isn't open in the winter, but I was wondering if, maybe, they flew out of Helena, where Jerry normally keeps them."

"So, you're just basically asking if we flew them at all during the winter?"

"Yes."

"Couldn't have, Clark. They were all down in Florida. We didn't get them back until April."

# Chapter 12

The tension in the command center had been rising since midnight when the latest weather forecast confirmed the worst: the high winds blowing from the south and whistling through the Jackson Hole, Grand Teton, and Yellowstone areas were expected to strengthen before daylight, urging the fires to even greater intensity.

Jim De Maio, the assistant director, had caught a few hours of sleep in his office downstairs and was back in the briefing room with six others as they took stock of the coming critical battle, and the assets they had with which to fight it.

"We've already lost the valley called 'the Meadows,'" Lynda Gardner briefed. "The flame front easily jumped the lines and climbed the east slope last evening and got north of Crystal Peak, and it's about to turn into the next valley, here. You can see on the infrared shot taken an hour ago . . . it's too late to stop it from jumping the ridge, so the entire valley north of Black Peak is our next stand."

"How about to the west?" De Maio asked.

"Just as bad. It's coming up to Sheep Mountain, and the winds are going to fan the flame front and push the head up the valley and into Kelly. We've got fifteen crews cutting line down that valley, and the choppers have been working out of Jackson; but it's a natural wind conduit, and I think we're going to lose a lot of structures."

"We need tankers?"

"Too late for tankers to help there."

Jim looked around the table. "Who's got the update on the new spot fires north of there?"

"I do, Jim, and it's equally grim," Alex White replied. "We had firebrands raining down through the night almost to Gros Venture Road, and since we had two helishot crews over south of Kelly, we had to rely on our ground crews to race up and down this valley all night. They've got most of the spot fires contained, but our problems are north of Gros Venture Road, as you can see here." He pointed to another white spot on the map indicating intense heat in the mountains to the north.

"We're looking at Grouse Mountain?" Jim asked.

"Southwest of there a few miles, south of Green Mountain. This is a lightning strike from two days ago we thought was contained, but the rapellers lost it last night and got chased north." He paused and looked around the table, making sure they were all paying attention before turning back to De Maio. "Jim, we're going to need everything we've got on this one today," Alex said. "This is a potential killer. If it gets north of Green Mountain, it'll go all the way to southern Yellowstone."

"These are all the same class of forest, I assume?"

"All of them. Primed, dry, ready to go. And here . . . this is a natural wind funnel as well."

Lynda Gardner had an index finger in the air, and Jim nodded at her.

"We're critical on tankers, as you know. We've got a single P-3 at West Yellowstone, and with the loss of two DC-6s, that leaves us five DC-6s, plus Stein has a few Jet Rangers and a Skycrane. Stein's only DC-7 will be staging out of Jackson Hole. But that's it. We should get three more tankers coming in from California tomorrow, provided they don't get diverted."

"Can West Yellowstone handle all that hardware?"

"No. But they'll have to. They're already bitching and moaning."

"I'll bet. How about the helos with buckets?"

"We can spare no more than two from Jackson, a Skycrane and a Chinook."

"This . . . this thing is already a half-mile wide. Is there any chance?"

"Like I told you yesterday, Jim. We've moved too late on all of it, but in this case, the hot spots got outflanked by the wind. Yes, there's still a chance, but the wind is rising as we speak. The first tankers are set to launch by seven-forty A.M., fifteen minutes from now. We'll hit it from the air until we time out the tankers."

"Someone mentioned jumpers?"

Another finger went up. "Yeah. We've got a Type One team staging at West Yellow, and we're going to have them standing by to go after any spot fires that blow up north of Green Mountain."

The meteorologist had looked increasingly uncomfortable since the subject of tankers had come up. He cleared his throat now. "Ah, you all need to understand that if wind speed exceeds forty knots sustained in here, the air tactical group supervisors will probably have to ground the fleet."

"Tankers and helos?"

"Everything."

"God help us," Jim said, half under his breath as he waved them to carry on and turned to go back to his office for a necessary call to Washington. The media had sniffed out the seriousness of the situation and used the story the previous evening. Now, in addition to the secretaries of interior and agriculture, he had to give an hourly update to Deputy Chief of Staff Jules Palmer, who was planted in a chair in the White House Situation Room, ready to relay information to the president on demand.

"Jules?" he said into the secure, dedicated line, hearing an instant response from the deputy. "Jim De Maio here. If you have the maps I sent you, pull them up and let me walk you through this."

"Bottom line, are we in trouble? Are you guys going to need the Guard's MAFFS-equipped C-130s?"

Jim hesitated, considering the effectiveness of the Modular Airborne Fire Fighting System of portable tanks, which sprayed retardant out the open back door of the aircraft. To get the MAFFS system required a political call for help and activation of the appropriate Air National Guard or Air Force Reserve units at the state or national level. Due to laws passed to protect the airtanker companies, the civilian fleet had to be tapped out and essentially unavailable before the MAFFS units could be called.

He sighed. "The 130s aren't the cavalry. They can't solve the problems single-handedly, and there's a question of effectiveness in these winds."

"You mean, the 130s with the older tanks?" Palmer asked.

"Yes. If they don't have the new AFFS version of those tanks, they're going to be less effective for us, and they're going to be grounded even sooner than our geriatric airtanker fleet."

"If the winds keep up."

"Right. Which is what our forecaster is forecasting."

"But, they *can* help, right?"

"Yes. Of course."

"And," Palmer continued, "aside from the usual policy of not asking for help too soon so as not to be a political liability, you think we're going to need them? Yes or no."

"Yes."

"Okay, Jim. We'll get that moving. I've got the map up now if you'll walk me through."

"One thing more," he said. "We may need more than the 130s, if . . . today doesn't go well."

There was a crescendo to the sudden silence on the other end of the line. "You're not considering what we did in '88, are you? Calling in the Army and National Guard troops and using the Air Force?"

"Could happen. We're at that planning level now, and I've decided we're going to fill out the request later this morning and submit it tonight if we think we're going to need it. After all, it'll take at least four days to train people and bring them in, and even then they'll be only on the safer sections of the line."

"In the final analysis, Jim, we didn't make much of a dent in '88. We still burned a third of Yellowstone, thanks mostly to our 'let it burn' philosophy."

"You're right. But we've got to try everything possible."

"In World War Two, General Patton tried to get good weather for a pivotal battle by ordering his chaplain to arrange it. We got a friendly pastor or priest around here?"

"I've already thought of that. We're looking."

FOREST SERVICE AIRTANKER OPERATIONS. WEST YELLOWSTONE
AIRPORT, MONTANA—SEVEN A.M., DAY TWO

Daylight was flooding in the windows of the Forest Service Ops by the time Clark pushed through the door.

He paused to take stock of the frenetic activity within, noting that most of the pilots had already arrived and a glut of them were now surrounding the crew desk with jokes, gestures, impromptu briefings, and yawns at the relatively early hour. The volume of background conversation in the room was already rising on a tide of radio calls between mechanics on the ramp and those pumping the fire retardant into the aircraft. A hint of cigarette smoke from someone flaunting the no-smoking rules joined the mixed aromas of fresh aftershaves and colognes and the worn leather smell of old flight jackets. The tempo of the cacophony was increasing as well, as if an unseen maestro was purposely quickening the piece with each downbeat, whipping the orchestration of the morning launch into a fever pitch of action and determination. The pace was actively boosting the adrenaline levels of all present.

In the distance somewhere on the ramp, the cough of a powerful R-2800 engine coming to life amid a cloud of blue smoke could be heard, followed by the melodious, throaty sound of the same two thousand horses smoothing out in the practiced hands of an unseen mechanic making some preflight adjustment.

Clark had moved into the room, actively calculating his desperation for caffeine, when a large hand touched his right shoulder. He turned to find Bill Deason smiling at him.

"How're you doing, Clark?"

"Hi, Bill. I'm okay," he replied. "Sleepy, confused, marginally functional, but okay. Unless the FAA is asking, in which case I'm officially bright-eyed and bushy-tailed."

"I hear you. I have to be careful how I use that phrase, though. I called Judy bushy-tailed once and she nearly slugged me." The well-weathered face crinkled into a large smile, a familiar image that most of the airtanker fraternity considered to be the face of the perfect grandfather. Bill Deason, who had for over a decade been known as Tanker Sixty-one—the tail number of his grounded PB4Y-2—now used the call sign of his newly-issued P-3, Tanker Ten. Bill was the father of four and the grandfather of seven, a pilot who'd begun attacking forest fires with large airplanes four years before Jeff Maze had left crop dusting. The Deason style of flying—in both the lumbering old four-engine PB4Y-2 tanker he loved and the newer P-3—was almost as artistic as it was effective, and if his longtime copilot, Chuck Hines, ever decided to quit, there would be a long line of applicants to take his place.

"You look a little fuzzy yourself, Bill," Clark said.

"Well, it was a short night for all of us."

"Misty keep you awake?"

"Oh, considering everything the poor girl's been through, she did pretty well. But even the biggest motor homes are a bit snug when you have a guest aboard who can't sleep."

"How's she doing?"

Bill shook his head and studied a distant window for a few seconds before meeting Clark's eyes again.

"She . . . was saying some strange things last night."

"What about?"

Deason hesitated, gauging how much to say, and Clark watched him pass an internal decision point and sigh.

"She was talking about Jeff, of course. That's what you'd expect. But it wasn't the usual rants we've all heard and loved. These were . . . things about the Caribbean, and about Jeff's airplane, and . . . frankly, Clark, I'm not sure what to make of it."

Instinctively Clark glanced around, satisfying himself no one was making a point to listen. He turned back, studying Bill Deason's genuinely worried expression.

"She said something like that last night when she was overboosting the band's microphone at the Coachman."

"Judy told me about that. But Misty said a lot of other stuff later on, when she was with us. You . . . have any idea why she'd be talking about the Caribbean? You know how Jeff hated the Caribbean."

"Not a clue. Did you ask her about it after she sobered up?"

Bill smiled. "I will, but the sobering's gonna take a while. She was still in a Jack Daniel's coma when I left this morning."

Clark had been moving slowly toward a less-crowded corner of the room with Bill following. He turned now to look the big pilot in the eye.

"When we both get back this evening? Maybe the two of us should have a quiet talk with her."

"Good," Bill replied. "I was kind of hoping you'd suggest that."

Clark cocked his head slightly.

"Why?"

"Well, I tend to look on the bright side of things and figure that Jerry's going to treat his fleet with loving care during the winter, but truthfully, we seasonal pilots don't really know where the planes have been each winter. Jerry does, I'm sure, and Jerry's always looking to turn a buck. And what's more, we know from experience that some of the operators have some pretty close ties with the CIA, and guess what Misty goes and talks about. Jerry being with the CIA, or dealing with them, or whatever she said."

"That's pretty far out, Bill."

"Is it? I don't know. But I do know that when a DC-6B comes apart in the air, that raises some really tough questions in my mind about where these old girls go in the winter and *if* they're being flown, *how* they're being flown. And then here comes Misty making some very worrisome comments about where Jeff and his airplane might have been."

"But, Bill, the flight time he'd logged seems right."

"You looked at the logs?"

"Well, in part."

"So, what's real, Clark? Can we trust what Jerry says and the times in the logbooks? Or is someone running the airplanes off the books during the winter? Did Jeff go fly one somewhere? Was someone else flying the fleet not using logbooks? I had to hold Chuck Hines back today on all the conspiracy theories."

"Your copilot's a conspiracy theorist?"

"Yeah, but he's made some good points. So, as I say, what's real?"

"I don't know."

"Well," Bill replied, keeping his voice low. "You made quite a case for being suspicious in that article you wrote last year."

Clark's eyebrows shot up in surprise before he winced.

"You, *too*? How could you possibly know I wrote that article? Did Rusty tell you?"

"No." Bill smiled, doing his own quick scan of the room for overinterested ears. "No, it just sounded like you."

Clark was shaking his head and looking down. "Am I the only one on the planet who thought I was anonymous?"

"Oh, most of the guys probably haven't figured it out yet."

"How about Jerry?"

Bill shrugged. "Well, you're working here, aren't you? However, you know Jerry. He could already be aware that you're the one who launched that missile, but he might not want *you* to know he knows until he can use it as leverage. Or, he could have completely slept through that part of the show. Either way, you were absolutely right in the points you made, and someone needed to have the guts to speak up."

"I appreciate that."

"Now," Bill continued. "Maybe Misty *was* delusional last night, and maybe on the other hand she knows something very worrisome about Jeff's activities. But you can be sure that if she knows something that might cast a shadow on Jeff's posthumous image, it'll take a crowbar to get it out of her."

A surge of voices approached, and two crews passed by engaged in animated conversation.

Clark pointed toward the ramp, asking Bill's P-3 lineup position.

"We're number three, just before you. Which would theoretically mean that you're number four on the launch schedule. I see they've got you back in your favorite flying machine, old T-Eighty-eight."

"Yep." Clark smiled. "I have her figured out. You get up enough speed and pull and the houses get smaller."

Bill shook his head. "Yeah, yeah . . . push and the houses get larger. Rusty flying with you?"

"As far as I know."

"And you two . . . haven't been briefed yet?"

"No. Just came in."

"Okay. This'll be a tough day, Clark. You'll hear in the briefing. We're going to be working north of where we were yesterday and trying to catch a blaze that's already grown large enough to scare everyone."

Clark nodded. "Everything we did yesterday failed. Every time we tried to contain it, the damned winds pushed it past our lines and over the next ridge."

"I know. Boise's ordered more tankers from California. And it's hit the national news. Peter Jennings was talking about it last night on ABC, and the other networks have picked it up, too. They're talking about what happened in Yellowstone in 1988. When things get that loud and public, I'm not optimistic, because it means the Beltway spin doctors are already trying to cover their posteriors by letting everyone know how overgrown and dangerous these forests are."

Clark spotted Rusty waving to him across the room. He glanced at Bill and arced a thumb in his copilot's direction.

"We'll hook up as soon as I get back on the ground this afternoon, Bill, okay?"

"You bet."

Clark moved quickly to the crew desk, where Rusty was waiting with an irritatingly broad grin, his maps and papers spread out on the counter.

"Okay, what's so funny?"

"Sorry?"

"This is a serious fire, Rusty, following a terrible tragedy yesterday."

"I wasn't thinking about the fire or the crash. I just couldn't wait to compliment my leader on the fine job he apparently did of beating up our director of maintenance, the man who keeps us all safe."

Clark rolled his eyes. "Where'd you hear that drivel? Jones just shoved me a bit, and I threatened to hit him if he did it again, that's all. He backed off with a few growls. I've seen bigger battles in church."

"Uh-huh. To hear those two over by the coffeepot tell it, Trent Jones came staggering out of that bar looking like he'd been dancing with a grizzly."

Clark glanced around toward the coffee bar, finally spotting the pilot Rusty had indicated. He turned back to Rusty Davis with a scowl.

"That's Butler, for crying out loud! Haven't you learned yet that Joel Butler is the biggest BS artist in here?"

"Maybe. But he said you came to the rescue of Trent's wife, who got banged up a bit. According to Captain Butler, it was a real furball for a few minutes."

"No one got banged up."

"Really? Not in the bar?"

"No. Why?"

Rusty's expression turned serious, the smile evaporating. "Ah, Clark—"

"*What?*"

"I was at the hotel a while ago, and Jones's wife . . . Karen, is it?"

"Yes?"

"She was at the front desk when I was heading for breakfast, and it sure looked like she had some bruises on her face. I was pretty taken aback until I talked to Butler."

"*What?*"

"Well . . . you know. Black eye, maybe. She was wearing dark glasses, but they weren't covering everything. From what Butler said, I thought it had happened last night in the bar."

Clark glanced around for a clock, then at his watch, which was beneath the cuff of his jacket as he struggled to free it.

"You're sure it was Karen?"

"Cute little blond smokejumper? Yeah. She had on a leather jacket with the Missoula jumpers' logo and her name. It was her."

"What time do you have?" Clark asked quickly, his voice sharp and urgent.

"Uh, seven-eleven. We have a wheels up of seven-forty."

"Run the checklists and get her started. I'll see you out there."

"What? Clark, we—"

But Clark had already raced away and pushed through the door to sprint to his truck, where he fired off the engine and raced back to the hotel. He braked to a halt in front of the entrance six minutes later and ran inside to the front desk.

"Has Karen Jones checked out?"

The desk clerk looked at him with an uncomprehending expression.

"Sorry?"

He repeated the question, glancing around the lobby while the man pecked at his computer.

"No. She's still registered."

"What room?"

The hawk-faced young man snorted. "I can't tell you that."

"Okay, then, where's the house phone? I need to call that room."

The clerk shrugged and picked up a phone behind the desk, dialing in several digits and handing the receiver to Clark, who listened as the line rang and shifted to voice mail. He turned his back to the clerk, speaking in a low voice.

"Karen . . . this is Clark. I've got to go fly in a few minutes, but my copilot saw you this morning and said it looked like you'd been beaten up, and I'm absolutely flabbergasted and very upset if it's true. Did that . . . did Trent come after you last night after we left? I'm worried about this. I'll be back on the ground to reload about nine or so. Could you please leave me a message at Operations and tell me where I can find you? I just . . . I'm just very worried. The last thing I want to do is cause you any trouble."

He handed the receiver back with a mumbled thanks and dashed back to his truck, unsuccessfully scouring the hotel parking spaces around back for her Suburban before glancing at his watch and heading back to the field, his stomach thoroughly roiled.

If Trent Jones had physically attacked his wife, he had to have either followed her upstairs to her room or enticed her downstairs—or perhaps he'd
bribed the night clerk.

*Who else could have hurt her?* he thought. The memory was all too clear of
how infuriated Jones had been to find him with Karen.

A flicker of concern that he was reacting like a protective lover flashed
across his conscious mind as he locked his truck and broke into a dead run
toward Tanker 88, which already had engines three and four running.

Rusty would brief him on the mission after takeoff, he calculated, even
though he knew he should have gone through the formal briefing and pre-
departure sequence in Operations and personally checked the weather and
the notices to airmen they called NOTAMS. But the thought of Karen's
beautiful face being bruised by a jealous husband was leading to darker
thoughts about what else he might try to do to her, blowing away both restraint and reason and even eclipsing the mission. He knew he was preoccu-
pied, but he couldn't help it. The next few hours were going to pass in
tortuous slow motion, and he would be counting every minute until he
could get back and find out exactly what had happened.

Clark realized he'd automatically climbed into his DC-6 and strapped in
by rote. He hadn't given a thought yet to actually running checklists or flying the airplane, and he could see Rusty was clearly alarmed.

"May I ask what that was all about, skipper?"

"Too complicated. I'll tell you later."

"Hookay."

The before-taxi checklist was on the copilot's lap, and he picked it up and
waved it like a fan, trying to catch Clark's attention, without success. He
cleared his throat, adjusted the microphone on his headset, and tapped the
mouthpiece.

"Hello? Anyone out there?" he said over the interphone.

At last Clark looked around at him with a blank expression.

"Sorry?"

"I said, would you like me to run the before-taxi checklist now?"

"Oh, sure. Before taxi, please."

"I'm . . . not flying this one solo, am I?" Rusty asked.

Clark chuckled in response. "No, of course not. I was just a bit preoccu-
pied there for a minute, but I'm fully back in service now."

They ran the checklist items, and Clark gave the taxi hand signal to the
ground crew and pushed up the throttles, holding the nose steering wheel
with his left hand as he tried to coax the aircraft into moving. The sound of
the big engines revving up was accompanied by the DC-6 rocking forward
slightly on the nose gear piston, but nothing more.

Puzzled, Clark pushed the throttles up even more as he cast worried glances left and right and tried to figure out what was wrong.

"What on earth . . ." Clark muttered.

"Captain?"

"Yeah?"

"May I make an observation?"

"Of course."

"Typically, the DC-6B's ability to roll forward is greatly enhanced when the parking brake is off."

Clark glanced at the parking brake and groaned. He pulled the throttles back and released the brake as he glanced at Rusty.

"Smart ass."

"Captain! I'm truly wounded!" Rusty said in mock alarm.

Clark worked the nose steering wheel as the four-engine Douglas began moving smoothly out of the blocks.

"You may be wounded," he chuckled, "but you're still a smart ass."

# Chapter 13

Sam Littlefox reached for the thermos of coffee again, this time snagging the handle with his fingertips just before it rolled off the right side
of the empty copilot's seat. He carefully opened the top and braved taking the coffee straight as he banked the aircraft to the left and continued
trying to decide how to array the inbound tankers for the first round of attacks.

Three separate spot fires topped his new target list, and the first one already had a hand crew of firefighters in place on the slope below the blaze,
which was steadily chewing its way through the forest on the north side of a
low ridge. He'd talked to the leader on the ground and flown over it twice
now to figure out the best alignment for the tankers, but the approach still
didn't feel right, and he decided to try to cut in closer to a saddle in the ridgeline and descend down the north slope.

The pall of smoke spreading from the growing conflagration of fires east
of Jackson Hole appeared majestic at first, especially in the morning when a
combination of calmer winds and an inversion layer kept the strata of
smoke below the mountaintops. But the wind was coming back up rapidly
and mixing the evidence of a disaster in progress. There were blue skies
above and the majesty of the Tetons just to the west, but the south wind was
making a bad situation worse. *It is tough to appreciate the beauty,* he thought,
*when confronted with such a beast.*

The air-to-air frequency came alive with the second inbound call as
Tanker Eighteen checked in. Sam gave the crew the coordinates and assigned holding, double-checking his kneeboard to make sure he hadn't
placed two aircraft at the same altitude. Tanker Forty-four was already in a
temporary holding pattern, and he would lead that ship in first, after deter-
mining the best flight path.

Once more he flew past the burning ridge and throttled back the Baron's
engines as he rolled into a steep left descending bank and set up an east-west
run along the north side of the ridge. The winds were howling over the top

and creating heavy chop, but his plan was to slip in just below the worst of it and bring the tankers down over the fire line about two hundred feet below the ridge.

*One hundred ten knots,* he thought to himself, checking the airspeed and dropping below the ridgeline as he bounced his way along. There were a few wisps of disturbed vapor just ahead, and he thought he could see them roiling, but he was wholly unprepared for the sudden wall of turbulence that rattled his eyeballs at the same moment it flipped the Baron almost on her back, ripping the headset from his ears.

Sam instinctively firewalled the throttles and rolled the light twin back left, pulling hard on the yoke as soon as he had more sky than mountain above him.

The horrifying sight of burning trees rushing at him, completely filling his windscreen, dominated the world for a split second before a major plume of smoke consumed the entire airplane, plunging him into zero visibility. The intense heat kicked the aircraft around as if it were blazing across potholes on a country road at ninety. He could almost make out the wildly vibrating attitude indicator on the panel ahead of him as he tried to make sure he was still upright and pulled, hoping he was going up instead of down. His jaw was clenched in determination and fear until the altimeter ever so slowly began climbing again, bringing a rush of relief.

The structure of the light twin was straining and squealing and banging around as he broke out of the smoke plume and into blue sky again, somewhat surprised to find himself nose high and slowing dangerously.

Sam jammed the yoke forward, putting the aircraft into a zero-g condition as maps, pencils, headset, and thermos floated up toward the ceiling.

*Check airspeed . . . throttles up . . . nose on the horizon . . .*

He relaxed the forward pressure, allowing gravity to return, and all the airborne debris crashed to the floorboards and the seat. He grabbed for his headset and struggled to get it back on his head as the Baron slowly returned to controlled flight, leaving him somewhere between stunned and terrified. His stomach was still flopping around, his eyes still creating vibrations of their own as his finger curled around the transmit button.

"Ah, Tankers . . . ah, Eighteen and Forty-Four, continue holding. That run didn't work."

His feet were vibrating on the rudder pedals, and he could feel his hands shaking as well, but he was pretty sure his voice was steady. He didn't want to sound anywhere near as shaken as he was.

*Jeez that was close!* he thought to himself, mindful of how disoriented he'd been and how easy it would have been to roll more toward upside down and into the mountainside.

*I would already be dead,* he thought.

"Lead Four-Two, this is Tanker Forty-four. We saw you doing aerobatics down there. You okay?"

"Yeah, just fine," Sam lied, wondering how much the other pilots had seen.

"You sure that thing can fly aerobatics?" the tanker pilot asked with a chuckle.

Sam chuckled. "Yeah, Tanker Forty-four. Just trying to keep you guys entertained."

A brief flicker of worry for the sanctity of his aircraft's structure ran through his mind, but he dismissed it. The Barons were tough airplanes, and he had to maintain an almost blind trust in their ability to take the constant beatings.

Once more he rolled in, this time completing the dry run with no problems by staying a bit higher and to one side. He pulled up again into a downwind and formed up Tanker 44 behind him for a full salvo of retardant.

A third tanker checked in on the frequency, and Sam recognized the call sign as that of the lone P-3 on the scene and its captain, Bill Deason. After assigning him a holding pattern, Sam took a deep breath. This time he'd give the ridge a slightly wider berth and bring Tanker 44 right across the targeted line of trees from a safer angle.

"Okay, Lead Four-Two is rolling in," he announced, verifying that the DC-6B was close enough on his right side to get in the correct position behind him.

Once more Sam slowed the Baron, this time giving the actual ridgeline the same respectful berth he'd used on the successful dry run. He slid over the saddle and descended.

*So far, so good,* he thought, holding the yoke steady and letting his peripheral vision track the progress of the trees whizzing by on his left.

Once again the fire's main smoke plume was approaching, and he altered course a bit to the right again to avoid it.

Where he'd found safe passage four minutes before, suddenly there was a massive, roiling horizontal hurricane of wind. It grabbed the Baron and flipped it up on one wing, this time to the left. Smoke, fire, trees, and mountain converged at once in the windscreen as he rolled the yoke full to the right and followed with rudder and full power, watching with horror as the tops of the trees ahead rushed up to grab his aircraft, succeeding only in handling the bottom of the fuselage as he firewalled the throttles and the

Baron's nose pitched up and it clawed its way back through the washboard of rising heat and smoke to deliver him once again into blue sky.

Sam grabbed for the transmit button.

"Tanker Forty-four, abort! I say again, abort! Alter course to the right and climb. It's much too rough, and there's a standing rotor there."

He turned to his right and banked in the same direction, hoping to see the DC-6B following his commands and climbing away.

Instead he could see the four-engine airliner holding its course, its flaps extended, as it aimed directly for the target line.

"Tanker Forty-four, did you copy? Knock it off! Recover northward and climb."

There was no answer, and Sam continued turning sharply back toward the east, holding his breath as he watched the red fire retardant begin to stream from the belly of the old Douglas dead onto the target line. The four-engine ship finished the drop at last and began climbing, altering course to the right slightly as it approached the plume of smoke. He could see the wings rocking as the crew fought to stay upright, but they were succeeding, and as the DC-6 disappeared into the plume, one of the crew keyed the radio.

"Well, that was special," the laconic voice of Dave Barrett—Tanker 44— said. "Not sure I've ever seen white caps in my coffee before."

"Didn't you copy my 'abort' call, Forty-four?" Sam called, aware his voice was probably too shrill.

"Yeah, but heck, we were already in the neighborhood, and it takes a lot more to roll a DC-6 than to shake up your Baron," Barrett added.

Sam knew Tanker Forty-four all too well. Dave Barrett had been around almost as long as Jeff had, and was almost as uncontrollable at times. He felt his left hand still vibrating lightly on the yoke. The thought of leading anyone else through that nightmarish horizontal tornado was horrific. It had almost killed him twice.

Barrett's voice returned to the frequency.

"Well . . . that turbulence was just about at my limits, Sam. I'd recommend not sending anyone else through there until the winds calm down. It's that eddy over the ridge that's creating the problem. It must be howling over there at forty to fifty knots."

*Thank God,* Sam thought as he hit the transmit button. "I fully concur."

He picked up the hand microphone to relay the bad news to the crew on the ground that there would be no more tanker drops. He knew there would be a brief argument, then a call for the helicopters, but they all knew it would be too late. The firefighters on the ground would have to escape to the north now and join the others on the next spot fire, letting this one go.

He quickly checked the map for the next coordinates before looking up and visually spotting another angry, growing plume of smoke four miles over the next ridge.

It was not even ten A.M. and they'd already suffered their first major defeat.

Misty Ryan emerged from the compact bathroom of the Deason's plush, forty-foot-long motor home, scratching her head and looking sheepish as Judy Deason looked up from a book she was reading.

"Judy, I am so sorry!"

"Why?" Judy asked. "What about?"

"I . . ." She looked around and gestured to the daylight. "I didn't mean to be unconscious for *hours* and . . . and tie you up."

"That's no problem. I wasn't going anywhere, and you needed the sleep. How do you feel?"

Misty rubbed her forehead and sat hard on the edge of the divan, tears reforming in her eyes.

"Surreal, you know? Like it was all a bad dream."

"Yeah."

"I mean . . . the news about Jeff."

"I understand."

"And that's aside from this horrid hangover. How much did I drink last night?"

Judy chuckled. "Well, let me put it this way. The county wasn't dry until you closed the bar last night."

"That bad?"

"What did we used to call it as teenagers? Wasted?"

"Yeah, or shit-faced."

Judy cleared her throat. "I think I like wasted better."

There was a short silence, punctuated by the rumble of another large aircraft passing by as a gust of wind rocked the forty-foot coach.

Misty's tears were flowing freely now. "I just can't believe Jeff's gone, y'know?" she sobbed.

"I know. But each season the risks feel the same to me. It's like being a military wife during wartime, spending your days praying the chaplain doesn't come driving up to your door in lieu of your husband, and trying to act like there's no danger."

"Yeah," Misty agreed. "Except I never achieved the wife part."

"You said that last night, too."

"I did?"

"On the microphone at the bar."

Misty's eyebrows went up. "Really?"

"Quite a show, actually."

"Oh, no! I don't remember anything, Judy. What else did I say?"

Judy studied her for several very long moments before answering. "One thing you said, Misty, has me very concerned."

"What?"

"Something about Jeff's airplane flying south for the winter and doing, I think you said 'stuff,' and because of whatever you were referring to, you said he couldn't keep it glued together. I don't know what that means."

True alarm had replaced the curious, embarrassed look on Misty's face, and Judy took careful note.

"I said *that*?"

"Yes. You also called Jerry Stein a very bad name, accused him of killing Jeff, and, I think, accused him of being with the CIA, and you said you weren't supposed to tell anyone about it."

Misty tried to laugh to cover her alarm, but it wasn't working, and she could see that Judy was pressing for real answers.

"I was . . . just delirious, I guess."

"Why would you think Jerry was connected with the CIA? I mean, Misty, you know Jerry. Is there a less likely candidate in North America?"

Misty laughed again, the sound even more forced and nervous than before. "I have no idea why I said that. Probably mixing up a movie with real life, you know?"

"Would you like some coffee?"

"Please!" Misty replied, relieved for anything to break the line of questioning.

Judy moved to the galley and began grinding coffee beans while Misty rubbed her head and tried to avoid her friend's eyes. When the coffee was ready, Judy poured them both a cup and came around to sit beside Misty. She handed her a couple of aspirin and started rubbing the back of her neck.

"I know you're hurting inside, Misty."

Misty nodded. "I had to live without him a lot, as you know, and he was anything but faithful to me, but . . . there was always the knowledge that he'd come blowing back into my arms like a hurricane. That big goofy smile and all."

"You always said he looked like a movie star. Like a cross between Tom Selleck and . . . who's the actor with the really suspicious, bad-boy smile?"

"I don't know."

"It was a canary-eating smile. Oh! Dennis Quaid. It was that same 'I've been up to something really bad and you'll never catch me' smile."

"Yeah, that was Jeff," Misty agreed.

"But, you know, Misty, the rest of us girls have still got lovers out there driving those old tubs around the sky. We still sit here and keep our fingers crossed that nothing's going to go wrong."

Misty was nodding.

"So, if there's something you know . . . *anything* you know . . . that would threaten our guys, I hope you'll tell us. Or me."

Misty looked trapped again as she raised her head and looked Judy in the eye.

"There's nothing, Judy. Really!"

"You're sure? Bill's always said that alcohol removes inhibitions very much like sodium pentethol, the so-called truth serum."

"No, really."

"When I mentioned what you said to Bill, he got real worried."

"Why?"

"Misty, Bill knows precisely where his airplane was all last winter. But all the rest of the fleet was out of town, and Jeff's just fell apart in the air. How about the other DC-6s? Is there some reason they shouldn't be trusted? Did something happen to them? Or was it just Jeff's airplane?"

"I was just babbling, Judy. I don't even remember saying that stuff." Misty got to her feet suddenly and swayed in place as she grabbed her head and closed her eyes. "Oh, wow. I've got to get myself together. I need to shower and then go work on funeral arrangements, you know?"

"Bill wants to talk with you when he gets back."

"Okay."

"You going to walk over to Stein Operations?"

She nodded.

"And then you'll come back here, right?"

"Sure," Misty replied, avoiding Judy's eyes as she pointed to the bathroom. "Okay to use your shower now?"

"Sure. Your towel's already in there with shampoo and everything," Judy said, watching the tall redhead move quickly down the corridor and open the bathroom door.

Judy looked outside as one of the DC-6Bs broke ground, realizing with a sick feeling in her stomach that she was half expecting it to suddenly nose over and crash. She hated the fact that Bill was flying today.

Misty knew something, but it was the fact that she was too scared to talk that was chilling.

# Chapter 14

The need to get out of the command seat was suddenly overwhelming.

"I'm going to walk around the cabin for a few minutes," Clark said to the copilot. "You want anything from the cooler?"

He watched Rusty evaluate the question against the distance and time remaining to the drop zone.

"We're still fifteen minutes to descent, right?" Clark added.

"Right," Rusty acknowledged.

"Okay. I really will be back in fifteen minutes, provided I can leave with your approval."

Rusty smiled. "Since when do you need my approval, Clark?"

"Well, while I'm gone, you get to pay for anything that gets broken."

"No problem. I'm broke anyway. And I could use a Diet Coke."

Clark nodded and threw off the seat belt, negotiating his way past the center console and back into the empty, cavernous interior of the DC-6B, wondering exactly why he'd felt such a need to get out of the cockpit.

The noise level in the cabin without his noise-canceling headset on was startling. Much of the insulation Douglas had originally stuffed in the walls when the aircraft had flown passengers had been removed over the years, as had the padded and upholstered walls themselves. Only aging insulation pads were left to line the metal skin of the aircraft, and the stench of thousands of gallons of fire retardant filled the air as if to confirm this was now a hostile environment.

He moved toward the aft end of the cabin, his mind on Karen and the possibility that her husband had assaulted her. Had the police been involved? At least she was seen walking and functional, but what on earth had happened?

*Why do I feel so damn guilty?* Clark wondered, glancing at his watch to see how many of those stated fifteen minutes he had left. *After all, she's a big girl and we were just talking.*

Deep inside he knew. Karen — or the thought of Karen — had been playing in his mind like a concerto ever since he returned to West Yellowstone, the harmonies and colors of the idea becoming a secret retreat of his mind, generating happy if random and impossible daydreams. After all, she was married.

There was a small compartment built into the sidewall toward the back end of the cabin, beneath a window. He'd paid very little attention to the details of the uninteresting cargo interior before, but now the presence of the compartment seemed to jump out at him. He knelt down and worked the two Zeus fasteners, then lifted the lid to find a jumble of cargo straps and metal pieces dumped inside.

The aircraft had a floor-restraint system for locking down cargo, consisting of heavy canvas cargo straps with large metal hooks on the ends that fit into receptacles built into the floor. There was a cargo door on the forward left of the airplane that had been installed decades after the last commercial passenger had flown aboard. He started to close the lid, but a piece of folded newsprint caught his eye. Curious, he reached in and pulled out what appeared to be the sports section of a Spanish newspaper, printed—according to the top line—in Cali, Colombia.

Clark resecured the fasteners and headed forward, absently carrying the newspaper with him.

"Ah, good. You're just in time," Rusty said.

"For what?"

"Sammy's putting us in a holding pattern. So if you want to go jog around back there or sleep awhile, we've got time now."

"And leave you up here alone to play with the switches?" Clark joked. "I don't think so." He handed Rusty the Diet Coke he had grabbed from the cooler. "You ever wonder how many people flew in this old bird, Rusty? All the human stories, the pathos, the emotional anguish as people flew away from loved ones, the drama when they were flying to someone, or something? For instance, did you ever wonder how many people were flown in this airplane in handcuffs on their way to a prison?"

Rusty was staring at him with an amused expression. "And this would be, what, your Andy Rooney impression?"

"No, I just . . . just wonder sometimes, about the rich human history of an old airliner. You know. What if she could talk? Make a great movie."

"This old tub? Tanker Eighty-eight?"

"Hey, don't call this old lady a tub."

"Sorry."

"She'd probably cuss you out for that insulting reference."

"If she could talk, Clark, she'd be begging us to stop trying to barbeque her belly with these cockamamie fires we keep buzzing."

"Not a romantic bone in your body, is there, Rusty?"

"Nope. I believe in practicality, straightforward communication, and not wasting time."

"In other words, you get slapped a lot on dates and no surprise you're still single."

"How'd you know?"

"We romantics can tell." Clark gestured to the plumes of smoke that were ahead, filling the sky to the south and southeast. "Not looking good, is it?"

The copilot shook his head without comment.

"Check in with Sam and put us in orbit, Rusty." Clark picked up the newspaper. On the front page was a photo of a soccer match somewhere in South America. Other lengthy tables of names and numbers—presumably scores—adorned various little boxes on the same page.

Rusty's voice crackled through his headset.

"Lead Four-Two, this is Tanker Eighty-eight orbiting southwest at thirteen thousand."

Clark heard Sam acknowledge between calls to the other tankers, one of whom was departing after his drop. The only other tanker ahead of them now was Bill Deason's P-3. Deason, also known as Tanker Ten, was lining up behind the lead plane for his first run at the fire.

Rusty pulled the power back to slow to 190 as Clark casually scanned the front of the old newspaper.

He ran his eyes toward the dateline.

*February 10,* he read, reexamining the last four digits to make sure he'd read them correctly. *Two thousand and three? No. What would a current newspaper from Colombia be doing aboard this* . . .

Clark felt a substantial chill spread through his bloodstream, and he fought the urge to jump to conclusions. A Colombian newspaper section could have come aboard in a thousand ways from a thousand innocent sources. Maybe it had been insulating material in some package, or perhaps some recent immigrant crawled aboard during the winter when the plane was parked down south.

Andy had said the DC-6 fleet had been gone all winter, and the inspection shop in Florida confirmed they had left their airfield in October. So where were they in the meantime, and doing what?

The sports section from Cali offered another explanation Clark was reluctant to consider.

He reached around behind the seat where the maintenance log was kept and pulled out the metal binder, ignoring Rusty's puzzled glances as he rifled through the entries from the Fort Lauderdale inspection work and repairs all the way up to last night when Tanker 88 had rolled out of the hangar. There was virtually nothing to indicate the aircraft had ever been serviced, inspected, refueled, or even landed in South America.

"Here we go, Clark."

"Sorry?"

"He just cleared us in for our first pass. Tanker Ten is on pullout."

Clark nodded and replaced the log, stuffing the newspaper at the same time into his brain bag. After all, even if Tanker 88 and all her companions had flown to Colombia, they might not have needed fuel, and there wouldn't necessarily be an entry in the log.

"Okay, I've got her."

"You okay?"

"You keep asking that, Rusty. Yes, I'm okay."

"It's just that you really look spooked."

"Yeah?"

"Yeah."

Clark adjusted his seat forward a notch and tried to smile. "Well, that's because I had a life-changing personal revelation back there."

"Really?" Rusty asked with complete sincerity.

"Yep. I discovered that I'm scared of forest fires."

WEST YELLOWSTONE AIRPORT, MONTANA

Jerry Stein called from his house and ordered the main doors of Hangar One opened so he could drive his new Hummer inside. He sailed in under the wing of a DC-6 and squealed to a halt a few feet from the stairs to his office. As planned, Trent Jones was waiting for him as he got out.

"Where is he?" Jerry asked.

"Over at Forest Service Operations right now," Trent said, tilting his head toward the last place the field investigator for the National Transportation Safety Board had been seen. "He asked that I call him when you got here."

Jerry brushed past his chief of maintenance with the key in his hand and gestured Trent inside.

In the plush leather chair behind the desk, Jerry folded his hands over his stomach. "I was going to come out and stand by to fly a mission anyway, so I didn't mind racing out here, but tell me again precisely what he said."

Trent was holding a cloth shopping bag, and Jerry nodded to it.

"What's that, by the way?"

"The logbooks—all of them—on Tanker Eighty-six. The NTSB asked for them."

"Are they copied? Every damn page?"

"Of course."

"So what does he want?"

"He said there's been a tip, or report, about the crash."

Jerry's brows almost came together, punctuating the severity of his frown. He leaned forward and shoved an expensive desk model of the DC-7C aside for an unobstructed view of Trent's face, which was dead serious and somewhat flushed.

"What the hell does that mean? What kind of tip?"

The fact that Trent Jones licked his lips while studying the wall had already alerted Jerry it was going to be bad news.

"Jerry, someone's called NTSB headquarters claiming that Jeff's airplane was brought down by sabotage."

"WHAT?"

"The caller claimed that the wing was taken off by some sophisticated method the NTSB will have trouble finding."

"Bull!"

"I'm just—"

"Yeah, okay." Jerry was on his feet. "Who's the investigator?"

"Steve Zale is his name."

"How experienced is he?"

"Not very, at least at NTSB. Three months with the board, and before that, I don't know."

"Oh, jeez! In other words we didn't kill enough people for Washington to send someone competent, right?"

"That's . . . probably not fair. He does have an A&P license."

"Has he been to the crash site?"

"Yes, he has."

"Has he inspected the wreckage and the wing attach points?"

"I think so."

"Then he's got to know the allegation is so much bullshit."

Trent was staring silently at him, and Jerry's anger began rising.

"What?" Jerry snapped.

"I'm just . . . nothing."

"What do you know that I don't?" Jerry said, coming from behind his desk.

"Well . . . you say it's BS, Jerry, but we don't have any idea what happened, do we? I mean, there wasn't supposed to be anything wrong with those wings, according to the inspections. So if they didn't miss anything when they tore into the wing box and the attach fittings and the pins and everything in Florida, why would we . . . or you . . . suddenly think that sabotage wasn't a possibility? I mean, Jeff had a lot of enemies, some of them angry husbands. And apparently they found something very suspicious in the wreckage, and they're sending parts in for chemical analysis."

"What do you mean, suspicious? What parts?"

"Jerry, let me call the man, and you can ask him rather than have me give you secondhand information."

Jerry sat down again in dark agitation and nodded, while Trent used the desk set to call the NTSB investigator's cell phone.

Within five minutes Steve Zale appeared in the maw of the open hangar headed for the office, and Jerry pointed to him.

"Trent, you haven't said anything to him about Jeff leaving a long trail of angry husbands and creditors, have you?"

"No, of course not."

"Good. Don't. This had nothing to do with the crew."

"I don't understand."

"You don't frigging well have to understand. Just keep quiet."

# Chapter 15

"We're losing it, guys," Sam Littlefox was saying on frequency as Clark stabilized the DC-6B on a high downwind again after his first of two runs over the fire.

Rusty started to respond, but Clark motioned to him and punched the transmit button.

"Four-Two, did we miss the target line back there?"

"Negative, Tanker Eighty-eight. You did great. Everyone's done great getting the target, but . . . I'm talking to the division supervisor and the fire's already crowning and moving so fast, even if we can put enough retardant on it before it reaches the shoulder of that pass, it's probably going to jump the line, just like yesterday. It's the winds that are killing us."

"Okay, Lead, we have one more set of gates available, and you've got two more tankers inbound, so let's just roll in right now and see if we can accelerate the time line."

"Eighty-eight, I'm getting worried about safety down there. You felt that wind. The downdrafts are just about out of limits."

"Let's drop one more, Lead. Come on, Sammy. Start your roll in. We're on your tiny little Beechcraft tail."

There was a hesitation, then a laugh and assent from the lead-plane pilot; Clark watched him roll into a steep left bank and prepared to do the same. Within three minutes the light twin was lining up for the last drop with the churning might of Tanker 88's four engines booming through the smoke behind him, less than a half mile in trail.

"Eighty-eight, I'm bringing you in the same as before, into the wind, which I'm computing at around forty-five now, and a hundred feet over the ridge. We need to soak that line of lodgepole pine just over the top. That's where the fire's going to jump. Can you see it?"

"Negative, Four-Two. Too much smoke," Rusty replied.

Clark raised a finger and turned to Rusty. "Tell him to give us a mark the second he comes over the ridge. I'll figure it out from there."

Rusty repeated the message on the frequency.

"Roger, Eighty-eight, standby," Lead Four-Two replied. "I'll be over the ridge and over the target coming up now on my mark, three . . . two . . . one . . . *mark!*"

Rusty glanced at Clark and saw his lips moving silently, the words "one thousand" clearly formed in front of each number. They had the flaps at twenty degrees and airspeed at 130 knots with a groundspeed of 85 knots, and he'd calculated exactly how many seconds ahead Lead Four-Two had been. Clark's thumb was once again poised over the release button on the control yoke as he watched Sam's Beech Baron suddenly become visible through the smoke, his wings wobbling left and right as the light twin's pilot fought to stay upright and begin the pullout.

Rusty's eyes shifted from trees to the Baron at the same moment Clark did the reverse, his eyes on the approaching ridgeline with less than two seconds remaining in his count. The rumble of the DC-6B's engines began to combine with the slap of the propellers biting large side gusts and the impact of the roiled wind currents on the big airplane.

"Jesus CHRIST!" Rusty yelped, yanking Clark's attention from the drop for a split second.

"What?"

"He . . . GOD! His left wing is failing!"

They slammed through the same jarring impacts of updrafts and mixed-up downdrafts as Clark caught sight of the Baron for a fleeting second, then forced his attention back to the ridgeline. He mashed the release button and held the DC-6B as steady as possible while his mind processed the image he'd just seen.

The left wing of the Baron was tilted up where it joined the outboard side of the left engine, not vertically, but at an angle the manufacturer had never contemplated.

With the last of their fire retardant streaming out of the belly, Clark looked back toward the last location of the Baron through the smoke and haze and could see nothing.

"My God . . . is he down?"

"I don't know!" Rusty said. "His left wing was folding . . . or failing . . . canted up, y'know? He's gotta be down!"

Clark rolled the DC-6B as steeply as he dared to the left, searching the burning forest below for any sign of a Baron or a fresh impact or anything that might reveal the fate of Sam Littlefox. At the same moment, an incoherent jumble of words an octave above normal range came through their headsets, followed by silence.

"What was that?" Clark asked.

"I think it was Sam."

A quarter mile ahead of the DC-6B Sam Littlefox felt the blood rushing to his head and the seat belt and shoulder straps cutting into him as he pushed harder on the yoke and goosed the throttles, somehow simultaneously aware that his airplane was now flying inverted and that he had no other choice.

The horrific groaning of the metallic structure of his left wing as it had partially failed and started bending upward had riveted his attention to a lesser degree than the sudden roll to the left as the tilting wing gave up some of its lift. The next few seconds were too bizarre to believe, but they were replaying in his head even now, as he struggled to make sense of an impossible situation, trees and smoke and ridgelines all appearing in the top of his windscreen with blue sky in the bottom as he hung upside down and pushed the inverted nose even higher to avoid the next ridgeline and get enough support from wings that were not designed to create downward lift.

He recalled rolling almost uncontrollably to the left.

And there had been the other sound, a horrendous metallic *clang* as the left wing—suddenly pushed *downward* by the relative wind of an inverted airplane—had snapped back into position.

There had been no time for anything but instinct. The Baron was inverted, the left wing was where it should be for the moment and apparently holding. Those realities flashed through Sam's mind in a microsecond, his aviating instinct dictating he stay that way.

What was getting tougher was the dyslexic feel of trying to decide how to turn left or right while upside down and disoriented. The pain from the shoulder harness and the seat belt he could ignore. But to avoid a mountain peak that was really to the left of his flight path and now in the right side of his inverted windscreen, he had to appear to bank toward it in order to turn in the opposite direction, all the while keeping forward pressure on the yoke.

A hundred questions seemed to cascade through his mind at once, as if he were mentally multitasking at warp speed. He could almost count the passage of the propeller blades, even though the engines were driving them at nearly two thousand revolutions per minute.

The fact that he was probably going to die in seconds became merely an observation. But the fact that some metallurgical fluke was permitting the left wing to stay on when upside down, but not when right side up, was some sort of bizarre celestial joke that seemed to hold out salvation when none was possible. He couldn't land successfully upside down. There would inevitably be a crash at the end of this tunnel, Sam knew. So should he prolong the flight as long as possible?

On another detached plane of thinking, it had even become intriguing, an opportunity to demonstrate his aeronautical prowess. His airmanship.

*Okay . . . the wings will produce lift upside down as long as I keep a steep enough angle and enough power. Why is that wing holding? Who cares . . . it is for now. Okay, okay . . . to turn left, bank right . . . no, roll right slightly, gently . . . keep pushing. Steady out.*

*Oh my God, the engines! Wait, wait . . . can these engines run upside down? YES! They're fuel injected! How about fuel supply? I remember something about fuel supply on these tanks that makes it okay . . .*

He banked left to adjust his course to the right again and realized the altimeter and rate of climb instruments were working fine. He checked the rate of climb, pushing even harder on the yoke.

Finally the needle began showing a small, steady climb.

There was a nine-thousand-foot range of mountains ahead of him, and his altitude was less than eight thousand. He tried to flip the memory of the topographical map of the area around and see it inverted, then decided that was even more confusing.

South. He had to turn south and find the low spot in the mountains leading to Jackson Hole.

Sam realized his finger had been pressing on the transmit button but he'd said nothing coherent. He forced the button down once again and tried to make his voice work, hearing nothing but a squeak in his headset.

*Oh . . . that's me!*

He cleared his throat and tried again.

"Ah . . . Tanker Eighty-eight, are you okay?"

The answer followed a brief hesitation, and he could hear strain and complete puzzlement in the voice in his ear.

"Sam? *Sam?* Are *you* okay? Where *are* you?"

"I'm . . . I guess roughly on the normal exit route, but . . . I'm trying to climb and turn south . . . and it's hard to figure out."

"Wait, Sam, we see you now. Good God, you're inverted."

"Yeah . . . that's . . . the wing is staying on this way, but . . . I don't think I can turn over. It was folding up . . . about ten, maybe fifteen degrees. It rolled me and then banged back into place."

"But you're stable now?"

"Yeah, I guess it's against the stops or something."

"We're pushing up the speed to join up on you, Sam. Hang in there."

There was a loud chuckle on frequency.

"Yeah, hanging in here is exactly what I'm doing. Can you kind of help guide me toward Jackson Hole?"

"Affirmative. Make gentle control movements."

"*Absolutely* I will make gentle movements. I don't know how long this wing's gonna stay on."

"You don't . . ." the voice trailed off, but Sam knew precisely what the thought had been.

"Negative, Eighty-eight . . . we don't carry chutes."

A flurry of radio transmissions followed as the two other tanker crews tried to ascertain what was happening and Rusty tried to quiet them down with a burst of information.

"Lead Four-Two has a major emergency, so everyone stand by while we escort him. His left wing is failing and he's inverted, headed for Jackson Hole. Someone get on another frequency and notify Jackson and everyone."

"Tanker Eighteen will do it, and we're gone," an instantly tensed voice said. "Good luck, Sammy."

In the cockpit of the DC-6, Clark glanced at Rusty and tapped his microphone, indicating he wanted to take over the radio.

"Sam, this is Clark Maxwell. You hear me okay?"

"Yeah, Clark. Any suggestions?"

"Well, for starters, you might want to change mechanics."

"Got that right!"

"We're about a half mile from you, Sam. You're looking good and steady, but you're going to need to change course a little bit more to the left . . . ah, which would seem to be your right."

"Give me a compass heading, Clark. Right and left are too confusing."

"Okay. You're flying about two zero zero right now. Come to a heading of one eight zero."

"Got it," Sam replied, banking the Baron very gently by rolling left and letting the course slowly come around.

"Okay, when we're almost clear of the peaks between us and Teton Village, I'll have you come the other way to a heading of about two hundred and forty degrees."

"Roger . . . and then south to the airport, right?"

"That's right."

"Clark, you have . . . any wild ideas what I can do when I get there? I mean, I was just thinking I could probably ditch this thing in Lake Jackson, but the windscreen would probably break on touchdown."

The thought of a wall of water cascading through a failed windscreen at over a hundred knots flickered through Clark's mind as it did through Sam's. It would translate to certain death. He would stand a better chance skidding along a concrete runway upside down.

Rusty's right hand was waving around in Clark's peripheral vision, and he looked over and punched the interphone.

"What?"

"There's . . . something like this happened to an aerobatics pilot a few years ago, I think in a Zlin. His wing was failing, he flipped it over and the wing relocked, just like Sam's."

"Did he survive?"

"Yeah, but that's what I'm getting to, Clark. It was the way he landed it."

Sam Littlefox's voice was on the frequency, the tension palpable.

"Any thoughts, guys? I . . . really don't have a clue what I'm gonna do with this thing. I don't even know why she's still running."

"You've obviously got some sort of a flop line or an inverted trap in your fuel tanks, Sam. With fuel injection and that feature, the engines will keep going. Stand by on the ideas."

"Clark," Rusty continued, "what the guy in the Zlin did was make the approach inverted, and when he was just about his wingspan over the concrete, he snap rolled it upright and plopped it down and rolled off in one piece."

"You're kidding!"

"No, honest."

"He can't snap roll that Baron! The roll rate's too slow."

"What other choice does he have? If he hits the concrete inverted, the tail hits first and then slams the cabin into the concrete and the windscreen's going to fail, and even if the cabin doesn't collapse on him, he's got things coming in his face at a hundred knots, like broken prop blades."

"He could duck under the instrument panel, maybe?"

"Maybe. But maybe this would work, too. The wing was bending, it didn't break."

Clark punched the transmit button and relayed the idea. "You'd have to extend your gear while inverted, Sam."

"You're serious? Roll it just above the runway and slam it on?"

"We don't know which one is a bigger risk. I know that bird doesn't roll too fast."

"I . . . I can snap roll it with rudder, but at twenty feet or so . . . if I screw it up or the wing folds too fast, I'll just roll it up sideways."

"Sam, you may need to experiment with your speed to see how slow she'll fly like that. And start changing your heading now to two hundred twenty degrees."

"Roger. Two two zero degrees. Clark?"

"Yeah, Sam."

"Ah . . . I think . . . maybe I . . . what if I slow down and test my stall speed like this?"

"You just need to feel the burble, Sam. Not a full stall. Remember your wing produces lift upward normally, so upside down you're at a much steeper deck angle to produce inverted lift, and I don't think anyone knows how slow the wing can fly that way. It won't be as slow as normal, of course."

"I'm holding one hundred and forty knots right now. Maybe when I get over the valley in a few minutes I can slow up."

"What's your normal stall speed clean, Sam?" Clark asked.

"Ah . . . clean stall is around eighty. Seventy-six to be exact."

"Okay, my best guess, Sammy, is that wing, upside down, will probably take you safely to a hundred knots. But before you go that slow, you're going to have to test it. Wherever it begins to burble the airflow over the wing, you'll need to add ten knots to that. But . . . the same winds that are blowing up the fire will actually help us over the runway. It's kicking up nearly thirty knots down the runway at Jackson."

"Yeah. Clark? If I tried that snap roll, which way do you think I should roll? Left or right? My head's swimming right now, and I can't figure it out."

Rusty's voice cut into the frequency.

"You'd roll right, Sam. That way, if the wing starts to fold on you and creates a left rolling moment, you're already rolling right."

Clark hit the interphone button. "No, man! That has the aileron putting upward pressure on the bad wing that wants to fail to the up position."

"Clark," Rusty said, "the rolling moment is more important. The aileron pressure isn't enough to be significant, and he'll also need some right rudder as he comes through ninety degrees."

"You're sure?"

"My degree was in aeronautical engineering with wind tunnels. Trust me."

"Tell him, then."

Rusty repeated the instructions on the radio.

"Okay," Sam replied, walking through the steps slowly. "Roll right and push as hard as I can with heavy right rudder, unload the back pressure as I come upright and quick flare it right over the runway with power back."

The transmitter aboard the Baron remained open as Sam gripped the switch unconsciously, not aware his personal mutterings were being broadcast.

"Yeah, right," he was saying to himself. "I'll screw this up and curt wheel down the runway in flames or collapse the landing gear and do the same thing. Jeez! What a cockamamie idea. Bob Hoover couldn't pull that off."

Sam pulled his finger off the transmit button as he discovered the mistake, and Clark jumped in immediately.

"You *can* do it, Sam, and Hoover would tell you the same thing," he added, wondering what Hoover, the dean of aerobatic flying in light twins, would really say.

"Sorry, guys . . . I'm just somewhere north of terrified up here."

"Bring your heading to two hundred forty degrees now, Sam. We'll turn you south over the valley in about another five miles."

"Clark," Rusty said, "take a look to the right. We've got company."

A giant Skycrane helicopter with a water snorkel hanging beneath was obviously flying at almost maximum airspeed to keep up as he angled in toward the DC-6B and the upside-down Baron.

"Tanker Eighty-eight, this is the Skycrane to your right, Skycrane Eight Echo Romeo. We're trying to figure out a way to get back on the ground and rig a sling. Maybe we could snag him and carry him down."

Clark and Rusty looked at each other with raised eyebrows, and Clark shrugged.

"Skycrane Eight Echo Romeo, Tanker Eighty-eight, you have a sling strong enough to carry a Baron, and big enough to capture him? How the hell?"

"Man, I don't know, we're just trying to figure out a way. We heard you talking about his slowing to a hundred knots and we thought maybe we could do it."

"Hey, Skycrane Eight Echo Romeo, Lead Four-Two . . . thanks, man, that's a great idea, but I'd take you out tryin' it, and even if I could somehow get the nose in the sling without chopping it up with my props, I'd probably slip out backward."

"No, no, Lead Four-Two. We could use two slings. Get you steady, we fly over and from behind, get the back sling around your tail and rear fuselage, then lower the forward sling and catch your nose before you shut down your engines."

"No, man," Sam replied, his voice calmer. "Nice try, and I appreciate it a lot, but there's just no way."

"Hey, Four-Two," the Skycrane pilot replied, "you were right about the cockamamie reference to the snap roll at twenty feet. You won't make it. At least this gives us a fighting chance."

"Skycrane Eight Echo Romeo," Clark interrupted, "you don't actually know that rolling it upright on short final won't work. It worked once before. The problem with your idea is you're not going to be hovering. At a hundred knots your slings would be streaming behind you, and even if you could get one around his tail section, how in hell could Sam get the forward sling around his nose without catching it in the props? Your slings, if I recall, are all hung from the same place. You'd have no control."

There was a telling hesitation from the helicopter crew and a new voice from the ground coming in on a different radio not audible to the other aircraft.

"Lead Four-Two, Jackson Helibase on AM. We've been listening to you on an aviation scanner down here, and Skycrane Eight Echo Romeo alerted us. We're looking for slings and we've got a second Skycrane on the ground. But one of our guys has another idea, and we're working it. How long can you stay airborne, Four-Two?"

Sam keyed the transmitter and hesitated before speaking. "Ah . . . I have no reason to think these engines will keep running past the next thirty seconds. I have no idea what my usable fuel is while inverted. I had about a half tank, but . . . God only knows in this condition."

"Sam, how're you doing?" Clark was asking on the air-to-air frequency, unaware of the conversation on the air-to-ground radio.

"Stand by a second, Clark. I'm . . . talking to Jackson."

"Okay, look," Helibase continued, "we're trying to get a big flatbed eighteen-wheeler. If we can make this work and get him up to a hundred on the runway, you could set down still inverted right on his flatbed. That's the idea."

"Okay . . . thanks . . . hang on." Sam switched back to the air-to-air. "Ah . . . Jackson Helibase has an idea, guys, about getting a flatbed truck to run down the runway and have me land on it inverted. What do you think?"

"This is Skycrane Eight Echo Romeo . . . that runway's only a bit more than a mile long. Can a big truck accelerate that fast?"

"Hold on," Sam replied, switching back and repeating the question to Jackson.

"We don't know, Lead Four-Two. But if you can stay up there and orbit awhile, we'll do our damndest to find out."

"Can you guys come up on a regular aviation radio?"

"We're . . . hold on . . . someone's bringing a handheld."

Suddenly the air-to-air frequency exploded in competing transmissions as several other pilots tried to jump in with ideas.

"Whoa, whoa, whoa!" Clark interjected. "Hold on, everyone! This is Tanker Eighty-eight. We're escorting Lead Four-Two along with Skycrane Eight Echo Romeo. Take it one at a time, please, and let Sam direct the traffic since it's his neck. And Sam, before you answer, we're coming out over the valley now and I see you're already turning south. Come to a heading of one seven zero degrees."

"Okay. Roger. Jackson Helibase, are you up on the air-to-air?"

A weaker version of the same voice came back. "Roger. We're on the handheld and monitoring."

"Roger," Sam replied. "Look, everyone, I . . . I need to test my stall speed first. Please keep working on ideas, but quietly, and I'll call you back in a second. I'm slowing now, Clark, to a hundred."

"Just feel it along, Sam. Don't fixate on the numbers."

"Thank God it's clear, except for the smoke," Rusty added in the interphone. Clark had extended the DC-6's flaps to the ten-degree position, but he called for flaps twenty now to be able to stay in formation with the stricken Baron as it slowed. Clark watched as Sam increased the angle of his Baron, the inverted nose describing a greater and greater angle above level as the wings tried to hang on to level flight. He saw the Baron begin to shake as Sam pushed his throttles back up and stabilized himself.

"Okay . . . well, that was scary."

"What'd you get on speeds, Sam?"

"She wanted to stall around ninety-five. So one hundred five is my slowest approach speed."

"Hey, Sam? Skycrane Eight Echo Romeo again."

"Yeah. Go Skycrane."

"We've got a better idea. We think there's a big cargo net in the hangar that would hold you, and all you'd have to do is slam into it. Like a Spiderman catch. We're gonna peel off to base, dump this load, and see if we can rig it in time."

"Might work. Thanks, guys," Sam said. "Man I'm getting one hell of a headache up here hanging like a bat. I can't believe people used to pay money for a rack in the basement to do the same thing."

The fright was clearly audible in his voice and Clark knew he was fighting hard against the debilitating tendency to hurry up and end the suspense regardless of the danger.

"Sam, Clark here. You're going to want to think about orbiting north of the field in case you lose power."

"Yeah, good point. I'll start a gentle turn here. Ah, Clark?"

"Yeah, Sam."

"Could I ask you a big favor?"

"Anything."

"If . . . if I don't make it out of this, would you please talk to Lisa, my wife, and my little girl, Kelly, and tell her we did everything possible?"

"Of course, Sammy, but you're going to tell her yourself. You're going to make it."

"Tell them I love them endlessly, and I'm sorry I didn't listen about this job . . . the dangers and all."

"Sam . . . you're going to be fine, but . . . if lightning strikes or something, of course I'll talk to her."

"I'm not giving up, Clark, but . . . it may be that the only reason the Big Guy is giving me a few more minutes here is to relay a good-bye."

Clark started to reply, but hesitated, realizing Sam's mike was still on.

"See, I . . . feel the left wing wobbling now. . . . I can see it. I don't think it's going to hold."

# Chapter 16

Jerry Stein had been on the Forest Service flight line preflighting his company's only Skycrane when one of his employees notified him of the tense drama in progress eighty miles to the south. He stood for a moment by the cockpit door, trying to decide whether to go back to Forest Service Ops or take off as planned, but too many years of experience told him the mission would have to be changed anyway.

He sprinted all the way to Ops and moved straight to the main desk, where Rich Lassiter was standing.

"Our Skycrane's ready to go," Jerry said. "Do they need it in Jackson?"

"Let me check," Lassiter replied, pulling up a receiver and punching up a tie line to the helibase at Jackson Hole's airport. He spoke urgently and quickly before replacing the receiver and turning to Jerry.

"The answer is yes, and do you have a cargo net of any sort capable of carrying a six-thousand-pound airplane?"

Jerry Stein stared at him.

"What?"

"Uh . . . they tell me they're trying to find a way to, ah, net the Baron lead plane since he can't land."

Jerry cocked his head with a disbelieving smile.

"Come on . . . get real."

Rich Lassiter wasn't smiling.

"I'm just telling you what they told me, Jerry. Can you check on the net?"

Jerry shook his head and pulled his cell phone from his belt. He punched in the number of one of his men and relayed the question.

"Okay. Get it and the harnesses out to the Skycrane within the next two minutes. Just . . . just do it!"

He clicked the phone back on his belt as he pushed through the door and jogged to the helicopter where his copilot was already waiting, passing a high wing turboprop Twin Otter jumpship from Missoula preparing for departure with a crew of smokejumpers aboard.

Jerry's eyes landed on an attractive blond fully decked out in her jumpsuit and parachute as she stood in the open cargo door of the Otter. Her face seemed familiar, and he wondered why. He turned away and pulled himself into the right seat of the Skycrane and turned his attention to an orderly departure.

IN FLIGHT, EAST OF JACKSON HOLE, WYOMING

"We're fat on fuel, boss," Rusty said, "and West Yellowstone says to stay with Sam as long as we need to. They also said to tell you Jerry is just launching from West Yellowstone in his Skycrane and he's bringing a net himself in case it's needed. He won't make it in time, but he's on his way."

Clark nodded as he widened his bank to stay about a thousand yards to the side of the still-inverted Baron as they monitored radio calls flashing back and forth. A growing team of people was laboring under the pressure of time to find a way to bring Sam Littlefox back to earth unharmed, and the traffic on the radio was becoming unbearably heavy. Sam was keeping the Baron slightly to the north of the airport at five thousand feet above ground level in case the engines quit. The wing, he'd reported, was vibrating slightly, and he had no illusions that he would be doing anything but dying rapidly in a vertical descent if it came off.

On the roads below, cars were pulling off the highway to watch the tense recovery effort as a local radio station located near the airport broadcast the airborne dilemma. Two television helicopter crews sent to Jackson Hole to report on the growing fires were preparing to launch from the east ramp.

"Lead Four-Two, Helibase Ops. We've got a truck in position right now, and they're getting ready to test his acceleration time. Can you hang on about five more minutes, ten at max?"

There was silence for a few seconds before Sam Littlefox came on, his voice more labored now, as he began his answer with a sigh.

"Every second is borrowed time with this crippled wing, but I think I'd better risk it. Yes."

"Okay. I'll get back to you as quick as I can."

Rusty could see the flatbed eighteen-wheeler rolling onto the end of the overrun of the Jackson Hole runway six thousand feet below. He could make out a heavy puff of smoke as the driver apparently headed southbound and rolled onto the hard surface of the runway, accelerating steadily. Rusty watched him dash past the midpoint of the field and get to within three hundred feet of the end before slamming on the brakes. Even from five thousand feet up, he could see smoke curling from the tires, and he watched in fascination as the tractor trailer steered slightly to the right to avoid the approach lights as he rolled onto the overrun, stopping less than a hundred feet beyond.

"Lead Four-Two, Helibase Ops."

"Go ahead," Sam replied.

"Okay, we've got it figured," the voice said. "We've got two engineering degrees, one masters in math, and a physics major working this out. The wind is steady at thirty knots down the runway. You said you're going to maintain an approach speed of one hundred ten knots, which is eighty over the ground. The truck will be just about at the midpoint of the field by the time he hits eighty. We've calculated he'll have to hit the gas when you're exactly fifty-eight hundred feet from the threshold of the runway, so we've got someone racing down there fifty-eight hundred feet from the end with a radio, and he'll give the Go command to the truck the second you pass over. If we're anywhere close, you and the truck will be in formation and right together by midfield. You think you can set her down in the remaining distance?"

"I think so, but I'll be prepared for a go-around if it doesn't look right. Tell the driver the props will probably chew into the trailer and make a hell of a racket, so don't let that, you know, spook him."

"Roger."

"Okay," Sam replied. "He'll feel the impact of the bird when I . . . come aboard. It'll probably work just fine to have him really tromp on the brakes as soon as I'm on, because that'll just snuggle me up safely on the forward side of the trailer. Tell me when you're ready. I'm going to start positioning for the approach."

"We've got the fire equipment standing by, as well, and it'll take the driver about five minutes to get back in position."

"Got it."

Clark keyed his radio.

"So, you're going to go with the truck, Sam?"

"Yeah . . . I'd like to think I could do the trick of rolling it upright on short final, but the wing's wobbling out there, and I can see it just breaking off if I tried. If I miss the truck and go around, I can always try the rollover as a last resort."

"Remember, they're still trying to configure the Skycrane, and there's a second one at Jackson and a third on the way. They might be able to fashion a two-helicopter sling out of the nets."

"I can't see that working, Clark. Wish I could. I can't figure how they could rig the net to catch me safely, even with two of them, and if my plane slipped out, the wing would undoubtedly break off and I'd have nothing left to work with."

"Understood."

"It's . . . a great idea, though. Maybe I'm wrong. You think I'm wrong?"

"Lead Four-Two, this is Skycrane Eight Echo Romeo. We're going to keep working on it. We're on the deck now and our crew's attaching the lines to the net, but go ahead with the truck and we'll try to be a backup. The second Skycrane's getting ready, and we are thinking about how to do the sling thing . . . suspending the net between the two of us and letting you fly into it. But if you can make the truck work, do it."

"Roger, guys, and thank you," Sam said, his strained voice taking on an almost eerie tone.

A voice from another helicopter pilot popped up on frequency.

"News helicopter off the east end of the runway, this is Jackson Helibase Operations. Please get the hell out of there! Cross to the west side and orbit at least a half mile west."

"Helicopter November Eight Seven Bravo, roger. We'll orbit the west side. Sorry."

"What's he doing?" Rusty asked.

"That's Channel Five's chopper out of Salt Lake. I'll bet you anything they're sending this live to CNN right now."

"Wonderful. Sam's spooked enough as it is," Rusty replied, almost under his breath.

"Clark?" Sam asked. "Any advice on how to do this? You did airshow stuff for a while, didn't you? You've seen guys land on moving trucks before."

Clark felt Rusty glance at him in surprise. He'd known nothing of that aspect of the senior airtanker pilot's past.

Clark let out an even breath and hit the transmit button.

"I'm surprised you remember that conversation, Sammy. In principle it's a piece of cake. Your biggest challenge is stopping your forward progress right over the truck, so you're flying perfect formation with him, because if you get it wrong, he'll pull away from you as you slow down. So I'd recommend you don't try to feather the props or change the power setting from whatever works, but also don't take too much time. Fly her all the way on, and when you plop it on the trailer, hold full back pressure to keep her there. Remember, you're going to get one hell of a burble from the truck, so it won't be smooth air, and the bow wave will tend to kick you up like an updraft just at the last second."

"Got it."

"What I'd do is keep a little forward momentum and just plan to fly it right onto the trailer, and aim to kind of smash your nose into the forward guard of the trailer at maybe up to ten knots closing speed. Not much more."

"I was thinking the same thing, Clark. I know there won't be much runway left to work with. It's just that I . . ." There was a sigh, and the transmission ended.

"Sam? Remember the frequency we discussed last summer that the Military Airlift Command used to use on VHF?"

There was a hesitation.

"Yes. Why?"

"Meet you there, if you can change the radio."

"I'll use number two."

Clark waited a few seconds for Sam to swap the frequencies before calling.

"I'm here, Clark."

"Sam, you're doubting your ability to do this, right?"

Many seconds of dead air went by before Sam triggered his transmitter again.

"Yeah, I am. I don't mind telling you I'm scared to death."

Clark steeled himself and took a deep breath. "Sammy, you're an incredible pilot, and this is nothing more than a new challenge. It doesn't have to be pretty or perfect. This isn't a check ride, and there are no procedures. Just common sense and judgment, which you've got, and skill, which you have in spades. Trust yourself, keep breathing steadily, and don't pay a minute's more attention to whether or not you can do it safely, because you can. Okay?"

"I appreciate the pep talk—"

"Sam, it's just aerodynamics. We're not waiting for a jury."

"One mistake and I'm dead, Clark!" he said, his voice trembling slightly, almost undetectably.

"Sam, quit feeling sorry for yourself!"

"I'm not feeling sorry for myself. Jeez! Don't you understand what I'm facing? The wing may come off at any second, or the engines stop running. I'm screwed, Clark!"

"No, you're screwed *up*, and you're going to stop thinking like this. You're going to do the best job of preparing as humanly possible; then you're going to go land that thing on that truck like you do it every day. Hell, Sammy, in the low-level environment we live in every day any single decision could kill you. You know that! You're *used* to that part of the job. So, this is a bit unique, but the same challenge. Now go back to the main frequency and get on with it."

"Roger."

Clark switched back and called Helibase.

The voice from Helibase below replied instantly.

"Go, Tanker Eighty-eight."

"Can you get a handheld aviation radio to the driver so the driver can alert Sam when he's going to have to brake at the end? Give him a few seconds to pull up if it's not working?"

"Already done it," was the reply. "Hopefully you'll be happy to know that our physics major is in the truck cab with a radio and a stopwatch."

For the first time in many minutes the frequency fell silent. The inverted Baron was flying north and descending as Clark throttled back his four engines and followed in a gentle descent, waiting for the turn back to the south.

"What are his chances?" Rusty asked over the interphone. Clark glanced at him in irritation. It was an unspoken rule fueled by ego and testosterone that in the throes of a life-threatening aviation emergency, pilots did not discuss the odds of living through what might be coming.

But Rusty was unapologetic.

"I think he's got a good chance, don't you?"

Clark gave up and nodded. "Yeah. Provided, when his tail hits concrete, he's in the right position."

"You think the tail will hit first?"

"Maybe."

"I think the truck's trailer surface is probably high enough so that won't happen. The Baron's vertical tail is stubby."

The Baron was sliding into a left turn now, and Clark followed, keeping the big DC-6B outside the arc of his turn and well within view. Ahead at the airport, Clark could see two Skycranes lifting off with something hanging underneath between them.

"Gear down, before-landing checklist, and flaps forty," Clark ordered. Rusty repeated the commands and positioned the controls, monitoring the gear lights before starting the checklist items.

"Down and three green," he reported, meaning that all three wheels of the landing gear were down and locked in place.

"Roger, down and three green."

The Baron was falling back in the side windows as Sam decelerated to his final approach speed of 110 knots, just barely enough airspeed to keep the big Douglas in the air. Clark throttled up his engines against the increased drag of the flaps and gear and checked the airspeed at 115 knots.

"Sam, this is Clark. I'll call your airspeed, okay?"

"Thanks."

"You're one hundred fourteen and steady. You have the visual glide slope lights?"

"Roger, I have the VASI," Sam said, repeating the acronym for the visual approach slope indicator, a series of three lights stacked vertically that were showing him to be exactly on the angled path to the runway's end.

"This . . . is the weirdest approach I've ever flown!" Sam said. "I'm hanging like a bat, everything seems reversed, and yet somehow this is getting comfortable. Go figure."

"We're four miles out, Sam. Keep her coming," Clark said, as the voice of the Helibase Operations manager returned to the frequency.

"Lead Four-Two, everything's prepared and ready. Aim for about the three-thousand-foot area of the runway, and just like a forward pass play, the truck should be there when you get there."

"Roger. Ah, Jackson Hole traffic, Baron One Four Seven Zulu is short final, runway one eight, full stop I hope, Jackson Hole."

"Sam, I think they know you're coming," Clark chuckled into his mike.

Sam unconsciously keyed his transmitter, his microphone picking up and broadcasting his rapid, somewhat ragged breathing as he talked to himself.

"Okay . . . okay . . . flatten it a bit . . . the flatbed's sitting on the end. When is he gonna go? I guess . . . there! He's moving. Why isn't Clark calling airspeed? Oh."

Sam realized he'd been squeezing the transmitter rocker switch and let up, clearing the radio frequency for a response.

Clark jumped in instantly.

"Sam, your speed is good at one twelve. Stay off the transmit button. Don't try to reply to me. You're one mile out, speed one hundred ten . . . right on. Positioning good."

Sam tried to shift his weight against the shoulder harness that was cutting off circulation, but only succeeded in creating a more severe pain in his leg from the seat belt. The top of his head was brushing the ceiling of the cockpit, and for the first time since qualifying as a lead-plane pilot, he wished he was wearing a helmet.

*Okay . . . keep it steady . . . remember the tail's hanging down . . . stay above the truck's level.*

The threshold was crossing his vision at the top of the windscreen now, the truck still more than a thousand feet ahead, twin plumes of black smoke streaming from the twin silver stacks.

"One hundred eight knots," Clark reported from somewhere overhead.

Sam pushed on the yoke, a bit too hard at first, and realized that the runway was now too far above him. He brought the yoke back a bit, letting the Baron settle closer, making sure he could still see the top of the eighteen-wheeler's cab less than five hundred feet ahead.

*Closing speed's still high, but that's okay, he's still accelerating,* he thought.

Sam could see the runway's remaining distance markers, and the five-thousand-foot marker had just come into view ahead. The dynamics of what he was about to attempt seemed straightforward suddenly, as if scales had fallen from his eyes and the job was essentially simple. He felt a calm surround him, a certainty of purpose and a supreme confidence that even permitted the thought of an orderly go-around. He no longer thought about the tenuous left wing. In some perverse way he was almost enjoying the challenge, not unlike the feeling he'd had on his first solo flight, scared to death and exhilarated at the same moment. It was as if he'd come too far for Providence to turn against him, even though that thought was coupled with an understanding of the unbelievably high odds against his living through this.

The truck was just ahead, at the top of his windscreen and upside down, of course, but slowing as he slid toward it. He could feel his hand retarding the throttles slightly as Clark Maxwell called out his airspeed as one hundred eight, a tiny bit slow.

Even the turbulence from the stiff winds seemed handleable, and he automatically compensated, bringing the Baron now just past the trailing edge of the trailer and still closing, with perhaps less than a fifteen-knot difference in speed between the two vehicles. The aircraft was hanging a bit too high, fifteen or twenty feet above the speeding trailer. He saw the four-thousand-foot-remaining marker slide past and began relaxing a tiny bit of forward pressure on the control yoke to let the Baron descend, as he aimed the nose to crunch into the forward guard of the forty-foot-long trailer.

*Too fast!* he thought, pulling back on the throttles a bit more.

But the trailer continued to slip by beneath him, and the speeds weren't matching. The cab was ahead now, at the top of his windscreen. His aim point disappeared as he soared too far in front of the truck. He grabbed the throttles, yanking them back to idle.

One second the truck had been sliding behind him, now it was accelerating out ahead of him, and he could feel the need for more forward pressure to stay airborne.

*Down! Just plunk it down!* He pulled too hard on the yoke, causing a momentary dive that scared him into pulsing the yoke back forward as he scooped up the throttles and jammed them forward to get more speed.

Sam saw the two-thousand-foot marker pass by.

Once again he tried to stay above the level of the flatbed and the truck cab, but a violent swirl of turbulent air streaming off the speeding truck caught him and without warning his inverted wings were banked perhaps twenty degrees to the runway as he struggled to right them and climb push—back to a safe altitude. There was grass in the windscreen now and the truck disappearing to his left as he fought to level the wings and climb, his finger finding the transmit button by rote.

"Waving off! I'm . . . ah . . . going around. I couldn't quite make it work." He let up on the transmit button momentarily as he began a serious climb back to traffic pattern altitude of fifteen hundred feet above the terrain.

"Roger, Four-Two. We'll reposition the truck," the Operations manager said. "You do want to try it again this way?"

"Yes. Everything the same. I'll get it this time."

Sam goaded the Baron to climb as he tried to ignore the pain of the straps cutting into him. He could see the DC-6B still shadowing him to the right and heard the Skycrane pilot saying he and his companion were taking off.

His shoulders hurt, his head was pounding, and the calm he had felt was still there, but the beginnings of a renewed urgency to end this agony was making itself felt in the corner of his psyche, and he tried to bat at it, to keep it from influencing him.

Sam climbed back to fifteen hundred feet and completed his turn north. The confusion of which way to bank was still dogging him, and almost every turn started with a bank in the wrong direction.

Sam triggered the transmitter.

"Lead Four-Two, on downwind. Please tell me when he's repositioned."

"Four-Two, the winds have dropped a bit. That may explain your overshoot. They're showing steady now down the runway at twenty-two knots. We'll work out the different start point for the truck."

"How're you doing, Sammy?"

Clark's deep voice was like a soothing balm, a rescue in itself.

"Physically, this is a new adventure in pain, Clark, but otherwise, as long as this old girl holds together, I'm . . . hold it . . ."

Something had changed in the hum of the left engine, and he tensed as it changed again, the power surging for a few seconds, then returning. Even in the middle of the surreal upside-down cockpit a familiar instinct took over and guided his eyes to the fuel tank gauges, which were wholly unreliable.

He glanced at the fuel selector as well, finding nothing wrong.

The engine had recovered, but the cause of the fluctuation could be anything, including the possibility that whatever had been keeping the fuel flowing to the engines was about to stop doing so.

*Fuel boost pumps!* Sam reached to the forward panel and flicked on the boost pumps that provided positive fuel pressure to the engines, holding his breath.

The engines remained steady, and he slowly let his breath out again.

The truck was reaching the approach end and would be in position momentarily, and he could see something else in the distance, two Skycranes orbiting with something strung between them.

"Lead Four-Two, this is Skycrane Echo Romeo. There are two of us now with a net slung between us. We're going to get in position on the south end of the field in case you want to try it, and we're pretty sure this would work for you. We think we can accelerate to a hundred knots and still have it stay in position."

"I can see you from here, Skycrane, but . . . how would I do it?"

"We'll stay about a hundred feet apart. The net is strong enough to take ten thousand pounds or more, and it's suspended in four places, like a big trampoline. Don't ask how. You'd have to fly between us, being really careful not to come up into our rotors, equalize airspeed, and let down onto the sling the same way you were trying to do on that truck."

"Jesus, guys, will that work?"

"We think so. It's your call. We're here."

"Lead Four-Two, Helibase Ops. The truck is in position again whenever you're ready."

"Roger, stand by," Sam replied, fatigue clouding the necessity of making a decision. Was trying to land on the truck more dangerous than trying to land on an airborne net?

He had almost made it to the bed of the truck. He could do it on the next pass. But landing in an airborne net might be safer, and he realized in a flash of horror that the never-been-done aspect was almost urging him to try it.

*This is my life I'm dealing with!* he reminded himself. This wasn't a testosterone check.

*No. I'll try the truck again. I'll go for the net only if all else fails.*

Once more Sam steadied out the Baron on final approach, unaware that an audience of millions was watching over CNN and Fox as two news helicopters hovered off to the west with their lenses trained on him. The links had been set up in less than ten minutes through several ground satellite trucks already in Jackson for the fires, and fed to the cable networks, which put them on air immediately.

"Can anyone think of anything I've forgotten?" Sam asked in the blind.

The only answer was the delayed click of Clark Maxwell's transmitter.

"I think you're ready, Sam. Nail it for us."

As before, Sam could see the plumes of black smoke as the truck driver floored his eighteen-wheeler and started down the runway on the unheard command of a spotter on the ground.

He checked his airspeed again, reading 110 knots dead-on. The VASIs were visible and showing him right on the glide slope. He worked the throttles and increased his descent slightly as he glanced at the altimeter.

*Over the threshold at fifty feet, level out and hold . . . hold . . .*

The truck was a thousand feet ahead, in the top of his windscreen, black smoke streaming out of both stacks as he closed on it, pulling the throttles back slightly. The driver was still accelerating, he could tell, but the closure rate looked reasonable and he held his breath as the back edge of the flatbed passed the top of his windscreen, the closure rate dropping steadily as he held the Baron some fifteen feet above, waiting for precisely the right moment for what he'd planned.

He hadn't noticed the sandbags before, but now they beckoned as a soft target midway on the flatbed. They formed a cradle just waiting for the top of his fuselage to come to rest nestled within them.

*Now!*

Sam goosed the throttles, feeling the Baron jump forward in a surge of power and speed for just a second, the truck suddenly beginning to move backward once again in his perspective. It was exactly what he needed to see.

He immediately yanked the throttles to idle and feathered the propellers, simultaneously relaxing his forward pressure on the yoke to bring the top of the fuselage down onto the surface of the trailer and maybe even right into the sandbag cradle. The plan was very precise in his mind.

The Baron's nose was over the front part of the trailer, but the trailer was beginning to move forward again, and he was still ten feet above it.

He had to walk the upside-down airplane into the cradle faster than he'd planned or impact it too far back and slide off the trailer and onto the runway at nearly a hundred miles per hour. There was very little runway left ahead of the driver, and he knew the truck would have to be stopped very soon.

"Braking in five seconds," a voice said on the radio. He assumed it was the driver. The seconds were evaporating, but for some reason he couldn't bring himself to just yank at the yoke and plop the aircraft down.

The feeling of utter calm that came over him seemed so completely natural it was easy to surrender to it. The concentration it gave him was suddenly total. There was no thought of an audience watching, nor of the need for anyone's approval. There was merely the intense desire in those few remaining seconds to do the job and do it well, nestling the top of the fuselage in the sandbag cradle now two or three feet above—or below—him. He could see the front of the sandbag cradle slide into view, and his hands nursed the yoke backward as the last of the runway loomed ahead and a voice from somewhere outside crackled through: "Nail it, Sam! Now! You're out of time!"

The turbulence from the truck was massive, but there was a soft thud and the sight of sandbags around his windscreen as a massive deceleration gripped him. He felt the truck slowing and the Baron sliding forward slightly on the sandbags and stopping as the front of the vertical tail fin— which was merely an inch or two above the concrete—caught the back end of the trailer with a crunch and held.

He had been afraid the Baron would tilt left or right and catch a wing and be pulled off, but the cradle was holding its wings level, and somehow the propellers had stopped rotating before he'd touched.

Sam reached forward to the panel to cut off the master switch, but not before the radio exploded in shouts of victory and the squeals of too many transmitters relaying congratulatory messages at once.

He turned the switch off. All motion and sound had stopped only to be replaced now by sirens and the urgent noises of people scrambling up on the trailer to yank his door open and help him out of his upside-down position and out of the cockpit.

Sam stood too fast on the wooden surface of the trailer as the blood rushed from his head to his extremities. The world went fuzzy, then dark as he collapsed benignly into the arms of two firemen.

# Chapter 17

The newly confirmed secretary of agriculture, Charles Bower, an old Washington hand with little knowledge of his new department, pressed his nose to one of the Air Force Gulfstream's passenger windows and tried to make sense of the scene unfolding below as Sherry Lacey narrated.

"Okay, see the column of smoke over there to the east of Teton Village?"

"I think so."

Lacey, the director in charge of wildland fire fighting for the Forest Service, had been talking nonstop for the past ten minutes and was now pointing to the full-color display on her laptop computer as a topographic map unfolded on the screen.

"The fire front is in the process of joining up with the two plumes you see on the left. We managed to contain two others closer to Lake Jackson, but the backcountry fires took more time to reach, and with the relentless winds, we lost control of them. Now, the southern fire that started due east of Jackson Hole has roared north and is in the process of joining with these other formerly isolated blazes to form a huge front. We were concentrating all our efforts on this area around Pinnacle Peak until an hour ago when the winds exceeded safe operational limits."

"So . . . now we're doing nothing?"

"No, no, no. We've had to suspend airborne operations, but not ground. Of course, that's a huge problem, because some of these isolated spot fires need smokejumpers and retardant. We've got a growing force of several hundred firefighters on the ground and everything moving in by logging roads, but what they're trying is probably not possible. We needed the airtankers and especially the helicopters to keep the spot fires outside of the main line so none of the fire crews get caught. So now . . . with the exception of the inbound smokejumpers"—she pointed to the computer screen once again, and his eyes left the confusing reality outside the window to follow her finger—"nothing's happening by air until the winds subside."

"Where are the jumpers headed?"

"See that small saddle between the two mountain ranges running north-east and northwest?"

He nodded, not entirely sure he did.

"Well, we'll drop them right there to cut line as fast as possible, and back-fire it to slow the head of the fire before it crests the ridge."

"Whoa. You're dropping them right in front of this blaze? I read about a major fire somewhere in Canada years ago that killed a bunch of smoke-jumpers because they got trapped in a valley and couldn't outrun the fire. Something gulch?"

"Mann Gulch, and that was in Montana, Mr. Secretary. And yes, this valley does have a rough resemblance to the Mann Gulch area, but there are differences. I mean, it *is* dangerous, and more so than normal. But the jumpers know what to do, and we can yank them out by chopper if it doesn't work."

"Even in these winds?"

She grimaced and shrugged. "I think so. But if we can protect that ridge and keep the fire out of that next valley, we'll split the main blaze and have a better chance to contain it on the north side. But there's far more at stake. Can you see what looks like a small clearing down valley?"

"Yes."

"That's a town. It was nothing but a scattered collection of old mining claims belonging to a disparate list of families and companies around the country until the late seventies, when a couple of very bright people figured out that mining claims are very difficult to void. These folks quietly staked numerous claims in the mouth of that valley and created a wonderful little thorn in our side called Bryarly. There's one primitive road in and out of there, and six hundred well-heeled, well-connected residents, and if the fire jumps that ridge, they're next."

"Have they been evacuated?"

"Not yet. They've been too busy burning up the phone lines to their con-gressional angels demanding protection."

"And you said Yellowstone's beyond?"

She nodded. "If we lose it here, or if splitting the fire around this huge valley doesn't work, we'll end up with a firestorm roaring into Yellowstone within two days, and from there it'll look like 1988, or worse, all over again."

The secretary looked away from the window and studied Sherry's face for a few seconds.

"So, how did this happen, exactly?"

"What? Tactically, strategically, or generically?"

"Well, I suppose— I huh, I stand I'm still trying to figure out what I'm supposed to ask."

"Tactically we failed to send the maximum number of airtankers and choppers in at the first sign of smoke. Of course, part of the problem is that we've grounded too many tankers. We don't have enough. I need an air force, and I don't have one. And I need my nineteen lead planes back, and I only have eight that are still airworthy, and with what happened an hour ago, I've now had to permanently ground them. Now all I've got for lead planes is a Cobra helicopter from California and a couple of Cessna Citations from Alaska, but we haven't been able to get the Citations here yet. We were in the process of leasing King Airs, but one of the vendors who was an unsuccessful bidder on the contract filed a protest, so everything is on hold. Anyway, even though we scrambled, we didn't scramble fast enough because we didn't anticipate the sustained winds. And strategically? We've been ignoring the fact since 1988 that these are still exceptionally dry, so-called thousand-hour fuel forests, primed and ready to explode. The possibility of a dry lightning storm coming through to light them up in mid-summer is hardly a novel idea. And generically? Whether it's a politically popular reality in the White House or not, global warming is real, it's here, and it's going to continue making things dryer and hotter sooner each year. In other words, Mr. Secretary, sooner or later these forests are going to burn, despite the current mandate to minimize such fires."

"So, gratuitous political swipe aside, we should have had a force already fully assembled."

"Yes. Plus we don't need the constant pressure on the fire budget from members of Congress who want to cut it each year," she added.

He was nodding. "Okay, and I understand that the so-called cost pools that the other branches of the Forest Service, Bureau of Land Management, and Park Service take off the top of the budget for administrative support each year are also hamstringing your capabilities."

She motioned to him to wait and spoke into a telephone handset connected to the cockpit.

"Major Wallace? Would you please bring us back across the same route but just about fifteen miles farther north? Then we can land back in Jackson Hole. Thanks."

She turned back to him.

"Okay. We should've had more resources. We had a team ready, but I have to take a bunch of the responsibility for this, Charles, and if you want my resignation, you'll have it. My staff and I were too focused on the current wildland fire situations in Idaho and Nevada, and we didn't see this coming, and didn't preposition enough personnel and equipment. Yes, we should have assembled a big force, and I should have been standing on your desk begging for help with Congress and funding and solving the airtanker and Air Force problems. But we didn't, and here we are."

"Bottom line, how bad could this get?"

She shook her head and sighed. "Well, we're about to lose another third of Yellowstone, and we'll very likely lose most of the east valley of Grand Teton National Park when the winds shift, as we expect them to. We'll lose several small towns, probably including Bryarly, and if the winds should entirely reverse, we could lose parts of Jackson Hole along with billions in very expensive private real estate."

He sighed. "So what do you need? Military help? Money? National Guard?"

"Mainly we need luck. And some National Guard and Air Force Reserve assets. But mostly luck. There's no time for anything else."

IN FLIGHT, TWIN OTTER JUMPSHIP N555N

Karen Jones stood in the open doorway of the twin-engine de Havilland jumpship and wrestled with the overwhelming feeling of sadness that had enveloped her quite without warning. There was no question that the startlingly beautiful alpine forest unfolding a thousand feet beneath her had less than a day to live, and that knowledge was an unwanted burden. The growing northbound blaze was just fifteen miles away. Only a major shift in the weather could alter its course, and she had somehow been appointed the bearer of that terrible news with the inevitable roar of backfires and the whine of their chain saws.

She knew all about the enlightened philosophy of fire being a natural process essential to the long-term health of forests, and of the century-long policy that had spawned Smokey Bear and the national will to let no forest burn—a policy now considered somewhere between controversial and sadly mistaken. The results were a tinder-rich, bone-dry, overheated western United States, filled with centuries of unburned fuels and clogged with massive encroachments of housing developments and towns and cabins whose owners demanded protection from wildland fires as well as so-called controlled burns.

But enlightened policies or not, Karen's lifelong love of verdant mountainsides and cathedral forests inevitably made forest fires painful, and purposely burning timber in backfires—part of her job at times—was equally disturbing.

And in this case, she knew, success would require a rapid sacrifice of many of the trees below her, some of which were a hundred and fifty years old or more. The forest at her feet would become the crude, denuded battleground on which they would try to slay the oncoming thermal dragon.

But first they had to get *to* the ground, which would mean jumping with a static line from the open door of the Otter and trying to land on a tiny meadow as they approached on the shoulders of too high a wind, at speeds as high as forty knots. That would be a ridiculous chance she wasn't about to let her people take.

She looked around the interior of the Otter, glad to bc back in this particular jumpship. N555N was known as "Triple Nickel," the same as the famous Triple Nickel unit of the U.S. Army, the 555th Parachute Infantry Company, an all-black unit that in 1943 began smokejumping over northwestern forests to meet the threat of Japanese incendiary balloons launched to cross the Pacific for the bizarre purpose of starting American forest fires. The Triple Nickels became adept at putting out the few that started, and made more than a thousand jumps.

Karen checked her watch, hoping her nervousness didn't show. She smiled at the spotter standing close by and nodded her head toward the streamer in his hand. He was ready for the next pass. Streamers helped them evaluate the wind and drift over the drop zone, and the last one had rendered startling results, with a lateral drift factor of more than twenty-five hundred feet.

The zone was behind them as the pilot got ready for the course reversal and return, which would be the fourth time the Missoula jumpship had passed over the zone at her request. Even though she knew what her decision along the south flank would have to be, she needed one more chance to see it nose to nose and think through all possibilities.

In the jumpship's cabin behind Karen, the eight members of her squad sat in pronounced discomfort, getting hot and airsick while they waited, all of them crowded together on low seats with their parachutes and gear strapped on and double-checked. They were as ready and eager to go as she was, but none of them was interested in committing suicide. It didn't take much experience to know that hitting even the softest of meadows in a forty-knot gale was as physically perilous as leaping from a moving car at the same speed. For a smokejumper mechanically attached to the chute, however, there was the added danger of being dragged by the winds through rocks and other sharp objects, and sometimes even over cliffs, as well as getting hung up in a tree and having to use a "let-down rope" to find the ground.

Karen's eyes watered from the effects of the windstream in her face as she leaned partially out of the door. She reached up to wipe her eyes, hoping none of her team members had noticed the extra makeup she was wearing. She rubbed carefully with her fingertip, making sure not to strip the flesh-colored coverup from the bruise that was already turning a mild shade of purple. To allow herself to be hurt in such a way was deeply embarrassing to a woman who prided herself on being her own protector. She was determined not to be the object of well-meaning sympathy she didn't need.

And she was equally determined to set straight any man who thought he could be her self-appointed protector. If that was in Clark's head, she would have to put a quick end to the idea.

The Otter was in a gentle left bank and getting ready to make the next pass. It would be several more minutes before the streamer could be released.

*Clark.*

Suddenly she wasn't sure what to believe about Clark, and maybe it was a natural protective caution overtaking her at last. He'd been a fond memory for four years, and suddenly she was dealing with the fact that she didn't know the real Clark Maxwell at all.

*Trent had complicated the whole thing,* she thought, *showing up drunk and saying that Clark had threatened him with some sophomoric message on his windshield.* She'd dismissed it completely. But then she'd learned that Clark had charged over to the hotel in the morning looking for her. If he was trying to engulf her and protect her, he could expect a quick end to whatever promise was brewing between them. It had been comforting to think of the possibilities with Trent out of her life, but the last thing she'd need was another possessive male.

What she *did* need was the chance to concentrate on her work and shut out the rest of reality.

Two vectors of her internal frustration met and merged, and Karen felt a rage giving birth to a scream she had to stifle. It would be comforting simply to yell into the wind, her words mattering less than the act of defiance. But with her squad watching her every move, it would be an indulgence she couldn't afford. They needed to see steadiness and stoicism in their leader's actions.

The target meadow was a treeless saddle cradled ten thousand feet above sea level at the strategic point where two mountain ridges joined together. It guarded the entrance to a long, widening valley to the north.

All of it was coming in view again. The jump spot where all nine of them were supposed to land and wait for the subsequent drop of their equipment was only a hundred yards wide, bordered on north and south by steep drops into the beautiful, peaceful forests below, and on the east and west by gentle ridges to the adjacent mountains, which were heavily forested and covered with snow during winter.

All the snow pack was gone now, she noted. In the years before the recently confirmed acceleration of global warming, there would still be patches of the previous spring's snowfall in the northern shade of large rocks and at the northern base of large trees beyond the meadow's edge. She loved snowfall, and the thought pulled her away again, imagining what the terrain below looked like in the middle of a gentle winter's storm, the image merging with log cabins and roaring fires and soft evenings.

She shook her head to restore her grip on reality.

Once more the drop zone was beneath them, and for a moment the fact that nothing stood between her and the low grasses of that tiny meadow became a demented lure, a physical siren song cynically beckoning her to step out the door.

Karen gripped the handhold in response, steadying herself as she double-checked her safety strap and watched the last streamer descend. It confirmed her analysis. *About two thousand feet of drift,* she decided.

The winds below were exactly the same as five minutes ago. She could see the graphic evidence of the small hurricane rushing up the south side of the slope as it rose four thousand feet from the adjacent forest and howled over and through their drop zone, bending the adjacent trees, kicking up a small plume of dirt and dust, and rippling the grasses in great waves she could track even from a thousand feet up. The wind howled through the trees on the northern rim of the meadow and plunged with equal speed and vengeance down the north side.

Once again Karen moved from the door to the cockpit and plugged in her headset. Herb Jellison, their pilot, looked at her, his eyebrows raised in a clear question. She shook her head even before her finger found the interphone button.

"It's impossible, Herb, until the winds die down. I was looking for sheltered alternates, but there are none."

"I'm not pushing you, darlin'."

She thumped his shoulder lightly with her thumb and index finger then pointed at his nose.

"You know better than to call me pet names, Herb."

"You're right, darlin', I do." He grinned, even more amused at her eye roll. Herb had been piloting Missoula jumpships for twenty-three years and had three grandchildren and the trust of everyone, but he loved to yank everyone's chain with innuendos and jokes that sometimes crossed the line.

The pilot checked his fuel gauge and clock before looking back at her. "So, do we go back? I've got enough fuel to loiter, but—"

"I had the same weather briefing you did, Herb. No change for at least twelve hours. We have no choice. And we're going to lose that ridge, and the whole valley and that little town if we can't get in there in time."

Herb nodded, pointing in the general direction of West Yellowstone Airport to the northwest through the new, rising plumes of smoke from the broadening flame front.

"I'll let Ops know we're returning, Karen. We'll be on the ground in thirty minutes."

"Okay."

She patted his shoulder and pulled off the headset, leaving it in the empty copilot's seat before moving back to brief her squad members on a reality they'd already figured out. There would be no question of their understanding the reasons. There would be disappointment, of course, the same as a psyched, winning baseball team filled with excitement but suddenly denied their game by rain or a last-minute default.

They took it well. She returned to the copilot's seat and pulled on her headset, watching the fire-threatened greenery pass as she shifted her mind to the subjects she'd been avoiding all day.

The scheduled jump had been a welcome balm, and she'd thrown herself into the planning process, from the successful eight A.M. return to the doctor's office for her medical sign-off to the extraordinarily detailed briefing she'd given the squad when they'd all assembled. It might take two days, she'd said, internally grateful that for the same length of time she would not have to think about Trent and divorce filings and logistics of where to live and how to avoid ever being in his presence again.

The smoke plume from a new fire dangerously close to the eastern boundary of Grand Teton's valley was sliding by on their left, but she took note only in passing, nodding without comment as Herb pointed it out.

She remembered the snarl on Trent's face when she'd opened her hotel room door in the early hours of the morning after stupidly agreeing to let him talk to her face-to-face. He'd shoved his way inside, drunk, furious, and belligerent, yelling about her "damned boyfriend." The blows had come when she'd tried to push him out, and she'd been astounded at the anger and ferocity of his attack. The only other time he'd hit her had been little more than slaps and a squeezed arm. Suddenly he was trying to slug her. She knew that the attack was propelled by a deeper frustration, but that was no excuse.

There could be no excuse.

She'd finally landed a few blows of her own and thrown him out of the room and into the adjacent wall in the hallway with a thud that brought other hotel guests to their doors.

"You tell Maxwell to stay the hell away from me!" he'd snapped as he pulled himself to his feet, about as unsteady as she'd ever seen him.

"What are you talking about, Trent?" she'd asked. "I was right there. He didn't threaten you."

"Yeah, right. He left a message on my windshield after I left the bar."

"What message? You're making this up."

"No, I'm not. He wrote it in soap, like on a used car. He wrote that you belong to him now, and if I get in the way, he'll get the FAA after me."

She'd hesitated as she stood there and almost felt sorry for Trent.

Almost. But she knew better. Once she'd looked down her nose at abused women, branding them as too stupid or too blind to understand that once abuse happens, it will always happen again. And yet, Karen O'Farrell Jones had rationalized *herself* into a version of the abused wife. It was frighteningly easy, she realized, to fall into that trap of believing that abusers could be redeemed or changed.

Until last night.

"Karen? You hear me?" Herb was asking.

She shook her head and smiled at him as she punched the interphone.

"Sorry. Just thinking. What did you say?"

"You want to consider scaring up a Chinook crew to try dropping the squad on the ridge?" He took his left hand from the yoke and matched his right in pantomiming a two-rotor helicopter.

Karen shook her head. She knew enough about the operational capabilities of helicopters to know that while a Chinook was probably available and could carry far more than all of them and their gear, landing in such high winds would be anything but safe and assured. And in many ways—even though she knew it was illogical—she feared being killed in a crash far more than she feared falling victim to a fire or a parachute jump gone bad.

No, they would return to West Yellowstone and regroup. It was the only rational decision, and she relayed that fact to Herb, who merely nodded.

# Chapter 18

The early return of Jerry Stein's entire ragtag fleet of airtankers had all but overloaded the ramp by nine A.M. when Clark landed and parked his DC-6B. He left Rusty to grapple with the usual postflight duties and returned to the unexpected cacophony of Operations, which was just as packed as it had been before the morning launch. Animated conversations were in progress in all directions. In calmer times, the paperwork would be sent out to the pilots, but the intensity of the battle had changed the dynamics. Groups of pilots had converged on Ops and were leaning over topographic maps while others made phone calls and checked weather reports, as if the synergy of their determination by itself could calm the winds and relaunch the fleet. In the corner of a table too rickety to be fully trusted, someone had set up a well-worn twenty-one-inch TV and spliced it into the building's cable service to display CNN's Headline News—which was reportedly running a story on the growing forest-fire disaster threatening Yellowstone and the Tetons. One of the pilots had been posted to watch for it and was waiting to sound the alarm.

When he came in, Clark had been almost instantly sidetracked by one of the small groups of pilots and almost missed the small tug on his sleeve. He turned, and one of the staff held out a portable phone.

"It's for you, Clark," the young woman said.

"Me? Who is it?"

She smiled. "Sam Littlefox."

Clark pressed the phone to his ear and automatically strolled toward a quieter venue down the hallway.

"Sam, thank God you're safe. Congratulations on a job incredibly well done," Clark said. "You okay physically?"

"Yeah, I'm fine," Sam's slightly wobbly voice intoned from Jackson Hole. "I'm a bit fuzzy-headed, but okay."

"Good." Clark could sense the lead-plane pilot had something serious to say that was catching in his throat, so he continued to make small talk to give him time. "From what I heard, I don't think you even scratched the plane or bent the props, not that it will matter much now."

"Yeah, the Barons are permanently grounded as of the last few minutes, and you wouldn't believe how fragile that wing looked up close. I don't know how it held together."

"Well, thank God it did."

"Clark, thank you, man."

"No thanks necessary. I—"

"I was losing it, Clark. I was shaking so badly at one point I couldn't think."

"You'd . . . never have known it from your radio voice."

"Okay, I'm a good actor. But what I want to thank you for is saying precisely the right thing to me at the most critical moment. And don't tell me anyone would have done it, because you were there and you got me through it, and I wanted to thank you, and, so, there it is."

"Well, you planning to straighten up and fly right from now on?"

Sam groaned and chuckled at the same time.

"Like I haven't heard that about ten times in the past hour."

"Too good to pass up."

The silences became rapidly awkward, and they disconnected with a promise to get together soon. Clark took the portable handset back to the right counter, overhearing the last snippet of a radio message from the Otter.

"Is that the Missoula jumpship?" he asked.

The Forest Service radio operator nodded.

"Where is he? Did they drop their jumpers?"

"Nope. The mission aborted. They're on the way back," the radio operator explained. "The winds were far too high to permit the jump. Of course, the fire's taking full advantage."

"I'll bet. Who's the squad leader?"

"Jones. Karen Jones. You know her?"

Clark smiled involuntarily. "Yeah. What's her . . . their ETA?"

"Maybe twenty-five minutes."

"Thanks."

Clark turned to find Bill Deason tapping him on the arm.

"Got a moment?"

"Sure, Bill."

Deason inclined his head toward the ramp and Clark followed him out, walking in formation and in silence down the flight line. They stopped near a tree, opposite the permanently grounded PB4Y-2 that Bill had flown for more than a decade. Clark found a sawhorse to lean on as the senior captain turned, his eyes on the distant Operations building and his hands shoved in his pockets, his deep voice resonating with concern.

"Misty's lying, Clark. Judy and I are convinced of it. She knows something really serious and probably very nefarious about Jeff's activities, and she's spooked, just like we figured."

"Did you talk to her some more?"

"Judy did."

He related the conversation Judy had tried to have with Jeff Maze's girl-friend before Misty had hurried out of the motor home.

"She hasn't been back, and that worries me on two levels."

"Yeah?"

"You know, I'm asking myself, has she run off? Is there any chance she really could be in danger?"

Clark look startled. "She thinks she's in danger?"

"Well, I'm interpolating, but why would she be so nervous when the subject of Jeff's activities came up if she weren't? I mean, I'll admit that's only one of several possible explanations for her reactions, but there are unexplained things going on around here, and when a wing falls off a sturdy airplane like the DC-6 and then I hear the NTSB is investigating sabotage—"

"*Sabotage?*" Clark interrupted. "Who said anything about sabotage?"

"One of the mechanics overheard Trent and Jerry talking with the NTSB investigator, who thinks Jeff's wing may have been blown off." Bill looked at him quizzically. "That's a really strange look on your face, Clark. What are you thinking?"

"If anyone planted a . . . a bomb or whatever on that airplane, it would have had to be done earlier, and maybe the night before, right?"

"Probably."

"Bill, *I* was scheduled to fly that airplane. Jeff was a last-minute substitution. And I'm the guy who wrote the anonymous article everyone already seems to know came from me, and that article could be considered a threat to . . . to—"

"Jerry, or any of the other owners?"

"Right."

Bill sighed and looked away for a bit before meeting Clark's eyes again.

"I think Jerry's up to his ass in trouble, Clark, but you know him as well as I do. If Jerry wanted to murder you, can you imagine him imperiling one of his precious airplanes to do it?"

Clark smiled in response.

"No."

"Yeah, remember this is Jerry we're talking about. He might come after you with a shotgun, but he'd do it nose to nose and in person. Of course, he'd also use discounted, no-brand ammunition he'd bought at a gun show to save a buck. But he's no midnight coward skulking around the flight line with a flashlight."

The reference stopped Clark momentarily, as he recalled how easy it had been for *him* to skulk around the flight line for reasons other than sabotage. Clark shook off the thought.

"Why do you think Jerry's in trouble, Bill?"

"You remember those guys who ended up doing time in a federal prison for selling and misusing C-130As the Air Force sold them for fire fighting?"

"Who doesn't?" Clark asked.

Bill nodded.

"Well, I strongly suspect Jerry's been skating very close to that line, too, during the winter. And Misty may have the key."

"I'm not following you."

"Clark, what if someone's flying our fleet in the winter off the books? What if the planes are handed over to Central Intelligence, or one of the CIA's phony baloney front companies, and then flown like the C-130s were, I don't know, in the middle of South America, then quietly returned, but without any of the missions being logged?"

"Off the books?"

"Totally."

"Where we don't even know about the flight time?"

"Uh-huh."

"And . . . and you mean not just one season, but perhaps two or three or more?"

"Maybe for years, Clark. These airplanes could be far older than we know in terms of usage. Hell, Jeff's wing may have come off due to a level of fatigue the mechanics never suspected could occur in a DC-6B with X number of flight hours, because it wasn't a bird of X flight hours, it was X times two."

Clark felt the blood draining from his face.

"Look, Bill, there's something I need to tell you." He related his midnight foray onto the flight line and the inspection bay that had been far too dirty to have been opened only a couple of hundred flight hours before, as well as his peek into the maintenance files.

"And, you called that shop in Florida?" Bill asked, when he'd finished.

"Yes, and one of the mechanics told me the fleet had left right after the inspections in October. But, Bill, they didn't show up in Helena until midspring. So where were they in between?"

Clark also told of his chance discovery of a Colombian newspaper in the back of Tanker 88, and the business card of a Colombian tavern he'd found in the wreckage of Jeff Maze's aircraft, acutely aware that Bill's expression had darkened as he turned again to check that no one was approaching.

"Clark, we gotta tell someone. Right now. Before another wing comes off. We've gotta make a call."

"To whom? The FAA's impotent and scared of this fire-bombing business to begin with, and the NTSB has no power beyond reporting on cause."

"Hell, I'm not a lawyer, but isn't there a new law that says these airplanes can't be used out of the country?"

Clark nodded. "Yes. It was passed last year, but I think it only applies to the ex-military airplanes, like your P-3 Orion. I'm not sure if it covers the DC-6 fleet."

"That sonofabitch," Bill said, almost under his breath.

"Who? Jerry?"

"Yes, Jerry! Who else? The little weasel isn't making enough money? He's got to go renting his fleet to the CIA to rake in more and then imperil all of us with secretly beat-up airplanes? Jeez!"

"Bill . . . we'd better be cautious here. Maybe Jerry doesn't know. Maybe it isn't what it appears to be."

There was a sharp, derisive laugh from Bill Deason as he threw his head back and shook it. "How could he *not* know? If your entire business solvency depends on your fleet of airplanes, you think you wouldn't be acutely aware of where they were at all times? Remember, we're talking Jerry here. The king of micromanagers."

"I'm just saying, not out of loyalty but out of caution, that we shouldn't jump to that conclusion."

The two men fell silent for a few moments, each examining his own horizon before Clark turned back.

"How about the FBI?"

Bill nodded without comment, and Clark continued.

"I know there's a field office in Helena. I'll go make a call and get an agent down here and just, you know, at least alert them to the possibilities. You agree?"

"In a heartbeat" was the reply as Bill turned to look Clark in the eye. "What was it Yogi Berra was supposed to have said? I don't want to wake up dead tomorrow and find I could have done something today to save myself."

Clark chuckled. "Berra said that?"

"Who knows, but it sounds like him."

"Yeah. Well, you're right to be cautious. For one thing, Judy would kill you if you made her a widow."

You got that right.

They walked back to the Operations building and Clark quickly slipped away to find an empty back office and phone book. The phone number of the nearest FBI office was in the governmental listings, and he made sure no one was listening outside the door before dialing and working his way through a secretary to the agent in charge. Clark kept the explanation short and urgent, pleased that the agent agreed to come to West Yellowstone.

"You know a good, reasonably safe location where others wouldn't expect to find you?" the agent asked.

Clark gave him directions to Strozie's Tavern, agreeing to meet at four, then quickly returned to the Forest Service complex and the standby shack to quietly relay the information to Bill.

"Okay," Bill agreed. "I'll meet you there. You going to be around the flight line in the meantime, Clark?"

"Any chance we'll launch again this afternoon?" Clark countered, aware that Bill had been at the Operations counter.

"Almost none."

"Then, yes, I'll be around, but there's something I need to attend to."

"I'm going back to my motor home, Clark. You want to join Judy and me for some coffee later and go over what we should say?"

"How about now?"

Bill grinned.

"No, son, I mean later. I just got a beep on my pager, and my incredibly beautiful wife is waiting right now with some more personal activity in mind that doesn't involve coffee or company."

"What?" Clark teased, "She beeps you when she's in the mood?"

"Actually, she's pretty much always in the mood, which is why I'm an incredibly lucky guy, but you're prying. Just come by after two."

"Okay." Clark followed him outside but reached up and caught his shoulder.

"Bill?"

"Yes?"

"Maybe I should go alone. At four, I mean."

"Why's that, Clark?"

Clark shoved his hands in his pockets and watched an aircraft click on its landing lights in the distance as it lined up with the runway. He looked back at Bill Deason.

"I don't want to sound paranoid, but if someone is gunning for me, there's no sense putting you in the same crosshairs. Besides, I have all the details."

He fully expected Bill to wave away the concern. Instead, he nodded solemnly.

"You could be right."

"Okay. So I'll take care of it and report back."

"Well, check your six, Clark. Okay?"

"You mean my DC-6, or the six o'clock position relating to my posterior?"

Bill smiled. "Both, actually, although in archaic fighterpilotspeak that refers to your tail feathers."

"Roger, Orion Lead, I'll watch my six. Not to worry."

Bill was hesitating, Clark could see, grateful to be off the hook but embarrassed to be worried just the same.

"I don't mind telling you," Bill continued, "this talk about sabotage is very worrisome."

"Yeah, it is."

Bill waved and turned, his six-foot-three frame ambling off toward the motor-home parking area, his gait slightly lopsided from a crop-dusting accident years before that had left one shattered leg a bit shorter than the other.

Clark turned his attention back to the airfield. The landing lights he'd been watching were closer now, and Clark squinted to make out the craft, wondering if the ETA estimate on Karen's airplane could be wrong. Maybe this was the Twin Otter jumpship. He felt an involuntary burst of excitement at the thought that she might be climbing down to the ramp momentarily, and had to remind himself of the circumstances. Rusty thought she'd been roughed up, and if so, guess who was responsible for having irritated her husband.

Clark turned to go back into the standby shack, pausing in momentary confusion. Had she had time to get the message he'd left on her hotel room phone? Probably not, he concluded, which meant he'd be approaching her cold, and in the presence of her "bros," which might embarrass her.

He could feel his cheeks flushing.

*No,* he decided. *I'll watch from a distance when they arrive.*

After all, he wasn't her protector, though that could change.

And the thought brought a smile back to his face.

# Chapter 19

Joe Groff sighed and sat back in the empty office, letting his mind roam through the possible solutions. He loved solving unexpected problems and proving his own brilliance to himself. And he was used to his employer grousing that he spent too much time finding solutions to problems that had yet to develop. But clearing away problems had always been his forte, and he was good at it. Jerry Stein had the visions and the entrepreneurial zeal, but it was up to the invisible man named Joe to make sure that no one interfered with those visions.

He shook his head and smiled at a private joke, thinking again how smart he'd been to leave his detective shield behind in Miami six years ago to follow the pied piper of aging airplanes and serve as Jerry's security director. Stein always introduced him as something else, of course. Some days he was a business associate, and other days he was Jerry Stein's personal pilot, even though he barely knew how to fly small Cessnas. And some days, Joe knew, his were the real brains behind Jerry's success. He was the shadowy operative who anticipated major problems and did something about them just in time.

Of course, Jerry was the wily one who realized how many professional enemies he'd acquired over the years, and how vital it was to know more about the employees, the customers, and the other companies than they knew about him. It was, in other words, a dream job for a frustrated clandestine operative.

It also helped, Joe thought, that he had a plain vanilla face that could suggest dozens of different people. Not a chameleon exactly, but over the years he'd found he could meet the same person two or three times during a year and never be remembered.

Such as now.

Joe drummed his fingers and thought through the next move. Clark Maxwell's determination to bring in the FBI at this point was a very dangerous move, given the sensitivity of things. The attempt had to be thwarted. But while he pondered, an alerted FBI agent was getting ready to drive down from Helena to hear what Maxwell was worried about. Undoing that momentum was going to be tricky.

*Thank God I saw Maxwell looking for an empty office,* Joe thought. Ducking in the parachute room and watching for the right line to light up had been a spur-of-the-moment reaction. Tapping into the call had been fairly easy for someone of his experience, especially since he'd already been shadowing the veteran captain. Maxwell had been on his close-watch list from the moment Joe had been told he was coming out of retirement for the season. He was well aware of Maxwell's scathing article, though he hadn't discussed it with Jerry. After all, they were short of pilots, and he figured he could keep careful watch on any seditious activity.

Joe picked up the phone and punched into an empty line, using the memorized number from the small telephone pad decoder he'd used to intercept the number Maxwell had been calling.

The field office receptionist answered in a now-familiar voice, and Joe dropped his voice to Clark's range, matching inflection and volume.

"Well, you can, if you are so inclined, connect me with Agent Blackson. This is Captain Clark Maxwell. I just talked to him not five minutes ago."

He waited for the FBI agent to come on the line.

"Agent Blackson, I'm sorry to bother you again. This is Clark Maxwell. But . . . I was just talking with a colleague here who's as worried as I am, and apparently he's already talked extensively to your Denver office, so I guess I bothered you for nothing. I'm told they're already on it. If you still want to meet, however . . ."

"Well, it's a pretty busy period. You say there's someone in the Denver office actively taking your information?"

"Yes, sir. The name is Special Agent . . . well, I can't read my note on the name. Could be Brown, Black, or . . . I'm not sure except that it starts with a 'B.' "

There was a brief hesitation, and Joe held his breath until the agent's sigh was followed by the reply he wanted to hear.

"Well, that's okay. I don't need the name. I'm glad you called back, Captain. If you do need my involvement, however, call me again."

"I will. I'm sorry."

Joe replaced the phone and wrote a careful note to himself of the time and the number, little details that could prove critical later on—or could be completely worthless. You never knew.

He checked his watch and thought through the question of whether he'd ever talked face to face with Clark Maxwell. He was very careful not to interact with Jerry's employees unless absolutely necessary. The strict application of that policy had kept him a ghost with the ability to glide around Stein Aviation without raising an eyebrow.

But Maxwell?

*No,* Joe concluded. *He's a virgin contact. I can do it safely.*

JACKSON HOLE AIRPORT, WYOMING

Jerry Stein was bored and, as usual, doing something about it. Time to kill was time wasted.

He checked his watch in irritation as he listened to the response on the other end of the cell phone and simultaneously watched the last adjustments being made to attach the removable water-tank system beneath his Skycrane.

"Hey!" Jerry barked into the phone before shifting it to his other ear. "Look, I'm trying to give you a news tip, and you want to play stupid telephone tag games with me?"

Once again he was put on hold, and he tried to stifle his growing anger by letting his eyes roam over the huge, ungainly helicopter, which resembled a metallic praying mantis. *Amazing machine!* he thought, indulging in a little pride that Stein Aviation owned one.

Even though the Skycranes were the most expensive aircraft of all for the Forest Service to use on an hourly basis, they could suck up over sixteen thousand pounds of water in one gulp from any nearby lake using a huge hose and high-speed pumps, then dump the water exactly where it was needed and go back to the lake for another gulp. Unlike the tankers that had to land to refill, the Skycranes could keep up the tempo for hours—although water was less efficient than retardant at keeping trees along the line of an advancing fire from exploding in flame.

There were three Skycranes already in operation on the Jackson Hole fires, and the Stein Aviation Skycrane would make four. Even with the winds above limits for everyone else, the Skycranes were heavy enough and stable enough to continue operating.

Once again someone came on the line, and Jerry turned his attention back to the phone.

"What? No, dammit! Connect me right now to the reporter covering that crash yesterday of the airtanker in Yellowstone. I don't need the name; I need the reporter."

For the fifth time the insipid hold music started up, and he found himself seriously wondering how far he could toss the phone to demonstrate his frustration. He didn't do counterproductive things like that much anymore, which put his reputation as a wild man in jeopardy. But he was tired of pretending whatever temper tantrum he'd pulled hadn't been costly as well as totally ineffective. *No,* he decided. He liked this particular cell phone.

Another voice came on the line, a male who introduced himself timidly, as if he were going to drop the receiver and run at the slightest hint of controversy, anger, or rage.

Jerry instantly adjusted his approach to fit.

"Mr. Fulton, is it?" he asked gently.

"Yes."

"I am truly sorry to bother you, Mr. Fulton, but there's a bit of information the authorities aren't telling you about that Yellowstone accident yesterday."

"And, before I ask you what that is, may I get your name, please?"

"I'm sorry, but I have to remain anonymous. However, I thought you needed to know that even though the NTSB isn't admitting it, they think that the DC-6B crash was the result of sabotage. That's why they're being so quiet."

"Really? Do you have any proof of that?"

"The proof has already been spirited away from the crash site by a helicopter rented by the NTSB. But you can take this to the bank: DC-6s are essentially incapable of losing their wings. That one was blown off."

"Why? Why would someone attack an airtanker?"

"To make it look like all the nation's airtankers are dangerous so that we'll ground them and end up losing Yellowstone and the Tetons and Rocky Mountain National Park and a lot more. Don't let them BS you. That DC-6 crash was not an accident. I have to go."

Jerry ended the connection and clipped the phone back to his belt as he walked toward the Skycrane. One of the maintenance crew was signing off the logbook, and the copilot was just completing his walk around as Jerry hailed him and pointed up.

"You ready to go make some money?"

"We're launching?"

"Immediately. Hope you brought your lunch."

The copilot nodded. He'd already learned the hard way that flying with Jerry Stein was a thinly disguised weight-control program.

"Jerry, how's it looking over there?" the copilot asked with a worried expression, pointing generally at the Forest Service Ops area.

"You mean the fire?"

"Yes. Who's winning?"

Jerry grinned at him. "We are, kid. I hate to say a mature forest fire is good business, but when the winds quiet down we'll be bombing this one for weeks. *Ka-ching, ka-ching.*"

Karen waited until every member of her squad had alighted from the Twin Otter before motioning for their attention.

"Since we're all in the same hotel, I think we can stow our gear and go back there as a group, but as per normal, we're on until eighteen hundred local, and if they want to hold us over on standby—"

"Twenty hundred. We know," several of them chorused. Karen rolled her eyes at the usual joshing and motioned them on toward the Operations building, amused at the vague feeling that she looked like a mother duck with her ducklings in tow.

*Except that they're all bigger than I am,* she reminded herself. Even with the frustration of having to abort the jump, they were all in great spirits, as was she, and that fact suddenly seemed strange.

She reminded herself how the day had begun and ran her fingers over the covered bruise on her face, suppressing another flash of anger. The enjoyment that came from focusing totally on her guys and the mission was too good to give up, and she forced away any thoughts of husbands and assaults and self-appointed stalking boyfriends.

"Miss Jones? Got a note for you," one of the Operations people said, leaning out the doorway as she walked by. The initials "CM" were in the upper-left-hand corner of the envelope, and she stuffed it into a pocket of her jumpsuit before anyone else could ask. For some reason, the arrival of the unread note was aggravating, and if it contained the sort of message she expected, she was going to have to put a quick end to this.

Karen was back in her room at the hotel before she'd calmed enough to open the note. There was a message light blinking on her hotel room phone, and she wavered for a few seconds over which to attend to first.

The note won out. Might as well get it over with.

*Karen,*

*I'm quite concerned that you're okay. My copilot said he saw you early this morning and your face appeared bruised, and I'm worried Trent might be behind it. Again, I'm deeply sorry if I put you in undeserved jeopardy of any sort. Please call me when it's convenient and let me know you're all right.*

*Clark*

His cell phone number was written below, and she reached for the phone and punched it in, a carefully phrased response assembling itself in her mind. But she reached his voice mail instead and balked. What they needed to talk about should be done in person.

Karen sat heavily on the end of the bed in thought, trying to meter the emotional need to tackle the problem before thinking it through. That tendency had landed her in trouble more than a few times, damaging friendships, ending promising romantic relationships, and causing unnecessary hurt feelings more times than she cared to count.

*We're on standby. I shouldn't leave the hotel until six,* she told herself. Afterward, she could find Clark's local address and go talk to him when she could be calm and poised. Calm and reason would be much better than landing on him like an angry cat with claws and fury.

# Chapter 20

By midafternoon it had finally became irrefutably apparent to Misty Ryan that if she intended to honor Jeff's wishes, she should not return to the Deasons' motor home, regardless of their hospitality.

Earlier she'd thought of just moving into Jeff's room at the Best Western, sleeping in the spot he'd occupied and trying to find solace there. But when the manager let her in with a master key, the enormity and permanence of his absence chased her out in embarrassed confusion.

The hotel had yet to match up the names of the pilots killed in the accident with their guest list, so Misty informed them of Jeff's death and arranged to have his things boxed and sent to her home in California. Afterward, she left the hotel as quickly as possible and walked aimlessly into the neighboring countryside, acutely aware of every departure and arrival from the airport as she tried to decide what she was supposed to do now.

Seeing to a decent burial for what was left of Jeff's body was step one. From a forgotten corner of her mind the wreckage of a Catholic upbringing rose up to nag her again, this time about the proper funeral for a loved one. Rules. Always rules. Obligations and promises and rules dictating what she should do for a funeral and with the body.

But Jeff had sworn allegiance to no religion other than himself, and in a tiny, ultimate act of revolt she decided a simple nondenominational service would be sufficient. If she arranged a mass, he'd probably rise up out of the coffin and strangle her.

And then there was the matter of what was to become of her financially, although right now that seemed wholly irrelevant. Her supervisor at the Forest Service District Office knew she was in mourning and had promised a few days of personal leave anyway, so she wasn't going to worry about it. If they wanted to fire her, she'd all but welcome the closure.

*Be my guest!* she could imagine herself saying in response to such an imaginary dismissal. The defiant thought pleased her, then faded on another tidal wave of emotion, another small river of tears best shed in private.

During the early afternoon she'd wandered through two of the taverns in town and added a moderate amount of alcohol to her confusion before deciding to leave immediately for California, then changing her mind and deciding to stay, and finally deciding not to decide anything for a few more days.

But by two o'clock the thought of remaining anywhere close to West Yellowstone became torture.

Misty walked quickly back to the airfield carrying her set of keys to Jeff's truck. She slipped behind the wheel, luxuriating in a residual hint of his cologne, and started the engine. It would take a while to get to one of the interstates, but she didn't care. She needed to be anywhere that West Yellowstone wasn't, so any road toward the Pacific would do fine.

CRASH SITE, YELLOWSTONE NATIONAL PARK

Steve Zale snapped another picture of the broken wing-bolt assembly and stood for the first time in ten minutes, letting the blood regain circulation in his legs, a process that made him dizzy. The smell of burned wood was everywhere, though the blaze that the airtanker's crash had started was now several miles to the north and barely contained.

He glanced at his watch, wondering if he should get back to the hotel room he'd rented and try to transmit the close-ups he'd taken to Washington before the end of the day, or whether anyone there was paying attention. So far his urgent recommendation to launch a modified Go Team had been laughed at and labeled as the alarmist blathering of a newly minted NTSB field investigator who didn't yet understand the basic politics and dynamics of allocating precious National Transportation Safety Board resources.

"Look, I know this stuff. I was with the Forest Service for twenty-four years," Steve had told the head of the air accident investigation division. "These people only have about twenty or thirty big airplanes left for fire bombing over the entire U.S., and a lot of them are old DC-4s, DC-6s, and DC-7s. If there's a basic flaw here and the Forest Service grounds that fleet, they've got nothing left, and this whole area's already on fire. We need to make sure we get this one right, and I'm just one guy."

There had been a sigh on the other end, as if his superior had been forced to give the same tired explanation a thousand times.

"Steve, *if* we start getting heavy political guns on Capitol Hill demanding more attention to this, then we'll give it more attention. But the board is stretched very thin right now, and you've got a very simple situation out there. A wing fell off. Okay? You said so yourself. This isn't a hairy human factors deal where a captain flies a perfectly good airplane into a perfectly good mountain for no apparent reason and leaves us needing to hire the great Kreskin to read his very deceased mind. Just, plain and simple now, the damned wing came off. So go find out *why* the wing came off. It can't be that difficult. Send us samples, send us pictures, send us small portions of critical parts. Follow your training and the book. The lab will work its magic and let you know about anything you submit, and in the end I'll review everything and help you reach a logical conclusion. That's how we do field investigations, especially when it's nothing but metallurgy involved. Well, metallurgy and maintenance history, of course."

He'd reholstered his cell phone feeling as if he'd been spanked, but that had been nothing compared to the embarrassment of the call an hour later.

"Steve? This is Ron, back at the board, your long-suffering boss. Do you have any reason whatsoever to believe the wing came off that DC-6 due to some form of sabotage?"

"Sabotage? Good grief, no. I'm standing right here at the—"

"Then what the hell are you doing speculating about sabotage in front of the operator?"

"I haven't mentioned the word or the concept. Who's saying I did?"

"Apparently rumors are running rampant out there and spilling into the media that the NTSB is investigating the possibility of terrorist-based sabotage. I just got a call from the Department of Homeland Security, for God's sake, and you *are* the NTSB out there for the moment. So tell me, so I won't be the goddamned last to know. *Are* we investigating the possibility of terrorist-based sabotage?"

"Ron, I . . . no! Of course not. When I talked yesterday with the owner, Jerry Stein, and his chief of maintenance, they asked *me* about the possibility, and I told them it was far too early to identify any particular cause. I thought that was a nutty question, the terrorist part. But I said precisely what I was supposed to say."

"Word for word?"

"Yes, sir."

There had been a blessed pause and a telling snort. "Okay, I think I get the picture."

"What?"

"I'll tell you later. Just refuse to touch that issue, and discuss nothing else with those people. We'll do the denials from here."

Steve shook his head to expunge the cold chill the call had caused. He toggled on the digital screen on the back of his camera and pulled up the close-ups he'd taken. He needed to compose the words to go with them.

*Let's see . . . the break apparently began at the lower forward attach point in the wing box–mounted fitting itself.*

The critical point looked a little like the cross section of a door hinge, a metal loop on the wing root that fit snugly between the two metal loops on the fuselage wing box, with a carefully engineered metal pin inserted through the combined loops and holding the assembly tight.

*When the casting attached to the fuselage broke, it caused the wing to rotate upward and overstress and break the remaining fittings. The pin was still in place, but it shows signs of excessive wear and fatigue and some corrosion, as does the entire attach point.*

*The next major step,* he thought, *aside from sending the pictures in and arranging for the critical pieces of the flange and wing pins to be shipped to Washington, is to plow through the maintenance history of Ship 86.* There had to have been a growing crack for some time. Maybe there was something in the records that could explain how it could have gone undetected.

But of one thing he was certain. There was zero evidence of sabotage.

STROZIE'S TAVERN, WEST YELLOWSTONE, MONTANA

Mentally, Joe Groff had already joined the FBI by the time he pushed through the door of the bar.

He loved projecting himself into role playing. He knew he would have made a great actor, too, if he'd had the tolerance to put up with the meat-market aspects of making it in Hollywood.

But this was almost as good.

He'd had to scrabble through his on-the-road wardrobe for a black suit and a conservative tie to wear with his one white shirt. FBI agents had far more latitude in dressing these days, he knew, than when J. Edgar Hoover ran the bureau, but he was dressing to convince a man just old enough to think of federal agents as closer to men in black than anything else.

Joe scanned the bar's smoky interior for someone who matched the file photo of Clark Maxwell from the computer database he kept of Jerry's employees. The accompanying information contained no indication that a face-to-face meeting between them had ever taken place, so at worst Joe's face might seem vaguely familiar, as someone once passed in the hall.

There was, of course, the problem of federal law, and that had stopped him for a few moments. Impersonating a federal agent was a felony, but the solution he'd come up with should keep him safe from prosecution.

*There you are,* Joe thought, spotting Maxwell at the back of the bar beneath a precarious display of beer mugs and other paraphernalia. Six feet, well built and trim, it was his roundish face and the way his mouth seemed permanently engaged in a warm smile under a full head of dark hair that made the I.D. complete. He'd been nursing a beer.

"Captain Maxwell?" Joe asked, taking the pilot's large, outstretched hand.

"Yes. Agent Blackson, I presume?"

Joe sat next to him and shook his head, keeping track of the bartender who was eyeing him suspiciously and moving his way.

"Actually, no, sir. I'm Randy Michaels. Agent Blackson ended up stuck in Helena, and even though in truth I've only had part of my Quantico training, and therefore I'm not technically a federal agent as yet, I've been tasked to come in his place." *Good touch,* Joe thought. He'd been through Quantico as a Marine decades before, but the name was synonymous with the FBI Academy. "I hope that's okay with you, sir," he added, eyebrows raised in anticipation of a judgment as the bartender arrived across the bar.

"Oh, of course. I just assumed you'd been around awhile."

Joe laughed. "I have, but in other capacities. They gave me a great opportunity to make a late career change." He looked at the bartender. "I'll have an Oly Light, please."

"We don't have that anymore."

"Okay. A Bud Light, then."

The man moved off to retrieve the order, still wearing a disapproving look.

Clark had been waiting to reply. "I just appreciate anyone coming on such short notice. But did Agent Blackson brief you?"

Joe nodded, repeating the essence of Clark Maxwell's end of the phone call with impressive accuracy.

He could see Maxwell relax.

"Okay, good. That's exactly right." Clark Maxwell looked around, gauging whether anyone else could hear them, or might be trying.

"Perhaps you should start by telling me in detail what you've uncovered about your employer's fleet and why it leads you to think that these aircraft are being used illicitly," Joe prompted.

"All right. But please understand I'm not formally accusing anyone of anything. It's just that, with so many strange things going on and the loss of our friend in that DC-6B yesterday, a number of us are very worried about whether our aircraft can really be trusted."

The beer arrived with a perfunctory thud. The bartender was ambling back to the front of the bar.

"You're worried about maintenance?" Joe asked.

"No, we're worried that there could be extensive unrecorded use of these planes, and that maybe that extra use has made them much more vulnerable to failure."

"Okay."

"And," Clark chuckled ruefully, "I guess I'm also just a bit nervous about being a target."

"A target? I don't understand."

"Well, you know, if there happens to be sabotage going on, it's possible that the crash was caused by someone trying to kill me."

"Why would someone want to kill you, Captain?"

Clark sighed. "Considering you're FBI, is it safe to assume that nothing I tell you will be turned over to Stein Aviation or its owner or anyone else?"

"You mean, will your identity be safe? Yes, it will. But you're not worried that Jerry Stein is watching you, are you?"

"Not really."

"Or secretly flying formation with you in his Lear?"

A sudden look of puzzlement descended over Clark Maxwell's face like a dropped veil, and Joe realized too late his mistake.

"Ah . . ." Clark began, trying to assess the meaning of an FBI representative suddenly knowing the make of Jerry Stein's personal aircraft.

Joe laughed and sat back. "Oh! Sorry. I did some quick research on Jerry Stein, and found him quite a character, and I love aviation, so I was interested in his Lear. Nothing from our files, of course. Just his overall reputation in this business, and through the Internet."

"Oh."

"Sorry to startle you. Checking up on what someone owns can be important."

The veil lifted. "Not a problem."

"You were saying? Or rather, I was asking if you had reason to think Mr. Stein was trying to hurt you?"

"No, I have no direct reason."

Clark related the sudden substitution of Ship 84 for Ship 86, and Joe nodded solemnly as if carefully mulling over the details before answering

"Well, again, Captain, I'm not a real-life agent as yet, but it seems to me that the crew substitution would be pretty good indication that the company was *not* trying to get rid of you, since they pulled you off that flight."

Clark nodded. "It could be read that way, but I need to tell you why I could actually be someone's target." He explained the anonymous article and his shock to find out that apparently a wide variety of people knew he was the writer.

"I don't want to sound paranoid, but it's bound to have angered a few people."

Joe was nodding again. "Reminds me of that great poster of W. C. Fields looking over a deck of cards with the legend, 'Just because you're paranoid doesn't mean they're not out to get you.' "

Maxwell was staring at him in silence, and Joe mentally lashed himself for being too glib.

"Sorry, Captain. I just have one heck of a memory for cartoons and funny greeting cards and such."

"Okay. Look, let me explain something. We fly these planes through hell every day, Agent Michaels, and—"

"Just call me Randy, please."

"All right, Randy. What I was saying, and what you need to know, is that these planes are on the ragged edge all the time. We dive over ridgelines through clouds of smoke and burning gases and rising debris into massive turbulence that knocks us all over the cockpit and puts tremendous stress on the structure. And last year, after the wings came off two different types of airtankers, we all finally found out that there's no one on the planet who really knows whether or not these airplanes can take what we're dishing out, whether we're inspecting them adequately, how to repair cracks, nor even the exact amount of turbulence the average retardant run puts us through. We've all been too busy flying them and putting out fires to do the research, and the operators—fewer than ten companies—aren't eager to pay for anything not absolutely mandated by the FAA or the Forest Service. But over the years, at least we were able to depend on one thing, or so we thought, and that's how many flight hours these old birds have been flown and where and how they've been used. Man, if that assumption is wrong, *too*, then we're just expendable test pilots without a cause, and more of us are going to die."

Joe thought of pulling out his digital voice recorder and securing Maxwell's permission to turn it on to give Jerry the precise tenor of the captain's protests, but handwritten notes would have to do. Montana had a law against recordings obtained under false pretenses, and he didn't want to spook the big pilot with such a request.

"Let me get all the details," Joe replied, "and then the bureau can start looking into whether any laws are being violated. Mind if I take notes?" Joe pulled a small steno pad from his briefcase.

"No. Of course not. Frankly, I'd be concerned if you didn't."

# Chapter 21

Bill Deason leaned toward Clark Maxwell's ear, speaking low.

"If this isn't eerily reminiscent of a World War Two mission briefing, I've been watching the wrong movies."

Clark laughed and nodded, his eyes on the uniformed member of the U.S. Forest Service standing at the front of the room with a pointer and a projected map covering the wall behind him. The man was thin and perhaps six feet tall, with a small mustache and an ill-fitting uniform that seemed to hang from his lank frame like an afterthought. With a mane of scraggly hair and a sad expression below a pair of permanently startled eyes, he looked more like a living cartoon or an actor sent in for comic relief.

"Somewhere between Barney Fife and Ichabod Crane, don'tcha think?" Bill asked.

"Sh-h-h-h!" Clark whispered back, genuinely afraid the man would over-hear and have his feelings hurt.

The atmosphere in the room was mostly somber, but Clark could see a number of the pilots were slipping into the same sense of the surreal; the shock and upset over the loss of Jeff Maze melding with the raised personal stakes in wondering who would be next was creating a suppressed giddi-ness. He felt like laughing outrageously and crying at the same time, and that made no sense. Worse, it was something you didn't discuss with an-other male, and certainly not another pilot—even Bill.

Virtually all the pilots flying Jerry Stein's aircraft were arrayed around the interior of Ops, which had been essentially converted to a briefing room for the occasion. The call had gone out at five-thirty P.M. for as many personnel as possible to attend a special Ops briefing as soon as all the aircraft were on the ground. Neither Bill nor Clark could recall a similar event, and curiosity was running high. On top of it, Jerry Stein and representatives of two other companies whose pilots were working out of West Yellowstone wanted the airtanker pilots to stay for a few minutes afterward.

The pilots, a community of rangy tomcats unable to contain their curiosity, were quietly making bets about everything from a shutdown to an immediate federal takeover.

Jerry Stein was in the room, standing off to one side and watching quietly. The entire assemblage knew he and his copilot had done yeoman's duty in the Skycrane into late afternoon, but he was also a qualified airtanker captain, rated to fly the DC-6B and the P-3 Orion. The fact that he wasn't on the schedule to fly such tankers in the morning had already become gossip fodder, and it was considered anything but inspiring.

"There's a pool on whether he'll go for the Skycrane or a P-3 in the morning," one of the pilots had whispered before Jerry opened the briefing.

"Nothing wrong with the P-3s," Bill had whispered back. "I'll lay money on the Skycrane versus a DC-6, though."

"Okay, people, can we have your undivided attention now?" Rich Lassiter asked. The Forest Service Operations chief looked alarmingly out of place as he waited uncomfortably for Rich to hand it over to him.

"Look, tomorrow morning will likely be the busiest this base has ever seen. It's gonna look like a combat launch out there, and we need to plan for it and talk about it and deal with some crew-duty time issues and the status of the fires."

"We already know the status, Rich," Joel Butler said quietly on the front row. "The forest is on fire. We know it's serious."

Rich looked wounded. He glanced at the Forest Service representative for support, then back at the group.

"In a nutshell, tomorrow will tell whether we catch these fires or lose them like in 1988. Ed Burch here, of the Forest Service, whom many of you know, has come over from Boise to take command of the air ops, and he wants to lay it out for you which fire is which, what the strategy is, and how we're going to keep going with the Baron lead planes permanently grounded and a small hurricane of a south wind propelling things." Rich turned to Burch. "They're all yours, Ed."

Ed Burch nodded, raised a small lavalier microphone to his mouth, and boosted his baritone voice into the room with startling volume from the single-speaker amplifier.

"You say they're all mine?" he repeated, looking at Rich, who was nodding, then back at the group. "Now I really am terrified."

There were a few small chuckles, but Burch realized the group was far too depressed for humor. He formally introduced himself and launched into a detailed recitation of where the six major fires had begun, the damage they had caused so far, and the latest grim assessment of potential control. Dutby hit the story moved north to the V-shaped valley containing the tiny town of Bryarly.

"Thirty percent of our efforts tomorrow morning will go toward containing the Sheep Mountain fire because it may turn. It's forecasted to head for Teton Village and Jackson. Most of that can be handled from the ground, however, so no aerial assets are needed. The Breccia fire and Deer Creek fires have merged. We'll call them the Breccia Complex from here on out, and right now, the majority of the damage is done. We've got hand crews working the north flank, so, as with the Sheep Mountain fire, the only aerial assets we'll need would be light and medium choppers with water buckets for spot-fire suppression. The rest of it, folks—all of our aerial assets—go to a make-or-break goal-line stand right here, at what we're calling North Fork Ridge. We lead off with smokejumpers who will cut line along the ridge while we're bombing the living hell out of the south side of the ridge, and the ground crews will try to outflank the fire in this valley and burn out from the northern flank. Our prospects are dicey. We needed the smokejumpers in there this afternoon, but the winds were too high. The fuel load is moderate to heavy. These are steep slopes with lots of brush and large snags. The fire can be expected to roar up and over the ridge by fourteen hundred. As we've discussed, if it gets past us here and does jump the ridge, not only will we lose Bryarly in this valley beyond to the north, along with anyone still in there, but it's a short shot to Yellowstone."

"Haven't they evacuated Bryarly?" one of the pilots asked.

"There was a bridge there, but one of our well-intentioned vendors did an effective job of demolition on it. He made a nutty attempt to walk a D-8 bulldozer over the rickety thing to get into town. The sign said maximum weight thirty thousand pounds, and the nitwit drove a seventy-three-thousand-pound dozer onto it. We're still trying to remove the dozer and almost lost the nitwit at the controls, but the only way out of town now is by air or on foot, and the foot part involves negotiating this very steep gorge the bridge once spanned. An evacuation is supposed to get started early using three of the Chinooks staging out of Jackson Hole. The Air National Guard is coming in from Missoula to help if needed."

"Are we getting more planes from California, and if so, what type, and when?" Ralph Battaglia asked.

Burch nodded. "Yes. As soon as possible. We just don't know if it's tomorrow morning or what. In fact, as of this afternoon, with the premature departure from Mr. Stein's employment of a captain and two copilots who were presumably spooked by yesterday's accident, we're short on crews as well as airplanes. I mean, we've got essentially two more airplanes than we have crews to fly them. You'll very likely be employed for the entire summer and fall."

Several more questions and answers flowed back and forth as Burch skill-fully dealt with the group before stopping them with an upraised hand and waiting for the background noise to die down.

"Okay, I appreciate you taking the time to hear this. I'd like to speak just to the airtanker pilots for a few minutes. The rest of you, thanks. Get some sleep, and we'll see you in the morning."

There was the usual scuffling of chairs and the buzz of conversation as the room began to clear of all but the airtanker flyers. Burch waited until they were essentially alone.

"Okay, I know you're aware of all the various things at stake here, but just so we're sure we all understand the same thing, and how vital your role is, here's the deal. This is informal and off the record, by the way."

He paused and the room grew even quieter.

"As always with big disasters or near disasters, the country is watching. Now, I'd get in trouble with higher management for saying this, so I didn't, but our country is jaded, ignorant of forest fires, virtually clueless about avi-ation, and geographically challenged to the point that many are going to think Grand Teton is one of the Florida Keys. But here's the point. With the tragic crash yesterday, and Congress looking at whether it should federalize all airtanker activity, all it will take is another aviation accident to pretty much write off this industry. I'm officially neutral because I have to be, but if you still want to be doing this stuff years from now without wearing an Air Force uniform, I suggest you pay attention to safety like never before! No more crashes. No more missing comrades. Please! Hit the targets as best you can, look out for one another, but for God's sake, follow the rules to the letter and don't take any inordinate risks. We'll have enough *ordinate* risks tomorrow as it is."

He glanced at two others standing in the wings.

"I've arranged a reasonably quick weather brief, and we've got the NTSB's man here, Steve Zale, to fill you in on progress regarding Maze's crash."

A meteorologist took over to explain the lull in the winds expected by morning, along with the bad news that they would be back to forty knots by late afternoon; then he turned the meeting over to a middle-aged man in a dark blue jacket with NTSB across the back, who moved to the front of the room from where he'd been standing near the back. Clark looked over at the door, surprised to see Trent Jones standing with Jerry Stein, both with serious, watchful expressions.

Steve Zale introduced himself.

"Folks, just a quick word on the crash investigation," Zale began. "You all know the right wing of Captain Maze's DC-6 failed. It failed at the attach point. We're sending a lot of parts back to D.C. for metallurgical analysis, but there's one thing I *can* tell you. There's been a rumor going around about sabotage, and someone has been purposely stirring up the media and relaying false information about the investigation. You can get sabotage out of your thinking, okay? No one sabotaged that airplane, and at no time did I or anyone at the NTSB ever say we were leaning in that direction."

He looked around the room. "We're dealing with metallurgic failure, guys, plain and simple, and it was not caused by human intervention. In fact, more than likely, and from what I'm seeing, there's a pretty good question of whether one of the causal factors may be the *lack* of human intervention. In other words," he paused, glancing quickly at Stein, "the possible lack of appropriate inspections and maintenance over the years has to be a considered factor."

Jerry Stein was seething inside, his focus so tight on the NTSB investigator that he missed the blur of motion on his left as Trent Jones pushed through the pilots with a look of rage on his face.

"I want to talk to you, Zale!" Trent snapped.

Steve Zale turned toward Stein Aviation's director of maintenance, his voice low and intense.

"You have a problem with my addressing the pilots, Mr. Jones?"

"I sure as hell have a problem with you slandering my maintenance shop and implying we caused that crash."

Zale was nose to nose with Trent and unblinking.

"I did nothing of the sort."

"You know absolutely nothing about this community, Zale! How dare you—"

"I put in twenty-four years with the Forest Service, Mr. Jones, most of it involved with fire fighting. And I'm a pilot. And a licensed A&P mechanic. Care to duel on the basis of pedigree?"

Trent seemed slightly staggered, but regained his voice.

"Okay, so maybe I'm wrong about your background, but what right do you have to crash one of our meetings in your NTSB role?"

"I happen to be standing, do I not, on a floor owned by the United States Forest Service, speaking to a room full of contract pilots hired by, and answerable to, the United States government. Am I right?"

"That's not what I'm talking about, you little—"

"Shut up, Trent!" Jerry said, his voice low and urgent, stopping him just prior to the oncoming epithet. Jerry's hand came down hard on Trent's shoulder, yanking him back slightly. "Mr. Zale, I've got to add my protest to Trent's, though in more measured terms. You as much as slandered us just now."

"That would be a matter of opinion, Mr. Stein, as well as a matter that triggers the question of whether the shoe fits."

"What?" Trent asked, acid dripping from his tone.

Jerry shot Trent another angry glance and pushed him back as he stepped between Steve Zale and the mechanic and answered over his shoulder.

"He's saying we shouldn't feel slandered unless we're guilty of doing something wrong. Right, Mr. Zale?"

"That's correct. And believe me, gentlemen, if I or the board were ready to spotlight a failure in maintenance by your company, I wouldn't beat around the bush, I'd say it straight out. Fact: There is extreme fatigue evident in the structure. Fact: What I've seen so far at that attach point would have been very difficult to ignore in any adequate inspection."

"Mr. Zale, I don't think you have any idea how much abuse these old birds take," Jerry said.

"I know what corrosion looks like, Mr. Stein. And I know what slow propagated cracking looks like. I know what stop-drill holes look like. I know what corrosion control looks like, and I know a lot about inspection techniques. Don't try to snow me. You've got the whole NTSB looking at you over my shoulder."

Jerry inclined his head toward the door.

"May we talk privately?"

Zale nodded as he turned to the pilots.

"Thanks for the chance to speak with you," he said, glancing back at Trent, whose face was almost purple from the effort to restrain himself.

Jerry and Steve Zale pushed through a door into an interior hallway and let the door close behind them.

"Look," Jerry began, "I respect your position, and, now that I know about your background, I respect your experience. I understand you're trying to do the job of a dozen people by yourself, and I also understand you may be incensed by what you think you've found. But you're playing with my reputation and livelihood when you suggest that some massive failure to maintain one of my aircraft has caused a crash and the deaths of two good pilots."

"I call the facts as I find them, sir, and only the facts. That's all I said. I'm sorry if that offends your—"

"Wait! Dammit, listen to me," Jerry said, his hand up.

Zale moved back a half step, as if expecting Jerry to take a swing at him.

"I'm listening."

"You're screwing around with the morale and confidence of a room full of finely tuned, high-strung pilots who are essentially gearing up for combat. You just suggested to them that maybe they can't trust any aircraft maintained by me, and that's virtually everything they're flying."

"I call it like I find it."

"Yeah, well, you also live on planet Earth, and we share the same realities, and here's one for you. If someone pulls out of a dive a little too slow tomorrow morning and crashes because he's afraid the wings aren't strong enough, thanks to your little confidence-eroding speech tonight, are you going to take responsibility?"

"That's a ridiculous analogy."

"Zale, you're not only wrong, you don't know what the hell you're talking about! I've run this outfit for decades, and I know exactly what it takes to keep these airplanes flying. Having a smart-mouthed, arrogant federal jerk in here trying to scare my pilots into mediocrity is very dangerous. You go do your investigation and write up your facts, but stay the hell away from my people."

"You can't intimidate an NTSB investigator, Mr. Stein."

Jerry stood silently as his internal pressure-relief valve failed to squelch the explosion that had been brewing.

"Oh, I don't have to intimidate you, Zale. Your chairman's going to do it for me, as soon as I have a little chat with him. I'd start thinking of alternate employment if I were you."

Steve Zale started to turn away, but Jerry caught his arm.

"You think I'm bluffing?"

Steve carefully pried his hand away before looking him in the eye.

"You know something, Mr. Stein? I honestly couldn't care less."

———

The remainder of the group had begun to leave the Ops area when Ralph Battaglia caught Ed Burch on the way out the door.

"Mr. Burch, excuse me. I need a clarification of what you were saying back in there about Jeff Maze?"

"Sure. And you are?"

Battaglia introduced himself and stood with his hands on his hips, and Ed Burch responded with hands thrust deep in the pockets of his ill-fitting uniform pants.

"Are you implying that Jeff Maze was taking a risk flying straight and level? I'll admit Jeff was a cowboy at times, but he was also the best damn pilot I've ever met."

Battaglia's tone was hard and hostile.

"Absolutely not," Ed Burch replied. "I wasn't implying that Jeff Maze was doing anything wrong, not that he hadn't been a hot dog in the past, as you just acknowledged. I'm just saying what I'm saying: Please do your best not to litter the parks with shredded aerospace aluminum."

"We are doing our best, thank you, and I think your tone is patronizing and offensive."

Burch sighed heavily and leaned toward the pilot. "I'm sorry you took it that way. Look, remember where the priorities are in terms of political acceptability, okay? I'm trying to help you guys see the bigger picture, not insult you. This program hangs by a thread as we stand here. Politically."

"Hey, you know what, Mr. Burch?" Battaglia replied. "I don't give a rat's ass about politics, okay?"

"Well, you'd better wake up if you want to be dropping pink stuff on fires for a paycheck much longer. We've got to be sensitive to everything from safety to basic environmental issues."

The copilot snorted. "Environment, huh? I wondered when this discussion would somehow get around to the preservation of useless species. We've got to worry so the bunny huggers won't get their knickers in a twist, right?"

"We're all environmentalists, Mr. Battaglia, but that's only part of the public equation." He studied the copilot's face. "I'll admit their sensitivities are often *as* misplaced as those folks who build houses in the middle of the forest and refuse to clear the brush and fuel around them, yet get irate when we can't immediately save them from wildfires."

"The environmental groups couldn't care less how many of us die fighting these fires," Battaglia snapped.

"That's simply not—"

"To the average hysterical environmentalist, okay, our broken bodies on the forest floor simply constitute unacceptable pollution of the pristine nature of the ecosphere."

"You're very bitter, aren't you?" Burch asked him.

"Damn right. I'm merely giving voice to the fact that in their wild-eyed view we humans are a fluke of the universe who have no right to be here. Forests are for bears. Barbecued or otherwise."

Burch nodded, studied his shoes for a few seconds, and looked Ralph Battaglia in the eye.

"Let me put it this way. You work under contract for the U.S. government through the Forest Service, and we serve the entire plurality of the people of the United States. That includes homeowners encroaching on wildlands as well as environmentalists of all stripes. They're not your enemy, Mr. Battaglia. And frankly, neither am I."

# Chapter 22

"So what do you think, Clark?" Bill Deason asked as he unwrapped a cigar and searched for his lighter.

The Forest Service building and the Operations room were fifty feet behind them as they stood in the waning light watching as orange and diffused reds filled the western sky in alternating light and dark streaks over an adjacent mountain range. The deep blue of the sky overhead was already revealing a tantalizing sample of the starfield beyond Earth's gaseous envelope, as if the process of sunset was a slow curtain pull in preparation for a stellar nightly show too many never thought to catch.

The winds had diminished across West Yellowstone, relaxing into a stiff, pleasant breeze of fifteen knots and sixty-eight degrees, carrying the perfume of the surrounding forests and fields and an occasional hint of wood smoke from various fireplaces in town.

"The night is attended by metallic ghosts," Bill said rather absently, drawing a quick and puzzled look from Clark, "and they be searching for their masters."

"What?"

Bill laughed and shook his head apologetically. "I'm light-years from being a poet, but evenings like this inspire even the roughest attempts at verse. And our ramp *is* overflowing with aerospace fossils."

"Ah, yes . . ." Clark agreed.

Bill finished snipping the end from his varietal cigar and, working against the fifteen-knot wind, fussed with igniting the tip with his propane lighter.

"God can inspire poems in the night," Bill said between establishing puffs.

"That's a beautiful line, Bill."

"Not mine. Comes from a book published down in Austin and written by a wonderful, indefatigable Texas poet named Peggy Lynch. I think she said 'songs,' though, rather than 'poems,' but it has the same ring."

Clark pushed his hands deep in the pockets of his leather flight jacket against the gathering chill of the evening.

"You asked what I thought?"

"Yep."

"It's a jumble of worries. Did you notice that little hallway confrontation between Jerry and the NTSB guy?"

Bill nodded as he took a long puff on his cigar and smiled at Clark.

"My manners are slipping, Clark. Would you like one of these cigars? I have several."

"No, thanks, Bill."

"Sorry to interrupt. You were saying . . ."

"Well, I've dumped everything we know into the FBI's hands, for all the good that will do. But we're still standing here asking the same question. Is it safe to fly our airplanes?"

Bill nodded, his eyes on the emerging starfield overhead and Venus, which was sparkling like a diamond in a spotlight. "It doesn't help to have the sabotage theory quashed, although I couldn't quite figure out who would want to sabotage us or why, you know? It didn't seem logical, even if someone was angry with you over that article."

Clark nodded. "That was a chilling little announcement back there, but knowing the wing failed on its own just brings us back to what I found out here early this morning, and I just don't know what to think. I'm flying Tanker Eighty-eight again in the morning. Should I be gentle on her? Should I . . . should I go out there right now and claw open the wing-root inspection panels and see if it looks like anyone's stuck their flashlight in there in the past decade? Hell, Bill, I think your P-3 is safe, partially because it's nowhere near as old. But I have a very sick feeling that the repair shop in Florida somehow helped Jerry or Trent slide at least a few of the airplanes away from the Sandia people."

"You mean, escape the inspections?"

"Yeah. Somehow."

"Just pencil-whipped the logs, you mean?"

"Well, Sandia would never do that, but they could have been hoodwinked somehow."

"Or, as you pointed out, there's another possibility. The inspections were done, but someone's flown the heart out of these birds off the books since then."

"Which is why having Misty run away today is also very worrisome."

"I hear that."

"You're sure she's gone, by the way?"

Bill took a deep breath and grimaced. "Jeff's truck disappeared in mid-afternoon from the parking lot, and Misty never came back. Judy called the funeral home handling Jeff's body. They've got shipping instructions from

Misty to send it back to California. No, Clark, she's gone. She didn't want to talk to us about what she knows. And we have no legal right to have her stopped."

"Do you suppose Jerry's responsible for her leaving?" Clark asked. A sudden thought came to him. "Hey, wait a minute!"

"What?"

"You think there's any chance Jerry actually *owns* that shop in Florida?"

"On the sly, you mean?"

"Yep. I hope I'm wrong, but one of the things we were all relying on was that an independent shop had inspected our wings on the DC-6B fleet. If that's *his* shop and it was all an exercise in building false confidence—"

"There would be ownership records somewhere, right?" Bill interrupted, his interest equally piqued.

"I don't know. If it's a private company, maybe not, but I can get on the Internet and check. I mean, Bill, you know I don't want to do anything to hurt Jerry."

"Of course. Unless he's cheating or putting us in jeopardy."

"That's the only exception. I mean Jerry and I have been friends for a lot of years."

"But you can't trust him anymore than I can, right?"

Clark looked at Bill carefully, finding resigned sadness in the statement, as if human nature would always disappoint him but he was accepting of it.

"You know what I'd do if I were you, Clark?" Bill asked.

"What? Find a new line of work before morning?" he chuckled. "I wasn't even supposed to be here this summer."

"Leaving's an option, I suppose. But, no. Jeff's bird came apart while he was straight and level. When you lift off in the morning, keep it at ten feet above the runway, suck up the gear, accelerate, then pull the hell out of her at the end. Load the wings up very quickly. If the wing's going to fail, it'll fail right there and you've got a fighting chance of surviving a fairly short drop to a flat surface."

Clark started chuckling, the chuckle growing to a full laugh.

"What's the matter with that?" Bill asked with a smile.

"Just the improbability of surviving such a disaster, that's all. Plus the certainty that the NTSB would cite pilot error in loading up the wings after takeoff. It's kind of a catch-22. I can't prove the wings are ready to come off until the wings come off."

"Yeah. Another Yogiism. It ain't over till it's over."

"No, Bill, I think I'm stuck. I've got a job to do, and there's a huge threat out there in terms of the devastation that fire is wreaking, and that's with no proof that our airplanes are anything other than boilerplate reliable. Of course Rusty and I will do the best preflight we can tomorrow, but if there's a hidden failure waiting to make me a ballistic object for a very short downward ride, I have no professionally safe way of stopping the process."

"You'll be okay, Clark."

"I hope."

"No, my friend, I can more or less . . . well, you'll think I'm a nutcase."

"What?"

"Well, it's not auras or anything New Age like that. It's just that I can more or less feel something about most folks, and maybe it's nothing but agitation, but with Jeff the other night? I had a really sick feeling that something bad was going to happen. I shrugged it off, though. You can imagine what Jeff's reaction would have been if I'd said anything."

"I sure can. So, what are you reading about me?" Clark asked.

"That's why I say you're going to be fine. I can just feel it. It's like when I'm gardening, I can almost feel the plants and whether they need water and such."

"Hookay," Clark said.

"Yeah, I know. Just indulge a dotty old man."

"So I'll be okay?"

"You bet. You'll be fine tomorrow. You'll be back here ready to go to the Coachman and pick up something very female."

"Yeah, right," Clark replied, his head filled suddenly with the image of Karen Jones. He shook the image away. All in good time.

"How much longer for you, Bill?" Clark asked, wondering if it was appropriate to bring up the subject of retirement.

Bill Deason removed his cigar and looked at Clark as if he'd never seen him before. "Not long, I imagine. But I can't read my own future."

"No, no, no. I didn't mean about your *life*. . . . I meant, over how many more seasons are you planning to bomb fires with airplanes?"

Bill's easy laughter was a relief. "Oh! Until they stop me, I suppose. Judy and I have some money socked away, but jeez, this is such a sweet deal. Work five months doing something you love and play seven months with the resulting income? That's pretty good. And I mean, I've got my motor home, my lady, and my bedroom all in the same place, and Judy's happy. No, I'm pretty happy, too, Clark. I'll stick around until we run out of burning trees, or until Congress fires us."

# Chapter 23

The need to talk to Karen Jones had become a mild fever by midafternoon, but Clark had kept it at bay. He couldn't deny his disappointment that she hadn't called or responded. Surely she'd been handed his note and heard his phone message. He'd been resisting the temptation to call her hotel again, convincing himself he could handle the discontent of no contact the same way he'd learned to resist aspirin for a headache.

*She'll get in touch when she's ready. She probably doesn't want me to see her bruises.*

He'd accompanied Bill to the Deason motor home but turned down Judy's offer of dinner, knowing she'd be quietly relieved to have Bill to herself. Instead, he drove to the Coachman, lured by the feeling that Karen might be in the lounge. He pulled up in front of the hotel and sat idling for a few minutes, trying to decide what he would say or do if she really was inside.

*Why am I here?* he asked himself. *I'm exhausted. I should go back and get some sleep.*

Going inside would undoubtedly result in his having to engage in unwanted conversations with some of the pilots, along with buying drinks and telling stories and pressing the limits of his endurance. His independent nature was pulling at him, suggesting that real men didn't worry about fatigue and that only wimps ducked the opportunity to buy their fellows a round, but the core of quiet responsibility that still governed him managed to overrule the rebel.

Besides, Karen was not likely to be there.

Clark put the truck in gear and quietly pulled away to drive the four blocks to his darkened rental house, his headlights catching the eyes of some small animal peeking around the corner as he pulled into the driveway.

*What is that? A raccoon, maybe?*

The glowing eyes disappeared and he got out, standing for a moment in the cool of the night air, trying to reload the memories of how much he'd enjoyed this log house in past summers, and especially the large river-rock fireplace that drew so well and was even wide enough to cook in. But tonight there was a loneliness to the place he hadn't felt before. It left him puzzled as he turned the key in the door and felt the coldness of the darkened living room suck at him like a vacuum, as if the plasma of warmth and personal contentment that had marked his residency over time had been draining away and he'd failed to notice.

He snapped on as many lights as he could on the way to the kitchen, then returned to the fireplace and busied himself with old newspapers to build a quick, roaring fire before returning to the kitchen to grind the beans for a late pot of coffee. He turned on the satellite music system, switched on a floor lamp, and cracked open a window. With his coffee in an oversized mug and bearing just the right percentage of condensed milk, he returned to the small living room and pulled one of the easy chairs in front of the fire, wondering absently if he should call his mother.

*What am I thinking?*

The sudden pain of remembrance that she was no longer on the other end of that long-memorized number jolted him for a second. Her death two years ago had occurred with her only son at her side in a Tampa hospital, but he kept forgetting. After Rosanna had left him, his mom had become his only real confidante. There had been a mature ease in talking to her from wherever he happened to be in what had become his almost gypsyesque aviation career after leaving the airtanker business. He remembered the long calls to her during his temporary postings in Malaysia, Australia, Africa, and Saudi Arabia over those two years, and the steadiness of the advice and love that had helped sustain him.

"Who's your best friend?" she asked him once.

"Why, you, Mom," he'd replied.

"No, Clark, a mother is a mother. Surely you have someone, male or female, to talk to when the days are hard. Right? Someone you can call other than me?"

"I did. Her name was Rosanna, Mom," he'd answered, grateful that she'd dropped the subject without further digging. The truth was that he had many acquaintances but no best friends, and that saddened him.

The sounds of a car maneuvering into a parking place out front escaped his attention at first, but the soft knock on the front door instantly cut through his thoughts. He opened the door to find Karen Jones on the doorstep, a stern expression on her face.

"Karen! What a nice—"

"Just invite me in, please," she interrupted.

"Well . . . certainly." He stepped out of the way and let her pass, closing the door behind her. "Let me pull up a chair by the fire for you."

"No, thanks," she said, turning. "I'll stand. I can't stay."

"All right." Clark stood in confusion, one hand out in a questioning gesture. "Could I at least get you some coffee?"

"No." The retort was far more sharp than she'd intended, but there it was. Karen cleared her throat, glanced at her feet as if positioning her toes on some imaginary mark, and locked eyes with him. "If I want an all-encompassing male protector, I'll go to the web and advertise for one. Understood?"

He was shaking his head slowly, his hands pushed deep in the pockets of his slacks. "Not really, though I am concerned about the bruises I see on your face. May I ask what you're talking about?"

"I told you last night that what happened between me and my estranged husband was not your responsibility, right?"

"Well," he began slowly, watching her response, "Karen, I apologized for anything I did that appeared to put you in a compromising position, and you said not to worry about it."

"That's right. And that's where it should have ended."

"That . . . *is* where it ended."

"Oh? And I suppose rushing over to the hotel this morning and embarrassing me with an impassioned plea to the desk clerk for information on where I was, and how I was, and which room I was in doesn't count?"

Clark sighed and cleared his throat. "We were getting ready to go early this morning, and my copilot said he'd seen you at the front desk looking like you'd been beaten up. And I can tell by looking at you now that he was right. I'll admit I was worried. I left you a message."

"Like you left a message for Trent?"

"Sorry?"

"Like the sophomoric 'Leave my woman alone' thing you wrote on his windshield?"

Clark shook his head slowly and began moving toward the fireplace before stopping to look back at her intently. "Karen, I have absolutely no idea what you're talking about."

He could see her expression change as a look of uncertainty clouded her lovely features.

"Are you going to tell me you didn't scrawl a message on his windshield last night after we said good night?"

"On his *windshield?* Absolutely not. I don't even know what his car looks like. And for heaven's sake, Karen 'Stay away from my ............!' " He laughed, a short staccato sound. "That is decidedly *not* my linguistic style, even when I'm scribbling on windshields."

There was no reply, and he tried again.

"Karen, who in the world told you that?"

"You didn't do it?"

"No."

She broke eye contact and looked down with disgust.

"Was it Trent?" he asked gently.

She nodded.

"Well," he sighed, "if someone wrote anything on his car—"

"Truck," she interrupted.

"Okay, his truck. It was not me. And, I did nothing this morning in front of that desk clerk that would have embarrassed you. I asked if you had checked out, and I did ask for your room number, but when he snapped at me that he couldn't tell me, I asked for the house phone instead and very quietly, and out of his earshot, left you a voice message."

"That's all?" she asked, the intensity gone from her voice.

"That's all."

Karen moved to a chair and sat down, sighing. "I think I'd like that coffee now."

"Gladly," he said, moving toward the kitchen and then pausing. "Unless you'd like some wine or scotch instead?"

She smiled sheepishly. "Single malt?"

Clark brightened. "Yes, as a matter of fact. A new bottle, even."

Karen nodded as she pulled her hair back from her face. "Please."

He reached into the small pantry and removed a bottle of fourteen-year-old Oban, then retrieved two tumblers before returning to the living room and pulling a larger leather chair next to his by the fire. The air in the room was still chilly, and she nodded gratefully and moved to the chair, taking one of the tumblers and letting him pour, then waiting for him to settle in next to her as she kept her eyes on the fire.

"I'm very embarrassed, Clark."

"That's all right."

"No . . . I just automatically jumped to the conclusion that . . . that . . ."

"That I was a controlling male getting ready to suffocate you?"

She nodded. "And that you could have left him that stupid note. I was suspicious when he told me, and I should have listened to my instincts. He's obviously lying."

"Karen, other than the night four years ago when we first met on that mountain, we've only had one drink together. This is number two. Why . . . would you . . ."

"Think that?" She shook her head sadly, shifting her position, the creak of rich leather accompanying the movement. It was still slightly cold in the room, but the perfume of wood smoke and the crackling fire were working to transform it. There was the sound of the wind through the partially opened window accompanied by the moan of pine needles and the tones of a wind chime somewhere distant.

She tucked her legs under her. "I guess I'm conditioned."

"Trent, in other words?"

She tossed her head back and smiled at him briefly, the chagrin still showing, the orange and yellow light of the fire dancing off the contours of her face, bathing her in soft beauty as she pursed her lips and looked for a place to begin.

"It's a long story. I don't think I'm spring-loaded to an 'All guys are pigs' mentality. At least not completely. But, obviously, I *am* spring-loaded to *some* bad assumptions. I am so sorry."

"It's about possessiveness, then?"

"Yes. A bunch of boyfriends over time who must have been Saudis in disguise. All sweetness and caring until they thought they owned me, and then I became merely a possession, and I can't *tell* you how much I hate that attitude."

"I'm getting a pretty fair idea."

She turned to look at him. "But you're not like that, right?"

Clark shook his head. "God, no."

"I mean, I need to know that you don't have it in your head that just because a girl likes you, you then become her white knight, her protector."

He was shaking his head and laughing softly. "Is this an audition?"

"Sorry?"

"I mean, no, you're right, I do *not* presume to think that just because a woman agrees to date me that I'm somehow appointed her defender, nor that she even needs one."

"Good."

"Are you?"

"Sorry?"

"Agreeing to date me?" he asked, astounded that those words had actually left his mouth.

She looked at him in mild surprise for a moment, as if replaying her words in her mind, and then smiled.

"I . . . suppose so. After last night, why not?" she asked.

"No reason."

"Provided you ask, you know, sometime," she added.

"I will."

"Good."

"When you're ready."

A pregnant silence settled in between them for a few seconds, but even though she was looking at the fire, he could see she was smiling, as was he.

"Do you mind if I ask you what happened last night?"

"Not at all." As she told him the details of Trent's midnight attack, including her bodily tossing him into the hallway, Karen started to chuckle. "He was a very surprised boy. He didn't think this poor little piece of female fluff could fight back."

Even through his disgust, Clark found himself smiling. "So . . . it hadn't dawned on him that his wife leaps from airplanes because she's a physically fit and conditioned smokejumper?"

"Oh, but she's a girl, Clark! And you can beat up a mere girl all you want as long as you marry her first. That marriage license is really just a deed to the woman, you see. Anyway," she said with a dismissive gesture, "you're right. I can hold my own."

He reached for the bottle of Oban and added an inch to her tumbler, and she thanked him and sniffed the golden brown liquor, inhaling deeply.

"I can smell peat in this, and maybe a little salt air."

"You're sniffing Scotland, lass," he said.

"Ever been there?"

His smile turned wistful as he nodded, his eyes on the fire. "Long ago."

"Not a good memory, then?"

"An old memory, involving my ex-wife, Rosanna, from when things were good. We spent the summer there touring around. She was—is—a writer. Romance novels, mostly, but she's nosed into the mainstream now and is making good money. I'm really happy for her."

"But the trip to Scotland?" she prompted.

"Yes. She wrote it off as research and brought me along, and it was idyllic. Castles and ramparts and Loch Ness and making love in the heather, which has its hazards."

"I can imagine."

"Anyway, I love Scotland, Ireland, Wales, Cornwall."

"You're Celtic?"

He nodded. "Way back there somewhere. The Campbell clan, we think."

"I'm supposed to be mostly Irish," she said, watching as he gazed into the fire and letting a few more moments of silence settle in. "I think the divorce hit you pretty hard. Is that why you suddenly retired from the airtanker business?"

He nodded. "Flying these old tubs takes a lot of concentration, Karen. Concentration and a pretty good dose of self-confidence. Losing her kind of destroyed both for a while." He looked over at her and smiled. "But time heals all wounds."

She chuckled. "I always thought it was the other way around. Time wounds all heels."

"Do we *have* to talk about Trent again?"

She laughed more easily than before and smiled at him as she took a rather substantial sip of the scotch. She lowered the glass, reached for the bottle to pour some more, and watched the fire, her body swaying slightly and suggesting the possibility that the evening had included a drink or two before she'd reached his door.

"I'm really feeling this, but it is so good."

"You might want to take it easy on that stuff, Karen. It's eighty-six proof and . . . potent."

She smiled, her tongue playing around the corner of her mouth and her head cocked. "I may need potent right now. To starry nights." She raised her glass to his and clinked, sipped some more of the Oban, and then looked at him quizzically. "So where are you from, Clark? I don't think I ever asked."

"I'm from Montana, and the U.S. Air Force." He told her about growing up on a succession of bases, as well as the Washington crash that threw his young world into turmoil.

"I never met a Montana boy who didn't love horses. You, too?"

He smiled. "Oh, yeah. I spent a collegiate summer riding fence for a huge ranch in Idaho. I even rodeoed for a while after college. I was pretty lucky to get through it without breaking anything valuable. But . . . I quit all that when I learned to fly and got my first flying job."

He looked at her closely.

"How about you, Karen? I mean, where did you grow up? Where did you go to school? Why did you develop this odd propensity for jumping out of perfectly good airplanes, that sort of thing."

"I'm a Seattle-area girl from a little place called Gig Harbor, across the bridge from Tacoma. We had horses, too, and my dad loved to camp. He's still a practicing surgeon who probably should have been a mountain man. I'm the youngest of four kids, three raucous brothers and me. We grew up with constant tents and hikes and campfires, just looking for the next excuse to be outdoors. I loved it! My mother suffered through it. Roughing it to her was sleeping on unpressed sheets, but she was always there to remind me how a young lady should handle the wilderness."

"How?"

"In a proper dress with makeup," she said with a laugh.

"But the leaping out of airplanes thing?"

"Well, that was . . . my undergrad degree was in forestry at the Univer sity of Montana, and I discovered this smokejumping outfit on the edge of town. . . ."

He nodded, well aware of Missoula and its prideful association with the Missoula Smokejumpers and their dangerous art of jumping into forest fires.

"Anyway, after two summers with the Helena Hotshots, I rookied in Missoula. I jumped every summer afterward. It was great money, too, for college. Dad may have been a successful doctor, but we were taught to pull our own weight financially."

She yawned and fell silent for a while, and Clark tried unsuccessfully to stifle a sympathetic yawn of his own as he patiently watched the fire, letting them both enjoy the silence of the moment. There was a soft buzzing sound in the room audible now over the hiss and crackle of the fire, and he realized it was Karen snoring.

He turned and watched her before leaning over to move her tumbler to the hearth. Reluctantly, he glanced at his watch and read a few minutes past ten, wondering whether to wake her. There was a shadowy feeling of guilt hovering around his enjoyment of her closeness, but he refused to consider it. The comfort of having her so relaxed in his presence was profoundly soothing.

Nevertheless, she had to be sharp and alert in the morning, and would need to get ready in her hotel room several blocks away. As much as he'd love to sit and watch her all night, duty was calling.

"Karen?" he said softly.

An eyelid fluttered, then closed again.

"Karen, do you want me to take you back to the hotel now?"

She almost nodded, then stirred, her eyes opening briefly.

"I'm sorry," she said, rubbing her eyes. "I fell asleep."

"Just for a few minutes."

"Lemme . . . rest a few . . . minutes more. Okay?"

She was asleep again before he could reply.

He got to his feet quietly and moved to the kitchen to tidy up the counter and load the coffeemaker for morning, then returned to the deeply satisfying self-appointed task of watching her sleep, until it was obvious she wasn't going to wake up easily.

Clark moved to the bedroom and pulled down the covers, then returned to the fireplace and gently scooped Karen from the chair, took her into the bedroom, and carefully laid her in his bed, removing her shoes before pulling up the covers.

She snuggled into the pillow and smiled in her sleep before turning on her side, and he stood looking at her for the longest time, amazed that his thoughts were not of possible future intimacy with her or how beautiful she was, but just how good it felt to have her trust—even if the scotch had inadvertently helped relax her in his presence.

Clark left a small night-light on in the bedroom and pulled the door shut behind him after retrieving his windup alarm clock, which he set for five forty-five. He pulled a blanket and pillow out of the living room closet and lay down on the sofa, falling asleep almost instantly.

# Chapter 24

The television station helicopter pilot nudged the Bell Jet Ranger a few degrees to the left as he worked the joystick camera controller with his left hand and watched the image in the high-definition monitor. The autofocus feature of the sophisticated 75 to 1 telephoto lens on the ball-turret camera under the helicopter's nose played with the sharpness of the picture momentarily, its servo motors moving the set point back and forth before it steadied out, leaving a crystal-clear image of the amazing sight below.

"Are we up on the bird?" he asked, referring to the communications satellite. The operator of the satellite truck parked on the edge of West Yellowstone below answered in a sleepy voice, affirming that the video picture was being received back in Atlanta. The pilot could tell the man was practically sleepwalking after driving the truck all night from Denver.

But, he thought, all the effort was going to be well worth it. It was a huge story with a goal-line stand against the possible reignition of Yellowstone Park and the fight to keep the eastern side of the Grand Tetons from burning.

The image on his screen looked for all the world like a bomber launch from wartime England, and it was going out live over CNN worldwide. Dozens of large propellers turned slowly on the airfield below as a long procession of airtankers trundled toward the end of West Yellowstone's single runway, preparing for battle.

"Stand by," the director was saying back in Atlanta as the voice of the anchor introduced the shot.

*"We're going to go live now to West Yellowstone, Montana, for this helicopter shot of what will be one of the most massive airborne attacks in recent memory against a forest fire. The airport is on the west side of Yellowstone Park, and you're seeing the start of what will be an extremely critical fight today to control four major, and dozens of minor, wildfires seriously threatening the two parks. The force of fixed-wing airtankers on your screen include DC-6s and DC-7s, former airliners converted to drop thousands of pounds of fire-*

*retardant fluid. In addition, there are several ex-Navy P-3 Orions and a vari-
ety of other support airplanes and helicopters. We'll be bringing you live
coverage of this aerial battle during the day from West Yellowstone and Jackson Hole, where no fewer than forty-two helicopters are also battling the
blazes."*

IN FLIGHT, TWIN OTTER JUMPSHIP, THIRTY-FIVE MILES SOUTHEAST
OF WEST YELLOWSTONE—SEVEN-THIRTY A.M.

*At least I'm awake now!* Karen thought to herself as she rubbed her eyes and
balanced the thermos coffee mug on her knee. It was amazingly cold inside
the passenger cabin of the Otter with the entry door removed for the upcoming jump. It would be a lot warmer in the cockpit in the empty copilot's
seat, but if her jumpmates had to suffer with the cold, so would she.

Karen hunkered closer to the sidewall in the uncomfortable cloth seat
and sipped the coffee, recalling her surprise at waking up in the wee hours
in Clark's bedroom still clothed but tucked in beneath a warm comforter.
Her postsleep confusion had been brief, and a quick look at her watch had
told her it was time to get moving.

She remembered the pleasant conversation in front of the fire, but she
couldn't recall how she'd ended up in the bedroom. Clark was sound asleep
on the couch, and she was going to leave him that way, but his alarm clock
corked off as she was tiptoeing back to the bedroom to look for her shoes.

He got up and made coffee, and she lingered as long as practical at the
door to thank him, luxuriating in the warmth of the rekindled fire and feeling as if she'd been pulled from a delicious dream that she'd rather stay and
finish. She wanted to recall more of what they'd talked about, but so far it
was a comfortable blur, and a nice counterpoint to the freezing reality of
the Otter's cabin.

Herb Jellison had been irritatingly bright-eyed when she'd reached the
briefing room. He was looking around at her now from the captain's seat,
flashing a thumbs-up sign and mouthing, "Ten minutes." The winds, as
briefed, were apparently holding within limits for the jump.

The North Fork fire had already consumed six thousand acres, and by
four A.M. the flame front had closed to within nine miles of the critical ridge
they were aiming for. Karen knew the fact that they'd lost an entire day
in getting to the ridge might mean the effort was doomed from the start,
but they were all up for the try—especially with a fleet of tankers preparing
to follow them onto the ridge with tens of thousands of gallons of retar
dant.

Once more Herb reached around from the cockpit and motioned for Karen.

She hurriedly finished the coffee and stowed the thermos lid before moving forward and climbing into the copilot's seat, where a headset awaited.

"Can you hear me okay?" he asked.

"Roger that, Herb."

"We'll be over the target momentarily."

"I see it ahead," she said, her eyes fastened to the right on the huge plume of smoke from the advancing blaze. The sun seemed barely over the horizon, and through the smoke a soft version of daylight was bathing the area. The sunlight would become more harsh and challenging through the day as it rose higher in the rarified atmosphere, the rays punching through increasing veils of smoke to deliver light and warmth and damaging UV-B radiation as well. The entire squad would need to keep drinking water to stay hydrated.

"Okay," he briefed, "I'll bring us around into the wind, southbound."

Karen pulled off the headset and patted him on the shoulder before climbing out of the seat and getting in position in the doorway. The spotter, who had just returned and strapped into his safety harness, was already there. Herb turned when they were just past the ridge, then circled around and returned again, flying north to south over the small meadow as Karen nodded and the spotter released the streamer to test the wind. They watched it fall, then reversed course and dropped a second one, calculating the windspeed and the impact point, which was almost squarely in the targeted meadow.

"Drift is about a thousand feet," Karen said, noting the spotter's nodded agreement.

"Much better."

"Okay, Herb!" she yelled above the roar. "Next time is a live run."

All the members of her squad were on their feet now, the first two coming forward and hooking on to the static line, a fixed piece of wire running the length of the Otter's cabin that yanked the parachutes open as the jumpers left the door.

"Winds are about eighteen maximum right now, from the south," she relayed. "Come in as hot as you can . . . the air is very turbulent right over the target."

"Gotcha," George Baird replied, slapping his partner on the shoulder as the spotter watched the terrain unfold again below and timed their exit.

"Now!"

In rapid succession the "stick" of two men jumped from the doorway, their round chutes opening instantly. Karen felt the same visceral thrill as always watching the two canopies suddenly go rigid, jerking each jumper from 120 miles per hour down to a gentle descent rate in the space of a few seconds.

They watched the first two overshoot the zone slightly but land safely, one of them getting his chute under control and unholstering his radio almost immediately.

"Hey, Triple Nickel. Adjust your drop path another hundred feet south."

"Roger that," Herb replied on the air-to-ground channel.

The second stick nailed their landing, and with two more passes and two more sticks, it was Karen's turn.

Stepping out the door of an airplane in flight was an incredible rush, no matter how many times she did it, but getting to the door with almost eighty pounds of gear was awkward.

Karen thrust herself out of the Otter and into space a quarter-mile south of the meadow and more than twenty-five hundred feet above the steep, forested slope directly below. The bracing rush of cold air and the immediate snap of the harnesses as her chute opened were exhilarating, and she let out a small yelp of glee before getting down to the business of modifying her chute by pulling free two of the lines on each side. The so-called "four-line modification" gave her a slight ability to steer by banking left and right and riding the wind.

Karen checked her speed and banked left a bit, calculating the descent rate, aware of the strong aroma of burning wood in the air, the calling card of the approaching inferno. The sky to the north was incredibly blue against the deep green of the forest, and it was hard not to drink in the beauty of the living portrait before her and just enjoy the ride. But miscalculations could be very dangerous and land her in a tree, or worse.

She tore her eyes away from the horizon and concentrated on the quick mental calculations needed to make the landing. All but the first sticks had sailed right into the middle of the drop zone, and she was on the same course. She would let her flexed legs absorb the impact of landing and roll in what was called a PLF, or parachute landing fall, then race to unhook at least one of her shoulder harnesses to collapse the parachute. Any delay in getting out of the harness in a stiff wind could give a billowing chute time to yank its jumper back in the air and over a cliff, or drag him or her through trees and rocks.

She could see her entire squad on the ground working hard to stow their chutes, and almost before she'd become used to the ride, it was over and she was bouncing back to her feet to release and collapse her chute before verifying that everyone was in good shape. The Twin Otter made its approach for the equipment drop, and three chutes bloomed overhead, the packs landing almost perfectly in the middle of the tiny meadow. There was one last, low pass, and Herb dipped the wing before heading back to base, leaving the squad in the process of unpacking the rest of their gear.

When the chain saws had been fueled and the other equipment readied, they spread out quickly to scout out and tie in any natural breaks and light fuel before returning for a quick tactical briefing.

Karen spread a laminated map on the ground, and they gathered around to review the plan.

"Remember, we're going to split the squad with half of us cutting line this way, east, and the other half working away to the west. This saddle is less than a mile wide, and when we're comfortable, I want to test burn out some of the line, then plan to backfire from the scratch line. So we'll need a scratch line wide enough to burn out from. When we get the tankers in, we'll start them on the north side, then down the ridge south of us, running east to west, and soak a line clear across the mountain, and have them work up toward where we want the burnout boundary."

"How long do you think we have, Karen?" Scott asked.

She shrugged. "At least eight hours, maybe longer. The plan for us, as soon as the flame front gets close enough, is to take up a safe defensive position along the ridge up there to the west side and wait. If we succeed in stopping it and it doesn't jump the ridge, we can get into the valley quickly to douse any remaining firebrands and spot fires that blow over. Otherwise, we hike out along the ridge westbound. We're literally standing on the Continental Divide, so if we stay out of the trees and grasses, we're okay, except for any lightning strikes."

Four chain saws came to life as the squad split and moved out in opposite directions. Karen checked her watch and glanced again at the veil of smoke approaching from the south. On the radio they would be known as "Jones plus eight." On the ground they would be scrambling. *This fire is breathing down our necks, and there's no question,* she thought, *that this is going to be a close race.*

<br>

FOREST SERVICE OPERATIONS, WEST YELLOWSTONE AIRPORT

Rich Lassiter glanced out of the Operations window again, confirming that the DC-6B with "84" on its tail was still sitting on the ramp fifteen minutes past departure time. He could see the propellers on engines three and four turning, but one and two were still static, and the crew entry steps were still snuggled up to the entrance door.

*Dammit!* Rich thought, pulling the phone up and punching in the number of Jerry Stein's office across the runway.

*He's going to be placed out of service shortly.*

Timing would be everything today, and if even one airtanker came and went out of sequence, it would be a problem, especially for the number of tankers and the short turnaround time.

Rich rubbed his eyes as he waited for the line to ring. He'd had less than an hour of sleep because of all the careful planning, and his temper was razor-thin.

Jerry answered on the second ring.

"Yeah?"

"Jerry? Rich. Are you flying Eighty-four or not?"

"Yes. Of course. I . . . just got delayed here with a call."

"Man, I need you off the ground, or I need you to put a relief pilot in your place."

There was a hesitation on the other end, and Rich felt a wave of disgust roll through him at the thought that this might be one of Jerry's orchestrated little charades. He'd made a huge deal during the morning brief of flying one of his own DC-6s to calm the rumors that he was afraid of them, and now this. "Jerry?"

"Hey, scramble the relief captain. I'll get in the saddle when he returns to refill."

"Jerry, dammit, did you plan this?"

"Plan what?"

"To bail out and not fly that bird."

"Of course not! I'm running a goddamned business over here, too, for chrissakes. Look, Rich, screw the relief pilot, if that's your attitude. I'll be there, but I'll need five minutes."

"We don't have five minutes, Jerry. I'm pulling you out of service if that ship doesn't start its taxi in five minutes."

"Fine. Whatever. Scramble the other guy. I'll take over on the return."

Rich replaced the receiver knowing full well Jerry would find another excuse when Eighty-four got back. The rumors were apparently correct. Jerry Stein was afraid of his own fleet.

"Jill?" he all but bellowed across the desk, regretting his irritated tone.

"Yo?"

"Please find Captain Tate and tell him to get out there and take Tanker Eighty-four immediately."

———

Two hundred yards to the south Jerry pushed out of his desk chair and opened the door, spotting Trent Jones across the hangar.

"Hey, Trent. Come here."

Jones turned and nodded with a sullen expression, handing a clipboard to one of his employees before crossing the hangar and entering the office.

"Yes?"

"We're short one Jet Ranger pilot, and I need you to substitute. Call Jackson Hole Helibase about the destination, but get moving. We just got the assignment."

"Jerry, I'm up to my armpits in snakes right now."

"Well, shove them aside and scramble your ass to the chopper, okay? Whatever's going on can wait. If you're a decent manager, your guys can take care of it anyway."

"Jerry, you don't understand. I've got an FAA inspector on the way—"

"DO IT, goddammit! Don't argue with me when I give you an assignment!"

Trent sighed deeply and worked to control the white-hot flash of anger that ripped up his back and through his middle. The words "sanctimonious bastard" formed in his brain, but he denied them voice, instead turning and heading for his locker to retrieve his David Clark headset and make the call to Jackson.

*So let the FAA ground his whole damned fleet!* he thought.

"Oh, Trent?" Jerry added. "Take that new kid with you, okay?"

He turned, genuinely puzzled. "What new kid?"

"He's over at Forest Operations on standby. Watson. Wallace, or something. He approached me to fly as copilot for free to prove himself. Take him along and see if he knows how to scratch his ass and whistle at the same time."

Trent nodded with forced civility as he turned and resumed the trek across the hangar floor to the nearest phone.

# Chapter 25

The profusion of ruddy colors undulating over the edge of the eastern horizon were much too beautiful to ignore, and Sam reached back to his flight bag, rummaging around for the tiny camera he always carried. He snapped off a few frames and stuffed the camera back in one of the many pockets of his fishing vest as the orange rays illuminated his face.

He looked down at the control head for the autopilot and smiled to himself at the luxury of letting the plane fly itself. He would get enough hands-on stick time later, but right now this was the best job in the world, being chauffeured around the sky by an obedient silicone brain while he took pictures and reflected profound thoughts on the status of Sam Littlefox.

It was true, he decided, the old saw about the wisdom of immediately getting back on a horse that had bucked you off. He needed to be here.

And he was lucky to be alive.

*No,* he corrected himself. *I'm ecstatic to be alive!*

There had been no time to lose in getting back in the air, and it had been surprisingly easy to do so. The takeoff from West Yellowstone some thirty minutes before had been his only rocky moment, his left hand shaking slightly on the yoke as his right advanced the throttles on the Beechcraft King Air's powerful turboprop engines. It felt right and wonderful to blow down the runway and leave his apprehensions behind. But on the other hand, it was a shotgunned commitment, forced past the point of no return by a combination of airspeed, pride, and determination.

And in less then thirty seconds he had been airborne again and out of reasonable options save one: fly.

*I am so very lucky!* he thought, rolling the statement over in his mind again, pleased with the way it sounded and felt, and the inherent little prayer each repetition implied.

It had been no easy feat to become the lead-plane pilot on what he expected would be the most critical day yet of the Teton Yellowstone fire siege. All the Barons were now permanently grounded, and even if there had been a plane to fly, the command structure expected him to sit it out for a few days after his harrowing brush with a collapsing wing.

But Sam Littlefox was not about to be grounded. True, his shoulders ached like hell from the harness, but otherwise he was sound. He would, he promised, go talk to the Critical Stress Debriefing Team later. After all, they were still busy interviewing those affected by the loss of Jeff Maze's air-tanker.

It had taken wading through endless, heartfelt hugs and handshakes at the helibase before he could locate and thank the people who'd produced the flatbed out of thin air. Once that was completed, he hunkered down to phone the dispatch center in Bozeman and beg his regional aviation officer in Ogden, Utah, to let him get back in the game.

They wanted him to rest, but he was determined to fly and take care of the incident reports later, and even more so when he discovered they had located a turboprop King Air owned by the Bureau of Land Management and were bringing it in as an emergency lead-plane replacement.

"It's on its way to West Yellow, even as we speak."

"Well, that's *great*! A King Air. I'm current and qualified on King Airs."

"I didn't know that. But if I let you fly it, Sammy, we have to treat this bird very gently."

"I will. I promise."

"The plane has a pretty good radio package aboard, but not what you're used to, since they only use it to haul their poobahs around."

"Put me on the schedule for the morning launch on the North Fork fire. I know you're planning to make a massive stand there, and I need to be the pathfinder."

Another sigh from Ogden had been followed with the words he wanted to hear. "You got it."

*A King Air!* Sam thought. *Cool.* Two 550-horsepower jet-prop engines and a big cockpit and cabin. Of course, the radios *would* be a big problem, since there was no way to install the extra transmitters that had been built into the forward panel of the Baron. Instead, he would be forced to use separate walkie-talkies stuffed in his fishing vest with the portable microphones clipped to his collar, triggering the right one at the right moment to communicate with the firefighters on the ground and the command post.

Sam brought himself back from the memory and looked around the interior of the King Air's cockpit. Fortunately it had a GPS navigation unit, and he checked the readout now, confirming his visual estimate. Ten miles remained to the targeted ridgeline, and it was time to get busy. He knew smokejumpers were already on the ground because he'd passed their empty Otter five minutes before as it headed back to West Yellowstone.

Sam toggled one of the handheld portable mikes on.

"Jones plus eight, this is Lead Four-Two. How copy?"

A surprisingly lovely female voice came back.

"Good morning, Four-Two! You *are* bringing us a thundershower of red slurry, I trust?"

"Yes, ma'am. I have a small fleet closing behind me right now. Any modification to the plan we briefed?"

"Negative. We're working to reinforce line along the ridge. If your guys can start wetting down everything downslope north of us first, as planned, that will help. We're popping a smoke canister to help with the wind, but I can tell you it's about fifteen knots south to north right over the ridge and stiffening."

The ridge was coming into view now in his windscreen, just to the left, and he could see the thin stream of smoke coming from the clearing and bending horizontally northward as the wind swept it down the opposite slope.

The first part, as he'd figured, would be fairly simple. But when the time came later in the morning to put the tankers on the windward side—the south side—it was going to be brutal, with eddies and updrafts and all sorts of turbulence making it very hard for the tankers to get the slurry on target. The plan would be to extend what they called the "black"—the backfired area from the squad's scratch line—southward as far as possible to meet the main fire advancing from the south and up the ridge.

Sam calculated the turn point for his first dry run and banked the King Air around to the north and then to the west, throttling back as he dropped toward the altitude of the ridge, and then below it, displaced just to the north of the ridge as he descended to less than a hundred feet above the sparse clumps of trees. He flew laterally along the slope, the trees seemingly close enough to brush the left wing tip, holding the aircraft level against the downdrift effect of the air flowing over the ridge from the south. There were bumps and lurches to be sure—enough to drive an uninitiated passenger into an airsickness bag in a microsecond—but once it became apparent the King Air wasn't interested in flipping over on its back, he felt himself relax and began to enjoy the ride.

"Back in the saddle, again!" he began to sing, his smile broadening once more.

The King Air, despite her generic name, was an elegant lady to fly. Stable as a rock and powerful, he'd loved skippering them around with executives in the back before joining the Forest Service, staying comfortably in the middle of the flight envelope and delivering airline-smooth flights. It was going to be interesting to fly a King Air again, especially down in the weeds like a fighter as a lead plane.

Sam reached the end of the run he would have the tankers follow and banked sharply right, away from the slope, throttling up and gaining altitude as he turned to go back for a second run.

The tankers were checking in one by one as they arrived from West Yellowstone. He issued holding instructions to the first two as he completed the second run and pulled up to a downwind once more. There was no sense in waiting. He had every intention of rewriting the record books on how much fire retardant could be applied in a given number of hours.

*By the time we get through with these trees,* he thought, luxuriating in the bravado, *you won't be able to ignite them with a blowtorch.*

He checked his kneeboard notes. First up was Dave Barrett in one of the DC-6Bs, but he needed to alert the smokejumpers.

"Jones, Lead Four-Two, how copy?"

There was silence on the frequency, and he tried again twice, wondering if their radios had failed. He could see the members of the squad busily felling a few last trees, and preparing to do small test burns along the south side of the wider line. A drip torch would be next, as soon as they were ready to light the backfire.

*Okay, set up my tankers first,* he told himself.

"Okay, Tanker Forty-four, I'm off your left wing now, and if you and Tankers Eighty-eight and Ten are ready, let me brief you on what we need to do."

NORTH FORK RIDGE DROP ZONE

Even with the walkie-talkie strapped to her belt, Karen could hear nothing above the cacophony of the chain saw next to her. But there had been a distant noise, like a handheld radio corking off far, far away in her conscious memory. She motioned for her companion to idle the saw for a few seconds and listened, but there was no break in squelch.

*I must have imagined it.* She glanced around and took a quick nose count of her squad in both directions.

Behind her to the east she could see the King Air rolling in with a tanker following, and she forced herself to resist the desire to watch them make the first pass. It was always surreal to stand on a ridge and look *down* on a huge airliner flying past below, but there was too much work ahead to play observer, and she throttled up the saw and started to place the blade against the trunk of a twisted, windblown pine when the subject of volume crossed her mind. She idled the saw again and reached for her radio's volume control, embarrassed to find it was at the lowest possible setting.

She unclipped the microphone from her yellow fire-shirt pocket and boosted the volume to maximum before pressing the transmit button. "Aircraft over North Fork Ridge, this is Jones."

"Yeah, that was me, Jones. Stand by, please. I'm briefing my tankers and we'll be ready inside two minutes. You might want to start getting your squad farther to the south of the ridge for our first pass. We're going to be right over the tree line bordering the north of your drop zone meadow. There are two sixes and a P-3 Orion."

Karen acknowledged the call and kept the transmit button pushed.

"Attention, Dave. Please acknowledge."

She could hear a chain saw dropping to idle behind and spotted Dave waving to her as he held his radio to his ear. She repeated the warning in the radio and watched him nod and begin to round up the four members of the squad on the east end of the ridge as she was doing the same on the west. It was both dangerous and messy to be caught in the cascade of heavy red fire-retardant, and she wanted to give it a wide berth.

A gust of wind blew at her from the southern slope, ruffling the adjacent trees and forcing her eyes closed against the dirt and ground-rock flour the zephyr had puffed into the air. She rubbed her eyes clear and looked south, wondering if the forecasted increase in wind speed was already happening. The huge low that was now moving south over Idaho was expected to intensify, pulling even higher winds into its vortex.

The angry plume of smoke from the North Fork fire was inching closer, and she could see the beginnings of crowning behavior less than four miles from the base of the ridge.

IN FLIGHT, TANKER 88

Clark slowed the DC-6B to 185 knots in preparation for his first turn in the holding pattern as he watched Dave Barrett—Tanker 44—make his second turn in holding along the south flank of what they were calling North Fork Ridge. The smoke from the advancing fire was not yet thick enough to blot out good visibility over the ridge, and Sam was taking advantage of it by changing the plan.

It was good to hear Sam back in the air, and Clark thought how easily the previous day's emergency could have gone the other way. When Sam showed up for the morning briefing and announced he was moving up in the world by flying a King Air, his determination had buoyed everyone.

The King Air could pull up and come around far faster than the lumbering bulk of a DC-6, so Sam at first had wanted to wheel around and lead

Clark in next, then do the same thing with Tanker 10—Bill Deason. But something had inspired him to change the plan again.

"I'm going to work you guys one right after the other, in loose trail formation," Sam explained. "I know it's totally nonstandard, but this is an emergency pre-treating mission and I think conditions are clear enough. So, if no one objects, it'll save a lot of time."

The frequency remained silent.

"Okay, I'll bring in the lead ship, which is Forty-four, and Tanker Eighty-eight will follow in trail, offset a bit to the right, with Tanker Ten behind him, offset again to the right. The object is a trail drop the entire length of the line they've flagged and constructed, as rapidly as possible."

"And . . . you want us in trail, right?" Bill Deason asked.

"Yeah, Bill. Ten. Like the pictures you've all seen of Operation Plowshare in Vietnam, without the toxicity."

"I was there," Bill Deason replied. "And that's a good plan."

"Thanks, Bill. We'll keep doing it this way until it's time to shift to the south side. So you guys will need to maintain formation in loose trail on Tanker Forty-four, and Forty-four? You're lead."

"Roger," Barrett replied.

"Jones? This is Lead Four-Two," Sam called on one of the handheld radios, gratified that this time the voice came back immediately.

"Jones here, Four-Two. Go ahead."

"Okay, is your squad clear of the line? This will be a live run. I've told the tankers we'll be doing a continuous drop."

"Roger," Karen replied. "Everyone's clear of the line."

Sam rolled the King Air into a left bank for the first release with Barrett on his tail as Clark throttled his DC-6B back to descend and follow. Bill Deason—Tanker 10—was out of Clark's sight above and behind, but he knew the four-engine turboprop would be sliding in behind him.

They were lining up, Clark could see, on the top of the tree line where it thinned out into the northern edge of the meadow that served as the drop zone. He knew the winds would be blowing the slurry away from the mountainside, and he watched closely as Barrett began his release and immediately readjusted his flight path to the left and slightly lower, keeping as close in as he dared, his left wing tip clearing the taller trees by probably no more than fifty feet.

"How do you know how close to come to the left side?" Rusty asked in a show of excessive diplomacy. Clark could see how wide his eyes were with a quick glance.

Clark adjusted the controls and pushed the nose down against the heavy winds flowing over the ridge, trying to avoid the wake turbulence from the lead tanker. "You mean how do I keep from snagging the left wing tip and cartwheeling us into the mountainside to certain death?"

He could see Rusty swallow hard.

"Ah, yeah."

"Well, it's an old tried-and-true captain technique, Rusty."

Rusty looked across to the left again at the trees rushing by in breathtaking proximity to the left wing tip.

"What technique?"

"It requires a good copilot who can make loud noises on cue."

Rusty turned back to look at him as Clark triggered the release button.

"What do you mean, copilot noises?"

"You aim the airplane into the mountain, flying just below the ridgeline with a closing angle of maybe fifteen degrees."

"Uh-huh."

"Where, if you don't eventually change course, you'll crash. Understand?"

"Maybe."

"Then I hold that course, and hold it, and hold it . . . until my copilot—you—gasps audibly. *Then* I turn to safely parallel the ridge."

Rusty shook his head in disgust. "I had to fall for that. I just *had* to fall for that."

Tanker 44, Barrett, was beginning his pullout ahead with a gentle climbing turn to the right as he followed the King Air. Clark ended his dump sequence and prepared to follow.

"Good show, everyone," Sam was saying. "Standby for a BDA."

"A *what*?" Rusty asked, noting that Clark was chuckling.

"BDA. Bomb damage assessment. Remember that Sam is a former windforce jockey. They tend to talk like that, in acronyms and abbreviations."

"Oh."

A minute went by as all three tankers continued to fly to the west and the King Air peeled off to the south.

"Okay, guys," Sam said at last. "Jones tells me we soaked the top rung really well. I'll work the other inbounds farther down the mountain and see you guys in an hour."

"Do you have the FM radio tuned, Rusty?" Clark asked.

Rusty leaned over his flight bag and pulled a Motorola portable from its depths.

"It's inop. But I brought a handheld." There were times when airtankers had to make drops without a lead plane, and FM radios enabled direct contact with the ground teams. He held up the walkie-talkie for Clark to see.

"It's already on her frequency, but I haven't turned it on."

Clark gave him a startled look. "Her?"

Rusty shrugged. "What can I say? Her name is Karen, she's cute as a bug, her marriage is history, and she likes you, and, given your performance this morning, you like her a whole bunch, too. What? You thought I didn't know?"

"Yes."

"Well, I do."

"Okay."

"So does everyone else," he said under his breath, smiling at the thoroughly startled reaction.

*"What?"*

"I'm kidding, Clark. Calm down."

"Everyone else?"

"I just made that up."

"But . . . how did you, I mean why—"

"Clark, you ask me to make sure we had the radio, which we're always supposed to carry anyway. We're going to be working with a particular smokejumping squad that has only one female in its number. I know you're not gay, so that kinda triangulates things right there. Plus, there are all these rumors about you KO-ing her husband, and I've already asked you about that."

"Apparently you know more about how I feel than I do!"

"Yeah, well . . . forgive me, Captain, sir, but you're a little transparent."

"Thanks a lot."

"And . . . you have good taste in women."

"For chrissakes, Rusty, she's still married."

"Not for long."

"And we're not dating! We had a drink."

"Not counting last night?"

*"What?* Okay, now, dammit, that does it!"

Rusty was grinning from ear to ear as Sam's voice cut through their headsets.

"All right, group. Tankers Eighty-eight, Forty-four, and Ten are released back for reload. Thanks, guys."

"Tanker Forty-four, roger," Barrett replied.

"Tanker Eighty-eight, copy," Rusty echoed.

"And Tanker Ten, roger."

Clark was staring at the occupant of the right seat. "All right, Rusty, what about last night?"

"Must have been beautiful, Captain. At your house, I presume?"

"You can't . . . what are you doing, spying on me?"

"Aha! I guessed right. It *was* your place."

"I didn't say that."

"You'd make an easy interrogation target."

"Look, I'm not kidding—"

"Maybe we should kind of turn back in the general direction of West Yellowstone?"

"Yeah, yeah, I am. But you're going to tell me how you know anything at all about Karen and me."

Clark glanced to his right, away from the dynamic image of the DC-6B ahead, to see Rusty holding an envelope out to him.

"What's that?"

"A message from your lady."

"Dammit, Rusty, stop that!" He took his hand off the throttles and snatched it away.

"I've got her."

"What?"

"The airplane. I've got her, and I'm making a clearing turn to the right."

"Whatever," Clark said, even more irritated by the copilot's chuckling. The envelope was sealed, and he tore it open and extracted the folded note, scanning the rounded, well-formed script.

> Clark, I appreciate last night more than you can know. You're a true gentleman, and a gentle soul, and I can't recall feeling more warm and comfortable in any man's presence. Thank you! Karen

"How did you get this?"

"Captain," Rusty said with mock seriousness, "I'm flying. Please snarl at me later."

Barrett's DC-6B was already a receding dot on the horizon as Rusty banked around to the north and announced the turn to a puzzled Sam.

"What are you doing?" Clark asked.

"You'll see."

Clark was holding Karen's note in his right hand.

"All right, Rustoid, answer the question, please. How did you get this?"

"That beautiful young woman who answers to the name of Karen we were just discussing handed it to me to hand to you. I asked her what it was about, and told her I pass no notes to my captain without an explanation, and she just smiled and said it concerned last evening." Rusty let a few seconds of silence mature between them. "Way to go, Captain!"

"Rusty, cut that out! I'm serious."

"Well, she thinks so."

"Jeez!"

"Sorry, Clark. But I am happy for you." He adjusted something on the handheld radio and pressed the transmit button.

"Jones, this is Tanker Eighty-eight. Are you on frequency?"

Karen's voice came back instantly puzzled.

"Ah, roger, Eighty-eight."

"Stand by, I have Captain Maxwell on the line."

Rusty handed the radio to the red-faced occupant of the left seat.

"She's waiting for you. That's why I'm turning, to keep us in line-of-sight range."

Clark snatched it away, his expression softening immediately.

"Hi, Jones. This is Maxwell."

"Hello," she replied, somewhere between professional and startled.

"Sorry to bother you. My copilot thinks he's funny. He finally delivered your communique, which I deeply appreciate . . . not his delayed delivery, but your thoughts. . . ." He let the transmit button go, and Karen's voice returned.

"Ah, this is a heavily monitored command-tactical channel, Tanker Eighty-eight, and . . . we're kind of all monitoring it down here. Can we, ah, deal with this later?"

Clark felt his face flushing even more.

"Roger. Sorry."

Rusty was laughing openly, and Clark shot him a withering glance. "Damn you, Rusty!"

"Okay," Rusty said between laughs. "*Now* everyone knows!"

# Chapter 26

Jimmy Wolf had never taken much of anything seriously in life, and that attitude—plus a modicum of musical talent as a singer-guitarist, a daunting stage presence, and a world-class ability to hustle—had earned him more than a hundred million dollars and the fifteen-thousand-square-foot home and recording studio built on the last mining claim in Bryarly.

There was an artistry to not caring, but even those who were best at being blasé and unimpressed knew that there were moments that required stepping out of character and actually showing concern. And if the cold feeling in the pit of his stomach was any guide, today had the potential to be a major life-changing example of just such a moment.

Jimmy emerged from the driver's seat of his Humvee after skidding it to a stop in the heart of the small-town square to emphasize his discontent with being interrupted at seven A.M. by the community emergency siren. He looked at the siren for a second, as if unconvinced it had stopped yowling. The racket it made could shatter his thinking anywhere on his property, and he hated the thing—even though he'd voted to approve the expenditure that had purchased it.

"We need a quieter system that won't wake up the bugging dead!" he'd complained, brushing aside the counter assertion that a community emergency warning horn that wouldn't wake anyone up was as dumb as a police department with an unlisted emergency number.

He stood for a moment staring back up the mountain to the south, but could see no smoke flowing over the top of ridgeline. He could, by long practice, make one hell of a scene just for the fun of it based on the lack of visual evidence that a threat even existed, but most of the well-heeled residents of Bryarly knew him well enough now to be unmoved by such displays. And there was the unspoken, dark reality that, as he got older, he seemed to be drifting into a state of greater responsibility. Officially, the very concept shook him. Privately, he was tired of the tantrums, unless they were done for the cameras in L.A. or London.

The satellite map he'd downloaded from NOAA—National Oceanic and

Atmospheric Administration—an hour ago told the tale with frightening clarity: The North Fork fire was out of control and headed toward them, whipped by high winds. With the lone bridge out of town destroyed by a boneheaded guy working for the Forest Service, he was feeling trapped and anxious.

The town government of Bryarly, such as it was, occupied a three-room log structure in the center of the one-street town. Gentry Wells, the aging star of countless tough-guy movies, was the usually absentee mayor, and thirty-four-year-old Larry Black was the long-suffering city manager they'd hired to run the town—which meant little more than keeping the water and lights on, and hiring the right lawyers to fight the Forest Service whenever they tried to suggest that maybe Bryarly shouldn't exist.

Jimmy leapt on the porch and blew through the door of the town office.

"And where the bloody hell is Black?" he bellowed, ignoring the startled expression of the young brunette sitting at a desk in what was laughingly called the "outer office."

She got to her feet in some confusion, well aware that the tall, lean apparition in jeans, shades, and a stylized broad-brimmed cowboy hat was one of the richest of Bryarly's residents.

"Mr. Wolf, he's on the phone right—"

"Yeah, yeah, yeah. Buzz off."

Jimmy opened the door to Larry Black's small office. The city manager looked up and nodded to Jimmy as he covered the mouthpiece.

"Have a seat. I'll be off in a minute."

Jimmy made a move to rip the receiver out of Black's hand to demonstrate yet again who ran things, then decided to be unexpectedly polite. He took off his custom-made Jimmy Wolf model Stetson and sat down in the offered chair, counting out loud backward from sixty. At zero, he assured himself, he would lean over the desk and rip the phone cord out of the wall.

But Larry Black was already replacing the receiver. He sighed and shook his head. "That was the dispatch center in Bozeman. The first choppers will be here in about an hour, and I've got to get the first group of thirty-seven assembled."

"Right . . . and where are the *focking* fire trucks, or planes, or whatever they're going to use to save my house, Mr. Manager?"

"I—"

"Have you seen the satellite map, mate? This whole place is gonna be carbon if they don't get help in here, and I've got a little bungalow up on the hill there that might just be worth saving, since I spent more than this whole state's worth building it! In fact, I think I'll throw some bags on one of the helicopters with some of the irreplaceable things, like the Grammys, just in case they send some moron with a bulldozer through my house rather than fight the fire."

"They . . . won't take personal goods, Jimmy. I'm sorry. People only."

"Wot d'you mean they won't take personal goods . . . the bastards knocked our bridge down and stranded our property in here. They'll take whatever I tell them to take."

Larry Black sighed. He'd been through these exchanges before. Jimmy had tried to fire him so many times it was almost a daily ritual.

"Jimmy, frankly, I'm pretty sure they don't care how many hit records you've cut or produced, or whether Cher and Tina Turner *are* your close friends."

"But they bloody well are!" He smiled.

"Yeah, I know. You introduced me to them last year."

"Did I now? But get back to the subject. Who's gonna save my 'ouse?"

"Fact is, Jimmy, as you know, they've never wanted us in their forest in the first place, and while they'll save all of *us,* I don't think they're going to be too broken up about the town, or your house, burning down."

"We'll just see about that! I know a senator or two who might want to be reelected."

Larry knew the Aussie rock star–cum–record producer had no clue how to curry or use political power as anything but a blunt weapon, but Jimmy was far easier to handle when he thought of himself as immensely powerful and respected rather than merely feared.

"Jimmy, as far as your possessions are concerned, I'd suggest the surest bet would be to hire your own helicopter and get it in here fast to haul your things out." He located a paper on his desk. "Here's a list of helicopter operators, but they'll have to coordinate with the Forest Service at Jackson and the FAA to get it in here."

Jimmy's voice dropped from an assaultive-braying level to a conversational-sober tone. "This is really serious, then, Lare?"

Larry nodded solemnly. "It is. We've got about four hundred people left in the area, and we've all got to walk away from everything we own and just pray they can stop the fire in time."

"How much time do we have before it gets here?"

"I don't know. I've heard everything from eight hours to three days to never, in turns of when it might jump the ridge. Despite the bridge incident, Jimmy, the Forest Service is throwing everything they've got into the battle."

Jimmy got to his feet and plucked his hat from the edge of Larry Black's desk, waving it at him.

"Well, I've got news for them. Tell them I trust them to succeed, and that's why I'm bloody well staying."

Larry jumped to his feet. "Jimmy, no! They don't need a show of loyalty. They just need to get us to safety. If the fire jumps the ridge to the south, it will be too late to get you out."

"Screw that. They can just pour enough water on my 'ouse to keep it from burning. We've got a lake, and they've got helicopters that can suck up the lake and dump it on our buildings. You take everyone else and go hide, Lare, and my blokes and I'll stay and save the town."

Larry eyed Jimmy carefully. You could never be sure where bravado ended and seriousness began with him, but once he dug his heels in, he was essentially unreachable.

"Jimmy, did you see any of the 1988 Yellowstone fire up close?"

"No, I was on tour. It was one of my best years. We played to eighty thousand people in—"

"Do you know what a firestorm can do, and how hot it can get?"

"Plenty hot, I'm sure. We had some real buggers in the Outback, make these things look like weenie roasts. Wot's the point, or do you have one?"

"Who's still at your house?"

"Hell, I don't know. Couple chicks, Janice, the staff. Some blond in my bed this morning. The usual."

"Jimmy, your people and your staff can't stay."

"I've also got my fishing rod, my hot rod . . . buncha rods."

"Jimmy—"

"My rods and my staff, they comfort me, dig?"

"HEY!"

"Wot?"

"Please listen. If the fire roars down the valley and crowns—that means it burns treetop to treetop—that flame front is like a plasma and burning at about eighteen hundred degrees Fahrenheit. Eighteen hundred damned degrees, Jimmy! If it gets that bad and becomes a firestorm, it will vaporize everything and everybody in its path, and no amount of water or fire retardant has a chance of stopping it."

Jimmy was staring at him. "I don't believe that! You soak a house, it can't burn. Period."

"Jimmy, please. Hire a chopper and evacuate your people and yourself and just hope the firefighters can stop the fire. If you stay and it comes, all of you will die."

The well-known sarcastic, lopsided smile that had leered off countless magazines and CDs spread across Jimmy's face.

"Right. Not bloody likely a piddling fire's gonna run Jimmy Wolf out of town. So, do what you're hired to do, Mr. City Manager, and save my town!" He turned and pushed through the door and back onto the street before Larry could think about, and reject, evacuating him by force. The effort would be useless, even if legal. Jimmy Wolf was his own ultimate authority—regardless of how secretly scared he might be.

WEST YELLOWSTONE AIRPORT—SEVEN-THIRTY A.M.

The harried ramp crew mixing and dispensing the fertilizer-based fire-retardant had started around midnight, using four huge, hastily-erected, plastic-lined portable tanks on the south end of the ramp and the fixed, regular metal tanks on the north side. The ramp crew had pumped that batch into the first wave of airtankers before seven-thirty A.M., and now the fleet was on its way back for a quick reload. All the tanks had been refilled, and the pumps were ready to transfer the tens of thousands of gallons of slurry into the newly emptied aircraft.

The DC-6B with the number "88" on its tail pulled into the chocks and shut down, and the loading crew immediately moved into position to start the process. Two of the men ducked under the wing and began opening the appropriate ports in the large, internal tank as the captain descended the rickety portable air stairs to find a runner from Operations waiting for him.

"Captain Maxwell? I have a message for you."

"Oh? Who from?"

"I don't know, sir."

The man handed over a "While you were out" slip of pink paper, and Clark held it as he turned back to watch Rusty alight from the cockpit. Rusty had felt sick on the way back from the last drop, and he looked weak and shaky as he climbed down the stairs and headed into the Operations building.

"How're you doing?" Clark asked him.

"I'm just . . . feeling kind of sick. I'll be fine."

"You're sure? We can replace you if you're too rocky."

Rusty smiled and waved him off as he walked by. Clark kept one eye on him as he opened the message and read the single line.

*Please call Todd Blackson in Helena ASAP.*

He refolded the note and followed Rusty to the pilot lounge, intending to call the Helena-area phone number from one of the lounge phones.

The name Blackson suddenly coalesced.

*That's the FBI agent I called. The one who couldn't come down,* Clark thought.

He stepped back out onto the ramp, pulled out his cell phone, and punched in the number.

"Agent Blackson isn't in at the moment," the receptionist reported. "May I take a message?"

"Well, I'll be in the air another two and a half to three hours, but I could check back when I get on the ground again. I'm returning his call."

He passed on his cell phone number just in case, then disconnected, mildly frustrated that he couldn't reach the man.

Bill Deason was just taxiing onto the ramp in his P-3 Orion, and Clark glanced at his watch, wondering if Bill had taken a sight-seeing detour on the way back. The P-3 could fly faster than the DC-6, and they'd both emptied their tanks at the same time, so theoretically he should have landed first. Clark made a mental note to needle him, aware that his mind was returning unbidden to the FBI call, and how much he needed answers about the safety of the DC-6B fleet. He'd been very gentle pulling Tanker 88 out of its bombing run the previous hour, but if the fire jumped the ridge as feared, and spread down the north side, things would become immeasurably rougher. He'd felt himself hesitate once already as he pulled back on the yoke in flight, wondering if his wings could take it.

*How would it feel to have them fold up like that C-130?* he wondered. He hated thoughts that drifted into fatalistic territory, but there was a morbid curiosity surrounding every crash as pilots commonly toyed with a "What if it had been me?" mind-set. The crew of the doomed C-130A in California the year before had just dropped its load of slurry and weren't even pulling g's when the wing box suddenly disintegrated. The wings—with engines still running—literally snapped off and flew up, like a bird's wings caught on the upstroke. They'd held that vertical position for a few agonizing moments before falling away. The whole sequence had been caught on video, which was shown over and over again on TV, and Clark had taped it and replayed it many times, analyzing, projecting, and wondering. It was a way of coping with the loss of three friends.

Clark felt an involuntary shudder move up his back. The shudder wasn't in response to the image of final impact. That had been painless and instant. The shudder was in response to a pilot's worst nightmare, which was loss of control.

He returned to the Operations room to get his paperwork, passing several groups of fellow FLOPP members who seemed to be grousing more than normal about something. He caught a reference to cowardice and another to greed in the same sentence as Jerry Stein's name, and he couldn't stop himself from turning and asking what was up.

"Did you know that Jerry was supposed to fly Tanker Eighty-four this morning?"

"Yes," Clark replied. "I heard Randy Tate took it when Jerry couldn't get off the phone."

"Yeah, off the phone my ass," Dave Barrett snorted. "He's scared shitless to get in his own DC-6 fleet, and he's scaring the copilots, and I'm not so sure any of us should climb back in. Everyone was buzzing about it when I walked in a few minutes ago, Clark. I tell you, I wouldn't be surprised if the whole fleet is parked and out of pilots by noon. That's how much damage he's done to morale."

Clark cocked his head. "He was supposed to take over on the first reload."

"Yeah, he was," Dave agreed. "But he's been hiding over there in his office. Tate just took off without him. Something's going on, and, frankly, I'm getting very worried. If he doesn't trust his life to these birds, why should we?"

Clark saw his copilot coming out of the rest room, his face a fine shade of ash. He met Rusty halfway across the room.

"You look terrible. How do you feel?"

"Ah . . . just, you know, throwing up," he said, looking weak and unsteady.

"You been eating at some cheap restaurant I don't know about?"

Rusty shook his head, and Clark realized he was actually taking the question seriously.

"I just need to sit for a minute or two, and then I'll get on with the preflight."

"Rusty, you can't fly like this."

"No, really, Clark, I'm okay." Rusty looked up, breathing hard, and shook his head. "I'll be fine. I'm just tired."

"You're sick as a dog, and I need a living copilot in the right seat."

"I'm living, Clark. You need me."

"I need you sharp and well. Stay here a minute."

Clark stepped away, leaving Rusty propped up against a wall, then returned with a heavyset older woman wearing a Forest Service uniform.

"You know Lynda from down there at the Ops counter?"

"Yes. Hi, Lynda."

"You're right, Clark. We'll need the coroner. I think he's already dead!" she teased in a gravelly voice as she looked Rusty over.

"Lynda's a nurse."

"Clark—"

"No protests. You may have food poisoning or something more serious."

"Just . . . let me go back to the hotel and sleep it off."

"No way," Lynda said as she felt his forehead. "If you went back to the hotel like that and curled up, and this is a case of ptomaine or botulism, you could wake up dead."

Rusty tried to laugh, but the effort made him wince. "You, too?"

"What?" she asked, glancing at Clark.

"He's bummed that you're also a fan of Yogi-isms," Clark explained.

"Yeah, I know," she said, taking his pulse. "I'm simply un-Berrable."

"Oh, God," Rusty moaned. "Now I truly am gonna be sick."

Clark waited until Lynda began guiding him toward the door and patted him on the shoulder. "I'll check on you on the next reload, Rusty. Get some rest and get better."

When they were gone, Clark moved to the Operations counter to report his crew short one first officer.

"Okay, well—"

"Don't call the replacement yet. Give me five minutes."

"Okay."

Clark pushed through the doors and jogged to his truck. He drove quickly around the end of the runway to the Stein hangars and Jerry's office, taking the stairs two at a time to find him at his desk with files and financial records strewn in every direction.

"Hey, Clark. What's up?"

Clark walked to the desk and stood, staring at him, unaware that Diana Stein was sitting in the far corner.

"Why, hello, Clark," Diana said, startling him. Clark looked over at her and tried to take it in stride.

"Hello."

"No, it's 'Hello, Diana.' "

Clark smiled. "Okay. Hello, Diana."

Jerry was sitting back and smiling at the exchange and, Clark imagined, rather enjoying his discomfort.

She got up and walked slowly toward the back of her husband's chair, her hands finding his shoulders.

"I don't like to be so formal around the crew members," she said, glancing down at Jerry, who had reached up to pat her hand.

"And," she continued, "I can see you've got some business to discuss, so I'll see you boys later."

"Bye, babe," Jerry said, watching Clark nod to his wife as she glided out of the office and closed the door. When she was gone, Clark crossed his arms and stood quietly staring at Jerry.

"What?" Jerry said, half in amusement. "Sit down, man."

"Jerry, did I do you a big favor coming back this season?"

"Sorry?"

"You heard me."

Ever cautious of a verbal trap, Jerry cocked his head and smiled. "Okay, what's up? More money?"

"Screw the money, Jerry. Please answer my question."

"Of course you did, Clark. You did me a big favor. You *are* doing me a big favor."

"Then I want one from you, right here, right now, friend to friend, man to man, no backing out."

All the caution lights in Jerry Stein's head illuminated at once, and he stood carefully, locking eyes with the big pilot.

"What's the favor?"

"My copilot's sick. I want you in the right seat."

Relief and amusement crossed his features. "Oh! Hey, we'll get you a—"

"No, Jerry. You. Your ass in the right seat of Tanker Eighty-eight in the next five minutes. Rusty's headset's still in there. You don't even need your brain bag."

A pained expression replaced Jerry's smile.

"Clark, hey man, I'm up to my ass in alligators—"

"*No*, Jerry!" Clark interrupted again, using a tone Jerry dared not challenge. "If you don't come with me *now*, you're going to be up to your ass in out-of-service airplanes because they'll have no pilots, then they'll void your contracts, and then the bankruptcy filings will follow. While you've been hiding in here, your DC-6 crews have been out there losing faith. We all heard your little pep talk this morning, and we were all a bit relieved that you were going to fly a DC-6 instead of the Skycrane today. It kind of told us that, just as we'd hoped, our old pal Jerry knew of absolutely no reason why the remaining DC-6s he owns aren't perfectly airworthy. Get it? The guy who would be expected to have inside knowledge? If he'll fly 'em, they must be all right. So you miss the first launch with Tanker Eighty-four, and we all wonder. Then Randy Tate leaves in Eighty-four for the *second* round, and there are pilots over there contemplating mutiny right now."

Jerry took a deep breath and licked his lips. He glanced at his watch, then out into the front of the hangar, then back at Clark.

"You *are* nervous, aren't you, Jerry?"

"No! No, I . . . of course I'm *worried*, because we don't know the cause."

"But you're willing to let us put *ourselves* at risk, right?"

Jerry sighed, a singular sound of defeat.

"Okay," he said, "Screw the paperwork. Let's go."

"After you," Clark said, his expression dead serious.

Jerry looked up and smiled. "What? You think I may run out the back door?"

"Your choice. But everyone will know. And we'll all be right behind you, running from the ramp."

"Screw your suspicions, Clark. Let's go kick some flamin' ass!"

Jerry grabbed his jacket and pushed open the door, bounding down the stairs with Clark in close trail.

The sound of an R-2800 engine rumbling to life on the ramp met their ears as they arrived on the eastern ramp. Dave Barrett was firing up his DC-6B, and Clark realized the reload crew had almost finished with his DC-6B as well. He left Jerry to go do the preflight and moved back into Operations to clearly inform everyone that Jerry Stein was flying right seat in Tanker 88. The news had an immediately positive effect, and he was pushing through the door again when a familiar face caught his eye as a man moved around the corner of the Operations building.

*Wait a minute! That's Michaels . . . Randy Michaels, the FBI guy. If he's here and poking around, they must be onto something.*

Clark started to head after Michaels, but stopped as he recalled the urgent need to keep the airplanes moving in sequence the way Sam Littlefox had worked it out. Reluctantly, he resumed course to Tanker 88 and climbed into the cockpit to begin running checklists, relieved to find Jerry there in the right seat hard at work.

As Dave Barrett was lifting off the runway and he and Jerry were finishing their runup before takeoff, the warbling "message waiting" signal on his cell phone caught Clark's attention. He reached down to his belt and silenced the warning. He'd listen to it in the air he decided, before they got too far out for the signal to work.

"West Yellowstone Traffic, Tanker Eighty-eight taking runway one-nine for VFR departure to the southeast, West Yellowstone," Clark intoned on the common frequency used in the absence of a control tower.

Clark found his mind drifting away from the disciplined thoughts he should have been thinking on takeoff roll. He needed to be ready to make instantaneous decisions on whether to stop or fly if an engine failed before liftoff, and if something went very wrong after liftoff, he needed to be able to handle the emergency smoothly and flawlessly, giving clear, calm orders. Yet, the presence of the FBI trainee, and what could be an unheard message from the FBI agent in Helena, melded with the diminished level of trust he felt in his airplane. On top of that, Jerry himself was sitting next to him, and there was little doubt he'd be considered a traitor for turning in his old friend to the feds. If Jerry was guilty of something, Clark would be responsible for ruining him, or even putting him in prison. The images were a disturbing mélange driving a growing sense of unease in the pit of his stomach.

*Maybe,* he thought, *putting Jerry in the right seat wasn't such a hot idea.*

"You've got her, Jerry," Clark said, when the big airliner was less than five hundred feet in the air. "I think it's probably against your policy, but I need to make a call and check on Rusty."

It was a minor lie, but it disturbed him. With Jerry sitting there, he was awash in the need for discretion if not subterfuge—on top of the already-weighty demands of the job.

"I've got her," Jerry replied, obviously concerned at the premature transfer of control.

Clark already had his headset off and his cell phone to his ear.

His assumption was right. The message was from Helena:

> "*Captain Maxwell, this is Agent Blackson. I apologize for not being available when you returned my call. I had called you because I had a concern regarding our previous conversation in which you told me that you had been informed that our Denver office was handling the matter you wanted to brief me on. You said you thought the special agent's name was Brown, or Black, or something with a 'B.' This concerns me, Captain, because I've checked with our Denver office, and not only are there no agents assigned there with a last name beginning with 'B' who know anything about the specific subject matter, but we did an all-office check and found that none of our agents by any name are aware of any such concerns or subject matter. Just to be sure, I also ran this through Salt Lake, and they, too, had no knowledge. So I really need to know who represented to you that this matter was being handled by the FBI, and by whom. If you're being inadvertently misled or otherwise, I don't want to let this drop. Matters like this concern the FBI very greatly because of the potential terrorist aspect. Please call me back as soon as you receive this message.*"

Clark saved the message and sat in silence for a few seconds, frustration overwhelming him that he couldn't make a call while airborne.

*Whoa, hold it. If I can reach the transmitter site to get the message, I can reach it to make a call.*

He hurriedly located the number in Helena and hit send, listening to what sounded like static on the digital connection as they motored farther away from the cellular tower. Clark made sure his headset microphone was too far away to pick up his voice and transmit the words to Jerry.

The receptionist answered, and once again he asked for Agent Blackson.

"This is Blackson.

"Agent Blackson, Captain Clark Maxwell here. Can you hear me? I'm in flight."

"Ah . . . a little scratchy, but go ahead."

He cupped his right hand around the bottom of the phone. "Agent, what are you talking about with the message about Denver? I spoke to you only once, and I never mentioned anything about a Denver FBI agent by any name."

There was silence on the other end.

"Hello?" Clark queried.

"Yes, I'm still here, Captain. I'm just . . . checking my notes. You called me again the same afternoon." He repeated the essence of the conversation he'd had with Clark Maxwell. "If that wasn't you, whomever it was knew precisely what we had said to each other earlier. Did anyone overhear your first . . . I guess your only conversation with me?"

"Not that I know of. Have you talked with Randy Michaels about that?"

"I'm sorry . . . I'm picking up some echo effect. Who?"

"Randy Michaels. The trainee you sent who interviewed me."

More silence, broken at last by the sound of Blackson clearing his throat.

"Captain, we've got a *big* problem if someone claiming to be from this office interviewed you. I sent no one, and we have no one here named Michaels, agent or otherwise."

"Then, who . . . oh my God, I just saw the guy . . . the Michaels character, or the guy who claimed to be Michaels . . . at West Yellowstone just before I left. What should I do?"

But there was silence on the other end as the cell phone lost signal and disconnected.

# Chapter 27

*The beauty of investigating the home of an unattached pilot,* Joe Groff thought to himself, *was knowing that said pilot couldn't show up unannounced when he was off flying.* It had taken just one call to Operations to confirm that Clark Maxwell was airborne, and thus safely distant—although the news that Jerry was with him seemed somewhat odd.

Joe drove past the log house and motored on down the street, deciding to park three blocks away by one of the hotels. He pulled a few tools from his briefcase before securing his car and pulling on a baseball cap and leather jacket, the same "uniform" many of the tanker jocks affected. Strolling down residential streets in almost any American city was easy for a man with a forgettable face, and his confidence level was always astronomical that no one would or could recognize him.

*And even if they did,* he thought, *the assumption would be that I'm where I should be.*

The front door lock was a fairly simple challenge, and he kept a newspaper under his left arm to look like a returning resident as he worked to get the tumblers in place. There was no evidence of an alarm system on the place, but his contingency escape plan was carefully constructed for the possibility of mistake or the sudden arrival of the police. He had a Stein Aviation I.D. card as a pilot with his picture and real name, and a note with Maxwell's forged signature granting access to the house.

The door swung open, and he moved inside with a confident air designed to alert no one, checked the rear exit and unlatched it just in case, then returned to the living room.

As a detective, he had studied forensics far more carefully than the average gold-shield carrier, and his techniques went far beyond just bagging something for later analysis. He'd learned how to stand or sit very still and gain a sense of a place, almost like reading vibrations—though he liked to sneer at people who seriously espoused such ideas as "getting in touch" with one's environment on a metaphysical level.

Joe moved to an empty chair in front of the fireplace and stood for a few moments, studying the small items on the hearth. Two tumblers, one of them with a little liquor remaining, a book of matches, and a scrap of a torn revenue seal from a liquor bottle.

He pulled on latex gloves before picking up the unfinished glass first, sniffing the aromatic liquor after swishing it around.

*Scotch. A good scotch, and he'd just opened it.*

He ran his fingertips lightly over the impressions in the two leather chairs. The one on the left had held a good-sized body, more than likely Maxwell, and if so, the pilot had slid forward before rising, partially obliterating the sitzmark in the loose leather cushion.

But the other was still rather precisely recorded, and had held a smaller posterior, probably petite, and almost certainly female. And whoever had made the impression had not scooted forward to get up. He thought about the possibilities. Either she had lifted herself vertically with her arms, or had been lifted from the seat. He smiled at the thought that Maxwell had lifted her and carried her to bed. He moved toward the bedroom, but on the way he noticed the thrown-aside covers on the couch, plus light indentations and a few blond hairs on the unmade bed led him to conclude that they had not coupled.

*Come on,* he chided himself. *You're being a voyeur. You have no need to know what they did sexually. This isn't a divorce investigation.*

He moved through the bedroom and began carefully examining Clark Maxwell's possessions, looking at each scrap of paper. It was the second drawer in the small bedroom desk that yielded the purloined copies of the DC-6 maintenance logs taken from the hangar office. He laid them on the bed and used a digital camera to record the contents, then replaced them in the same spot in the drawer. When he'd examined virtually everything and assured himself he'd left no trace of his presence, Joe returned to the living room and sat again for a few minutes on the edge of the hearth.

*Okay, so what do I tell Jerry, if anything? This bozo thinks he's gone to the FBI: he's copied maintenance documents, made calls to the Florida maintenance base, and yet Jerry needs him in the cockpit.*

He sighed, thinking it through. He could say nothing and just wait and watch; he could try to intimidate the man into frightened silence; or he could choose the third option, as distasteful as it was.

Joe sighed again and pulled off the latex gloves. He moved to the bathroom and flushed the gloves down the commode, remembering his mistake once of leaving a pair in a kitchen garbage sack, which the target later found. He relocked the back door, pulled on his baseball cap, checked that the street was clear of dog walkers or other potentially curious people, and moved outside, locking the front door behind him.

*Perfect!* he concluded. *Whatever I decide we need to do, Señor Maxwell will never see it coming.*

NORTH FORK RIDGE DROP ZONE—TEN THIRTY-FOUR A.M.

Karen wiped her forehead with the back of her glove and turned toward the south, facing into the stiffening wind. She could see the towering plume of smoke that seemed to stretch for as much as ten miles from east to west. She could already smell the smoke, and it was getting stronger, but the visibility was still good enough to see the flames as they chewed through the forest northbound, at times leaping more than a hundred feet in the air.

*Is it my imagination,* she wondered, *or is the flame front moving faster?*

She unclipped her radio mike before remembering that there were no forces of men and equipment between where she and her squad were working and the oncoming fire front. She kept the radio on the same frequency and keyed the transmitter as she scanned around to locate the King Air.

"Lead Four-Two, Jones. How copy?"

The voice came back crisp and clear. "Five by, Jones. How're you doing?"

"Steady progress, but I have a question. The wind seems to be picking up speed, and the fire front looks a lot closer. What's your estimate?"

There was a hesitation before Lead Four-Two's voice came back. She could see him off to the east, altering course to fly back toward her, and noticed that the plane was now descending.

"Okay, Jones, I estimate the flame front is now about six miles from the base of the mountain leading to your ridge, which means it's about eight miles from you. It . . . does appear to be moving faster, but over a broad front."

"Copy," she said when he paused.

"Ah . . . I'm coming at you to measure the wind speed. Stand by."

The King Air buzzed overhead and banked sharply left.

"Okay, my GPS tells me we're at nearly twenty-nine knots now. It's picking up faster than predicted."

"I was afraid of that," she replied. "We're strip burning and hot spotting some, and we're about halfway done with the reinforcement of the line, but please keep me informed of the distance between us and the fire."

"Roger. And we're going to resume the slurry drops in about five minutes."

She reclipped the microphone and hesitated, surveying her western part of the squad all with fusees in hand, and the eastern group now some 250 yards to the east and working hard to complete the last widening of the line with the saws. They needed to go only one more quarter mile along the ridge until there was nothing of significance to burn. The job of chopping away at the grasses and the accumulated brush that could provide a pathway for the fire across the top of the ridge to the unburned, tinder-dry forest on the north slope had gone rather rapidly. But the number of trees along the ridge had taken time to fell, and the task had taken a toll on everyone's energy. Karen had tried to calculate the speed of the flame front and divide that into the distance remaining, but there were too many variables. She'd watched each retardant drop as the airtankers finished working the ridge to the north and began soaking the forest to the south beyond their backfire line. Hopefully that would be enough, but if there was a magical method of cutting half the trees on the upper southern slopes, she would authorize it in a heartbeat.

She saw a DC-6B in the distance beginning a turn in his holding pattern, with another one just behind him. They were too far away to make out the numbers on the tails, but she knew who was flying Tanker 88, and she smiled at the mistake Clark had made earlier in assuming they were talking on a discreet channel. It was sweet of him to try to reach her, and that thought triggered a deeper feeling she suppressed as she picked up her Pulaski and returned to the job of following the thin burn swaths the squad was laying down.

BRYARLY, WYOMING

Larry Black shielded his eyes against the dirt and grit being flung into the air by the rotor blades of a powerful Chinook helicopter, and backed up slightly, a handheld radio clutched tightly in his right hand. As city manager, he'd been issued the radio to communicate with Forest Service personnel in an emergency, but it had remained in its charger base for the last six months.

Suddenly the radio was a lifeline.

Nearly eighty of the citizenry were arrayed behind him in the makeshift landing zone one block to the west of the tiny town square in what was a beautiful little park.

The Chinook pilot unloaded the rotors, and the craft hunched down on its struts as built-in stairs came out of the right side and two men in Forest Service shirts almost tumbled out.

*Jon Pardo and Charlie Foss,* Larry thought, trying to maintain a pleasant expression in the face of the rescuing enemy. Pardo and Foss, both Forest Service land survey officials, had fought long and hard in the courts to terminate the rights of Bryarly citizens to occupy the old mining-claim lands. They had failed, but not without a decade-long battle.

He waved, and they waved back as they moved in his direction, feigning pleasure at having the opportunity to help him.

*Come to think of it.* Larry mused, *they're smiling because the fire may do what they couldn't.*

He knew the two men especially despised Jimmy Wolf, and had long gone out of their way to sue, harass, and cite Wolf for violations on national forest land when even Larry had to admit the violations were petty and trivial at best.

There were the usual handshakes before Pardo spoke.

"Well, Larry, this is, of course, one of the reasons this place really isn't suited to be a town. One road in—"

"Don't start, Jon. Okay? Not today. I've already been nice to you. I sent Jimmy up to his little log mansion to keep him out of your faces."

Jon Pardo laughed. "So we haven't been on the ground two minutes and already you're name-dropping Jimmy Wolf. What are you thinking, Larry? If we don't see things your way, you'll send Jimmy down to babble incoherently at us?"

"Absolutely. Don't mess with me, dude. I have a toxic rock star, and I'm not afraid to use him!"

The laughter was a truce of sorts, a bonding of those who'd had the agonizing task of dealing with Jimmy, and it took the edge off the difficulty surrounding this encounter.

"How are we going to do this, gentlemen?" Larry asked when they had turned away from the idling rotors.

Pardo pulled out a copy of the evacuation plan and unfolded it, pointing to the particulars.

"We're going to assume thirty-seven passengers per flight, Larry, and we've got three CH-47s like this one, so if you've only got about four hundred in town, we can do this with about ten to twelve trips."

"And I assume it's only about twenty minutes back to Jackson Hole Airport?"

Pardo nodded. "Yeah, but we've got a landing zone set up for everyone closer to town, and we'll parcel them out to several school auditoriums, motels, offered homes, whatever."

"This isn't a needy crowd, Jon, as you know. They can afford hotel rooms."

Pardo laughed. "I heard you'd already been reserving hotel rooms. So much the better.

"Ah . . . I should ask, any room for pets and property?"

"Pets, yes, provided we're talking moderate-size cats or dogs in secure containers. Property is limited to a single suitcase of moderate size, and the loadmasters on the choppers are the final arbiters of what goes with the people, what goes after the people, and what stays. The more suitcases, the more weight, the fewer people we can carry."

Charlie Foss leaned in. "I think we'd better talk about timing, Larry. The flame front is less than five miles from the base of the mountain and moving at anywhere from three to four miles per hour. That means it can be expected to hit the base of the rise in a little more than an hour. From there, you remember the old rule about burning upslope with the wind? Even with all the fire retardant they're laying down, it'll accelerate in this low humidity to ten to fifteen miles per hour, and it has less than a mile to traverse. If they lose it over the ridge—if it blows up and starts down this slope, and especially if the winds stay above thirty knots, we'll have no more than an hour and a half, maybe less from the ridge, before it gets to where we're standing."

"That's if it crowns, right?"

Foss agreed. "Trust me. Larry, with that much energy, if it jumps the ridge, it will spot and rapidly rebuild into a wide front. That's why the Sky-cranes are going to be standing by."

Larry poked at a rock with the toe of his shoe and decided the subject of Sir Jimmy couldn't be avoided. He described the earlier encounter in brief.

"Bottom line? He says he's not going, and when he says 'he,' he means a herd of people up there from girlfriends to housekeepers to all sorts of other employees and hangers-on."

"And your question would be?" Pardo asked with a straight face.

Larry looked at him in shock before grasping the joke. "Oh. Well, anyway, I'm going to need the sheriff, I guess, to get them all out, and that will be against the backdrop of threats to sue all of us into penury."

"The sheriff's department is already on the way in one of their choppers."

"Okay. Then let's get 'em out of here."

IN FLIGHT, TANKER 88—TEN FORTY-FIVE A.M.

Clark was flying the DC-6B by rote, his mind almost completely back in West Yellowstone. Jerry had noticed Clark's extreme distraction following the postdeparture phone call, and he decided to raise the level of camaraderie through the normally accepted needling all pilots were used to.

"What're you thinking about over there, Clark? A woman?"

Clark glanced over and shook his head.

"Well, I hear rumors, you know," Jerry added.

"What rumors?" Clark asked, well aware that Trent Jones worked directly for Jerry Stein.

"About a new woman in your life."

"You heard wrong. That's the same old thing. A male and female can't be professional friends without someone making up stories."

"So, she's a professional at something? What?"

Clark sighed and turned toward the right, apprehensive about where the questions were going. "Jerry, please, and with the greatest respect, shut the hell up about that!"

"All right."

"My distraction over here has nothing to do with a woman."

"Okay. Then what does it have to do with? Wings staying on?"

Jerry watched Clark focus his eyes back on the horizon ahead, deep in thought as Tanker 88 approached the North Fork Ridge drop zone for the second time.

"No," he said, as casually as he could, his mind consumed with who Randy Michaels really was, and whether Jerry had any knowledge of him or what he was up to.

Jerry pushed the transmit button and reported in to Lead Four-Two. Barrett's DC-6B was already in holding, and Tanker 10—Bill Deason—was less than five miles in trail, as Dave Barrett's voice boomed through the frequency.

"Hey, Tanker Eighty-eight. Is that the amazing Mr. Stein?"

"Of course it is, Dave. What, you think I'm gonna let you guys have all the fun?"

"Are you there of your own free will, Jerry, or is someone holding a gun on you?"

Clark gestured to the radio in a "see there" gesture, and Jerry rolled his eyes.

"No, Dave, I'm here of my own free will. And no, I'm not attached to a parachute."

"Well, welcome to our job."

Once again they arranged themselves in a trailing three-ship formation and followed Sam across the south face of the mountain, hitting lower and lower levels of the forest until the slurry had splashed through the lowest pines on the slope and all three tankers had emptied their loads.

Three more tankers were inbound from West Yellowstone as Barrett, Maxwell, and Deason headed back for another "load and return." The flame front of the fire was less than eight miles away, the smoke becoming too thick around the base of the mountain for another low-level run. As they departed the area, Clark could hear Sam on the radio briefing the inbound crews that once more they would be starting at the edge of the ridgeline and working back down.

"The wind is picking up far faster than we'd figured," Sam was explaining. "You may notice the flames standing over almost horizontally in the wind down there, and that's going to start the fire climbing the slope viciously as soon as it gets there because the flames will bake off any of the water in the retardant we've been putting down. We've slowed the fire down, but the object of what we're doing now is to widen our line toward the top so it runs out of steam and can't jump the ridge."

### JACKSON HOLE AIRPORT, WYOMING

Trent Jones held the Jet Ranger in a reasonably stable hover as he rechecked the traffic around the airport. The empty water bucket and fifty feet of cable were safely stowed in the backseat, and the plan was to deploy it at Bryarly when and if the spot fires started. The helitack crewman gave him the all-clear signal a second time, and he began carefully raising the collective to increase both engine speed and lift, adding more power as he nudged the cyclic forward and transitioned to forward flight. He accelerated steadily, departing Jackson Hole Airport and passing an inbound television news helicopter as he aimed his helicopter toward the North Fork area and the town of Bryarly, where Dispatch had assigned him to land and stand by.

The angry columns of smoke from the fires now threatening the small town of Kelly and the resort areas within Grand Teton National Park on the east side of the valley were becoming thicker and more energetic with the rise of the wind. There was a permeable wall of dark smoke in his path, most of it boiling out of the Sheep Mountain valley and blowing north, northwest. Trent checked his map and altered course slightly so he could come around the northwest side of Bryarly, some forty miles away.

Despite the smoke and the crisis and the frenetic activity on the ramp he'd just left, he was in something approximating a good mood because he was flying again, an infinitely more pleasurable pursuit than what he'd temporarily left behind in West Yellowstone.

It wasn't just dealing with Jerry that was killing him, Trent decided. It was the apprehension, wondering whether the rest of the fleet was going to hold together and whether his worst fears had come true with the crash of Tanker 86.

The crash was a nightmare on several levels, including one he could talk to virtually no one about. The loneliness of that knowledge was like an acid steadily leaching away his confidence. It had already destroyed his marriage, and he suspected it was somehow destroying his health as well. He knew he was in over his head, confusing his maintenance team and making all the wrong calls about where to put the few resources Jerry gave him to work with. The mechanics were good people, good professionals, but they deserved better leadership than he'd been able to give them, and he was losing sleep over how many corners they had cut due to his inability to buffer Jerry's constant cost pressures. Somewhere out there in the fleet there was a part that should have been replaced, something one of his people had kept in service because of the pressures he'd put on them. Eventually, that bomb was going to explode and kill someone.

If it hadn't already.

Trent glanced at the left copilot's seat and the wide-eyed twenty-three-year-old would-be copilot named Eric Wright, whom Jerry had insisted he bring along. He'd been all but ignoring the kid, but not pointedly. *There were just too many things to think about—or avoid thinking about,* he mused. Maybe he'd talk to Wright a little bit on the ground in Bryarly, but he couldn't deny being irritated by his forced presence.

The thought of Bryarly forced him to peer closely through the windscreen again, this time spotting the tiny town in the pall of smoke and haze five miles ahead.

"Excuse me, Captain Jones?"

Trent shook his head and rolled his eyes. "Hey, Wright . . . I'm the chief of maintenance, not an airline captain, okay?"

"I'm sorry. How do you like to be addressed?"

"Just call me Trent. You had a question?"

"Yes, sir."

"Yeah, and that's another thing. Don't call me sir."

"Okay," Eric Wright replied, carefully programming himself to avoid the word. "I know Mr. Stein wanted you to evaluate me as a pilot. Would you like me to fly it for a while and let you relax?"

A flare of resentment soured his expression, and Trent felt himself turning on the young pilot like a cop turns on an assailant, his tongue the lethal weapon and restraint all but gone.

"*What?!*"

Eric Wright looked startled as he tried to decide whether to repeat himself.

"I . . . ah . . . just thought I'd offer to spell you on the controls."

*I'm sick of people trying to steal away anything I might enjoy,* Trent thought, his bitterness rising. His anger slipped the usual bonds of restraint and aimed itself at the copilot.

"When I want your damned help flying my helicopter, Wright, I'll ask for it. Is that clear?"

"Ah, sure. I apologize if . . . if that was out of bounds."

Trent glanced at him again and tried unsuccessfully to affect a smile.

"Look, I don't get much stick time. Understand?"

"You bet."

"So . . . your offer is kinda like trying to take a half-gnawed bone from a hungry dog."

Eric Wright nodded, his eagerness to please irritating Trent even more as he began slowing for the landing.

# Chapter 28

*Here it comes,* Karen thought, peering over the south rim of the meadow, *and we're not ready.*

The thickening stream of smoke howling up and over the ridge and into her face was the hot breath of the beast. With fifty- to eighty-foot flames crowning and leaning over almost horizontally, it had reached the base of the mountain and was starting its climb. Just under a million pounds of slurry had been dropped in its path, but the massive heat produced by the flames was able to effectively evaporate all remaining moisture content, preparing the trees and grasses for a sudden explosion of blazing heat. The retardant was slowing the process chemically, holding the rate of assent to a more sedate pace than an untreated mountainside, but it was inching toward them, and the moment of eye-to-eye encounter was approaching.

Karen motioned to three of the squad and reached the others by radio. They gathered with her quickly as she pointed downslope.

"It's time to test to see if we have enough pull from the main fire to get a backfire going."

Her strategy from early morning had been to prepare enough black along the scratch line to separate the north and south ridges, but leaving enough fuel downslope to the south to ignite once the main fire was close enough to create the inevitable inflowing wind. The flame front of a major forest fire sucked air at furious rates, and regardless of which way or how hard the winds had been blowing during the day, the fire would suck air back across the ridge from north to south for a brief period as it climbed toward them, causing a backfire to burn furiously *toward* the advancing flame front, and severely widening the unburnable black left in its path.

"We missed those two trees," Karen said, pointing down the south slope where two Douglas firs stood close enough to the meadow. Downslope from the two trees a stand of fir and larch and a few lodgepole gave way to a horizontal run of aspen, which were a slow-burning fire barrier. If the backfire could take out everything above the aspen, they had a good chance of stopping the main flame front from even reaching the ridge.

"Which ones do you want us to drop?" Peter Zable asked. "Those?"

"Yeah," Karen confirmed. "We have just enough time," she said, almost yelling over the roar of the wind.

"That slurry makes it slippery as hell," Peter replied.

"I know, I know, but if the backfire fails and those explode, the force of the wind will propel all those upper branches over the top. We didn't see that problem earlier."

"Okay, Dave and I'll go," Peter said, and Karen shook her head.

"No, we'll all go, and tie a safety harness around whoever has the saws. Three of you, two saws, the rest of us on backup."

They moved as a disciplined unit more characteristic of ground-bound hotshots who hiked, choppered, or drove in to handle the more volatile line work. Within three minutes, chips were flying and the trees began coming down, the sawyers having constant trouble keeping their footing on the red-stained dirt of the forest floor they were denuding. The wind was almost to forty knots again, and the force of it was helping them stay upright.

One young larch fell at once, and Joey Sampson turned his attention to a fifty-foot Douglas fir, using his chain saw as he struggled with his footing. He stepped back just as the remaining few uncut inches of the trunk snapped and the tree began to fall. Karen saw him step out of the path of the tree as it gathered momentum, but she was unprepared to see the sudden launch of his chain saw into the air as his feet slipped from under him and his body slid toward the path of the oncoming tree. Joey flipped his body around to face the ridge and clawed his fingers into the dirt. His squad mate on the other end of the tether reacted too slowly, stopping him with his lower legs in the crosshairs of the accelerating trunk. There was a simulta-neous scramble to yank Joey upslope as he fought to pull up, raising his right leg to his chest and digging his knee in for support as he tried to pull his left leg out of the way, but the tree thundered to earth at the same moment, catching the side of his heavy boot and driving it into the mountainside, the sound of delicate bones snapping within the partially crushed boot lost to the cacophony of the impact.

"Joey! Jesus!" Karen shouted as the saws went silent and the entire squad converged on their fallen comrade.

"Goddammit!" he was saying, over and over again. "Almost!"

Three more of the squad joined them, and all six struggled to roll the thousand-pound tree downslope and off Joey's boot as the others starting digging the damaged foot out of the dirt. They carried him back up to the meadow and laid him out; Dave, the one trained paramedic among them, removed the boot and did a quick examination.

"Well . . . you need some immediate attention, old boy," Dave said to

Joey, looking toward Karen at the very moment she was pressing the transmit button on her handheld to call for a rescue helicopter.

*Okay,* she said to herself, shaken by the injury and their new situation, which wouldn't permit the escape she'd planned before the fire's arrival. *We'll get Joey airlifted out of here and then get off this meadow.*

She turned to Dave and Pete.

"Where's our emergency shelter area?"

"Around the north side of the ridge to the east, Karen," Pete replied.

"Get up there and verify it's ready if we need it."

They nodded and moved off immediately.

She motioned to Scott.

"Did you test the winds for the backfire?"

He was nodding. "Yes! It's good enough. We're ready."

"Light it up," she yelled, motioning to the line of grasses and fuels on the southern downslope below the blackened area they'd prepared.

"Jones, Lead Four-Two," came across her radio as the first flames of their backfire were taking hold.

"Jones, go," Karen responded, feeling her heart racing.

"Jackson Hole Ops says to tell you they're sending the closest thing with a rescue basket. I think it's a CH-47 Chinook. The winds are too high up there for anyone to land."

"Okay."

"Remember to ground the basket first."

"Roger that. What's his ETA?"

He hesitated. "Ah, ten minutes, I think. He's coming up from Bryarly."

"Where are you, Four-Two?" Karen asked. "I've lost you in all the smoke."

"Just to the south monitoring the flame front. It's started up the slope, but it's been slowed down by the slurry."

Karen could feel her heart pounding, but the question had to be asked.

"How . . . how long would you estimate before it reaches us?"

Again a pause as she imagined him doing the math.

"Ah . . . this is just a guess, okay?"

"All right."

"It's hauling ass, Jones. I calculate it's moving about three chains per minute, and it has a bit over three thousand linear feet of terrain to traverse."

He let that sink in as she forced herself to do the same calculation.

"That's fifteen minutes!" Karen replied, feeling a chill up her back.

"Roger. At the earliest."

"How far is the Chinook?"

"Coming up the valley now. I'm talking to him on the air-to-air."

"We'll have only moments. He'll have *one* shot at it."

Karen turned and ran to the northern side of the meadow, searching the murky depths of what had been a crystal-clear valley when they'd arrived. She could hear the heavy thumping of rotor blades and finally caught the outline of the twin-rotor helicopter several thousand feet below and climbing. She squinted hard and was relieved to see the big helicopter rising out of the haze.

"Okay, I have him. We're three hundred feet to his twelve o'clock right now. Tell him how time critical we are."

"Ah, Jones, do you have an escape route?"

"Yes, but it takes a few minutes to use it. They can't pick us all up, can they?"

"Not enough time, and they wouldn't have enough room anyway. But I'll check."

"Karen!" She turned around to see that Pete had returned and was pointing behind him. "The rest of the squad is fortifying the place back there about two hundred yards. We already fired it, and Dave's back there clearing it farther."

"Good." She called to the others and pointed to the Chinook, which was now audible and visible and still climbing from the northwest valley. "Get Joey ready. Ground the basket, strap him tighter than hell, and wave them out of here. Then we drop all but the essentials and follow Pete."


IN FLIGHT, LEAD PLANE FOUR-TWO

Sam banked the King Air tighter this time over the ridge, watching the progress of the big Chinook as it approached. He wasn't qualified to fly helicopters, but he wondered if his assumption was wrong about its not being able to land in the high wind and whether they should have left the basket behind and just plopped the chopper onto the meadow, essentially *flying* it into the wind while the whole squad jumped aboard.

The fire was climbing like a determined panther, tree by tree, egged on by the wind whirling to fill the partial vacuum of the low-pressure ridge now west of the Tetons. He flew over the ridge to the north, spotting the small fire they'd started in a promontory of rocks on the eastern flank of the ridgeline; he knew what the leader was planning. Their backfire was just taking hold, and, as they'd obviously planned, beginning to burn downward in the suction of the massive advancing flame front. Whether it would be enough was unclear from his vantage point. The backfire looked puny and insufficient against the wall of flames roaring upward toward them.

"Lead Four-Two, Tankers Forty-four, Eighty-eight, and Ten are on your doorstep again," Barrett's pleasant voice reported in his headset. Sam had planned to start working the north side of the ridge, but the situation had changed.

"Okay, fellows, Lead Four-Two. We have a situation here." He briefly outlined the progress of the fire upslope, the extreme turbulence now filling the same airspace they'd soared through so many times during the previous hours, and the urgency of slowing the flames.

"We can't do this the same way we did before," Sam added. "We've got to buy them enough time to get their injured jumper aboard that Chinook. Forty-four, enter a hold at ten thousand. Tanker Eighty-eight, make it ten thousand five, and Tanker Ten, hold at eleven thousand. Tanker Forty-four, I'm coming up to get you and guide you in. No dry runs. Full salvo. We're going to nail the flame front."

All three tankers acknowledged, their voices dead serious. This time they would be attacking the beast personally, flying through the flames and the smoke and the horrid updrafts of superheated air, which would be throwing burning firebrands in their path.

Sam could see the Chinook moving into position over the ridge meadow, the basket swinging in the heavy wind as the crew tried to drop it gently in the middle of the clearing. The big chopper was undulating, the pilot struggling to keep a hover that, in fact, was like flying with a forty-knot forward airspeed. He saw the basket touch the ground, bounce, lift in the air and twist, then do it again.

And he could see the fire below climbing another rung. It was now less than a thousand feet below the summit.

Sam had Tanker 44 in his right windscreen as he shoved the King Air's throttles to maximum torque and came by his left side.

"Forty-four, Lead, don't turn . . . extend your run until I'm ahead of you. We'll roll off on this pass."

"Roger."

He shot past the DC-6 at a sixty-knot advantage and continued east for thirty seconds before throttling back and rolling into a left turn, knowing that Dave Barrett would be right on his tail. He steadied out westbound and adjusted the altitude, aiming right over the flame front.

The fire was moving with almost perfect horizontal symmetry, and laying down the retardant in an equally straight line would be simple. Getting through the smoke and the turbulence would be anything but.

Sam tightened his seat belt and boresighted the exploding tree line.
"Here we go, Forty-four."
He could see the Chinook a thousand feet above over the meadow.
And he could still see the empty basket swinging wildly.

————

Karen watched the basket impact the dirt twice, and when the Chinook crew slammed it down a third time, she'd had enough and ran from ten yards away to virtually tackle it, putting an instant halt to its gyrations.

They had Joey in the basket and cinched down to almost tourniquet strength in less than ninety seconds. She patted the grimacing smoke-jumper on the shoulder and leaned over him, aware the helicopter was struggling mightily to maintain position overhead and keep the line slack until they were ready.

"Hang on tight! This is liable to be a wild ride."

He smiled and nodded, taking her hand. "Thanks. Move away!"

Karen and the other two scrambled to their feet and scampered to one side as the pilot began pulling up.

They watched the basket begin to swing wildly in the wind and the ro-torwash, which was already overpowering the surface winds as the Chinook picked up a bit of forward speed and tried to gain altitude, then seemed to be blown backward.

The hurricane blast of wind up the southern slope of the mountain was now beginning to carry the heat of the approaching fire, along with a steady stream of heavy smoke that was getting thicker by the minute. Burning branches and sparks and other material propelled by the same hot wind lashed at the bottom of the helicopter and at Joey Sampson, and his squad members on the ground watched helplessly as he literally twisted in the hot, dry wind. With one final surge, the pilot forced the big chopper forward, and the Chinook finally picked up forward speed and sailed free of the ridge, the basket slowly stabilizing beneath them as they soared out over a three-thousand-foot abyss and headed toward Jackson Hole.

Karen turned and counted her squad, motioning to where Pete stood ready to guide them around the ridgeline into the safe area he and Dave had prepared.

There was a new roar from east to west just below the ridgeline, and she caught the flash of a DC-6B as she waited to bring up the rear. "88" was clearly visible on the tail. She hadn't had time to listen to anything the air-tankers were doing, but she knew who was flying Tanker 88, and she imag-ined Clark sitting in his cockpit and worrying about her safety.

"Come on!" Pete yelled as she sprinted after him.

The roar of the approaching fire sounded like a locomotive or a squadron of jet engines howling at full power. It was gutteral and deep and full of angry frequencies as it sucked in rivers of air and oxygen and moved like a big, angry dragon marking its passage toward them with as much sound and fury as heat. She could see the plasmic clouds of flame break away from the main fire and burst upward, hanging in midair for a split second before dissipating, only to be chased by another orange flare hundreds of feet across.

It was still downslope and slowed by the continuous slurry attacks, but it was coming, and the noise level was already soul shaking.

Karen brought up the rear around a promontory of rocks that divided the south part of the mountain from the north. She could see where they were headed, an overhang of rocks clear of trees. Pete and Dave had burned out all the grass or combustible materials in case they needed to use their shelters.

But it might be okay. The wind had shifted so that it was coming up from the southeast instead of due south, and even if it breached their line and jumped the ridge, it was unlikely to burn backward to the east and toward their position at the base of the rocks.

She reached the others and turned around, watching the stream of smoke and flaming debris and firebrands now sailing over the ridge and falling onto the forested northern slopes below. It would just be a matter of time before ignition began in earnest, but if they weren't threatened by the main flame front, there was a chance they could still do their jobs and go after individual spot fires.

"Lead Plane Four-Two, Jones. How copy?"

The male voice was instantly reassuring. "Loud and clear. Are you all sheltered? I saw the Chinook get your guy out."

"Thank you for holding the flames back. Yes, we're safe." She gave him their approximate location. "We're blind now. What's happening?" she asked.

"It's baking away the slurry as fast as we can lay it down, and it's crowning and about three hundred feet from the summit. You folks did a great job . . . that's a solid line you built and the backfire's helping . . . but I doubt it's going to be enough. I'm going to start my tankers down the north side now, dropping westbound from your position."

"Okay, we'll hunker down here and wait," Karen answered. "But please alert me in case it starts coming our way."

———

Sam acknowledged the last transmission and banked hard left. The three tankers were spent and headed back, and two new ones were arriving to take their place. There was no need to waste any more effort on the south slope. It was gone, but they'd saved the injured smokejumper and given the others extra time.

Another thought began to nag at Sam, and he flew to the east and around the back side of the wall of rock protecting the smokejumpers from the raging blaze on the south side.

*There's a back door, dammit,* Sam thought to himself. *The winds would have to shift around, but if the fire comes up that little draw I'm seeing in the rocks, it could ignite the other side and sneak up on them from behind.*

He started to relay his concerns to Jones but decided to wait. There would be time if he saw the problem beginning. In the meantime, soaking the north side of the ridge was the first priority, and he turned his attention to the task of bringing in the two new tankers for full salvo passes.

# Chapter 29

The Helibase Operations manager moved around one of the tables in the portable building normally used by contractors and tried to get a different perspective on the topographic map. The small enclosure was full of people and noise, with portable phones and several landlines in use, radios blaring, and constant shuffling of papers and maps. Coordinating the helicopter operations against what the nation was hearing described as the Teton-Yellowstone fires had reached the critical moment, and the force of rotary-wing aircraft at his disposal—from the giant Skycranes to the smallest Bell Jet Rangers—now numbered forty-eight. More were on the way from the Wyoming Air National Guard, which was very good news indeed, since they were one of the few units that carried upgraded radios and water buckets on each of their helicopters.

Grant Spano looked around the table at two of his coworkers who were standing ready to take notes. *After more than twenty-eight fire seasons, it was a familiar scene, although one thing had blessedly changed,* he thought. *No longer were such command posts awash in cigarette smoke and spit cups.*

"You say the new fires are starting right here?" Spano asked.

Janice Nelson nodded, placing the tip of a pencil on the ridge that had been the landing spot for the Missoula Smokejumpers many hours before. She was holding a cup of hot tea with the tag still hanging loose, and started to place it on the map, then thought better of it.

"They cut a great line up here, and the tankers have done their best, but what we have now is a steady flow of sparks and firebrands flowing over the top on forty-knot winds and landing all over the northern ridge."

"But the main fire is holding?"

"So far, yes. The line is holding, but some spot fires have started. We're hearing upward of twelve so far, with more to come."

"Okay, and the Skycranes are moving in?"

"It's a struggle with the wind, but yes," Janice replied. "Five-Eight Juliet Tango and Seven-Eight Delta Lima are working along this area, and sucking out of the lake four miles west of Bryarly. There are two Bell Super

205s with water buckets working a bit more eastward, but there's so much burning debris in here, and it's so dry, it could make another run very soon."

Grant Spano sighed. "We need to transmit all this to Bozeman as well. How about the evacuation in Bryarly?"

"Moving slowly, but moving. By the third flight, they ran out of people to take out."

"You're kidding! Even after all the warnings?"

"I know. I'm told there's a spot fire within a half mile of the town as well."

Grant didn't ask about the Chinooks. He already knew. The one taken out of the evacuation shuttle to medevac the injured smokejumper was just lifting off from the Jackson Hole Hospital to head back to Bryarly.

"Grant, Bozeman is worried about our putting all our air resources on North Fork and leaving the Sheep Mountain fire alone too long."

"Tell them we've got to throw everything against North Fork to try to save that town and that valley first. If it doesn't work, we'll divert everyone to Sheep Mountain and try to knock it down before it reaches Kelly. There we have some time."

"I already told them," she replied.

"Please keep them off my back for at least the next six hours. We'll know by then."


IN FLIGHT, TANKER 88

The last pass at the fire had been the roughest yet.

Clark and Jerry had followed Sam's King Air along the north side of the ridge and released their last load of slurry just past the rocks where Karen and her squad were taking temporary shelter. The mechanical turbulence had been brutal enough, but when in their westbound run they flew out from behind the protection of the same rocky ridge, the full force of the heat-driven southeast wind flowing over the ridgeline hit them sideways, flaring the spewing fire retardant to the right and violently shoving the old DC-6 sideways.

Sam had warned them, but still it was startling and malevolent.

Clark had begun his climb immediately afterward, turning northwest and trying to hide his personal concerns for Karen amid the need to race back to West Yellowstone and reload the tanks. There were three other air-tankers in the queue behind him following his aircraft and Bill Deason's P-3 Orion, and amazingly the fire had been halted at least temporarily at the ridge by the effective work of the smokejumpers. But it was a battle in progress, its outcome uncertain, and the intense drive to stay in the fight existed independently of his concern for Karen's welfare.

They leveled out at 16,500 feet for a cruising altitude, and Clark glanced at his watch. "We'll be there in fifteen minutes."

Jerry Stein looked over from the right seat and arched an eyebrow. "Did I miss something?" He smiled. "I don't recall asking."

"No, I was just thinking out loud."

"Okay."

"I suppose you'll want to get off on this reload, and that's okay, Jerry. You showed the guys what you needed to show them."

"I'm not going anywhere."

Clark glanced at him. "Really?"

Jerry smiled. "Hey, first, last, and always I'm a pilot, and even copiloting's better than flying a desk."

"Yeah, I agree with that."

"Besides, despite the dangers back there, that was a real rush."

Clark glanced at him again to make sure he wasn't being teased, and Jerry noticed and smiled. "What, you think that's mercenary of me, to be enjoying this?"

Clark shook his head. "No . . . I guess I'm just tunneled in on stopping that blaze."

"Well, I want to tell you something, Clark. I'm damn glad I called you for this summer, and I'm damn glad you accepted, because you're a masterful tanker pilot. It's a joy watching you."

Once again Clark looked at the owner of Stein Aviation as if he'd been replaced by aliens.

"Praise, Jerry? That's *praise*?"

"Yeah. High praise."

"Uh-huh. Okay, mister, who are you, and what have you done with Jerry Stein?"

Jerry laughed. "Yeah, I know, I don't give out enough back pats, but even though you wrote that stupid article, I'm glad you're working for me."

Clark could feel his face flush.

"Ah, what makes you think—"

"Hell, Clark, the entire Airtanker Fliers Association knows you wrote it. It was your reasoned voice. Of course, I *was* going to have you killed, but then I thought I'd wait and let you 'splain it to me personally."

Clark felt himself swallowing hard and trying to think of something appropriate to say without apologizing, which was decidedly not appropriate.

"Jerry, I guess I'm stunned. I figured if you knew I'd penned that, you'd never have called me."

"Hey, you want to know something, Clark? About the points you made?"

"What?"

"You're mostly right. I can't build new tankers, I can't afford new planes, and the ones we have are getting elderly. We *can't* get it right. Our days *are* numbered in this business. I know that. It was just rather . . . hurtful to have you swipe at us at a vulnerable moment."

"Hurtful?"

"Well, hell, man, I may respect your opinion and, as I was saying, even agree with it, but timing is everything, and your timing sucks."

"When would have been a good time, Jere?"

"I don't know. You stated facts; I'm stating a fact."

"Okay."

"On top of that, you're sitting over there convinced I'm up to something with these airplanes, aren't you?"

"What . . . do you mean?"

"Quit shadow boxing with me, Clark. You're really an amateur at it. I know you think I'm doing some sort of criminal deal with these birds off the books, and I'm telling you, man, that's not only not true, but that's something I'd never do."

Clark took a deep breath, feeling surprised and off balance. A rather loud voice in his mind was cautioning him to limit his tendency to trust. There were very large questions to be answered, and a bogus FBI agent out there who knew too much.

"Jerry, do you have any idea what happened to Jeff's plane?"

It was Jerry's turn to take a deep breath. He was shaking his head in apparent disgust.

"Yeah, Clark, I know what happened. The damned wing came off."

"I mean—"

"I *know* what the hell you mean, okay? And I know I owe Jeff, and you, a better answer."

"I have some suspicions. . . ."

"I'll bet. And they involve me being greedy and cutting corners, right?"

Clark altered course five degrees right and looked at him. "I don't make that assumption, Jerry. We've known each other too long. But . . . these are tough ships, and for a wing to fail after a big round of inspections . . ."

"Something has to be wrong with the inspections, right? Or it's the off-the-books thing about extra flying time. By the way, I do have a maximum tolerance limit for slander, you know."

"I'm not slandering you, Jerry. I'm just very, very worried. I don't make the assumption that if something's going on, you're necessarily involved."

"Well, who is, then? Hard to postulate without slandering, isn't it? Especially when you have absolutely no proof."

"No proof?" Clark asked, his eyebrows raised as he glanced at Jerry, feeling the restraints slowly slipping away from his temper. "Did you say 'no proof'?"

"Hell, yes!"

"How about Jeff? Isn't that proof that *something's* wrong?"

"It's tragic, but it's not proof that my airplanes are being misused."

"Jerry, I know you used a company in Florida for those inspections. Any chance they could have taken your money and not done them?"

"Is that what you told the FBI, Clark?"

A new shocked silence filled the cockpit. Clark felt his hand bobble on the yoke and felt the airplane respond, as if asking what he was doing. How could Jerry Stein know he'd called the FBI? And if he knew that . . .

"Obviously," Jerry began, "you want to know how I know that, right?"

Clark could only nod.

"Well, would you believe me if I said I was tipped off by another pilot with the same concerns?"

"No. You've stunned me twice in the past few minutes. My head's swimming. But no."

"Maybe I was tipped off by a pilot who doesn't automatically jump to the conclusion I must be guilty of something?"

"I never jumped to that conclusion, Jerry. I'm just not sure what's going on. In fact, I really made the assumption that if anything nefarious was going on, it probably *was* behind your back. But, there's only one other pilot who knew I was going to contact the FBI, and I cannot believe he would've told you."

"But somehow I know, right?"

"Right."

"Okay, Clark. Let me tell you how things are. Something *is* going on, and I haven't a clue what it is, but that's what I was doing when you snatched me away a few hours ago, going over the books and the logs and trying to find out if there's an obvious problem."

"With the maintenance shop in Florida?"

"Yes. Those inspections were supposed to be perfect. I paid a huge amount for them. How could they not catch an impending wing failure?"

Clark sighed and decided to tell about his midnight ramp inspection and the dust and dirt and apparent extra usage readable in the wing root of Tanker 74.

"Jeez, you're kidding?" Jerry said. "Tanker Seventy-four?"

"Yes. And no, I'm not kidding. I looked at the logs, and they seemed in order. But, Jerry, there's no way that aircraft's attach points were inspected a mere one hundred fifty-five flight hours back."

"Lord."

"Where did you keep them during the winter?"

"The DC-6s?"

"Yeah."

"Roswell. We ferried them to Roswell and bought some desert. Better than letting the snow and ice chew on them up here."

The explanation felt like a relief, the charred business card and the newspaper from Colombia momentarily forgotten.

"You don't own or have any financial interest in that repair station in Florida, do you?"

"What? Hell no. It was just the best contract price versus reputation I could get."

That did, indeed, sound like vintage Jerry, Clark thought.

They could both see the field looming ahead, and Clark altered course to bring them in for a tight left base, making the requisite radio calls before calling for the checklist. They were flaps and gear down in the final turn before Jerry spoke of the subject again.

"Clark, please trust me. I'm not the bad guy. In fact, I may be one of the victims."

Clark couldn't restrain himself from nodding, a result of his tendency to want to please. But even though he wasn't brave enough to state it, trust was not something he could manage on Jerry's word alone.


BRYARLY, WYOMING

Larry Black saw the dust being kicked up by the caravan of cars and SUVs before spotting the lead vehicle. They were barreling into the center of town from the southwest, which could only mean Jimmy Wolf.

"Hang . . . hang on," he said to the panicked homeowner on the other end of the cell phone. "No, look . . . just get down here right now. Bring the pet bunny. We'll do our best, but the main thing is to get yourself out of that house and get down here. I've gotta go."

He punched the phone off and turned to a harried young woman standing next to him with a clipboard fluttering with dog-eared pages listing every local resident.

"Mrs. Harrison. We may have to send someone with a gun up there to get her."

"Jimmy's coming," Andrea, his receptionist and town secretary, reported.

"I know."

The Rolls-Royce was in the lead, followed closely by a Lincoln Navigator, a Humvee, a Jeep, and two late-model pickups, all of them crammed full of people. The Rolls aimed directly at the two of them and braked hard to a stop before Jimmy jumped out and waved.

"Okay, Lare . . . you win. I'm kicking them all out."

Larry shook his head but tried to affect a smile. "It's not a contest, Jimmy."

"Wotever . . . but 'ere's my entire household in your care."

"We'll get you all out on the next departure in about ten minutes."

"No . . . I'm not going anywhere, mate. Just them."

"Jimmy, we've been through this."

"I want water on my house, Lare. Who do I talk to?"

"Look—"

"No, mate, *you* look!" Jimmy Wolf said, punching his index finger gently into Larry's chest. "I'm not crazy. I know the choppers will be tied up in short order with the spot fires. Before that happens, I want them to soak my roof."

"Oh."

"Not so crazy, then, right?"

A group of frightened-looking citizens was approaching from an adjacent street, and several others deputized to keep control and direct the residents to the impromptu helipad moved to intercept them, pointing the way to the green where one of the Chinooks was just settling down.

Larry sighed as he waved to them before turning back to Jimmy.

"Okay, look. Do you have your phone?"

"Of course."

He scribbled down the number. "This is the number of Jackson Helibase. I probably should have you talk directly to Bozeman Dispatch Center, but first you can ruin this guy's day. Grant Spano, the manager. He's in control, Jimmy. Not me."

"All right. Thanks."

Jimmy Wolf turned away, punching in the number as Larry made a mental note to earmark the date and time the rock star had actually thanked him for something.

The sound of another Chinook approaching captured his attention as three more residents hurried up to talk to him. He gave them a wait sign and turned to Andrea.

"I think I just saw two sheriff's deputies get off that chopper. Grab them and—"

"Get them up to Mrs. Harrison's, the Billings place, the Williamsons, and the other three who're refusing to go, and brief them on the impending problem with Jimmy, right?"

"Right. What are you, a female Radar O'Reilly?"

She smiled. "I like to stay ahead of you."

"You're scaring me," he said quietly with a quick smile, then turned to the three anxious faces standing patiently to one side.

# Chapter 30

"Good Lord, look at that!" George Baird was saying almost under his breath.

"I know," was the singular response from Karen as the entire squad huddled in the lee of the rock wall and peered westward along the north side of the ridge. The giant bubbles of flame and heat boiling off the south ridge were periodically rising into view and dissipating, but not before the infrared energy had flashed in their faces, instantly transmitting a sample of the intense heat.

"I don't think," Karen began, "that I've ever seen anything like this in my life."

Since shortly after they had reached the prepared safe zone, the shower of sparks and firebrands had been flowing like a hellish river from south to north over the ridgeline and then out over the valley, falling inexorably into the forest where spot fires too numerous to count were beginning to flare.

There were two Skycranes making rapid round-trips between a small lake two miles away and whichever spot fire they could catch first, and the effort seemed to be working. The line they'd cut along the ridge was still holding, the main flame front remaining on the south side, though straining to crawl across the divide and explode the northern forest as well.

"Look, that one just downslope. We can get to that one," Karen said, pointing to the nearest flareup several hundred yards westward from their position. "What do you guys think?"

Dave Sims scratched his soot-stained chin. "I don't know, Karen. Maybe we can try, as long as at least one of us remains as lookout. If the main front jumps over the divide, we'd have to get the hell out of there and back up here very quickly."

She nodded, pulling the radio to her to check with Lead Four-Two, who was still orbiting overhead and making runs along the northern slope, trailed by another tanker, approximately every ten minutes. The red dusty look of dispersed fire retardant and the distinctive smell were all too famil iar, and while it hadn't eliminated the spot flareups in the pine and larch on the north side, it was slowing the ignition process.

"Okay. Let's go. Pete? You stay here with the radio in hand and call us if you see anything threatening."

The squad scrambled out carrying the chain saws and Pulaskis and moving as fast as possible down to the tree line and toward the nearest spot fire, which had consumed only two trees so far but was already spreading rapidly. Karen could see one of the Skycranes straining to climb after sucking up another sixteen thousand pounds of water from the lake. Behind it were two Jet Rangers with small, orange water buckets, and she thought of trying to call one in, but thought better of it. The helicopters were attacking the fires closest to the town. She and her squad could take care of the ones nearest to the upper slopes.

For a while, at least.

She knew there was a chance of getting trapped by a sudden flareup coming over the ridge. If that happened, their only chance would be to run back to the rocks, and she knew all too well that sometimes wind-propelled fires could outrun the best sprinters, even if they were carrying no equipment. She mouthed a small, silent prayer that their line on the ridge would hold, and that Peter would know when to sound a retreat without waiting too long.

IN FLIGHT, LEAD FOUR-TWO

Sam had his hands full just coordinating the tanker attacks on the north side of the ridge, but his was also the best view for the choppers' crews working to douse the spot fires, and he'd ended up being their air-traffic controller as well. The portable radio microphones were constantly in and out of his hand and vest as he worked one, then the other, reporting on the effectiveness of a drop or swinging one of the Skycranes around to see a place they'd missed that was flaring up.

Down valley Sam could see the steady progress of the Chinooks in ferrying the citizens of Bryarly to safety. The helicopter manager on the air-to-ground frequency was reporting 60 percent completion of the evacuation, and he sounded increasingly worried as several spot fires broke out within a half mile of the town.

Sam checked his kneeboard. He had two airtankers in the queue with his favorite three due back from West Yellowstone in twenty-five or thirty minutes.

He banked over the ridge again, trying to decide whether to direct a few more drops on the leading edge of the fire, but decided against it. The intensity of flames and heat was just too extensive. Better to use the slurry as a prophylactic on the north side and keep hoping for the best.

He banked back to the north, noting the small procession of bright yellow-shirted smokejumpers moving rapidly through the green, out of their protected lair and toward a small spot fire down in the tree line. He was close enough to see one of their number holding back in the rocks, and figured he was a lookout. It was time to check on the back door that had concerned him earlier, just in case the fire was getting clever.

HELIBASE, JACKSON HOLE AIRPORT, WYOMING

At first, Grant Spano had declined to take the call. But when an aide returned to his elbow with the somewhat wide-eyed news that the Bryarly resident on the other end was none other than rock legend Jimmy Wolf, he couldn't resist. Grant lifted the receiver, not sure what to expect.

"Hello?"

"Is this is the bloody manager of operations?"

"Yes, it is. Grant Spano here. Is this Mr. Wolf?"

"Chrissakes, mate, it scares me when people say 'mister.' Just Jimmy'll do."

"Okay, Jimmy. I understand you're in Bryarly."

"Right. And I need a favor really quick."

"Tell me."

"I have a big home up here with a shake roof, and it's dry as a friggin' bone. I need one of your helicopters to wet it down for me."

Grant transferred the phone to his other hand. "Ah, Jimmy, you realize we're using everything we have up there right now to save not only your house, but the whole area and the town."

"Course I know that."

"Well, we've got spot fires breaking out all over the woods between you and the ridge, and we need every helicopter on the spot-fire suppression. I'm sorry, but we can't spare any assets for your house in particular."

"Look, mate, I'm not really asking, you know? Don't make me call the bleedin' congressional delegation to get this done. One load of water, and I'll stay out of your hair."

"We can't, Jimmy. I'm sorry. We have to think of the greater good."

"I'm watching one of those suckers right now, Director Spano, and he's sitting on his arse with a huge canvas bag that's empty a half mile from a lake that isn't!"

The news stopped Grant for a second. "Do you have his N number?"

"Yes." Jimmy read the registration number from the side of the Jet Ranger, and Grant checked his list.

"Okay, that one's on standby duty for close-in fire suppression. We absolutely can't spare him."

"That's nonsense! Get his bag wet! Then you have a fifty-fifty chance of having him filled with water when you need him."

"Jimmy . . . look. We're going to do the best we can to save your place. But the idea of dumping water on your roof in particular versus fighting the fires is out of the question. I've got to go. I'm fighting a battle here."

He handed the phone back to his aide, who hung it up.

"Tough one?"

"Somehow I doubt we've heard the last of him," Grant said. "Okay, get that map over here."


WEST YELLOWSTONE AIRPORT, MONTANA

Jerry Stein had scrambled out of the cockpit to get to his office as soon as they'd set the parking brakes, but only after promising to be back in the seat in exactly twenty minutes. He'd taken the steps to his second-story hangar office two at a time and closed the door behind him to call Joe Groff on his cell phone.

"Joe, who, exactly, told you about Maxwell's call to the FBI?"

There was a hesitation on the other end. "Why, Jerry?"

"Hey, don't ask me why. Answer the question, please."

"Jerry, there are things you don't have a need to know, and things you really don't want to know."

"You mean plausible deniability?"

"Exactly."

"Forget that in this instance. We've got a plane down and two crew members dead and one of my best captains trying hard to rattle everyone's cage because he's really concerned, and you know something? Maxwell asks some good questions . . . questions I can't answer."

"Such as?"

"You first, Joe. Which captain overheard his FBI call? And why are you sure the FBI hasn't responded?"

"Are you in your office?"

"Yes."

"Be right there."

"I've got ten minutes, Joe."

The line was dead, but within five minutes Joe Groff appeared, closing the door behind him.

"Man, I'm almost out of time," Jerry said, tapping his watch. "Now what's with this cloak-and-dagger stuff?"

Joe Groff laughed. "That's what I do, Jerry. Cloak and dagger."

"Come on, Joe. I'm in no mood for games."

"Clark Maxwell only *thought* he talked to the FBI."

"Sorry?"

"He talked to me. Not the feds."

*"What?"*

Joe filled him in on intercepting Clark's initial call, then calling off the FBI and meeting with him in the guise of an FBI employee.

"Jesus Christ, Joe! That's a felony!"

"No it isn't. Trust me. I did not represent myself as an agent. It's okay."

"I would have never approved this!"

"You want to know what he's worried about?"

"I already know what he's worried about, and he's not off target." Jerry summarized his conversation with Clark, and all the things he'd said were worrying him.

"Well, he's an honest man. That's the same laundry list he gave me as the surrogate FBI guy."

"So, Joe, you're my security guru, assuming they don't stick your ass in a federal prison. What *are* the answers? What the hell is going on with my airplanes? Have we been cheated, or what?"

"I'm still working on that."

"Well, you'd better work fast, because with the feds on the trail—"

Joe was holding his hand up with a smile. "Remember, they're *not* on the trail because he never actually *talked* to them."

"You're sure that'll hold? You said he actually did make contact?"

"Trust me, Jerry. It's cool. The FBI guy in Helena was overjoyed to blow it off. Case closed."

"I'm not going to be a party to illegal activities, Joe."

"You're not!"

Jerry stood and grabbed his jacket. "Earn your keep, okay? But for God's sake, do it legally. And if anyone ever asks you under oath or otherwise, I want you to remember that's what I've always told you."

"Yeah, Jerry. I remember."

"Now, why the hell did Tanker Seventy-four look uninspected, and did we have the same situation with any other birds, including Jeff's? That's your yesterday assignment."

"Okay."

"I'll be back in two hours, and I want answers."

"*Two hours?* Jerry, I'm not a mechanic. It'll take me two hours to figure out how to check on that Florida repair place."

Jerry brushed past him and turned on the top of the landing. "Do it, Joe. And if your little thespian experience blows up in your face, just remember that I knew nothing about it and never authorized you to do any such thing."

"I know, I know. You're clean. Jeez."

*But are you?* Joe thought to himself. Jerry was very good at seeding the record to appear exactly how he wanted to appear. So what kind of clever move was it to launch his own security guy on a trail that might lead right back to the boss?

*The most clever kind of all,* Joe thought, *hide in plain sight.*

———

A few hundred yards away Clark was restowing his cell phone, aware that the conversation with the real Agent Blackson had probably triggered a manhunt for the bogus agent. The fact that the FBI would be diverted from the main issue of what was happening to Jerry's fleet was undoubtedly going to relegate the more important issues to the back burner. He'd related everything he knew about the meeting in the bar, what the man looked like, and what he said. Somehow, Clark told him, the imposter had to be connected with either Stein Aviation, or the Florida repair shop that had supposedly inspected the DC-6 fleet.

Blackson had promised immediate action. "We get irritated," he'd said, "when someone pretends to be one of us."

Clark checked his watch and headed back to the aircraft, his step quickened by the thought of Karen on the side of a blazing mountain.

They were airborne again in almost record time, and slowing within twenty-five minutes as they approached the North Fork area once more. Clark was alarmed at the growth of the convection column enveloping the entire southern flank of the ridge where Karen and her squad had been.

Jerry had returned to the cockpit in a distracted and almost sullen mood. A result, Clark figured, of their previous airborne discussion. As the nonflying pilot, he was handling the radios, but his response to the latest transmission was far too slow, and Clark pointed to the microphone and hit the transmit button himself.

"Roger, we copy Lead Four-Two, Tanker Eighty-eight. By the way, how are the smokejumpers doing?"

The voice of Sam Littlefox came back rapidly.

"They're hanging in there, Eighty-eight. They're on the north side fighting the spot fires. I'm going to put you on hold right now behind Tanker Ten and three others while we watch this thing."

"Is the ridge holding?"

There was a significant delay in the response, and when Sam's voice returned to the frequency, it chilled Clark to realize he was choosing his words carefully.

"Yeah, but . . . I'm having some worries about protecting the squad's flank, Eighty-eight. I want to keep at least two tankers fully loaded and on hold in case we have to lay down an escape route for them, and you're my fourth and fifth arrivals."

# Chapter 31

Trent was snoozing in the right-hand captain's seat of the Jet Ranger, ignoring the sound and fury around the landing zone. He was not happy to be shaken awake by Eric Wright.

"What?"

"Phone call from Helibase for you," he said, holding the satellite phone out. Trent took it, metering his tone.

"Yeah?"

"Mr. Jones? We need you on a rescue, if you can handle it."

"What, with the water bucket?"

"No. Apparently three residents who were trying to get across the ravine, or canyon, that the bridge used to span have gotten themselves trapped near one of the spot fires."

"Okay."

"I'm told they're several hundred feet down, one of them's turned an ankle and can't climb, and there's a lot of burnable brush and fuel along the river bottom that's threatening to catch. Fortunately, one of them had a satellite phone. See if you can safely—and I emphasize safely—get down in there on one of the sandbars and get them out."

"Okay. I'll take a look. You have their exact coordinates?"

The precise latitude and longitude were recorded, and Trent motioned to Eric to off-load the cable and water bucket and get in, briefing him on the mission.

"Should I tell anyone here on the ground where we're going?" Eric asked.

"No. The helibase in Jackson Hole knows. That's good enough. When we get airborne, you can broadcast the altitude, direction, tail number, and type in the blind on the air-to-air frequency."

The copilot climbed aboard and secured the left-hand door as Trent lifted off from the small park and pivoted into the wind, swinging around to the west as he programmed the GPS.

The pall of smoke and haze in the valley was increasing alarmingly, lowering overall visibility, and seemingly coming from dozens of fires between

Bryarly and the ridge, where only occasional flames could be seen above the trees.

The entire mountainside seemed to be alive with helicopters. Chinooks and Skycranes were dumping massive quantities of water in an endless series of trips to the nearby lake, and small craft such as Jet Rangers were hauling smaller amounts to douse specific trees and minor clearings that had received a flaming branch blowing down from the ridge.

Trent checked the GPS readout. The spot was two miles ahead, and he could see a thick column of smoke rising from just to the south of where the wide ravine would be. He carefully brought the Jet Ranger in from the east, flying down the small canyon, which, at its narrowest, was about twice the width of the rotor blades' diameter.

*I think I can do this,* he mused. *But I'm not going down in there until I spot them.*

He walked the Jet Ranger westbound along the channel at less than ten knots, searching through the pall of smoke for something resembling a stranded group of people.

"There they are!" Eric called out.

"Where? Oh, yeah."

Two of the three were standing on a sandbar in the narrow river and waving energetically.

"Piece of cake," Trent muttered as he took stock of the wind behind him. "We'll turn around and come back so we'll be heading down valley."

He pulled a little pressure on the collective control in his left hand, increasing engine speed and lift and bringing the Jet Ranger some sixty to seventy feet above the treetops along the lip of the canyon and right through a thick blanket of smoke that momentarily blocked out everything.

"Good grief, where's that coming from?" Trent asked.

"Look left. That fire's really growing. The smoke is blowing mostly across the canyon, though. It should be clear down inside."

Trent swung the Jet Ranger around without comment and began moving into the canyon, below the lip, approaching the sandbar and settling onto it easily. The two people who'd been waving pointed to not one, but two people on the ground.

"Whoa, they said three total. We don't have the lifting power for six of us at this altitude."

"That's okay, Trent. I'll stay while you get them out if you'll come right back for me."

"Okay, that's a good plan. Take one of the fire shelters though, just in case."

Eric grabbed one of the firefighter's shelter packs and got out to help the four aboard, placing three in the backseat and one in the copilot's seat. He closed the door and waved them off as he moved to the same spot on the sandbar where they'd been waiting.

Trent pulled the Jet Ranger into a hover and pushed it forward, picking up speed as he gained altitude and lifted clear of the canyon.

Behind, on the sandbar, Eric found a log and sat down, listening to the babbling of the shallow stream and watching the smoke sail over the top of the canyon rim.

But there was something else going on in the canyon he hadn't noticed earlier from the air. His attention suddenly shifted to the east, down the canyon, where an increasing amount of smoke was coming not from above, but from along the bottom of the canyon, working its way toward him.

*Oh boy,* he thought. *Something's caught fire down there, and the wind's blowing it my way.*

He glanced at his watch. The Jet Ranger's round-trip time to Bryarly and back would be less than ten minutes, fifteen on the outside. But that was going to seem an eternity if whatever blaze was building in the riverbed began to race along the channel, burning the dry brush and grass and low bushes along the way.

He had one season's experience fighting fires as a member of a hand crew, and he wished now he had at least one basic tool, such as a Pulaski, the combination axe and hoe carried by many of the smokejumpers and hotshot crew members.

He glanced at the depth of the water and shook his head. It was barely deep enough to lie down in, and there was sufficient fuel all around him to be worrisome.

*Gotta stop trying to scare myself,* he thought.

But the smoke was definitely getting thicker, and as more of it reached him, he could tell by the smell that it was, indeed, burning grass and bushes, and such fires could travel very fast.

Eric fingered the seal on the fire shelter and jumped to his feet, looking for a stick strong enough to help uproot the dry vegetation on the sandbar on either side. It was too late to backfire the area, but the bar was mostly sand, and he could dig himself into it after rolling in the stream, if a sudden wall of flame came charging around the channel of the canyon.

Armed with the shelter and a plan, he sat down again on the log and waited.

### HELIBASE, JACKSON HOLE AIRPORT, WYOMING

"Grant, take a look at this latest satellite map," one of the Operations assistants said, unfolding the freshly printed image in front of him.

"How old?"

"This is a GOES satellite image, five minutes ago. Infrared scan. Look at the hot spots here between the ridge and Bryarly."

Grant Spano put on his reading glasses and studied the image, then picked up an Agfa magnifying loupe and looked more closely, whistling under his breath as he straightened up. "Good God, there must be thirty or forty of them."

"Over fifty. We just counted."

"Does that include ones we've dumped water on?"

"Grant, we're trying hard, but we're on the verge of losing it. We've got all three Skycranes flying their rotors off, but they're going to have to return for fuel in another hour. We have six Bell 212s and two Jet Rangers with buckets trying to put them out as well, and up on top of the slope the smokejumpers are attacking two hot spots, but the lead-plane pilot—"

"Is that Sam?"

"Yeah. Back in the saddle. He's reporting that it looks like one of those scenes where a grinding wheel is showering sparks off a piece of metal. He says it's a river of firebrands flowing over the ridge to the north and spreading all over the valley above Bryarly, and it hasn't diminished."

"Damn."

"I know, and—"

She was interrupted by another aide holding out a cell phone.

"Grant, you may want to take this."

"Who is it?"

"Senator Walthers."

"As in U.S. Senator Jobe Walthers of Wyoming?"

"The same."

He took the phone. "Senator, Grant Spano. What can I do for you?"

The voice on the other end sounded as weary as Grant felt as he laid out Jimmy Wolf's case for dropping water on his house.

"Senator, I've already told Mr. Wolf something he didn't want to hear, which was that our fire-fighting forces, such as they are, are not his private fire department, and that we can't spare a single chopper to go wet down his roof."

"Why not?"

Grant closed his eyes and rubbed his forehead. "Because, Senator, we're struggling against overwhelming odds to save the town. If we pull one chopper away for ten minutes to go douse his house, that could just be the pivotal element that loses the battle. Then his house and all the others get incinerated."

"How long would it take?"

"For what?"

"To pour some water on the poor man's house?"

"Well, he's hardly poor . . . but about ten minutes, as I say. But, Senator, you can't just—"

"With all due respect, Mr. Spano, and with great reluctance to intervene, I nonetheless have not heard any valid reasons why this man shouldn't get help with his house. I would appreciate it if you'd divert one of your helicopters and just get it done. The longer we argue about it, the more you're shifting your attention from the fight that matters."

"Senator, I'm sorry, but we're not going to do it."

"I was hoping you'd be reasonable about this, Mr. Spano. But stand by for a call from your superiors."

They ended the call politely, and Grant returned to the battle planning, only to be interrupted less than five minutes later by a call from Washington, D.C.

"Mr. Spano? Chuck Bower here. I'm told you work for me?"

"I'm sorry . . . who?"

"Charles Bower. I'm the new secretary of agriculture. You're Forest Service, aren't you?"

"Yes, sir."

"Well, I'll make this brief. There's an important fellow named Wolf needing water to protect his house in Bryarly, and you folks have been refusing his requests. Now I've got a couple of angry senators telling me about it. So I'm directing you to have someone accommodate the man."

"Mr. Secretary, you're *ordering* me to pull a helicopter away just for the purpose of dropping some water on his roof?"

"Yes, Mr. Spano. That would be an order."

Grant Spano rubbed his forehead and rolled his eyes. "Very well, Mr. Secretary. I'll need you to fax that to me in writing." He passed on his fax number, agreeing to take a handwritten version.

Bower passed on his direct phone number and disconnected as Grant turned to the section of the overcrowded command post festooned with radios. Even across the room, he could hear the fax machine coming to life, and he waited for one of the helitack to bring it to him.

"Thanks, Wally." He read the written order and checked the signature before looking up. "By the way, who's working helitack above Bryarly?"

"Judy and Carol."

Grant moved quickly to the alcove where two radio operators were monitoring the helicopters working to save the town.

"I need a helo to go dribble some water on that bastard rock star's house."

"You're kidding," one of the men replied.

"Don't ask, don't question. I'll tell you why later. Who's coming off the lake right now?"

The radio operator consulted his laptop, zooming in on a particular target.

"Ah . . . Skycrane Two Zero Echo Romeo."

"Can he do a metered release?"

"Yes. Of course."

"Just a trickle?"

"Yes."

"Here's the coordinates. Tell him to go piddle on the fool's roof and then get back to work."

Grant Spano turned to get back to his map table as the radio operator keyed his microphone to relay the order.

IN FLIGHT, LEAD PLANE FOUR-TWO

With the intensity of the fire on the south slope diminishing without crowning over to the north side, Sam began directing his efforts to the job of saving Bryarly. Tankers Eighty-eight and Ten were at the back of the queue in the holding pattern, boring circular holes in the sky, while Sam waited for the helicopters to clear the area and tried to keep an eye on Jones and her squad. It was clear that the people in the greatest immediate danger were the smokejumpers.

The task was going to be an air-traffic-control nightmare. No fewer than twenty helicopters were buzzing like bumblebees around the valley leading from the ridge to Bryarly, and access to the small lake they were using had to be maintained. Sam's portable radio microphones were being clipped and unclipped from his vest pockets at a furious rate as he worked to coordinate both the helicopters and airtankers on the tactical air-to-air frequency, as well as talking to "Jones plus seven" on the north slope of North Fork Ridge. After an agonizing fifteen minutes of preparation, Sam sounded the warning and led the first aircraft in for the drop, aiming to form a line of retardant just south and east of the town—a job necessitating a tight right turn across the mouth of the valley.

After the third airtanker had dropped his load and headed back for a re-

load and return, Sam pulled back up to the altitude of the ridge to check on
the smokejumpers, but other than the man left in the shelter area below the
rocks, he'd lost track of the others.

"Jones plus seven, Lead Four-Two, how're you doing down there?"

The female voice came back within seconds, sounding winded but
strong.

"We're just scraping our little hearts away down here, Four-Two."

"Yeah, but *where* are you?"

"Ah . . . we're working our way downslope essentially due north of the
shelter area."

Sam banked the King Air around to the right and dropped lower, throttling back and searching the forest for any sign of them.

"Are you working a blaze right now?"

"Affirmative. The only one so far straight north from that shelter, about a
half mile."

"I have the smoke. It's kind of wispy now—"

"That's what it's supposed to be." Karen laughed. "We are, after all, trying to put it out."

He flew on eastbound, turning around the end of the ridge and the
mountain that intersected the ridge, with the Continental Divide running
right down its twisted spine. There were very steep, heavily forested slopes,
a small lake, and a draw leading from the south slope to the north that was
itself heavily forested and untouched by fire retardant.

*Uh-oh*, Sam thought to himself. *That could easily become a pathway for the
fire coming around from the south.*

Considering that possibility felt like a form of paranoia, but it was real,
and the winds were shifting from southeast to east as the intense low moved
south over central Idaho sucking the air around northwestern Wyoming
toward it.

He pulled one of the radios from his vest.

"Jones, Four-Two. You guys are getting yourselves exposed if you get any
farther to the east or too far downslope."

"What do you see up there?" she asked, the caution in her voice apparent.

He explained the nightmare scenario once more.

"Roger," she replied. "But you'd see it coming if it burned around the
corner, right?"

"Affirmative. But it could happen fast, and I've still got some bombing to
do down valley near the town. We may be slowly getting an upper hand, but
remember that the winds are shifting."

"Okay, just please watch our tails whenever you can," Karen replied. "Is
our line on the ridge still holding?"

"Sure is. You guys did it beautifully. You saved it. The only thing we're fighting in the valley right now are spot fires, as well as laying down a protective retardant line. The main fire front stopped at the ridge."

"Thanks."

"Jones, I wouldn't get much lower around that slope."

"Copy."

IN FLIGHT, TANKER 88

The oil pressure on number-three engine had been moving in strange ways for the past fifteen minutes, and Clark had called Jerry's attention to it. Now both pilots were trying to interpret what it meant.

"Pressure's still good, but it's not steady, which means a gauge."

Clark was shaking his head. "I don't think so. I've been watching the oil temperature gauge, which doesn't work on one and two, by the way, Jerry, but does work here. Whenever the oil pressure dips, the temp goes up. I think we've got a real problem."

"Okay, I'll watch it."

"I know this isn't good news. More engine trouble." Clark glanced at him, his mind ranging over the dangerous possibilities of poor maintenance and inspections on the DC-6 wings and wondering just how deep the problems could be buried.

# Chapter 32

Larry Black stood in the doorway of the tiny city hall and began to cough. He loved wood smoke, but there was entirely too much of it now obscuring visibility in his threatened town. He consulted the clipboard list held out by Amanda and indicated his assent. All but fifty-three residents had been air-lifted out, and two-thirds of the remaining number were now on the park green waiting for the Chinook that was just touching down. Four sheriff's deputies were racing around trying to check houses and forcibly remove those who were being stupid enough to think they could just ride it out.

And then there was Jimmy Wolf. Larry had been surprised when he reversed his stance and let his entire household be evacuated, but Wolf himself had been parading around the middle of the street with his cell phone talking to God knew who in an effort to save his house. Suddenly, Larry noted, he'd jumped into the Humvee and burned rubber back up the road toward his house.

Larry resolved to send the deputies after him when virtually everyone else had left, but some perverse sense of curiosity was eating at him.

"Amanda, take over. I'm going to chase that silly bastard down," Larry said, handing her the clipboard. "I've got my radio if you need me."

"Don't be long."

He flashed her a thumbs-up and climbed into his Jeep, firing off the engine and following Wolf back up the mountainside less than a mile to his palatial home. Sure enough, the Humvee was in the front drive; but instead of being inside somewhere, Jimmy was standing on the circular drive with his hands on his hips and searching the sky.

At the same moment one of the giant Skycranes lumbered into view, the huge five-bladed rotors creating a stiff wind on the ground as it moved into position approximately a hundred feet over his house, the long snorkel hanging down like some vaguely obscene appendage.

*Bet they don't refer to that machine as a "she,"* Larry mused.

The Skycrane began releasing a small stream of water onto the roof from its cavernous tank. He assumed that it had just refilled from the nearby lake.

Normally the tank's contents would be loosed all at once to drown a spot fire, but only a small, insignificant trickle was sprinkling down on Jimmy's roof, and he seemed none too happy about it.

"No, dammit! MORE! PUT THE WHOLE BLOODY THING DOWN!"

Larry watched him yelling and jumping and waving his arms, then taking his hat and waving it at the Skycrane crew. Larry got out of his Jeep and began walking toward him as Jimmy suddenly stopped jumping around and pulled out his cell phone, punching the buttons frantically.

"Mr. Secretary? They're barely pissing on my roof! Would you please call that bastard Spano back and tell him to tell this throttle jockey to dump the whole damn thing now?"

Larry was almost at his side and reached out to touch Jimmy's sleeve to get his attention. But the aging rocker saw him and pulled away.

"Jimmy, you need to be careful. That water is very heavy—"

Jimmy whirled on him. "Shut up! I don't frigging have time for you!"

He leaned over, looked up, and leaned over again as he listened to someone on the other end.

"That's right! Sonofabitch is just dribbling water. Yes. All of it! Right now! Yes!"

"Jimmy, please listen to me," Larry said. "You don't want to do that."

Once more Jimmy turned to Larry, an almost feral expression on his face as he mouthed, "Shut up."

"YES, YES, YES! I DON'T GIVE A DAMN!" Jimmy yelled into the phone. "ORDER THE BUGGER TO DROP IT ALL NOW! YOU HAVE THAT SPANO BASTARD ON THE LINE? DOES HE HAVE RADIO CONTACT WITH THE STUPID PILOT? GOOD! DROP...IT... ALL...NOW!"

Larry's level of alarm was increasing. He grabbed Jimmy's shoulder and tried to turn him around, yelling above the noise of the rotors.

"JIMMY! LISTEN TO ME!"

"WHAT?!"

"YOUR ROOF CAN'T TAKE A FULL LOAD OF WATER."

"WHAT? WHY NOT?"

"STRUCTURALLY—"

But the remaining words were obscured by a new sound from above, as a loud *whoosh*ing noise announced the sudden opening of the entire dump valve on the bottom of the large metal tank, and the immediate descent of nearly twenty thousand pounds of water laced with confused rainbow trout and assorted algae, all of it accelerating at normal gravitational rates of thirty-two feet per second per second and impacting the middle of Jimmy Wolf's $14 million four-story lodge at just under fifty-five miles per hour. The combined kinetic assault was instantly accompanied by the cacophonous sound of splitting timbers and collapsing structure as the roof caved inward, pulling walls and various floors of the open atrium with them. The water backlashed out through the sides, blowing out what windows remained unbroken in a cascade of glass, metal, wood, and furniture, the tidal wave finally dissipating enough to break around the small grassy rise they were standing on.

As one of his favorite chairs floated by, and several frantic fish flopped around on his driveway, a thoroughly stunned Jimmy Wolf slowly raised the phone to his mouth. "Right," he said slowly, "I think that's enough."

"Good grief, Jimmy!" Larry managed to say. "I was trying to warn you—"

"God! Well, at least the sucker won't burn now," Jimmy said, his eyes still on the Skycrane, which was slowly turning, and as it dipped its nose southward, a hurricane gust of rotorwash knocked them both to the soggy ground.

THREE MILES WEST OF BRYARLY, WYOMING

Eric Wright was on the verge of ripping open the fire-shelter pack. The smoke was causing him to cough constantly, even though he'd wetted down the elastic cuff of his jacket and was breathing through it to filter the air.

The sound of the Jet Ranger returning was beyond musical, a sound of deliverance as clear as a cavalry bugle to a besieged wagon train in a John Ford western.

The helicopter flew overhead, pivoted carefully, and settled down in the same spot as before, and Eric raced over and clambered in.

"God, am I glad to see you!"

"Yeah, there's a fire down the canyon coming this way," Trent said as he pulled on the collective and fairly yanked the Jet Ranger back into the air. "And there's a big blaze burning right up to the edge of the canyon just ahead."

"Everybody else out of the town?"

"All except for a handful. The rest should already be in Jackson Hole by now. Hang on, I promised the city manager a call."

They were gaining forward speed, and Trent nudged the collective even higher. They rose above the lip of the canyon just as a powerful gust of wind pushed in from the left, carrying with it a hail of branches and burning leaves in a peppering rain of debris. The wind shoved the Jet Ranger to the left, and the craft weathervaned into the wind, pivoting to the right and taking another fiery gust laden with debris head-on.

Trent triggered the transmitter, speaking into the boom microphone on his headset.

"Bryarly City Manager Black, Jet Ranger Two-Three Bravo, how copy?"

A tenuous voice came back.

"Ah, loud and clear, Two-Three Bravo."

"I've got my guy, and we're on the way back to pull you out."

"Roger."

Both men saw the flaming firebrand coming at them, but there was no time for Trent to react on the controls as the cloud of debris from branches that had exploded in flame hit, the density great enough to clog the critical air intakes of the otherwise uncloggable engine.

Trent could feel the power of the turbine engine begin to fade as it gasped for air. They were at fifty knots and only a hundred feet off the ground, a critical place to be for an engine loss in a helicopter, and all he could see ahead were trees, the closest ones on fire.

"Jesus! We're going down!" Trent said, somehow squeezing the transmit button on the stick. "Mayday, mayday, mayday, Jet Ranger Two-Three Bravo, engine failure, going down two miles west of Bryarly. Mayday!"

The town was somewhere to the east, and the engine rpm's were fading fast, the engine temperature rising precipitously. The branches and other debris that weren't grinding through the engine were choking off the air supply.

"We need a clearing!" Trent shouted, his eyes frantically scanning the impossible scene ahead.

"Over there!" Eric gestured to the right, over the back of the burning trees into unburned green, where a stand of aspen appeared to open into a clearing.

The rotor rpm was decaying, the engine all but gone. Trent twisted the motorcycle-style throttle to maximum, but the turboshaft engine was slowly strangling, and its power output was nearly useless. He had mere moments to put it on the ground or run out of energy and simply fall. There was enough remaining rpm in the rotor for a soft landing directly below, but there were nothing but burning trees there. He would have to stretch another few hundred feet, holding the airspeed as the rotor blades slowed. It was against every instinct a helicopter pilot has, but still he held course, letting the skids almost brush the treetops below until they were over an unburned green with a tiny meadow ahead.

There was no time for finesse. It was going to be a crash landing.

"Brace!" Trent yelled, aiming the Ranger between trees ahead and getting her as low as possible before the inevitable impact with the rotor blades. They were still flying but now less than twenty feet above the ground, the rotor rpm below red line, the engine gone. He nudged the collective down to prevent ballooning and hauled back on the cyclic to raise the nose and slow the forward speed, trying to soften the impact. The forward airspeed was below twenty, the blades now chopping into adjacent light vegetation like a mower, when one of the blades caught the trunk of a tree too big to sever, and the world began to spin in an uncontrollable whirl of green and motion and yelps and mechanical sounds of tearing and crashing. The noises stopped, and Trent realized they were on their left side in a grove of trees, with the sounds of hot liquids hissing dangerously on metal surfaces.

He looked over at Eric Wright. The young copilot was unconscious, his head resting against the shattered corner of the Plexiglas windscreen.

Trent closed his right hand around the frame of the right door window and opened his seat belt, letting himself down as gently as possible on the copilot. He climbed out through the broken front windscreen and then turned back in, working to release Eric's seat belt and haul him out. There was considerable blood on his head, and Trent realized the young man was bleeding from his mouth.

He could hear the forest fire on the other side. He had to get the copilot out of the crushed interior of the cockpit before the Ranger caught on fire. They'd had more than two-thirds of a tank of jet fuel onboard, and the tanks had broken. He could smell the kerosene, and he knew it was pooling around the wreckage and waiting for a spark.

Finally, gingerly, he managed to pull the copilot through the crushed window frame and drag him a safe distance away. There was a rumble overhead at the same moment, and he looked up to see the King Air lead plane roar by less than two hundred feet overhead. He knew what would follow.

Trent quickly turned the copilot on his side and leaned over him protectively as a DC-6B thundered over at treetop height, spewing fire retardant that rained with painful impact on his back and head, thudding and thumping into the forest.

Obviously they hadn't seen the downed helicopter, and now—even though better protected from the fire—the wreck would be obliterated by a swath of red.

Trent wiped the slippery chemical from his face and took a closer look at Eric. Though he was unconscious, his pulse seemed steady. But the blood oozing out of his mouth was frightening, and it was obvious he was going to need immediate medical help. Trent began to turn back to the wreck just as the kerosene ignited with a *whoomp,* and a bright, hot orange flame began to consume the remains of the machine.

## Two Miles Above Bryarly, Wyoming

"Woohoo!" George Baird exclaimed, holding his Pulaski high in victory as the last of the flames from the spot fire they'd been attacking flickered out, done in by a combination of rapid tree felling and the effective line they'd cut to isolate the small blaze before it got out of hand.

"No rest for the weary, gang." Karen smiled, pointing east and down-slope a bit more. There's smoke down there as well."

They moved out smartly, drawing on the reserves of youth and the bio-chemical high of excitement, knowing their squad had played a pivotal role in saving the entire valley, a town, and maybe even Yellowstone and were still going at it, doing what few people would ever choose to do.

Karen brought up the rear, her nose so full of fragrant wood smoke it was nearly impossible to sniff anything new on the stiff wind now whistling almost directly at them from the east. The shift had been dramatic, from al-most due south at daybreak to almost due east in midafternoon, but it meant that any spot fires on the eastern side of the valley leading northward to Bryarly needed early containment.

She could still hear the sounds of helicopters working the north slope, and wondered when she'd need to admit their finite limitations and call for water on a spot fire too big to dry mop. So far, with four significant spot fires extinguished and a dozen other smaller blazes stomped to death before they climbed the trees, they hadn't needed helo support. But that could change.

Karen stopped suddenly, letting the rest of the squad move on ahead as she held back. She sampled the air and let her eyes roam the horizon, look-ing for Sam Littlefox in his King Air. She hadn't heard him fly past for fifteen or twenty minutes and imagined he was flying near the town and bringing the tankers through. The other smokejumpers were disappearing ahead of her, and it was a little worrisome that no one had noticed her absence. *Smokejumpers tended to be that way,* she thought wryly. They were a squad, but more a collection of mavericks at times, not like the hotshot crews who seemed to be far more disciplined and even militaristic in their methods.

She listened to the growing silence, finding nothing to be alarmed about. Yet . . . some sixth sense was very definitely alarming her.

*It's probably just a combination of Sam's cautions a bit earlier and that stiff eastern wind.*

Phil Dale, who had been just ahead of her, turned suddenly when he fi-nally realized there were no footsteps behind him. Peering through the trees, he spotted her thirty yards back.

"Karen? You okay?"

"Yeah, just checking to see how much you need me."

"Well, come on."

She laughed and trotted after him, her pack and gear feeling much heavier than they had a few minutes before. When she got within a few yards of Phil, she motioned for him to go ahead. "I'm okay. I'm going to range left and right here and check things out."

"You da boss lady," he replied with a grin.

Karen began working her way directly downslope before resuming an easterly course toward the spot fire. There were no human trails along the steep slope, but there was evidence of deer and elk and smaller animals, and here and there in the pine-needle carpet she saw a fresh outcropping of black dirt and a small hole for some animal's den. Out of curiosity she started scanning for additional ones, her eyes falling on a small, cavelike opening in the dirt of the mountainside just up from where she was pushing through the trees.

*Wow! I'll bet that's an old bear den. Maybe too small, but . . .*

It had been years since she'd stumbled on a bear's den, and she wondered if the occupant was home, but there was no time to check.

Karen glanced at her watch and forced herself to end the nature tour and get back to work. She got an audible fix on the noise of her squad's chain saws, checked the sky through the tall stand of larch, and resumed walking.

Karen rejoined the group as the first trees were falling, the flames still contained at the bases. She glanced up again to the eastern flank of the mountain, worrying that perhaps Sam was no longer on guard, but at that moment the distant whine and whirr of the King Air's turboprop engines buzzed overhead, and she unholstered her radio and decided to wait a few minutes for him to check on things.

The call wasn't more than ninety seconds in coming.

"Jones, Lead Four-Two, how copy?" Sam's voice was sharp and urgent, and it sent chills down her back.

"Go ahead Lead Four-Two, Jones here."

"You guys are going to have to bug out NOW! The fire's blowing up around the eastern side, and it's already crowning. I just got back here to take a look and didn't expect this. How far are you from that rock face and your lookout guy?"

Karen signaled to the rest of the squad as she answered. "Ah, we're about five hundred feet in altitude down the mountain and a little east of that position, over."

"Okay . . . look, it's coming around, and although it's hard to judge the speed exactly, it's running even as we speak and . . . the front is broadening in a uniform fashion. It's going to burn an almost vertical line rotating around from east to north. Understand?"

"Roger. Hang on." She turned to the squad, noting in the same second that all the saws had been idled. "The fire's blowing up around the ridge and coming at us! It's too thick in here to burn out around us. We've got to get up the rocks."

"Behind us?"

"Yes! Drop your packs and gear and saws now and run! George? Lead the way. Single file. Make sure you have your shelters and run. NOW! GO, GO, GO, GO!"

Packs and equipment hit the ground almost simultaneously as George Baird yelled for everyone to follow and started half jogging at a sixty-degree angle through the trees up toward the ridge.

Karen raised her radio again. "Okay, Sam, we're on the move."

"Run as hard as you can," he was saying as she brought up the rear. "There's a middle portion that's moving faster now, about two hundred, maybe three hundred feet from the top. It's burning westbound toward your position through the crowns. Keep running! I'm going to bring the tankers down to give you cover. Can you pop a flare for me?"

"Roger . . . stand by. Peter? Peter, this is Jones! We're running back to the safety zone. Get yourself there now. Copy?"

"Roger. Moving now."

Karen had just begun the scramble. She turned now and raced back to one of the packs, grabbing up a smoke grenade before resuming the run, staying forty feet behind Dave Sims. She worked the cannister release ring open, cutting her hand in the process, and yanked the lanyard, holding the orange smoke end up like an Olympic runner as she ran, jumping over the snags and logs and slowly catching up to Sims.

Somewhere in the background she could hear it again. They had contained the beast on the south side, and now, like a dragon searching inexorably for its prey, it had crept around the other side to catch them off guard. And it had succeeded. She could hear the roar and the whistle and the increase in the sounds from behind as she closed in on Dave at the exact moment he stumbled and went facedown in front of her before she could sidestep. The smoke cannister hurled out of her hand as she, too, tumbled head over heels, landing with a thud against a fallen tree trunk, her radio partly breaking her fall.

"Dave?"

"Oh, shit!"

"What?"

"I've broken something." He tried to stand again and went down. "Jesus, Karen! I'll use my shelter. Run!"

"No!"

"Karen, RUN!"

For a microsecond her mind flashed back to the Storm King Mountain disaster in Colorado, when they had all run for their lives. What had haunted her ever since was upon her again like a second chance. She remembered no voices from behind calling for help on Storm King, nor any twisted or broken ankles. Nor had she been the squad leader.

But three of her jumping compatriots had been left behind to die when the juggernaut of fire and heat overwhelmed them from behind.

And she had survived.

Never again would she be the survivor, wondering whether she could have done more.

"Come on," Karen said to Dave without hesitation. "You can lean on me. We're going to make it one way or another."

"No! Karen, listen to it back there. We can't make it this way."

"Well, you can't stay here! This is thick fuel we're in! It'll burn fast and hot, and we don't have time to fire out."

He grabbed her sleeve. "Karen, I'm not kidding! You get out of here."

She smiled at him. "Not a chance in hell, buddy! Hold on to me, and let's go. We've got to figure this out quick."

# Chapter 33

"Jones, are you there? I say again, Jones, are you there?"

Sam felt the muscles in the back of his neck almost knotting with tension. He'd spotted the orange smoke grenade. They were in deep trouble with the fire at their heels and still more than four hundred feet from the protection of the rocks, and now she wasn't responding.

He switched radios.

"Tanker Eighty-eight, we've got a situation on the eastern flank. Do you see my location?"

"Roger, Lead."

"Okay. Roll off the perch right now, and Tanker Ten, roll off in trail behind him. I'm going to lead you in for an emergency drop coming right over the saddle, then laterally diving you down to the east to set up a protective barrier. We've got the smokejumpers trapped and trying to reach safety near the ridge. Punch half your load."

"I'm coming at you right now, Lead. We're bringing the flaps out and ready to follow."

"Lead Four-Two, Tanker Ten's right behind Clark."

"Okay, guys, this will be tight. I'll need a hefty dive, but don't start the release until you're just past the rocks on the north side of the ridge. I'll call out when I'm there."

There were two terse "Rogers" as Sam pulled his throttles all the way to idle and ran the flaps to the "approach" position, then pushed the propellers up to high rpm for maximum drag, diving for the ridgeline from the south.

He held the nose low and skimmed over the ridge at less than fifty feet, feeling as if his right wing was going to be dragging the trees as he aimed for the fire front and just to the east of where the orange smoke had been. It was the hottest part of the day, and the temperature of the fire front would be higher than fourteen hundred degrees, making it even harder to slow.

The protective rocks flashed beneath the King Air, and he thought he saw the other smokejumper waiting there.

"Now!" he called on the radio. "Keep it dumping until you get to the edge of the fire, but not beyond."

The updrafts and side gusts were amazingly intense and buffeting him mightily, but his eyes were recording almost everything, and for just a split second he thought he saw two-thirds of the way down the outline of fire-fighters running through the forest in the opposite direction.

"Stay as low as you dare, guys! We need an impenetrable barrier!"

He was well aware that there was no such thing when the hottest crowning fire met fire retardant. You could slow it, yes. Extinguishing it was highly unlikely.

Sam began pulling out and pushing his throttles back up as he impacted the superheated gases and debris churning into the air at the flame front. The King Air bounced unmercifully, knocking him around and triggering a quick, rueful reminder of his promise to treat the executive propjet gently.

He banked sharply to the right, catching a glimpse of the last of Clark Maxwell's run as the DC-6B crossed the same fire line with red streaming from its belly.

"Tanker Eighty-eight is pulling up."

"Roger. Follow me for an immediate repeat."

There was a thirty-second interval before Bill Deason reported his pull up as well.

Sam heard himself breathing hard. He kept the aircraft in a fairly smart, right-climbing turn to reposition himself and the big ships behind him for another pass, then used the seconds in between to pull out the handheld radio and try once again.

"Jones, this is Lead Four-Two, how copy?"

Nothing.

He tried three times and replaced the radio, missing the response from Pete Zable, who had been on lookout by the rocks.

Pete tried again. "Station calling Jones, please identify and repeat. This is Smokejumper Zable. Go ahead."

This time, Sam heard the call as he banked back around to the right and once again lowered his flaps while yanking out the radio microphone.

"Zable, this is Lead Four-Two. Are you with Jones?"

"Negative. I heard her talking, but I can't raise her now either." He re-layed where he was on the mountain.

"Zable, they were running toward you."

"Yes, I heard you advise that."

"Keep trying to raise her." It was time to reclip the microphone and fly the airplane. "This is pass number two, guys," he said, violating just about every established standard for the procedural callouts. "Tankers Ten and

Eighty-eight, pull up to a left-hand hold in trail formation at ten thousand five hundred, just south of the ridge, and hold for me to dry run it again. I need to find them."

Once more Sam sliced over the ridge at too intimate an altitude and nosed it over, walking the rudders to keep on track and knowing that Clark and Bill would have to do the same behind him once he located the squad. To his dismay, he could see the flame front marching past the end of their last drop, the red-stained areas burning less brightly, but the trees exploding in flame nonetheless.

*Oh, Lord! We're coming the wrong way!* he realized.

The mistake was now so obvious, yet had been so obscure. If he'd had the tankers approach over the eastern shoulder of the mountain and lay down line directly in front of the flames, the retardant effect could have begun instantly. Instead, he'd left too much space between the slurry line and the advancing fire, giving it room to accelerate and grow.

"Shit!"

This time he had seen no sign of the smokejumpers, and no sign that they'd slowed the fire.

Somewhere down there on that steep mountain slope Jones and some of her smokejumpers were literally running for their lives. The sinking recognition that they might have created yet another Storm King disaster was bouncing off the margins of his mind and threatening panic, which wouldn't help.

Once more he pulled out, throttling up the King Air as he made a wide left turn.

"Okay, Ten and Eighty-eight, I can't see them, but I can see what we need to do for them. This time we're coming over the eastern shoulder, and we're going to draw a line in front of the blaze."

Two more full tankers reported inbound, and he quickly assigned them slightly higher holding altitudes and instructed them to fly over and watch Tankers Eighty-eight and Ten on the next pass.

"Keep it tight, guys, they need us down there," he said in the right turn, honking the King Air around too rapidly before remembering that the DC-6 and P-3 Orion following him couldn't make such a tight radius turn.

Once more he pulled out the handheld microphone and called, and once more he reached only a semifrantic Pete Zable.

"I still haven't raised them, and I can see the fire coming this way!"

"Call me when they show up!"

Tanker Eighty-eight was calling. "This is the last of my load," Clark warned.

"I have a thousand gallons left," Bill added. "Let's make this count.

*Dear God, do what he said,* Sam thought. The idea that any of the smoke-jumpers could be left unprotected was as unacceptable as leaving a downed pilot behind enemy lines.

Only this time, Sam reminded himself, the fire was the enemy, and this enemy took no prisoners.

————

Clark glanced over at Jerry, whose expression was hard and serious.

"I'm going to dive it over the ridge behind him at treetop level. I could ding a prop, Jerry."

"Keep us out of the mud, but do what you need to do. He wants to lay a protective line down in front of it, right?"

Clark nodded as he pulled back the throttles. "Flaps twenty, please."

"Roger, flaps coming to twenty."

"Flaps right to forty."

"Flaps forty."

"Yeah . . . that's what he wants. We may have wasted the first load."

"No you didn't," Jerry said. "Watch that updraft right over the edge, Clark. It'll shove us up fifty feet."

"Gotcha."

The King Air had crossed the ridge and was diving down the face of the steep slope paralleling the fire line less then twenty yards in front of it, and Clark worked the rudders and the yoke continuously to follow, aware that their speed was already increasing as he approached the ridge and pushed as far forward as he dared, mentally counting the remaining yards as the DC-6B hurtled toward the rocky shoulder and the trees beyond.

*Three, two, one, here we go!* he thought to himself at the moment the ridge flashed beneath them with the predicted updraft.

Suddenly there were burning, exploding treetops off the right wing practically brushing the wing tip, and he mashed the release button, feeling the tons of retardant begin to leave the belly. He was in a combination dive and slip. His hands and feet were in constant motion as if the controls themselves were part of his body. He noted the rising airspeed, holding the DC-6B at treetop level, rolling it right against the monstrous rising heat currents generated by the flame front, and all the time holding the release just in front of the fire to surprise the beast with a sudden barrier of moisture and chemical retardant.

"Pull out!" Jerry called from the right seat at almost precisely the same moment Clark closed the dump valve and rolled wings level, pulling hard to reduce the number of trees in the windscreen, and then rolling into a tight left turn to start gaining altitude down valley.

"Tanker Ten coming over the ridge," Bill's copilot, Chuck Hines, reported from the right seat of the P-3.

Clark and Jerry were far enough into their left turn to see the P-3 cross the ridge at exactly the same point, and they watched for the red retardant to start pouring from the belly as Deason and Hines followed the same profile, skimming treetops to dive down the slope and add to the protective barrier between the escaping squad and the monster on their heels.

———

The P-3 Orion took the updraft over the ridge just as Bill had expected, and with the thrust levers severely retarded and the huge four-bladed propellers in high rpm and acting as speed brakes, the military version of the Electra nosed over and stayed mere feet above the trees and almost exactly over the fire line. Bill toggled the tanks open, but for some reason could feel nothing leaving the plane. They were less than a hundred yards beyond the ridge, and the liquid should have been pouring out. He mashed harder, his eyes flicking to the indicator and seeing nothing that indicated they were dumping. His attention was distracted for less than a second, but it was enough for a slight amount of pressure on the yoke to the right, causing the Orion to slide over the fire line and squarely into the column of superheated plasma from below. The huge kick of turbulence beneath them was a scorching updraft, and Bill's hand pulsed forward slightly to oppose it, forcing the nose of the diving, skidding P-3 too far over at the same moment a small grove of lodgepole pine literally exploded beneath the left wing, the force of the fiery updraft rolling the P-3 to the right just enough to drop the engines on the right wing below the altitude of the burning trees.

The impact of the outboard and inboard propellers on the right wing with the solid canopy of flaming forest was enough to destroy the outboard propeller immediately, sending all four blades off in different directions, one of them cleanly slicing the hub from number-three engine and disintegrating its propeller as well. One of the fragmenting blades whirled across the underside of the P-3, punching gouges and holes and impacting the inboard left engine's propeller with a glancing blow that was insufficient to blow the prop apart but enough to unbalance it.

"Jeez!" Bill hauled back on the yoke and jammed the left rudder to successfully pull the ship out of the trees and regain control, reducing the descent rate with the extra airspeed from the dive and slowly dishing out until he was level and turning left down the valley.

"Tanker Ten, Lead Four-Two. Are you guys okay?" Sam called. They had no time to answer.

"What have we got?" Bill called out.

"Loss of three and four, Bill!" a wide-eyed Chuck Hines replied, his head jerking back and forth from the forward panel to the right window.

"Okay . . . checklist . . . ah, let's run the engine-loss and two-engine checklists, and give me max power on one and two."

Hines leaned over his set of throttles, adjusting the settings.

"Did we feather three and four?"

"Bill, the props are gone. They're just frigging gone!"

An intermittent heavy vibration was coursing through the P-3, and Bill's eyes went to the instruments looking for some indication of what was wrong.

"What *is* that?" he asked.

"I don't know . . . propeller on the left, maybe?"

There was a singular laugh from the left seat. "We can't afford to lose another fan."

Chuck Hines leaned forward, peering closely at the engine instruments.

"I think it may be number two prop," Hines said. "Can I pull it back?"

"No! I need every ounce of torque I can get. Ah . . . call Operations if you can reach them. Tell them we've got a severe emergency and are coming straight back to West Yellowstone. Wouldn't be a bad idea to get the fire equipment out for us as well."

"Roger," Chuck Hines replied, pulling his boom microphone closer and triggering the appropriate frequency.

"How's she flying, Bill?" Chuck asked while waiting for a response from the radio.

"Like an eighteen-wheeler pulled by a Volkswagen. We never got any of that last ten thousand pounds out of the belly, did we?"

"No. I don't know why the doors didn't open."

"Well, that's not helping, but we should be okay. I'm climbing a little now."

Once more the vibrations coursed through the aircraft, shaking the crew severely for a few seconds.

"God, we can't continue with that!" Bill said.

"Are we closer to Jackson or West Yellow?" Chuck Hines asked.

"I think . . . we'd better go north. We can follow the Yellowstone River to Yellowstone Lake and ditch this puppy if number two lets go. But right now, I'm climbing a bit."

"So, right turn over Bryarly here?"

"Yeah. Then down the valley. Make sure we haven't forgotten any checklist items."

"Roger."

"Holy shit, I never saw that coming."

"It's okay, Bill," Chuck counseled.

"No, it's not. I've never broken anyone's air machine before. Dammit!"

There was a burst of static on the radio, followed by Clark Maxwell's voice.

"Tanker Ten, are you guys okay?"

Bill held a finger in the air indicating he'd answer. He pressed the transmit button on the yoke without letting up on the pressure he was having to maintain to roll left into the live engines.

"Well, Clark, I really screwed up this time. We've lost our props on three and four, the ship's vibrating, and I think we may have damaged number two as well. But we're airborne and limping home."

"What happened?"

"Later, okay? I'm a little busy up here right now. But if Sam's on the frequency, you need to know we couldn't open the tanks on that last drop. All they've got is Clark's contribution."

"Roger Tanker Ten, Lead Four-Two here. I'm chasing after you now."

"Ah, negative, Four-Two. Tanker Eighty-eight's empty. Let him join up on me. You have more tankers in holding?"

"Roger. Three."

"Then use 'em immediately! Just tell them to stay about fifty feet higher than the treetops. I just got too low."

There was a hesitation.

"Ah, Lead Four-Two, get your tail back there and keep dropping, please! This is Clark. I'll take care of him."

"Roger. Four-Two is turning around, and if you guys can change frequency, I'll work the others on this one."

They all acknowledged, and the copilot dialed in the new air-to-air frequency as Jerry did the same thing on Clark's flight deck.

"Tanker Ten, Tanker Forty-four. Bill, where are you?" Dave Barrett asked. "I heard you guys go to this frequency. I'm empty and north of the lake."

"We're somewhere south of the lake, Dave, going down the river valley and climbing slowly but steadily," Bill replied.

"Okay, I'm going to circle back and join up with you guys."

"Bill, Clark. I've got you in sight about four miles ahead, and I'm going to come up on your right wing and take a look. Approved?"

"Hell *yes,* approved! Something's shaking the hell out of us up here every minute or so, and I suspect number-two prop."

"Roger. We'll take a look. But if you have any doubts you can make it, consider ditching in the lake."

"Yeah, I am, Clark."

"You guys . . . have chutes?"

"Roger. Two of them. Remember, I'm the old fool who refuses to fly without chutes."

"Thank God. I'd recommend you put them on and open a cabin door, and if it gets too gamey or you lose number two, put it on autopilot and jump."

"Well, I've been meaning to ask Jerry to get this autopilot fixed," Bill replied with a chuckle, knowing full well who was sitting in Clark's right seat.

Clark could almost feel Jerry grimace, as he raised a finger and hit the transmit button.

"Bill? This is Jerry. Don't try to save that bird if there's anything at all risky about staying in her. I'm insured, and you guys are irreplaceable. And I'm sorry about the autopilot. I'll kill Trent on return."

"Roger. But I'm a lot more concerned about that young woman and her squad back on the mountain right now than I am about a flock of old pelicans like us."

# Chapter 34

There was no question that the fire was going to catch them. The only thing to be determined was where they would try to survive it.

Karen could hear the roar of the flame front rising from the east and behind her as she tried to stumble along helping Dave a few feet at a time up the steep slope, and she finally realized that he was right. There was no way.

Going downslope would be fatal, even if they could do it rapidly. The valley would fill with smoke and flames, and there would be even more deadfall fuel the lower they went. Staying exactly where they were would also prove fatal, since they were up to their ankles in deadfall and bone-dry tinder that would instantly explode in fourteen-hundred-degree flames when the overall fire front arrived. The personal shelters repelled the radient heat, but they could do little for air temperatures approaching eighteen hundred degrees. There was no time to dwell on what death would be like inside a roasting shell of a shelter overwhelmed by heat, but the assurance of non-survivability was a given.

There had to be another solution, and she forced her mind to back off from the precipice of terror she was on and think. Dave was looking at her helplessly, convinced he was spending his last minutes on earth. The roar in the background was rising slowly and steadily, though it was suddenly broken by the whine of a diving airplane, the King Air, and then a DC-6, which Karen recognized instantly as Clark's, followed by Bill Deason's P-3.

"Oh, thank God!" Dave said, perceiving deliverance.

"They'll slow it, but they can't stop it," Karen said, her mind searching for a glimmer of hope. A solution.

*The bear den!*

She'd seen it when she was trailing behind the others. The problem would be finding it again.

She mentally retraced her steps, trying to resist the panic she felt and think clearly. How far had she been downslope when she'd seen the hole? There was no time to search. She'd have to go right to it.

She looked downslope, remembering the stand of aspen in the area of the den. She could make out aspen leaves in the distance. It was worth a try.

"Come on! Now! Lean on me, and we're going to do this like the old three-legged races. Coordinate our movements, okay?"

"Where to?"

"You'll see. Just work hard."

They stepped off together, falling once, picking themselves up, and trying again, her left leg serving as his right as he maintained half his weight on her left shoulder. A hundred feet later they had developed a workable, if painful, pattern, and she was becoming adept at finding her footing even with the added hundred pounds on her left side. They stumbled past a large rock and continued on for a second before she stopped them.

"Wait! Wait!"

"What?"

"Stay here," she said, dashing off a few yards and looking up and down, and suddenly pointing at something with a broad smile.

"I found it!"

"Found what?" Dave asked as another airtanker screamed down the slope behind them, whining and picking up airspeed as the hiss of falling fire retardant filled their hopes.

She came back and latched on again, guiding him the few steps to where she'd been standing.

"See that hole down there? Like a small cave? We're going to clear the brush from the entrance in about two minutes, hope the owner isn't home, get ourselves inside, pull the shelters around us, and hunker down."

"What *is* that?"

"A bear den, I think. I saw it earlier."

"But what if there's a bear in there?"

"There's a bigger, hotter, meaner bear out here! C'mon. Let's move!"

Quickly they worked their way down to the opening, and she pulled out her headlamp and dropped down on her stomach, aiming the light inside. She could see the back of the den, and, although it stank and was smaller than she'd hoped, it was empty.

With Dave working from one knee, together they pulled and hauled and scratched to clear all the vegetation away from the entrance, getting the fuels as far away as possible. Karen pulled her Woodman's Pal from its sheath on her belt and started slashing with its blade. She'd worn the tool since picking it up on an Alaskan assignment years before. She regretted now having dropped her Pulaski earlier when she ordered the squad to run, even though it had been the right order to give. She imagined the others had reached the rocks by now, provided they hadn't tried to double back to find

Dave and her. That possibility was worrying her greatly, but her radio was apparently broken. There was no way to connect with them to order them to go on. She had to rely on their common sense.

The roar was becoming more pronounced, and they both could see flames leaping from the tops of the trees in the distance back to the east.

Once more a DC-6B flashed downslope trailing red liquid over the fire, this time from a different direction. She imagined it was Clark, but she couldn't see the number on the tail. It was the middle of the afternoon, and the thick smoke was only allowing in a slight hint of the sun's orange glow. Less than a minute later, a P-3 followed the same path, although she couldn't see the expected cascade of red slurry streaming from its belly.

"Okay, Dave, unfold your shelter for me and shinny in there feet-first without it."

"What?"

"Both our shelters are going to keep the heat out of the hole. I need them together."

"Right," he replied, squeezing himself into the hole, his head slowly disappearing. "It's awfully tight in here."

"Something smaller than a bear owned it. Fold your legs!"

"I'm trying. It's hard with this ankle. Oh . . . okay, come on. I'm ready."

She spread open her own shelter and folded the two together before getting on her knees facing outward to began the task of worming her way inside. She was startled at how soon her feet touched the back wall of the den. She folded her legs and felt Dave helping to pull her in more, but her head was still partially exposed in the hole. Her heart sank.

*Oh, Lord! There's not enough room to maneuver.*

She shinnied back out, hearing his muffled voice.

"What are you doing?"

"Plaster yourself against the back, concave, your back against it."

She could hear the growing roar of the fire and also his scrambling around.

"Okay. This hurts, but come on."

She could feel the heat now, the flames visible through the trees, firebombs cascading above the tree line as the flames crowned from top to top, exploding their way even through the slurry that had clearly slowed it down.

She knelt again and folded the combined silver shelters, bringing the combination in after her as she wiggled in again, this time folding her legs and pulling herself completely inside with barely enough room to arrange the four layers of the shelters as a plug to the entrance.

"What are you doing?" Dave asked.

"Hold . . . on . . ." she managed, forcing herself to avoid claustrophobic thoughts of panic as she painfully rotated around with her knees retracted against her stomach and her back holding the plug firm against the entrance from the inside.

Their only chance was a fast-moving fire. If it lingered, burning the ground cover and saturating the air and the ground with intense heat, they would either bake to death or asphyxiate from lack of oxygen.

Karen had jammed herself into a painful fetal position, and she tried to slow her breathing and loosen her muscles and wait, but her whole body ached, and every muscle was screaming for freedom. She could hear occasional muffled sounds coming from Dave, who was pressed against her as inconveniently as any human body could be. He was speaking words of reassurance and fear, and they fully echoed her own feelings of terror greater than she'd ever experienced in her entire life. They were, indeed, in the belly of the beast.

The roar of the fire rapidly increased to a deep, moaning rumble, the very ground shaking around them, as an unearthly muffled howl rose in pitch and filled their ears, blocking out all other sounds and all other thoughts.

BRYARLY, WYOMING

Jimmy Wolf had heard the mayday call from the Jet Ranger on Larry Black's handheld VHF radio. The shock of having destroyed his own home had not worn off, but the reality that there had been a major defeat in the firefight had finally broken through his bravado. The entire eastern side of the far ridge was burning now, and moving westward along the steep, northern slopes. Unless something changed, the east wind was going to propel the fire down the funnel of the valley until it reached and obliterated Bryarly. Anyone left would likely die, and he was not ready to cash out.

"Who's going after the downed helicopter crew?" Jimmy asked as Larry tried to herd him into the Chinook that was sitting in the middle of the park.

"I've called Jackson Helibase. They're going to send one of the helicopters."

"Yeah, but they're needed for the fires."

"Jimmy, just get aboard. They'll take care of it."

"How about you?"

"I'm going with you. As far as we know now, we're the last ones out, except for any survivors on the helicopter."

"I know where he went down."

"Jimmy, it's okay. Let's complete the evacuation. You didn't listen to me before. This time, please listen."

Sixteen other residents were sitting in the maw of the helicopter gazing down their valley away from the flames now licking more than a hundred feet into the air back upslope. Destruction had been just a possibility before. Even with the spot fires, most of them thought the worst catastrophe could be avoided.

Now all hope had been lost.

Reluctantly, Jimmy put on his hat and climbed the short built-in stairs into the Chinook before turning and helping Larry up. The helmeted crew member who was tending the cabin, and was also the copilot, looked at Larry with a questioning glance.

Larry Black, city manager of the doomed community, gestured for him to go ahead.

The crewman leaned over and pulled up the door, securing it before speaking an all clear into his headset microphone. He turned and moved into the left seat to begin the before-takeoff checklist, unaware of the sudden motion behind him as Jimmy Wolf stood and flipped open the door latch, dropping the steps and clambering out, then raising the door back into place before Larry could respond.

"Whoa! Hey, wait!" Larry yelled as he rushed toward the resecured door. The pilots saw the sudden "door open" light illuminate, but Jimmy closed it almost as fast, extinguishing the light. With the noise of the engine and the rotors rising and their headsets on, neither pilot heard Larry yelling, and they lifted off.

Through one of the windows Larry could see Jimmy wave them off and trot back toward the village square. The copilot saw him, too, and motioned the pilot into a hover as he turned to Larry.

"You want to set down and go get him?"

They were in a hover fifteen feet above the park and turning slowly.

Larry shook his head and cupped his hands, yelling at the copilot who had his headset partially pulled back.

"No. I've done everything I can for that fool. Just notify the rescue force that they'll need to pluck him out of here, too. I figure he has about two hours."

———

Jimmy turned when he reached the town square and watched the big Chinook gather speed as it headed down the valley. He could imagine the consternation of the city manager at yet one more act of defiance from his troublesome citizen with the waterlogged house.

But Jimmy Wolf had another mission, and for the first time in too many years to remember, it felt absolutely right. When he'd first moved to his mansion in Bryarly, he'd looked around at the surrounding wilderness areas—nearly inaccessible canyons, draws, hills, and forests—and immediately paid nearly $150,000 for a custom-built, field-capable Humvee, with satellite communication, GPS, and even gas masks on board. In the years since, he had become familiar with nearly every foot of ground in a twenty-mile radius of Bryarly. He enjoyed pushing the Humvee to its limits.

Jimmy slipped behind the wheel of the Humvee, and fired off the engine, bringing up the GPS screen and working through the buttons until he'd isolated the point near the canyon he intended to reach.

*Probably a bloody song in all of this,* he thought as he maneuvered around the corner and headed west. *At least I can keep Leno laughing next time I'm on.*

———

The southern shore of Yellowstone Lake was moving under the nose of Bill Deason's P-3 with Clark Maxwell flying formation on the right side.

"Bill, I see some metal damage to the cowling on number-four engine, and there's a dent in the wing tip. Looks like one of the prop blades gouged the fuselage going from right to left, and it might have nicked your number-two prop. Is she still vibrating?"

"Yeah, every minute or so. We're experimenting with different power settings."

Dave Barret, who had backtracked to meet them, pulled up and joined on the crippled P-3's left wing.

"About another thirty-five miles, Bill," Dave was saying. "Hang in there."

The unusual sight of three large four-engine aircraft flying overhead in formation was turning heads on the ground as tourists and rangers alike looked up, but few were able to see that the propellers were entirely missing from the right engines of the Orion.

As they passed the middle of the lake, the vibrations returned, but this time they refused to dampen out. Bill again scanned the instrument panel as the severity steadily increased, building to such a violent shaking that he couldn't read anything on the panel. On the left wing, he could feel the inboard left engine begin to gyrate on its mountings, which meant it was seconds away from ripping off the aircraft.

Instinctively, Bill reached up and feathered number-two propeller, and as the huge paddlelike blades moved into alignment with the wind and the propellor ceased to rotate, the shaking diminished and stopped. They completed the engine-shutdown checklist and pushed the remaining engine to a slight overboost.

"Can we make it like this?" Chuck Hines asked.

"I think so," Bill replied. They were at 10,500 feet and beginning to lose altitude with thirty miles to go over terrain ahead as high as eight thousand.

Dave Barrett had seen the propeller on number two winding down.

"Bill, what are you doing?" Barrett's voice rang in their headsets.

Bill triggered the radio and explained the shutdown, and Clark's voice came back.

"Bill, you'd better think about ditching her."

"Naw, I think we're okay."

"If you get too far into the hills and can't hold altitude, your choices are going to get pretty slim."

Bill looked at the rate of descent and the airspeed and ran some rough calculations in his head before turning to Chuck Hines.

"I'm going to stick with her awhile and see if I can't get her back home. But it's too risky for me to commit you. You get in your chute right now, open the rear door, and jump while we've still got altitude and before we get over the geysers."

The copilot started to argue, and Bill cut him off.

"That's an order from the skipper of this aircraft. You're jumping. Why do you think I've taken the abuse all these years for being the only damn air-tanker captain to carry chutes? If I don't have you use one now, I never *will* live it down."

"I just thought you wanted ballast," Chuck said, trying to smile, his hand shaking slightly on the yoke.

"Naw, goes back to my sport-jumping days and a particular C-119 crash. I'll tell you the tale back in West Yellow."

"I've heard it, Bill," Chuck said.

"Okay, so go get it on. Now. And open the hatch," Bill said.

Chuck nodded.

"Are you sure, Bill?"

"Go, dammit! Don't forget to pull that D-ring the second you exit."

He toggled the radio. "Dave? Clark? This is Bill. Chuck is jumping. I fired him. Please mark his position, and tell me when he's away and you have a chute."

There was a hesitation, and Bill thought he could feel the slight vibration as Chuck jumped.

"Okay, Bill, he's out and has a good chute, and he'll be coming down in a safe location. We're relaying his lat/long's for pickup."

"Thank God. Okay, now to get her home."

Jerry's voice came on frequency, his voice terse and low "Bill, don't try this. I don't care about that airplane. Trim her slightly nose up, get in your chute, and bail out of there. Better yet, turn her around so you're facing the lake."

"Jerry . . . thanks, but I think I can do this. Really. If I have to fly down the west entrance pass, I think I can keep her up here long enough."

*If,* Bill thought to himself, *whatever tailwind has been helping me doesn't die off.*

The altimeter was unwinding through ninety-eight hundred feet, and he trimmed the nose up slightly to lessen the descent rate and accept the slower airspeed, realizing too late it had been the wrong aerodynamic move. He tried to regain the speed, but he'd have to trade altitude for every knot. There were two eighty-five-hundred-foot rises he would have to get over to make it back to West Yellowstone, and he realized it wasn't going to work.

"Okay, guys, I'm gonna turn around and put her in the lake. I'm going to fly up the valley here and come around a low spot there to head back east."

He glanced at the altitude, shocked to see it winding down through nine thousand. He was already too low to make it over the next ridge ten miles to the west, and he doubted he could turn tightly enough with one engine to follow the road.

For the first time, real apprehension, like cold groundwater around the feet of a trapped man, began to creep into his thinking. The descent rate at the slower airspeed was now three hundred feet per minute, and he'd lost the tailwind. He thought of bailing out, but the aircraft was not far from Old Faithful and the Old Faithful lodge area, and God knows where it might go with no one at the controls.

*If nothing else, I can just pancake it onto the nearest flat surface,* he thought. *This old girl's tough as nails. She'll stay together.*

"Bill, get out of that thing, now! This is Jerry."

"Too late, Jerry. Too much danger it might come down on a tourist bus or something. Stay with me. I'll make it back to the lake."

*Eighty-seven hundred!* Bill read on the altimeter. That was decidedly lower than he'd figured.

There was a particular turn point ahead, and he knew it led to a corridor of lower terrain that could take him back over the ten miles to the lake. Lake Yellowstone was seventy-three hundred feet above sea level, and the terrain he would have to cross was a little under eight thousand in his memory. Inevitably, he would lose additional altitude trying to make the turn, but maybe he could hold on to her.

Bill reached over to the only remaining live throttle and forced himself to push it above its torque limit, beyond the red line.

The small area known as Porcupine Hills slid beneath his nose as he banked and skidded the Orion from a northerly to an easterly heading. He was within a thousand feet of the surface now, and the surface was going to rise in altitude.

*How much higher is it this way?* Bill wondered, grabbing one of his sectional charts and trying to open it to the right panel while hanging on to the controls. Finally the contoured lines of the park fell into view, and he studied them with great speed, his heart sinking.

*Oh my God, it comes up to eighty-two hundred along here!*

He could see it wasn't going to work, and the airmen in the adjacent airplanes could sense it, too.

"Dave, this is Clark." The transmission was sudden and crisp. "This will sound nuts, but if we got our respective noses under Bill's wing tips and pulled some upward pressure, couldn't we get him from here to there? Buy him some miles?"

"What?" Dave asked.

"We might just be able to do it. Just a little buoyancy could stretch him ten miles or so."

There was a brief hesitation before anyone responded.

"You *are* nuts, Maxwell. Let's give it try. Get in position but don't make contact before we're both ready."

"Hey, guys, no! You could crash us all!" Bill was saying, torn between grasping at a straw and hoping for a suspension of the laws of physics. Without help of some sort, he almost certainly wouldn't make the lake. But if they fouled up, all three could crash. "Clark? Dave? Are you sure you want to try this?"

"Hang on," Clark said.

Both DC-6Bs were already maneuvering into position, braving the disruptive effect of the wake turbulence from the Orion's wings by positioning their cockpits just aft and below the respective wing tips of the Orion. Their altitude above the terrain of Yellowstone Park was now less than seven hundred feet. It was now or never.

"Okay, Dave, on my count of three, we engage by coming under the wing tips so as to lay them just behind our cockpits on top of the fuselage as we come up. Understand?"

"Roger."

"Are you in position?"

"Yeah."

"Bill, hold her as steady as you can, whatever happens."

"Roger."

"We may blank out your ailerons, but we'll be keeping your wings level on our own."

Clark realized both he and Jerry were holding their breath. Even though he owned all three airplanes, Jerry was saying nothing, five lives at stake completely overriding his usual penurious tendencies.

The right wing tip was less than three feet above the fuselage of Clark's DC-6, the wake turbulence not as severe as he'd expected. Clark pulsed the yoke to make sure of the feedback and the response, and triggered the radio as he came forward, aligning the front of the Orion's wing with his forward window. He could see Dave doing the same thing, and waited until the other ship looked steady.

"Okay, one . . . two . . . three . . . up!"

With an unpleasant crunching sound of metal to metal, the underside of the Orion's right wing tip made contact with the metal above the cockpit. Clark pulled back slightly on the yoke to compensate for the disturbed aerodynamics, fighting the roll and the turbulence and the tendency of the extra weight on the forward part of the DC-6B to push the nose down. Instead, the body angle of both airliners increased nearly five degrees as they fought to remain steady while exerting close to equal lift on the Orion's wings, doing what the single remaining engine could not.

"Jerry, push the throttles up a bit. Give me more."

Jerry's left hand gathered the throttles and nudged them forward.

"It's working, fellows," Bill said, his voice strained but excited.

"Rate of descent is down to zero," Jerry announced.

"Great!" Clark managed through gritted teeth, his control movements trying to keep pace with the asymmetric gyrations of the Orion, which was in effect resting with its wing tips on the backs of both DC-6s.

"Clark, we're still below the terrain we're approaching," Jerry said.

"Yeah . . . stand by . . ." was all Clark could manage. The control inputs he was making were not matching those Dave was using, and they were beginning to fight each other in a resonant gyration that was causing the Orion to roll left and right. There would be only moments left before the Orion would end up lifting a wing off one of them and crashing it back down, with possibly catastrophic results.

*Come on! Come on! Oh, no!*

"Break away!" Clark snapped on the radio as he pulsed the yoke forward and tried to disengage, feeling the Orion's wing following him down until Dave Barrett did the same thing on the other side.

Clark dropped thirty feet below the Orion as Bill tried to regain control, stabilizing the pitch of the crippled P-3 quickly, but beginning to descend again.

Clark saw Dave Barrett moving out to the left and climbing. He looked at his radio altimeter and read three hundred feet above a rising landscape.

"Dave, get back in position. We can do this."

Bill's voice came over the headset before Dave could respond.

"No, we can't, guys. Thank you for a noble attempt, but there's not enough time or room ahead. Move out to the right, Clark."

"Bill, dammit, we're not going to let you crash."

Jerry had hold of his right sleeve. "Clark."

"What?" Clark said, turning toward Jerry.

"He's right. Move out of the way of his wing tip."

With his throat dry and his heart pounding and his mind screaming *No!*, Clark banked right slightly and soared clear of the descending Orion. They were less than two hundred feet above the surface now, with another problem ahead. What had been a flat, burned-out moonscape with very little regrowth since 1988 was giving way to unburned timber standing as much as eighty feet high.

"Just my luck to find the one unburned forest in these parts," Bill radioed. "I'm going to shamelessly overboost your engine, Jerry."

"Go for it," Jerry replied, his voice small and strained, his eyes on the rising tide of green ahead of them.

Bill shoved the remaining thrust lever as far forward as he dared, hearing the huge Allison turboprop as it screamed at illegal speeds and temperatures. It was truly the last ounce of power he could wring from it, and it appeared to be working, flattening the descent rate but producing no climb.

"How far to the lake?" Bill asked.

"Ah . . . six miles, Bill. If you can clear this plateau ahead."

Clark moved to the left again, slightly higher than the Orion, seeing alarming readings on the radio altimeter. He could see Bill in the left seat holding on to the yoke, his head moving in various directions as he worked to find another solution. But ultimately they all knew it was a matter of Newtonian physics, of gravity and thrust and kinetic energy, and he was losing the battle. The tops of the trees were now less than thirty feet beneath the Orion's fuselage, and the plateau had flattened to level. The lake was visible in the distance, but the P-3 was still sinking slowly into the thick forest, and there was simply too much distance between it and the water.

"Bill, don't let go of her, man. We're so close."

"I guess I picked a bad plan here," Bill said. There was a pause and then an open channel and then another resigned chuckle in that familiar, friendly baritone voice. "Well, fellows, it's been a great career, if this doesn't work out. Clark, tell Judy . . . tell Judy . . ." His voice caught, then resumed. "You tell that cutie of mine that no matter where I go after this life, I've already been in heaven for all these years in her arms. Tell her that, please. And that I love her. Not all of us get to say good-bye, you know."

He released the transmit switch.

The trees were ten feet below the belly of the P-3, flashing past at 140 miles per hour. Clark pushed his transmit button.

"God bless you, Bill," he said, knowing nothing else to say and feeling impotent and stupid and helpless, tears obscuring his vision as he raged internally at the lack of anything left to do.

"Amen," Dave echoed.

There was a brief moment of beauty as the Orion settled gently into the treetops creating a bow wave that followed along like wind waves in a ripe wheat field. But beneath the uppermost boughs were bigger and thicker boughs, and like a million tiny hands reaching up to pull him back to earth, they padded and then clawed at the Orion's slick metallic belly and the one remaining propeller until the gentle brushing became lethal impact and the big aircraft seemed to submerge suddenly into the green canopy with a roar of fragmenting metal and wood clearly audible in each DC-6 cockpit overhead.

And he was gone.

Clark struggled to pull up before he, too, fell victim to the trees that were now falling away and sloping down to the lake just three miles ahead.

"I'm breaking right and climbing a little," Clark said on the frequency, his voice utterly flat.

"Roger. Behind you," Dave Barrett replied.

He brought them around to a westerly heading and then back north. There was no trouble marking the site. A tall, angry column of smoke was rising from the location, and a single pass overhead confirmed the worst: burning wreckage strewn in a line of broken trees through the forest.

# Chapter 35

Phil Dale had been the first to discover that Karen and Dave were no longer bringing up the rear. He'd glanced around, then stopped in abject surprise, searching the forest behind them for any sign of movement and scarcely believing that he couldn't see them. The roar of the fire was growing in the distance, and no one knew the dangers better than Karen.

He yelled back up the trail after the others, but the sound was lost to the noises of men crashing frantically through the woods. He reached for his radio but his hand found an empty holster. *Oh, no! I must have knocked it out when I was struggling to ditch my pack!* If he turned to go back now for Karen and Dave, they'd be looking for him, too.

He could see the ridge looming impossibly high above them and knew they were all exhausted from climbing on the run. They would need every minute to get to safety.

*Something terrible must have happened to Karen and Dave,* he thought, *for them to fail to keep up. Some sort of accident, or injury.*

Indecision was killing him, and he swore at himself as he swung around and took a few steps back down the slope, then stopped, cupping his hands to yell for Karen.

The only sounds were the primeval roar of the oncoming fire.

He turned back and began to run after the others, angry with himself for wasting so many precious seconds.

*Maybe one of the other guys has his radio!* he thought, the idea justifying a renewed sprint as he crashed through the underbrush, leaping over snags and trying not to fall. Fifty yards ahead he saw George at the tail end of the squad suddenly turn around, his eyes wide in surprise and searching back through the forest the same way Phil had moments before.

George turned and began moving back to intercept him, absorbing the fact that Karen and Dave were missing.

"Do you have your radio?"

"No, I must have dropped it."

"Dammit. What do we do, Phil?"

"Man, I don't know. It's a huge forest." Phil hesitated. "Look, George. Go after the others. Tell them I'm going back to find Karen and Dave. No sense in imperiling the rest of you."

"You can't go back," George said quietly. "There's no time. It's on our heels."

"But we can't just *leave* them out here!" He cupped his hands again, shouting at the top of his lungs. "KAREN! DAVE!"

"You know the training, Phil," George said. "We may not make it as it is. They know what to do, and they've got their shelters. There's no guarantee we'd find them even if we tried."

"Goddammit, George, look at your feet! Their emergency shelters won't help if they're sitting in all this fuel. They won't make it."

"Neither will we! Come on, man. Other than suicide, we've got no choice."

Tears of frustration were squeezing past the testosterone barrier as Phil finally agreed, every fiber straining against the decision. He resumed scrambling uphill toward the ridge and the shelter they'd prepared earlier, guilt already tearing at him, hoping he'd hear Karen's voice any second.

ONE MILE WEST OF BRYARLY

Jimmy Wolf steered the big Humvee around another fallen tree and then easily climbed over the next one. He was being thrown around against the seat belt in the cab of the machine, but he was loving it. To see through the increasingly thick pall of smoke, he'd switched on the row of halogen lights mounted on the roof, thinking how cool they looked stabbing into the murky forest.

*Must be hell to be lying there with a forest fire approaching wondering if anyone's coming,* he thought, feeling a flash of empathy for the downed helicopter crew, a long-dormant emotion he'd all but forgotten.

Jimmy checked his GPS again. He had about another mile to go to reach the place where he knew the Jet Ranger had gone down. He'd heard a helicopter overhead minutes before, but couldn't see it through the smoke. If the crash site was equally opaque, no one would ever find them in time from the air.

The fact that the main fire was coming down the slope from the southeast and accelerating toward the town was merely an inconvenience. He felt neither heroic nor foolhardy, just satisfied. *This is like writing a great tune,* he thought. The variations were all his, and whether the decisions he was making second by second killed him or made him a hero was immaterial. What he was engaged in doing was his creation, and he was never happier than when flying against the wind.

The Humvee bounced off another snag, the forward left wheel dropping into a hole and throwing him toward the windshield. He shifted back to low and let it right itself and crawl out before accelerating across a small meadow. *The U.S. Army did a crackerjack job of thinking up this baby,* he thought. It was impressive and tough.

Once more he checked his progress on the GPS, letting the Humvee lurch ahead while he studied the glowing screen, then suddenly slammed on the brakes.

The edge of the small canyon was no more than five feet ahead, with a 150-foot drop-off, and he'd almost rumbled over the edge.

*Right. Can't drive this thing on autopilot.*

Jimmy set the brake and got out, peering over the rim. The bottom of the canyon was a riverbed lush in vegetation, and it was on fire, the choking, grayish smoke flowing along westward like a hellish river. He jumped on the hood of the Humvee and looked around. Visibility was less than a quarter mile, he figured, which meant that he would almost have to run over the survivors to find them.

Provided there *were* survivors.

*Damn shame I can't see any smoke from the crash,* he thought. But they had to be somewhere out there in front of him.

There were sounds behind him, a roar of some sort, or he could be imagining it. Then again, maybe it was an aircraft. The smoky pall over everything was weird and played tricks with sounds.

He'd overheard a quick conversation in town about how incredibly loud the roar of a forest fire became as it closed in on you, and a small flicker of something approximating apprehension danced around his mind for a few seconds, spurring him back into action. He pictured the two men aboard the helicopter hurt but alive, with a monstrous fire bearing down on them, and he couldn't let that happen.

*That'd be a terrible way to go,* he thought. *Hang on, you buggers. If you're still alive, I'll get you the hell out of here.*

He made note of the GPS reading and decided to use a grid search like he'd seen in a movie once. Statistically, one of the characters had said, a grid search worked better than a random search. He wasn't entirely sure what a grid search meant, but he knew what a grid was, and it couldn't be too different.

Jimmy studied his GPS screen, deciding which direction to drive, how far to go, and how much to displace the return source to parallel the first. He marked the starting point electronically in the GPS computer and put the

Humvee back in motion, rolling all the windows down and silencing the satellite music system he'd been listening to, just in case the pilot could call out to him.

*Damn! I forgot I've got a PA!*

Jimmy put on a headset and adjusted the microphone before turning on the PA system and blasting his voice into the murk.

"YO! ANYONE OUT THERE? YELL BACK AT ME, MATE, OR BANG SOMETHING AROUND IF YOU HEAR THIS, RIGHT?"

A small meadow opened up ahead, and he stopped at the edge of it, killed the engine, and listened. He could almost imagine he was hearing a voice against the background of the low, rumbling roar in the distance. He started again and bounced across the meadow, moving into the trees at the same moment a rock bounced off his hood and caused him to brake.

"Hey! Wot the 'ell was *that*?" he said to no one in particular, a flash of anger crossing his mind that a rock would dare hit his expensive toy.

*Hold on!*

He killed the engine once again and jumped out. "Anyone there?" he yelled.

"Right in front of you," a strained male voice replied from somewhere in front of the Humvee. Jimmy hurried around the front to find two men, one of them unconscious, the other struggling to stand. "Jesus, man. You almost ran over us!"

"Sorry, mate. Could you hear me on the PA, then?"

"They could hear you in Canberra, for God's sake! Do you have a first-aid kit? My copilot needs immediate help."

"Bloody hell! Are you from the Jet Ranger?"

"Yes." Trent was leaning over, trying to lift the copilot by himself. "I'm the pilot, and my copilot's in bad shape."

"That's why I'm here, mate. Leave him there and let me have a look."

"Are you a doctor?"

"No . . . but I know a few things. There's a first-aid med kit in the back."

Trent was severely bruised but otherwise unhurt. He stood painfully and went to the Humvee's back hatch, finding the kit. There was an emergency defibrillator kit as well, and after a moment's hesitation he unclipped that, too.

Jimmy bandaged the worst cut on Eric's right arm and then checked his breathing and airway.

"One more item. There's a green emergency oxygen bottle in the right rear utility bin."

They retrieved it, and Jimmy slipped an oxygen mask on Eric's face and turned it on before directing Trent to open the rear doors and lay out a blanket. Together, they lifted the copilot as gently as possible and carried him to the Humvee, loading him in the back.

"You able to stay back here with him?"

Trent nodded.

"Good. It'll take us thirty minutes to get back and get a chopper in, if we can. The smoke's getting very heavy."

"What if we can't?" Trent asked, his defenses all but gone.

Jimmy grinned. "Nobody says no to Jimmy Wolf, mate!" He closed them in the rear hatch and moved to the driver's seat to get started, as Trent tried to ignore the dull pain in his back and mull over the bizarre reality of their rescuer's identity.

## WEST YELLOWSTONE AIRPORT, MONTANA

Clark Maxwell and Jerry Stein flew in silence through the twenty air miles between the crash site and the airport, speaking only during the approach in the staccato and sterile language of checklists and flaps and landing gear.

They ran the shutdown checklist and sat immobile in their respective seats as the props and the sounds slowly wound down and stopped, the puzzled ground crew approaching with increasing concern over why no one was moving out of the cockpit. The refueling crew and the retardant-refill crew were both waiting.

"I don't know what to say, Clark," Jerry said at last, his voice low and husky.

"I know. Me either."

Clark inhaled and sat up, looking over at Jerry. "But it is time for some hard answers about the DC-6 fleet."

"I know."

"That's my point, Jerry. I think there are things you do know that you've been hiding. What happened back there . . ." He choked up momentarily and fought to regain his composure, taking a ragged breath in the process. "What . . . happened back there, Jerry, while unrelated, has pushed this over the edge. What happened with the DC-6s? Where have they been? How much did they fly? And why?"

Jerry's head was bobbing slowly, but his eyes were unfocused and staring unseeingly at the instrument panel.

"The answers are going to come out one way or another, Jerry. Better they come from you. And I mean now, man! Go ahead and fire me for challenging you, but—"

"I'm not firing you, Clark."

"Okay, then, answer the damned question."

"The answer is, I leased them to the Company."

"I'm sorry? You leased them to your *company?*"

"This aircraft. Jeff's. All of the DC-6s. I'm not supposed to tell anyone."

"What are you talking about, Jerry?"

Jerry sighed, his right hand flailing the air in a resigned gesture. "It was, I was told, my patriotic duty not to ask too many questions."

"Who told you that?"

"Jeff. There was a lot of money attached, of course, and all I had to do was sign a few papers once the airplanes had reached Roswell, then bring them back up here in the spring."

Clark swiveled to the right, an incredulous look on his face.

"Hold it. *Jeff?* What . . . I don't understand what Jeff is doing in this equation."

"Well, he said no one would believe it if it ever came out that he was . . . what did he call it . . . an aviation assets procurer for the CIA."

"We are talking about the same Jeff here, right? Jeff Maze?"

"Yes."

"The ranking maverick of the whole group? The head of the Airtanker Fliers Association?"

"The same."

"Jerry, is there a less likely candidate?"

"I know, I didn't believe him either at first, but he had the papers, he had the money, and he performed exactly as he said he would."

More silence as Clark tried to work through the utterly bizarre idea that Jeff Maze could have been associated with anything more official than an FAA pilot's license.

"You leased them the whole fleet?"

"Not the PB4Y-2s or the other birds. He said the Company . . . Jeff said they really do call it that . . . just wanted the DC-6Bs."

"Why?"

"Simple humanitarian cargo runs that had no direct connection to the U.S. That's all I was told. I inspected the planes and the retardant tanks and everything myself when the birds came back to Roswell, and everything looked good."

"And the logbooks?"

Another sigh, and Jerry's head dropped. "God, Clark, I believed him. The money was too good, so I believed they were going to log everything carefully and put no more than a hundred hours on each plane. And all but one of them had exactly that range of just about a hundred hours."

"So how much did they *really* fly?"

"I don't know, but what you found in Tanker Seventy-four? The dust and the dirt? That shocked the hell out of me. They reported only about a hundred and fifty hours on her."

"Jesus Christ, Jerry! Is Southlight Aviation a CIA operation, too?"

He shook his head. "I don't think so. The deal started and ended in Roswell."

"But that's illegal! These airplanes are considered national resources. Remember that new law?"

"No . . . actually, what's illegal would be my renting or leasing them to nongovernmental parties. But this was our own damned government, Clark!"

"And you have no idea what's been done to these birds? Where they've been? Whether they were maintained, or not, and by whom?"

Jerry shook his head.

"God, Jerry. Rogue pilots not qualified to handle these engines could have been doing assault landings in the jungle, or flying off a Pacific beach too near salt water with corrosion going crazy, *and you don't even know?*"

The ground crew had rolled the steps up to the airplane's crew entrance and were opening the door.

"I just didn't ask. I got paid not to ask. Jeff knows . . . *knew* these ships, and I trusted him, especially with the lease contracts."

"The contracts were with the CIA?"

"No, no. One of those front companies. Kind of like the old Air America they used in Vietnam, except this one was called Standard Aeronautics."

"What does Trent Jones know about all this?"

"Same as me, I think. Maybe a little less. He didn't like it much."

"He and Jeff were close friends. You knew that, right?"

Jerry shrugged.

"Jerry . . . you know the FBI is going to be all over this, right?"

"Yes. I can't say I'm glad you called them, but . . . let the chips fall where they may."

One of the mechanics came in and stuck his head in the cockpit. "You guys all right up here?"

"Yeah. We'll be down in a second," Clark told him.

"Okay."

The mechanic backed out as Jerry started to respond but caught himself and sat silently until Clark sighed and continued. "It's coming unraveled, Jerry. You see that, I hope."

"Yes."

"You can't let these planes fly again until a whole new round of very thorough inspections has been done. I mean, you've just admitted you have no idea how badly they've been treated, or how many hours are on them, or where they went, or anything."

"I know."

Clark sat in the thick atmosphere of embarrassed silence for a few more seconds, staring at the fearless entrepreneur and remembering their decades of friendship.

"Why, Jerry?"

"Because I truly thought it was the right thing to do. It was a lot of money . . . more than the planes are even worth . . . and I knew we'd have, tops, maybe two more fire seasons before it would all be over anyway. This was . . . kind of a way to build my own golden parachute, and I did *not* know they were abusing our birds. It was our government on top of it all. You may not believe me, Clark, but—"

"Rationalization is a powerful hallucinogen, my friend."

Jerry sighed deeply. "You've got that right."

Clark swallowed his disgust. "Let's get out of here."

Jerry hauled himself to his feet and turned from the copilot's seat as Clark caught his sleeve. "Jerry, look, whatever happens . . . I mean, I'm deeply disappointed in you, but you've been there for me over the years, and I'm still your friend."

Jerry patted Clark on the shoulder. "I appreciate that."

# Chapter 36

The constant barrage of fire retardant from a procession of airtankers had continued as the smokejumpers ran for their lives westward and up the steep mountainside, trying to reach a modest-size step about a hundred feet above the base of the protective rock formation where Peter had been waiting. The fire retardant was serving the same purpose it had served earlier on the south side of the ridge. It wasn't enough to put out the fire, but it was enough to buy them the time to escape.

They came scrambling out of the trees onto the ridge utterly exhausted physically and emotionally, each of them well aware that two of their number were somewhere behind in the path of the flames. Tempers flared with a brief debate over what to do, but a quick radio check with the lead plane confirmed that there was literally no future in going back for Karen and Dave until the flames had passed and the smoldering remains of the lush forest were sufficiently blackened to be unburnable.

They were adjacent to a rocky draw near the ridgeline that had promised protection if the original blaze from the southern flank of the mountain had roared over the top. Now it was coming around the eastern flank of the mountain, and they needed to find a safer place.

"There's no reason to risk using the shelters here with this monster on our tail," Pete said. "Our original landing zone would be better. It's burned over already."

"What are you saying, we have to keep going? I say we stay right here!" George snapped.

"And *I'm* saying that any of us who'd like to live without the risk of third-degree burns or worse should follow me back to where we landed this morning."

"What about Karen and Dave?"

"How are we going to help them by staying up here, huh?"

The two men squared off silently for a few heartbeats, then broke away. The controversy was meaningless. The squad members shouldered the remaining equipment and retraced their path downward, around the ridge-line to the original landing zone.

"There's a small lake up there, a mile farther on according to the map. One of the Skycranes was using it a while ago," one of the other smoke-jumpers said.

"Yeah, but we're in the black here. Let's stay put," Pete replied. He tried calling Karen and Dave again on his radio as they all hunkered down to wait for the fire to pass.

They watched the smoke boiling off the oncoming fire, the flames leap-ing at times several hundred feet in the air, the endless oxygen provided by the stiff east wind now blowing through the funnel at the eastern end of the valley they'd labored so hard to protect.

"Oh, God, Pete. How could we lose those two?"

Pete was shaking his head, thoroughly stunned. "I don't know."

"Do you think there's any chance they could have made it through in their shelters?

Pete peered for the longest time at the flames, listening to the roar and tasting the smoke, before shaking his head at the chilling reality.

"No."

WEST YELLOWSTONE AIRPORT, MONTANA

Clark followed Jerry out of the DC-6B to the sound of departing helicop-ters, one of them carrying Steve Zale to the site of Bill Deason's impact with Yellowstone's forests. With the rising number of mechanical incidents and now the loss of a P-3, NTSB headquarters had finally launched a Go Team, but it would be hours before they arrived, and Zale, in the meantime, was the only NTSB representative on scene.

They walked in silence to the Operations building, and Clark trailed Jerry as they pushed into another wake. The only good news was that Chuck Hines from Bill Deason's P-3 had landed safely and been picked up by park rangers, and was en route back. Firefighters and search squads were already on the crash site, but from that location no good news was flowing.

Jerry moved to the Operations desk and flagged Rich Lassiter's attention. He picked up a notepad and wrote down the tanker numbers of every DC-6B in his fleet and handed it to Rich.

"I'm grounding all my DC-6Bs immediately, Rich."

"Say that again, please."

"I'm grounding my fleet for safety reasons, if the Forest Service hasn't al-ready put everyone on the ground. Who's still up?"

"Good Lord, Jerry! You'll gut our capabilities! Even if they put us down for a few hours—and you're right, I'm sure they will, like yesterday—we'll get back up and need everyone."

"Just do it."

"What's wrong?"

He shook his head. "I'll explain shortly. Who's still flying?"

"Uh, Dave Barrett is . . . no, he's on the ground. Clark Maxwell is here. Well, of course, you were flying shotgun with him. Tanker Seventy-four . . . let's see . . ." He thumbed through several sheets on a clipboard. "Okay. Two others are working the North Fork Ridge right now."

"When they're empty and back in, shut them down."

"All right, man. I hope it's really necessary," Rich said, clearly getting ready to yank up the phone and inform Bozeman Dispatch.

Clark had already turned to the crew desk for any information on the smokejumpers.

"It's good news, Clark. They were racing to get up to a safe place, and they made it. I just heard the lead-plane pilot talking about their escape."

Clark exhaled sharply and smiled, feeling immeasurably relieved as he thanked him and turned to find a man he'd never seen before waiting for him.

"Captain Maxwell?"

"Yes?"

He held out his hand, speaking quietly. "I'm Todd Blackson from Helena."

"Yes?"

"From the office you called in Helena a few hours ago?"

"Oh, yes. I guess I didn't expect you here so soon."

"Why don't we find some place to talk privately."

"Sure," Clark replied, instinctively glancing in Jerry's direction and surprised he had already disappeared. "Ah . . . let's go out on the ramp."

Clark led the way around the building to the parking area and turned to find Blackson holding out his credential wallet.

"That's okay."

"Well, you've already been tricked once."

"Yeah. You're here to talk to Jerry, aren't you?"

"Yes. But first I want you to tell me everything you know about this situation with the maintenance of these aircraft. I'm aware of Captain Deason's crash a while ago. I understand he was a friend, and I'm very sorry."

"Thanks," Clark sighed, feeling bone weary and still disbelieving, unable to let the reality of the crash he'd witnessed sink in. "Well, first of all, I've got a shocker for you. I just found out the CIA is involved.

"Mr. Stein told you that?"

*Strange,* Clark thought. *He didn't even blink.* "Yes." Clark related everything Jerry had said, as well as the wild incongruity that Jeff Maze could have been a CIA operative.

"We'll find out if it's true."

"Yeah, but you guys don't communicate well, do you?"

"CIA and FBI? Cats and dogs, but, since nine-eleven, we do a lot of talking. You might call it a shotgun wedding."

"I think Jerry's telling the truth," Clark said. "I've known him a long time. He was probably duped."

Todd Blackson leaned against a parked pickup and studied Clark for a moment of uncomfortable silence.

"Look, Captain. I'm not here to crucify Jerry Stein. I'm here to figure out if a crime's been committed with regard to the use of Stein Aviation's aircraft, and after all, you're the gentleman who called to tip us off that something was wrong."

"He just grounded all the DC-6s."

"That's good, considering your basic worry was whether or not the airplanes are safe."

"Right."

"But there's more at stake here, as you're well aware. And we'll need some time to sort this out. We're already working with the NTSB's representative on Captain Maze's crash."

Clark's expression changed from grim to startled. "There was a sabotage rumor going around yesterday, but . . . could Jeff Maze's crash have been connected with his CIA role?"

"That's one of the questions we need to ask and answer, because if there is any indication of sabotage, we take over the case."

"All right."

"I have your cell phone number. In the meantime, it's probably a good idea not to discuss my presence here, or our conversation. And before you ask, no, I can't tell you why."

"Okay."

"I will tell you there's another Stein employee I need to find immediately."

"Who's that?"

"Trent Jones."

BRYARLY, WYOMING

Jimmy Wolf had retraced his route through the forest in the Humvee while arranging for a helicopter on his satellite phone. As a result, the sound of an unseen Bell 212 came booming overhead as he rounded the last curve before town. The crew was waiting with an open door as he drove up, and they quickly brought aboard the still-unconscious copilot and Trent Jones. As soon as he'd parked and locked the Humvee, Jimmy climbed aboard as well.

"Glad you were here on time," the copilot said. "We almost couldn't find the landing zone, the damn smoke's so thick."

"How did you?"

"We had an exact GPS position and came down to a minimum altitude, and just barely saw it at eighty feet. You're sure there's no one else in town, right?"

"I can't say for sure, but I didn't see anyone."

"Okay. 'Cause we're the last train out of Dodge. No one's gonna make it back in here." He moved up to his seat in the cockpit.

The 212 lifted off through the pall of smoke, and Jimmy watched the details of the town fade and disappear, as if a dream were evaporating before his eyes. He could hear a soundtrack in his mind, but it was nothing he'd written. The music was grand and ominous and mysterious all at once, as if an American Indian chant had been woven into a symphonic suite, the music a lyrical reflection of the collision between nature and the onslaught of men and machines. Jimmy felt something changing inside himself, a feeling of belated respect for this beautiful valley, now that it was just hours away from complete destruction.

*I wonder if I've ever really seen it before,* he mused. *And now Mother Nature decides there should be fire in the forest, and here we stand, clever but puny little ants trying to refuse her that right.*

The pilot gained altitude up valley to the southeast, lifting above the main layer of smoke, and Jimmy could see that the entire southern flank of the cirque was on fire, the flames leaping a hundred feet or more in the air, the line of flames running from the top of the ridge down the mountain as it burned its way toward the northwest and the deserted homes of Bryarly. The battle, obviously, was lost, and the puzzle was why he didn't feel worse about it.

A fleeting image of his collapsed roof and severely damaged home crossed his mind, but he dismissed it. It was only money, and besides, the entire place would be nothing but ash and memories before this night was over.

The pilot banked to the right, aiming at a low point between the two ridges, and Jimmy could see a small meadow that had burned along with the entire southern flank of the mountain. It looked like a war zone, and, as the 212 flashed over the tiny plateau and turned southwest toward Jackson Hole, he thought he saw figures, soldiers of this war, along the edge of the clearing.

Trent Jones moved across the interior to sit beside him with his hand outstretched.

"Wot's this?"

"We were too busy back there for me to say thank you."

He shook Trent's hand quickly.

"No worries, mate."

"Well, I appreciate it. I hadn't realized until we got back that you stayed behind on your own just to get us out."

"Yeah, well, I'd rather not make a big deal of it, all right?"

"Sure. I just wanted you to know." Trent got up and began moving back across the cabin, then turned. "They would have never found us from the air, Mr. Wolf. You know that, right?"

Jimmy waved him off in dismissal and turned away, surprised at how helpless he was to suppress the smile on his face.

# Chapter 37

Judy Deason sat on her sofa in her motor home's living room, her arms tightly folded as she stared at Clark Maxwell. Her eyes were large and brimming with pain, but tearless in disbelief and denial.

"He's not dead," she said.

"Judy, we can hold out some hope, I guess, but—"

"Have they found him?"

"I don't know. I saw the crash site, Judy. It didn't give any hope."

She uncrossed her arms and leaned forward, placing a hand lightly on his forearm, her green eyes studying his.

"Clark, Bill and I are tuned to each other. I would know if he was dead. I would just *know*."

There was no point in arguing.

"Am I scared to death?" Judy continued. "Absolutely. What if he's dazed and stumbling around? There are bears out there, and geysers. But he's not dead."

"Okay."

She sat back, folding her arms again, her expression intense and determined, as if she would validate her words by mere force of will and love.

"That's what loving someone will do, Clark. You can feel it when they're in trouble. You can feel it when they're hurting. And you know it when they're gone. You go back to Operations, Clark. Get something to eat. Come back when you know where he is."

———

Clark had closed the door of the motor home behind him and walked a few steps when a feeling of sudden dread descended on him, flickering a maddeningly indistinct spotlight on a procession of people in his mind's eye, and stopping on Karen.

She and her squad were safe. That's what he'd been told. The extreme chances he and his fellow pilots had taken to clear an escape path—the effort that had killed Bill Deason—had at least accomplished its purpose.

But there was still fire on the mountain, and while Karen Jones did not need his protection, he couldn't help but wish she was safely out of the fire's grip.

It was a deep shame, he thought, that their combined efforts had not saved the valley and the town. They'd bought enough time to evacuate the residents of Bryarly, but now the fire would have a straight shot at the unburned portions of Yellowstone, and could easily spread back west to finish Grand Teton Park's eastern areas, even as a huge force of ground firefighters began to get control of the North Fork fire.

But Karen was still out there, and in the aftermath of an endless day, the floating beauty of their conversation the previous night mixed with the memory of their first meeting on that Oregon ridge and stirred a deep longing.

*I wonder how they're going to get out?* he thought, recalling how he'd inadvertently embarrassed himself and her earlier on the radio. He couldn't come flying in like a white knight to yank her from the mountain. She'd be furious. They probably had a Bell 205 or 212 on the way in any event.

But something felt wrong, and the feeling was growing.

Clark returned to the crew desk in Operations, finding Lynda still behind the counter.

"Hi, Lynda. Sorry to bug you,"

"No problem, Clark. You'll be happy to know that Rusty is fine. The doctor gave him some antinausea stuff and sent him to bed."

"Thanks, Lynda. I got the message you left."

"Good."

"Ah, do you happen to know whether or how the Missoula Smokejumpers are planning on getting off that ridge tonight? Are they going to hike like they normally do, or . . . get picked up?"

"Hold on," she said, dialing the number to Jackson Hole Helibase. She thanked her counterpart and replaced the receiver, looking at him a few seconds before responding.

"What?" he prompted.

"Well, there's apparently a problem. The squad is requesting search-and-rescue support."

"Why?"

"Two of the squad got separated just before the fire jumped them from the east."

"Two? Do you have names?"

Her concern was apparent as she watched his face, and the words that followed broke like a stomach punch.

"The squad leader, Karen Jones, and Dave Sims."

"Where . . . what happened?" He was working to keep his voice under control, but it was an effort. The memory of the vicious flame front and the accelerating speed of the fire as they'd bombed it was all too vivid.

"All I know, Clark, is that the squad had to race back to the safe zone they'd designated, and when they got there, apparently those two were missing."

He described briefly the struggle to save them that had led to Bill's demise.

She sighed. "Clark, it could easily be that they used their shelters and just haven't come out. The fire has passed their drop zone now, and the winds are in the process of changing. That's why they're asking for search support."

"Are we still attacking the fire?"

She nodded. "In the past half hour the winds have started to shift again and there's some hope of saving the town."

Clark moved to the nearest phone and yanked it up, punched in Jerry's office number, and prayed he would answer.

"Yeah?" The voice was subdued, but it was unmistakably Jerry.

"This is Clark. I need to borrow one of the Jet Rangers, Jerry. I'll pay for the time."

"Why?"

"I . . . can't tell you, other than that it involves helping with a search."

"Oh. Sure, Clark. Go."

NORTH FORK RIDGE DROP ZONE

The memory of the steep mountain slope where Karen and her squad had been threatened was etched in Clark's mind like a three-dimensional topographic map. During the thirty-minute flight to the North Fork Ridge, he mentally ranged through it and around it, astounded at how few places there were to hide from an approaching firestorm.

He'd glimpsed some of the escaping squad during one of his bombing passes and knew where they were headed, up and across the back of the ridge to an outcropping of rocks. In that microsecond of a glimpse he had seen them running single file. They would have dropped their packs and raced ahead of the flame front, he knew, but such a climb on a steep slope was tough going. It must have been a double hell for her, he thought. Having survived the Storm King disaster and having been one of the ones who made it to safety over the ridge, Karen would be driven to get her people to safety first. She would have brought up the rear, and something, obviously, had happened to their radios

Clark flew over the approximate location of Bryarly, pushing the Jet Ranger to its maximum speed. The town was still shrouded in heavy smoke, but he could see that the winds were now blowing from the northeast and slowing the main fire line's progress less than three miles from the nearest house.

He flew over the valley into the clear area to the east, toward where the squad had been trapped, amazed at the destruction. There were scattered trees with flames still flickering out of the torched upper trunks, but a sea of carbon marked what had been a verdant forest, lodgepole pine and larch and aspen with their branches scorched off, and a forest floor laden with ash white enough in some places to tell of incredible temperatures.

*Oh God,* he thought. *If she got trapped in that . . .*

He could see men moving down laterally to the east from the smoke-jumpers' drop zone, and he could see one of the 205s used for rescue operations perched in the middle of the blackened, burned-over drop zone.

He slowed the Jet Ranger to less than twenty knots and fought against the mechanical turbulence from the wind flowing over the eastern shoulder of the cirque. He began methodically searching the slope where he remembered bombing just ahead of the fire. He moved on toward the safe rock area the smokejumpers had used, and ranged from there downward.

He could make out nothing other than the yellow shirts of perhaps twenty smokejumpers and rescuers picking their way along the same burned-out war zone.

No one waved, and no one gave him a thumbs-up. The message was sickeningly clear: They hadn't found any sign of life.

Clark suppressed the growing feeling of loss and circled to the south side and along the ridge, looking for any sign that a human being had been there.

He maneuvered around and touched down next to the 205 on the blackened drop zone. Judging the winds not strong enough to roll the Jet Ranger off the side of the ridge, he shut down and alighted, looking around for someone he could question.

He saw Pete holding a radio loud with worried voices of those down the ridge. Clark walked over quickly and introduced himself, asking the obvious.

"We've been searching back over the same route," Pete replied. "We found the remains of our packs, so we know the route is correct, but . . . there's no trace of them."

"I'm going to go down there. I looked from the air and could see nothing," Clark told him. He showed Pete on a map exactly where he'd hovered and looked.

Pete handed him a spare handheld radio. "Keep in touch with that, okay?
I guess just use your name."

"I'm Tanker Eighty-eight. I'll use that."

"Okay. Take a Pulaski, too." He tossed him the tool, and Clark began
clambering down what was becoming the outlines of a trail through the
burned forest floor. He moved as resolutely as possible, tripping several
times on the slick, steep mountainside, but aiming toward the would-be rescuers strung along the line they'd established from the burned equipment
packs to the shelter of the rocks they were trying to reach.

While the fire began to burn out to the west under heavy air attack, Clark
searched for three hours, first looking higher than the baseline, then lower,
and finding nothing. The rays of sunlight were becoming longer, and he
calculated sundown was less than two hours away. He still had a $500,000
helicopter perched precariously on the ridge, and he had only a small flashlight.

*Three more hours of daylight.*

There was something downslope in the distance that caught his eye, and
he rejected it subconsciously before his conscious mind overruled the decision. There was something lying on the burned grasses and ferns, something completely blackened itself, but with a rounded shape that fallen trees
couldn't achieve.

He began moving downslope toward the object, his stomach contracting
at the horrific possibilities. Whatever it was appeared to be in a curled position, its charred back toward him.

He judged he was within twenty feet, but a few more steps revealed the
slight optical illusion. The object was a bit larger—and farther away—than
he'd thought, and as he came up to it he could see it was a deer, curled
around itself in death, its body as black and carbonized as a human body
would be.

*Thank God,* he thought, but the small deliverance brought only momentary comfort. Karen was still out here, somewhere.

He knelt by the deer for a minute, looking to the west and the setting sun.

Karen was dead, but she was not his life.

There had been promise, of course, although where it might have gone
neither of them knew. She had been beautiful and exciting and had helped
his love for life peel itself off the floor after Rosanna, but they had barely
known each other.

A shaft of sunlight probed through a growing cloud cover from the west,
just steep enough to match the slope and illuminate it like some giant
searchlight shining from atop the ridge. He squinted his eyes against the

brightness, and saw the utter dullness of the overall reflection from the burned forest. No drops of dew, no fluttering aspen leaves, nothing to catch the light and bounce it back.

But there *was* something, perhaps thirty or forty yards westward and across the slope, weakly reflecting the sunbeam.

Clark stood, running through a mental catalog of anything that could reflect light like that. Nothing matched exactly. The reflection was somewhat dull, not mirrorlike or bright, yet, there was something there.

He left the deer and moved toward the source of the reflecting spot of light, worried that the ever-changing sun angle would cause it to disappear before he could reach it. And just as he had feared, it suddenly blinked out.

Clark stood still for a moment, holding on to the memory of his last sighting and carefully triangulating against a row of burned and barren tree trunks standing like darkened markers in some native graveyard.

He moved closer, seeing nothing but the same ruined landscape until he was standing beneath the trees he'd used as a target. As he had feared, whatever had caught the light wasn't apparent.

Clark looked around, puzzled. All over the slope, trees had broken under their own weight when too much of the trunk burned away, or when other larger trees called "widow makers" fell and caused a cascade of falling timber among the shallow root systems. A large pine, perhaps 150 years old, had fallen near where he was standing, the victim of another tree hitting it. The bark had been badly charred, but surprisingly, much of the trunk was unburned.

He moved along its length, catching a snippet of human voice from one of the smokejumpers or rescuers somewhere above him.

*There!*

Something had caught his eye. Peering closer, he could see what looked like a piece of aluminum foil lying on the backside of the log.

And as he looked at it even more closely, it moved.

Clark stumbled along the littered forest floor to what he now saw was a silvery metallic material that seemed to be caught under the log. Someone or something was yanking at it from below and wiggling it.

"Hey! Can you hear me?" he yelled.

There was a muffled reply, and he got down on his knees and started digging around the piece of material, which was looking more and more like thermal shelter material. His hand found a deeper cavity, and he punched through it.

"Help!" The voice was clearer, and female.

"Karen? Oh God, is that you?"

"Yes! We're trapped in here."

A male voice, more distant and muffled, joined hers. "Something's block-ing the entrance."

"Hang on!" Clark said.

He stood and tried to roll the log, but it was far too heavy and deeply em-bedded. The radio was swinging from his belt, and he pulled it out now, pressing the transmit switch.

"Attention, everyone on this net. This is Tanker Eighty-eight downslope. I've got two alive, but they're trapped in some sort of hole. I need at least a half dozen of you down here to help me move a log."

Voices started coming back in a cascade of conflicting transmissions that Pete finally sorted out.

"Wave your arms and keep waving them until we see you in the glasses," Pete instructed.

Clark leaned down again to the hole.

"You have enough air for twenty more minutes?"

"Yes. We're hurting a little, but we're okay. I heard the transmission."

He balanced himself on the back of the log and began waving, keeping it up for nearly two minutes before the reply came.

"We've got you!"

He could see a new cascade of movement above as yellow shirts began moving downslope.

It took eight of them, a chain saw, and several tries to roll the section of the huge log away and expose the partially collapsed entrance to the den.

The two lost smokejumpers emerged with considerable help, unfolding themselves slowly, their legs and feet asleep and tingling from being de-prived of good circulation for hours. Dave's injured ankle was swollen to twice its normal size. Karen tried to stand prematurely and almost pitched headlong to the ground. Both were dehydrated and filthy, and Karen's back had been bruised slightly by the fall of the trunk, but the shelters had pro-tected them against the monstrous temperatures that had raged just outside the hole until the huge tree had sealed it from further flames and radient heat.

But the weight of the same tree had effectively buried them alive.

There were hugs and tears and explanations and apologies flying among the tight-knit squad and Clark stood back slightly, watching the process and feeling anything but the hero Karen had instantly dubbed him.

He watched her, thinking how beautiful she was even in her present state, and wishing he could be bold enough just to walk up and enfold her in his arms in front of her squad.

But he held back, feeling a calm that had begun to fill the void left by Bill's demise.

*No. Bill's sacrifice,* he thought. *After all, it was these people Bill had been deter-mined to help by flying lower and closer than safety would allow.*

He was immersed in the thought when she moved shakily from the em-brace of her squad and walked the few yards to him, sliding her arms around him and looking in his eyes as she mouthed, "Thank you." He was partway through "You're welcome" when she kissed him. A long and deep and very disturbingly sensual kiss delivered to the cheers and catcalls of her fellows.

# Chapter 38

A very tired Jim De Maio looked up from the newly delivered meteorological map spread before the command staff and suddenly thrust his right thumb in the air as he broke into a broad smile.

"Yes!"

Lynda Gardner, a small stack of papers in her hand, glanced at the four others in the briefing room.

"It's only a possibility, Jim."

"I don't care," he enthused. "Just the mention of the probability of precipitation means we've got a chance."

"The winds are a far more important element," she cautioned, smoothing her hair back. "And with the low suddenly on the move southeastward and the winds shifting to north-northeast over that valley—"

"And," Jim interrupted, "with the Air Force C-130 MAFFS units and the California P-3s, which will have at least two flights before dark, *and* with the helitack operations continuing on the spot fires, *and* with that temporary Army bridge they brought in to get the ground force back into and around Bryarly, kids, I think we're going to finally catch it and win one."

"Still too soon to tell," Alex White added.

"Did everyone see that live shot from the news helicopter we allowed over the valley?" one of the others asked. "It showed the main flame front slowing enough for our ground teams to cut line on the other side of the retardant drops about two miles from the first Bryarly house. The best guess is that with the wind shift Lynda mentioned, the fire will lay down overnight while the crews work, and we can hit it with a fresh aerial assault in the morning."

"Unless it rains, in which case we've got it," Jim added.

"Absolutely! There's a great chance it won't blow up if we get sufficient moisture on it."

The rescue of the two missing smokejumpers had already been reported and cheered, as had the formal containment of the Sheep Mountain fire threatening the Grand Teton Park facilities on the east side of Jackson Lake.

Lynda held up a newly received fax. "We moved a hotshot crew in on the fire started by the airtanker crash, and they stopped it cold."

"The copilot was picked up, right?"

"Yes. Uninjured."

"Any word from the crash site on locating the pilot's body?" Alex asked.

"I don't know. The last report said the wreckage is pretty mangled and very spread out."

WEST YELLOWSTONE AIRPORT, MONTANA

Clark finished shutting down the Jet Ranger while watching the intense activity around the Bell 212 parked a hundred feet away on the Forest Service ramp. He'd trailed the 212 all the way in from the North Ridge drop zone, wishing Karen could have been sitting in the copilot's seat next to him rather than with her squad in the other helicopter. She'd waved as she and Dave were hurried from the 212's cabin into a waiting ambulance for a quick trip to the local clinic and a medical checkover. Karen had promised to find him by phone as soon as they let her go, and Clark was looking forward to the call.

As the ambulance pulled out, the sight of Bill Deason's old PB4Y-2 caught Clark's eye and triggered an overpowering feeling of melancholy, born of fatigue and confusion and frustration, but mixed together with more intensity than he could handle at that moment.

Clark forced the indelible image of the P-3 sinking into the trees from his mind, knowing the respite was only temporary.

Darkness had covered the town, held back on the ramp by sodium vapor lamps, but closing in around them like a dropped veil. There was still purple and light to the west, but it was fading, and suddenly he had an irresistible urge just to get to his truck and leave.

Clark left the Ranger's keys and the clipboard on the pilot's seat and moved quickly to the parking lot. He slid into the driver's seat and was in the process of turning the key when Misty Ryan knocked loudly on the passenger-side window, causing him to jump.

"What? Misty!"

He fumbled with the window control to roll down the glass.

"Please let me in, Clark."

"Sure . . . wait . . ." His finger found the unlock switch, and she glided into the passenger side, closing the door behind her as she swiveled around partially sideways to look at him.

Her cascading mane of red hair was uncombed and windblown, and her missing makeup told of tears and anguish. She looked older than he recalled, yet there was a calm about her he hadn't expected.

The tears were beginning again.

"I found out about Bill a couple of hours ago when I got back."

Clark nodded, unable to add anything himself.

"Oh God, Clark! Judy was just comforting *me* yesterday! I . . . I was going to go to her as soon as I heard, but . . . I can't, and I don't know why."

"It's all right, Misty. You're still in shock."

She was nodding through her tears, which were flowing freely.

"I'm in shock in more ways than one," she replied, leaving a part of Clark's mind searching for the predicate to her words.

"We thought you'd left for good," he said.

"I had. I made it as far as Pocatello. I just wanted to put as much distance between me and this place as possible, and I guess I was lead-footing it because I got stopped by the Idaho State Patrol, who wanted to see registration and insurance for Jeff's truck. I found them in his glove compartment, which is where I also found this." She held up an envelope and several pages of paper in a plastic sleeve.

"What are they?"

She sighed.

"An envelope that says for me to open only in the event of Jeff's death. I guess I should have just kept on going and cashed in, but . . . regardless of whatever anyone thinks of me for being Jeff's girl . . . I do have some principles, and I draw the line at this stuff."

Clark leaned forward, truly puzzled. "Misty, I'm not understanding this. What was in the envelope?"

She nodded. "Let me . . . tell it from the start, okay? 'Cause . . . I don't know who to go to. I was going to go to Bill . . . and Judy . . . when I heard about the crash."

"And you waited for me?"

She laughed briefly. "Yeah. Something Bill said about how steady a friend you'd been. But it was getting cold out here. I was going to watch your truck until you showed up."

"I'm listening, Misty. Take your time."

"I'm cold, Clark. Could you—"

"Sure." He started the engine and turned on the heater. "It'll take a minute to warm up."

"Thanks. Okay. My biggest problem, Clark, has always been that I wanted to believe Jeff even when I knew he was lying. But women are like that, you know?"

"I do."

"No one knows this, but I saw Jeff in the Caymans late last October, when there was no reason for him to be there. He was with a little blond copilot and flying a DC-6B that looked suspiciously like one of Jerry's."

Clark shifted in the seat, his eyebrows involuntarily rising.

"A DC-6B?"

She nodded. "Turns out it *was* one of Jerry's. I don't know which one."

"The Caymans, you say?"

She nodded. "Yes. It took me weeks to catch up with the rat, and when I did, he admitted everything . . . or so I thought." She cocked her head. "Do you know about him being with the CIA?"

Clark searched her eyes, wondering if somehow this was a failed attempt at humor. "That's about the last affiliation I would have suspected. But, yes. Jerry told me this afternoon."

"Well, he was. And Jerry did know all about it because he leased Jeff all of his DC-6Bs, the one you fly, too, and the CIA used them for some South American thingy involving food and refugees or something. Jerry knew all that because the CIA paid him very well."

"How do you . . . I mean, do you know this for *certain*, Misty?"

She was nodding vigorously. "*Oh,* yeah!"

"Misty, Bill and I called the FBI yesterday because we found some very strange things about the DC-6 fleet that . . . well . . . that suggested maybe someone was flying them off the books during the winter."

"You were right," she said. "And you know what else? Jerry got paid millions. He leased his airplanes to the CIA through Jeff."

Clark realized he'd been holding his breath and exhaled sharply. "I was having trouble believing that, Misty. But apparently it's true."

"No, it isn't," she replied.

Clark looked at her in some confusion. "What?"

"Oh, it's what Jerry believes. That he leased the airplanes to the CIA."

"He *didn't*? You're saying he thinks he did, but he didn't?"

"No. He leased his airplanes *through* Jeff and collected a fortune, but the lessees weren't who he thought they were. Jeff fooled Jerry. And he fooled me. When I nailed his miserable hide to the wall on why he was in the Caymans, he gave me this long and detailed story and told me about flying DC-6s back and forth from maintenance in Florida to winter storage in New Mexico and then through the Caymans down to Ecuador and Peru."

"What . . . makes you think that isn't true?"

She leaned over and handed him the papers she'd been holding.

"The first sheet is just the instructions he left me on where to find a series of hidden files he'd planted on my laptop. The second is a copy I printed out from one of those files."

*To My Beautiful Misty—Your Eyes Only*

*Baby, if I've directed you to open this file, then I'm either dead or missing. In any event, you are as of this moment a very rich woman, and I want you to take the money and run. But first, you have to know how to take care of yourself.*

*I'm not with the CIA, babe. Never was. I hated lying to you about that, but you actually got the same story I gave Jerry to get him to lease me his airplanes. I'm not going to give you all the details, but let's just say that I was actually brokering aircraft for certain interests in Colombia, and they paid me handsomely. I have to tell you this because even though I earned it, they're liable to come poking around someday to see if they can steal it back.*

*I paid Jerry a great deal of money that he thought came from the CIA, and in return, my clients got the use of some old, indestructible warhorse DC-6s, and I got very healthy financially as a result. With a little friendly maintenance tweaking to fuzz up the extra flying, the planes slipped back into the fold each spring in great shape, and no one was the wiser. Result? Three offshore accounts in different banks and islands containing a grand total of $6.4 million, as of April 25, 2003. All yours, doll! I've listed below the account numbers and the passwords, and each bank has specific instructions on file to release any and all funds to you as long as you have a copy of the coded authorization form that's in this file. Document 2 of this group tells you how to keep your money safe and not alert the IRS, and what not to do! Document 3 is very dangerous, because it lists my Colombian clients, but it's something you need to know because you do not EVER want to do business with or otherwise get to know or be around any of them. Remember, this is earned money, not stolen money, and the only trick is to keep Uncle from taking two-thirds of it as taxes.*

*Also, do not confide in Trent Jones about anything, but especially this legacy to you. If he had any hint there was profit stashed away, he'd think he was entitled to some of it. He's not. He's already been paid handsomely.*

*Bottom line, as they say? You never saw any of this and you know nothing! That's the only way to stay safe. I know you like to be a woman of principle, but for God's sake and your own don't go to Jerry or the cops with this or you'll just blow it for yourself.*

The text went on to talk about how much he loved her, and how much he wanted her to enjoy being wealthy, and how much he hoped it was compensation for putting up with him and his serial womanizing.

Clark looked up, thoroughly shocked. "Colombian clients?"

"Yes," Misty said.

"What were they doing with our airplanes?"

"What else would someone do with a fleet of DC-6Bs in Colombia? I'm not going to have anything to do with drug money, drug kingpins, or fooling the IRS, or anything."

"And this was on your *computer?*"

"Yes. Embedded on my hard drive. I would have never found it. It's a strange little numbered file in an obscure subdirectory that looks like one of those gazillion files Microsoft embeds, and it was a 'hidden file' at that. He'd made me memorize a password a year ago, and I could never figure out why, but he'd test me periodically to make sure I still remembered it. Now I know it was to unlock the file."

"Good Lord!"

"I don't know who to go to, Clark."

"This is a kind of will, Misty, but he never had the authority to sublease those planes. And, oh my God."

"What?"

Clark swallowed hard and looked at her. "I'm guessing, because we don't know the cause of the crash yet, but I'm wondering if the wing came off Jeff's aircraft due to unlogged abuse he himself caused."

"Poetic justice, I guess," Misty said quietly.

"Something like that," Clark replied, looking down at the letter again. "He wasn't even scheduled to fly that airplane. It was a last-minute switch."

Misty shook her head.

"Clark, I loved the rat, but I wouldn't have stayed with him for a second if I thought he was breaking the law or helping drug runners. Please believe me."

"I do. Don't worry. This letter pretty well exonerates you."

The tears were flowing again.

"There's an FBI agent already investigating this, Misty. You need to . . . I mean . . ."

"Why are you hesitating, Clark?"

"Just . . . trying to work out the money thing for you."

She was shaking her head. "No. I'd rather wait tables than have blood money. I feel very strongly about that! That's not my money, regardless of what Jeff says."

"What if the FBI and the courts disagree?"

She shrugged. "I don't know."

"I'm no lawyer, but . . . this might really be yours."

"I'll let the law decide. I don't care."

Clark looked down at the printout again, digesting the amount of money Jeff had referenced. There was no choice, and she was right, but it was way beyond what his entire working life had produced, and that had staggered him for a second.

"How do I find the FBI agent?" she asked.

"His name is Todd Blackson. Hold on . . ." Clark fished for a slip of paper in his shirt pocket and punched in the agent's cell phone number to arrange a meeting. He closed the phone.

"He'd like us to meet him in ten minutes."

"Okay. Where?"

"Across the field. Hangar One."

———

There were footsteps on the wooden stairway leading to Jerry Stein's second-floor office.

Jerry had leaned back in his chair and closed his eyes, wishing he was somewhere else and doing almost anything else. But Special Agent Blackson was obviously coming back with a question or two he'd forgotten to ask in a nearly two-hour interview. Blackson had arranged for a light twin belonging to another company to take him to Jackson Hole to interview Trent Jones. Obviously the intervening time was going to be spent with more embarrassing questions about his DC-6B fleet—questions for which an owner should have had ready answers.

"You really just took the money and looked the other way, then," Blackson had asked at one point, and Jerry had reluctantly agreed. That was exactly what he'd done, trusting the CIA's representations all along, apparently to his detriment.

The footsteps reached the landing, and Jerry got to his feet with a tired sigh and looked toward the door, waiting for Todd Blackson to enter again.

Instead, Misty Ryan walked in, followed by Clark Maxwell and Todd Blackson.

"Misty?"

"Hi."

"I'd heard you were headed back to California," Jerry said.

"I was."

He surveyed their faces. "Okay, what's going on?"

Todd Blackson spoke first.

"New information, Mr. Stein. We thought you'd want to know what your fleet was really doing."

ORION CRASH SITE, YELLOWSTONE NATIONAL PARK

"Mr. Zale? I think we've located the front end of the plane."

The yellow-coated firefighter pointed back beyond the primary mass of smoking wreckage as he and the NTSB representative stood with eight other firemen waiting for instructions. The light was fading fast, and portable lights were being set up around the perimeter.

"You mean the nose and cockpit?" Zale asked.

"Yeah. You see that series of snapped trees back where I'm pointing?"

"Yes."

"Looks to me like it broke off and went that way quite a distance. That's why we didn't see it at first. It's a mangled mess—hardly recognizable as part of an airplane."

"Did it burn?"

He shook his head no. "Two of my guys are looking right now to determine, you know, whether they can get the body out without a cutting torch."

The portable radio squawked to life and the fireman acknowledged it, talking back and forth for a minute before returning the radio to its holster.

"I don't know if you heard all that, but he says he can see inside just enough to know the pilot was apparently thrown free of his seat. That means the body is intertwined in the mass of wires and debris, and he says he thinks he's spotted it."

"I'd better go take a look," Zale replied, following as the fireman nodded and began walking in that direction.

The other members of the Yellowstone Search and Rescue team and several park rangers were downing sandwiches and soft drinks. One of the rangers glanced at a firefighter who had apparently doffed his yellow protective gear and was now standing at a large water jug draining his third cup. The ranger glanced at his partner and smiled as he turned to the man, noting his brown leather jacket.

"Thirsty, huh?" the ranger asked.

The man looked at him and nodded as he took a deep breath. "First things first, y'know," he said in a tired voice.

"You bet."

"Did the crew get the fire put out?"

The ranger chuckled and cocked his head. "I don't know. You're the fire-man, aren't you?"

The man seemed winded, but he smiled broadly and wiped at what looked like soot around his hairline and streaking his forehead. His right hand appeared to be bleeding.

"Oh, sort of."

The ranger cocked his head and took a step closer.

"Whoa, wait a minute. You're *not* a member of this fire-fighting crew?"

"Well, no. Not really."

"Then, sir, you shouldn't be here." The ranger shifted to his official mode, his guard up, his partner coming to alert as well. "Okay, how did you get in here? This area isn't open to the public."

"I walked in from over there. I was just real thirsty."

"All right, sir, you know what? The only people allowed in here are those on official business. I'm going to need to see your identification, and I'm going to need a pretty convincing explanation of why I shouldn't arrest you for violating park rules. We want park visitors to remain out of these back-woods areas for very good reasons, and for your own safety. There are un-marked geysers and fumaroles and thin crust all over the place, not to mention bear and bison and other dangers."

The man looked confused. "I guess I'm here on official business, then."

"Yeah, right. Now that I challenge you, you're on official business," the ranger snorted. "Sir, this is the site of a major plane crash."

"Yes, I know," the man answered. "I'm the pilot."

# Chapter 39

To the captain of the Bell 212 helicopter maneuvering for landing, the crowded Forest Service ramp bathed in the orange glow of the sodium vapor lights looked like a movie set.

"It looks for all the world like the set of Spielberg's *Close Encounters of the Third Kind*," he said to the copilot. "You know, when the spaceship lands at the end?"

He slowed their forward velocity to less than ten knots and gently descended toward the designated landing spot for a gentle touchdown as he leaned back toward the cabin, his voice raised above the din of the engine and rotors.

"Bill, I'd say they've come to welcome you back from the dead."

An impromptu cordon of pilots and Forest Service workers had formed at the left side, and they began to move forward as Judy Deason broke through the group, eyes streaming, launching herself through the opening door to embrace her husband.

Bill Deason, sitting up on a stretcher, grabbed and kissed her to the raucous noise of sustained applause.

She pulled back then to look at him.

"I told all of them many hours ago that you'd made it, Bill," she said. "But no one believed me. Not even Clark."

"Hell, darlin', I was there and *I* didn't believe it either. I woke up hanging upside down in a crushed tin can, and I couldn't even remember for a while what had happened, or where I was, or anything. I still don't remember everything, and—" He pointed to one of the paramedics. "—I don't know why these boys think I've got to lie down. Hell, I walked out."

"Sir," the paramedic replied with a smile, "shock can mask a lot of problems. The fact that you walked out doesn't mean you should be trotting around until after they check you over at the hospital."

"He's just badly bruised, and nothing's broken, right?" Judy asked, but her husband answered.

"Yeah. All appendages are still attached and working, but I feel like I lost a fistfight with a locomotive." He paused to take a somewhat strained breath before smiling at her and continuing, "That's why we've got to go on to the Jackson hospital, so they can cluck around and see if I have terminal athlete's foot or something. I told them I wasn't going anywhere but to you, first."

"Well, I'm ready to go, and I've got your bag, too."

Dozens of others were pushing in, trying to remain polite but dying to shake his hand, and Judy inclined her head. "Your public awaits."

Clark Maxwell and Dave Barrett were in the lead, and as soon as Judy released him, Bill grabbed their hands.

"You guys are the heroes," Bill said, having to pause for breath. "I couldn't believe you were trying to literally pick that P-3 up by its wing tips and carry me to the lake."

"I'm sorry it didn't work, Bill," Clark said. "If we'd—"

Bill carefully raised his bandaged right hand to stop the apology. "We did the best we could. Point is, you guys risked everything trying." He spotted Jerry and nodded, wincing at the gesture. "You, too, Jerry. You could have vetoed the whole attempt."

Chuck Hines pushed forward to hug Bill as he gestured for Jerry Stein to come closer. Jerry complied with a broad smile on a drawn and anxious face. "I'm just incredibly glad you're alive, Bill."

"I'm sorry about your plane, old boy. I was getting fond of Tanker Ten."

"Forget it."

"Hell, Bill, you probably haven't heard," Dave Barrett chimed in. "We, you, all of us apparently saved the smokejumpers and the town of Bryarly, and we probably saved Yellowstone, too."

"Really?"

"So far, so good," Barrett replied.

"Bill," Jerry added, "we've got an impromptu welcome party planned for when you get back from Jackson, if you can handle it."

"Will there be any scotch?" Bill asked with a grin.

"You bet."

"Then I'll be able to handle it." Bill took a deep breath and winced before continuing. "Jerry, if you'll still have me as an employee . . ." He stopped to take another breath, smiling as if the effort were an amusing anomaly. "Sorry. Maybe I can requalify on the DC-6s."

"They're all grounded, Bill," Jerry replied. "But I made an offer to buy two more P-3s an hour ago, so keep your fingers crossed."

"You're going to need some rest anyway," Clark said.

"Rest, hell," Bill replied. "What I need is about a week in the hay with my wife. The best reason I know for being alive."

WEST YELLOWSTONE AIRPORT, MONTANA

Joe Groff carefully parked his car at the far end of Stein Aviation's parking lot behind Hangar One and surveyed the area before getting out. The call from Jerry had been exceedingly strange, and with the knowledge that the FBI was snooping around, he was seriously thinking of just leaving town for a few days—an intention he should not have shared with Jerry.

"No, Joe . . . I want you to come to the office. Now."

"Why now? I was going to have some dinner—"

"Now, Joe. Don't argue."

There were figures visible in the lights bathing the ramp, but they were going about their various jobs as Joe walked the outside wall of the hangar and swung inside. There were a couple of men in animated conversation just inside the hangar doors, and he ignored them as he moved past and headed for the stairs to Jerry's office.

He heard a voice calling someone's name, but it didn't register until it was repeated in a moderate bellow.

"Randy! Randy Michaels!"

The memory of the alias name he'd used snapped into place a microsecond before the caution that no one should be using it. He had already turned and automatically smiled before the second realization hit, and he tried to recover, shaking his head and waving off the individual who was across the hangar. He'd turned back toward the stairway instantly on guard when Clark Maxwell stepped from an alcove and blocked his path.

"Hello, Randy."

He tried to brighten and pick up the part.

"Oh! Captain Maxwell. How—"

"Or should I say, 'Joe'?"

"Sorry?"

Another voice was crowding him from behind now, and Joe partially turned to see another man within a few feet of him holding something in his hand.

"Mr. Groff, I presume?"

"Ah." Joe was panicked, his escape route cut off by the reality that running was a dead giveaway.

"Say something, Mr. Groff," the man said, holding a small, metallic device close to his face.

"Who the hell are you?" Joe managed, alarmed that the device suddenly flashed a green light and issued an audible tone. The man holding it turned it around so Joe could see the tiny panel.

"It likes you," Blackson said.

"What do you mean? Who *are* you?" Groff asked, his voice carrying a tinge of panic.

"This little device is a portable voice analyzer, Mr. Groff. It's loaded with the parameters of a specific voice, and it just told me that the voice that called the FBI to tell us not to come—and *your* voice—are the same."

"What are you talking about?"

"Captain Maxwell?"

Clark nodded. "This is the man who called himself Randy Michaels, an agent-trainee."

Blackson pulled a badge wallet out of his pocket. "See, Mr. Groff, I'm a *real* FBI agent."

Joe felt his blood running like ice water as beads of sweat broke out on his forehead.

"So? I didn't impersonate an agent. I specifically said I wasn't an agent."

"But you specifically said you were here on official business for the FBI as an employee of the FBI. Are you a lawyer, Mr. Groff?"

"No."

"Maybe you should have consulted one. At least you'll get your chance now." He reached out and snapped a handcuff on Groff's right wrist, turning the stunned man around to get the other in place. "You're under arrest, Mr. Groff, for impersonating a federal official. Whether you said the magic word 'agent' or not doesn't matter."

WEST YELLOWSTONE, MONTANA

Clark looked at his watch, his heart sinking slightly at the reality that it was past midnight.

Perhaps tomorrow he could talk with Karen.

He'd built a good fire and sat down to enjoy it with his cell phone balanced on his knee, ready to punch it on when her call came. He wasn't entirely sure what he wanted to say, but he'd built the last hour on the hope he'd get a chance to try.

Clark leaned forward and placed the phone to one side of the hearth, contemplating the half-consumed beer in his hand, which suddenly seemed less than appetizing. He'd barely pulled himself to his feet when a voice reached him from behind.

"Now. Where were we?"

Karen Jones was standing in the doorway to the kitchen with two tumblers and the bottle of Oban, a tired smile on her face.

"Karen!"

"You looked so peaceful in front of the fire, and the back door was unlocked."

He started to move to her, but she waved him back.

"Pull me up a chair."

"You bet," he said with a very pronounced smile. "How are you?"

She handed him a tumbler and filled it before filling her own and sliding into the companion leather chair he'd positioned.

"I'm thinking I want to hear more about that trip to Scotland, and your past four years, and a certain night on a mountaintop in Oregon."

"And then?"

She turned and smiled. "And then . . . I'll go back to my lonely hotel room like a good girl and get about the business of becoming a single girl again."

"Good."

"After which I won't have to think about such inconveniences."

"Like putting up with Trent Jones?"

"No," she smiled. "Like having to go back to a lonely hotel room."


CENTRAL INTELLIGENCE AGENCY,<br>LANGLEY, VIRGINIA—FEBRUARY 2004

The first assistant deputy director in charge of Covert Ops in South America leaned back in the simulated leather armchair and shook his head as he smiled at the man and woman on the other side of the boardroom-style table.

"You mean something finally worked?" Rod Campbell chuckled. "Isn't there a rule somewhere that dictates that can't happen?"

Janice Fosberg laughed in response. "I think you're referring to Murphy's Law."

"Ah, yes. The prime directive for Covert Ops. Whatever can go wrong will do so with maximum public exposure."

"And Murphy was an optimist," she added. "But in this case, even posthumously, the precaution worked."

"You told him it wouldn't, as I understand?"

She gave him an affirmative nod. "Of course. So did Ralph, here."

Ralph Davis smiled but said nothing.

"And he put it in place himself?" Campbell asked.

"He sure did. Drilled her in the password, set up the file and the program, and had it all oiled. He knew she'd take his truck if he was killed, and he knew she'd eventually look in the glove compartment for cash, because that was her habit. And he knew she always carried her laptop. So it was a rather straightforward equation."

"Bull, Janice. How could he possibly know she'd turn down literally millions of dollars and go do the right thing?"

"He understood her. Of course, for an outside operative, he also did a pretty good job feathering his own nest."

"Well," Campbell laughed. "That was the deal. He provided the aircraft, and we paid the bill. The money was his. Our clandestine flights were successfully accomplished with zero attribution, because of him. I'm just not happy about the implication that we damaged those planes."

"It does appear," Janice added, "that the crash that killed him was directly related. That almost makes him a killed-in-action."

"But there's no wife or family for us to quietly pay or support or take care of, right?"

"Correct. Only his girlfriend Misty, and we're watching to make sure she doesn't end up destitute. Oh, about the airplanes. We made sure Stein's entire fleet is being thoroughly inspected and repaired. And we made sure Trent Jones didn't lose his FAA licenses. He won't be working for Stein again, but he'll survive."

"Interesting, the legal battle that's broken out," Ralph added. "Stein is suing Jeff's estate, which still has possession of the funds, for the return of everything in those three accounts as damages. Misty, on the other hand, apparently got good advice and changed her mind about how dirty the money is, and she's suing in probate court to recover the money as sole heir."

"Yeah, and you fellows are aware, aren't you, that Jeff apparently stuffed the remaining four million somewhere else and we haven't found it yet."

"Are we looking?" Campbell asked.

"Not officially." Janice smiled. "But, unofficially, if it's not being claimed, Uncle might as well get it back."

"We've checked the usual places, but as expected, thanks to the extreme lack of cooperation of the offshore banks, there's no trace of it yet."

"The same old story. They won't let us check any other account name but his. He stashed it somewhere or spent it, and, of course, held out on poor Misty, which wasn't a surprise for Jeff."

Campbell sighed as he got up and picked up the folder. "Well, we can drink a toast to a good man who was willing to destroy his own reputation to protect the Company and his country. *I* sure wouldn't want to be remembered as an accessory to Colombian druggies." He picked up a glass of water and the other two did the same. "In the meantime, here's to you, Jeff Maze."

GRAND CAYMAN ISLAND—FEBRUARY 2004

Misty Ryan paused in front of the bank building and breathed in the fresh salt air, noting the presence of another cruise ship approaching the harbor. She turned left and began strolling south along the main avenue.

It had been easier to get through Jeff's funeral knowing he was a crook, and even easier, given her knowledge of computers, to make a certain listing disappear from her hard drive and from the individual files he'd left. That was a reference no one should ever see.

She reminded herself that she needed to call the law firm representing her claim on Jeff's estate. There was a real chance, she'd been advised, that she would win most or all of the funds, especially since Jerry Stein was having a hard time proving that his planes had been abused outside the scope of the lease contract.

Misty walked to the commercial dock at the south end of town where a rented forty-two-foot yacht was waiting for her. She stepped aboard and smiled at the captain, a young man resplendent in spotless white nautical shirt and pants. As he guided the boat gently out of the harbor, Misty climbed to the fly bridge and stood at the rail, breathing deeply of the sea air and feeling incredibly free.

*For a pretty good reason,* she thought.

When they were a mile off the west end of the island and rocking gently in a calm sea, Misty descended the stairs and moved to the aft deck. She reached in the tote bag slung over her shoulder and extracted a Ziploc bag of ground-up computer disk, the small floppy that was the last remaining record. She placed it on a small table by the rail and reached back in to get a pewter canister, which she also placed on the table. She unzipped the bag, emptied the contents over the side, then wadded up the plastic and stuffed it back in her purse.

An envelope was visible at the top of her purse, and she couldn't resist pulling it out and looking at the single sheet of paper it contained once again. The figures were amazing, but there it was: $4 million in U.S. dollars, already transferred and safely recorded in the numbered account she'd opened a week before in Geneva. Jeff's fourth offshore account had undergone an untraceable name change six months before, thanks to a "service" fee she'd quietly paid the right banker. Now it had been closed and expunged, as if it had never existed.

Misty opened the canister and slowly emptied the gray ashes over the side. Her eyes brimmed with tears as she watched the stream of gray ride the gentle waves. When they had almost floated out of sight she put her fingers to her lips and blew a kiss toward them. For several seconds she remained in that position, her open palm reaching out toward the sea.

*Good-bye, my love!*

# Acknowledgments

One measure of professionalism and dedication in any human endeavor is how passionate practitioners are when asked to explain what they do, and why they do it. In that sense, the men and women who helped me understand the nuances of aerial wildland fire fighting and airtankering passed the highest test: All of them are understated ambassadors for a world we seldom see, yet one that is of vital importance to all Americans.

Before naming a few names in appreciation (and realizing that you aren't interested in plowing through an endless list), I need to tell you in the strongest voice of alarm that the United States has some critical decisions to make *immediately* if we're to have the ability to subdue wildland fires from the air in the future. Each of us needs to be engaged in demanding that our congressmen and senators face and solve the problems created by aging airtankers and insufficient professionalism and capacity in the airtanker industry. The choices? Well, visit my website at www.johnjnance.com and click on "The National Crisis Behind *Fire Flight*" for more details. But in a nutshell, we need either to completely federalize and standardize airtankering by putting the Air Force or the Air National Guard in charge of dedicated units of highly trained pilots and crews with modern aircraft stressed for the job; or, we need a split system in which at least forty thoroughly modern, tested, and certified airtankers are provided under contract from private companies, and at least forty Air Force / Air National Guard aircraft (possibly dedicated C-130H or later models) are converted specifically for aerial retardant drops. And the Forest Service must be able to call in the Air Force / Air National Guard fleet at any time, not just when the private airtanker force has been exhausted. Finally, nothing is going to change until the wildland aerial fire-fighting job has been assigned to a separate agency with a separate congressional line-item budget. Only Congress can enact the necessary changes, and year after year the forests are getting hotter and drier. This is, without a doubt, a national emergency.

First and foremost, I want to thank the members of my great new publishing team at Simon & Schuster, starting with Executive Vice President and Publisher David Rosenthal; President Carolyn Reidy; my amazingly sharp and delightful Simon & Schuster senior editor, Marysue Rucci; and Marysue's Radar O'Reilly assistant, Tara Parsons; and my longtime force-of-nature friend and mentor Adene Corns who—along with Carolyn Reidy—helped bring me home to S&S.

Thanks, as well, to my agent emeritus, Olga Wieser, to whom this book is dedicated. Olga is stepping away from the front lines this year after decades of noble service, and the flag is passing to my new team at The Writer's House, Amy Berkower and Simon Lipskar.

As always, this work had benefited greatly from the professional efforts of my in-house editor and business partner, Patricia Davenport, and my thanks go as well to my University Place staff, Gloria Gallegos, Lori Carr, Todd Stringham, and Lori Ann Evans. Thanks as well to my wife, Bunny, for her ideas and review of the manuscript.

And my heartfelt thanks to fellow Air Force veteran and airline pilot and author John Halliday, whose close encounters with the worst of airtankering many years ago helped set the contrasts with today's force in perspective. Thanks, also, to Juan Browne, an experienced lead plane pilot who spent many hours in person and on the plane helping me understand that part of the mission.

In Washington, a longtime friend and colleague (and published author) from the Air Force days who now heads the Forest Service's Aviation Division, Lt. Col. Anthony Kern, USAF Retired, helped bring me up to speed on the many aspects of the fight to bring order to and reliability from what has too often been chaos in the federal government's stewardship of aerial attack of forest fires. In 2002 Tony received one of *Aviation Week*'s coveted Laurel Awards for having the courage to ground 25 percent of the airtanker fleet when it became apparent that the C-130As and PB4Ys could never be deemed as safe as necessary.

Perhaps my most profound appreciation goes to Mr. Jim Barnett, a veteran of the Forest Service and a colleague of Tony Kerns, who has spent uncounted hours assisting me in an unrelenting quest for accuracy in the portrayal of every aspect of wildland firefighting, and especially the aerial component. To whatever degree this novel—set as it is against the background of today's reality—helps to highlight the nobility of those who struggle with wildfires as well as delineate the tasks ahead, Jim shares a lot of the credit for the accuracy of that background. We're incredibly fortunate to have such men as Tony and Jim in government service.

Out in Missoula, Tom Eldridge, the spokesman for (and a veteran of) the famed Missoula Smokejumpers, provided a wealth of information and assistance as well as a review of the manuscript. I was especially pleased by

Tim's "thumbs-up" reaction to Karen Jones, who really is the prototypical female smokejumper today—strong, confident, capable, and always feminine. The fictional Karen and her real sisters share much with Kat Bronsky, my FBI agent from *The Last Hostage* and *Blackout* (and you'll be seeing Kat again in future works).

Thanks also to the folks at the West Yellowstone National Forest Service facility.

And ultimately, thanks to you for being a loyal fan and reader. The website's for you, www.johnjnance.com, and my email address is: talktojohnnance@johnjnance.com. I love to hear from you.

# About the Author

A decorated Air Force pilot veteran of Vietnam and Operations Desert Storm/Desert Shield, John J. Nance is also a lieutenant colonel in the USAF Reserve. He is the author of thirteen major books, four of them nonfiction. Two of his previous works, *Pandora's Clock* and *Medusa's Child*, aired as major, successful two-part television miniseries.